Damage Control:
Public Relations for the Perfectly Fine Family

Copyright 2018 © by Michael Horner
Cover image: Lev Chorney

ISBN-13: 978-1-944388-09-6
Library of Congress Control Number: 2017952869

Fomite
58 Peru Street
Burlington, VT 05401
www.fomitepress.com

Damage Control:
Public Relations for the Perfectly Fine Family

Michael Horner

Fomite
Burlington, VT

For my parents

1

Everything's fine.

Really.

I'm out in front of the library in a snowstorm, my minivan idling behind me, the headlights illuminating the snowflakes. Two of my three kids are accounted for. Tina's in her booster seat a few steps away and there's no chance that Rudd isn't at varsity hockey practice over at the Boys and Girls Club. It's just Jessica who's supposed to be here, right here at the library. After several jumping jacks in front of the automatic doors have no effect, I pull vigorously on the handle of the next door over and the handle on the next door and the one next to that. The thing is, with kids, you're finding and losing them all the time.

It is a little odd that my thirteen-year-old daughter just called from this very building, which is locked and dark except for the glow of the exit signs. Out here in the cold, the snow descends diagonally by the streetlights and onto the snow-covered parking lot that is empty except for one car. There are not even rectangles of pavement where cars had been. There's a distinct lack of recent footprints in the snow on the walkways. It's snowing hard, but not hard enough to cover all tracks in the fifteen minutes it took me to get here. This isn't that surprising. This is Jess after all.

I tug with both hands just to make sure each door is really locked and try another round of jumping jacks in front of the door sensor when finally a figure appears in the dusk of the corridor—surely my daughter.

It is not relief that fills me. Tina is not the only one inside the minivan. The windshield wipers edge up the glass reluctantly and then drop with a smack. Strapped in his own booster seat next to Tina in the middle row is her best friend, Burty. Both Tina and Burty are now stubble-headed six-year-olds when an hour or so ago they both had hair, and in Tina's case, hair that flowed almost all the way down her back. Where that hair went or how it went or why it went, I'm still not sure. And if that is not enough, up front, sprawled in the passenger seat is Rachel St. John, who is Burty's mom and also the very popular anchor of KNNK's Lowdown at Lunch. And, well, I'm sure we're all going to be laughing about this in a few days, even my wife, but Rachel's passed out and wrapped in Burty's vintage collector's edition Aquaman blanket pinned onto her with refrigerator magnet clips. Really, when you put it in perspective, this isn't that unusual as far as playdates go.

How will Jess view this? Whereas my sanity as a father and a spokesperson for GE stems from taking the wider view, my daughter's teen-driven insanity revels in the microscopic: one single clogged pore on the tip of her nose, a single hair out of its proper place, the constant parsing of the two most concrete words in the world: yes and no. These will send a planet off orbit, certain death will ensue, or worse her social status will plummet; whatever the case, lamenting emojis will be texted. Add to this minefield, Burty's wrapped mom? Tina with no hair? A phone that in a few clicks could deliver a photo to my wife two time zones away at her job in Arizona? Not so funny, probably. Something like this needs a little distance to see the humor at the bottom of it—time distance, not mileage. But the one thing I have going for me is that Jessica's thirteen and clearly in the middle of some crisis of her own, so unless something interjects itself into her personal pronoun, there's a chance she won't even notice anyone else in the car.

It is true I could have avoided this situation with one quick call to my mother-in-law, but Jessica said *emergency*, and, well, that means *Dad*.

As she breaks from the corridor's shadows, I smile to show how glad I am to see her. But it's not my daughter. It's a woman who comes to the door, a woman with a winter hat on, not a teenybopper who will risk frost-bite and all manner of illness so her hair will be just so: a pastel knitted hat pulled down over her ears and forehead, glasses, a scarf wrapped ten times around her neck and chin, and out of the thick of this a shirt collar wedged between the scarf and her quilted overcoat—a librarian, of course, and one on the edge of retirement. The complexities of parenthood are manifold: Here simultaneously I'm slightly relieved I don't have to broach the contents of the minivan with my daughter, I'm now slightly distressed because my daughter doesn't seem to have a known location, and most of all, I'm certain Jess will somehow get word that I mistook her for an elderly librarian—this will extend the time that she won't talk to me by another six months (she has spoken to me since her Big Birthday Disappointment in August but only in business transactions: "Sign this for school." "Ever heard of privacy?" "Hello! I'm like on the phone!" "We're eating that again?" "When's Mom coming home?" "Drive me to Sarah's." "Need to go to the library tonight.").

The librarian hesitates at the door, looking warily at me through the tinted glass. I search behind her for some hint of a daughter. I keep my grip on the door handle ready to help her out but she stays put. I'm not a person anyone should be wary of.

"You need a book badly?" Her voice barely penetrates the glass. "Should I contact the authorities?"

"I thought you were open until nine," I say. She squints wrinkles and then turns her head so her ear is situated toward the door. Over the years I've had run-ins with a librarian or two about late fines, but she doesn't look familiar. I shout it this time.

"We close at eight and open at nine," she responds, then adds, "in the morning." Her salesclerk smile tells me she'd be glad to help me bright and early. Then her eyes flash, a recognition of some kind, and she looks at the wall for something and then at her wrist. "It's after nine," she says, just to let me know that I'd be in the exact same situation. She looks at me and her smile disappears. Again I wonder if she's recognized me from the late fees. Her elbow squeezes her gangly purse against her side and her mittened hand protects the strap on her shoulder. She's not coming out. I want her to come out.

"Is my daughter in there?" I ask. "She's supposed to be here and she's not here. She's somewhere and she's not here."

And then, as if I told her my library card was stolen, a genuine look of concern comes over her. She loosens her grip on her pocketbook—apparently murderers, rapists, and biblioklepts don't lose their daughters at libraries. She leans on the door bar but does not push it yet.

"I know you," she says.

My stomach drops. She is one of the late fee demons. But she's smiling again. There's a positive vibe here through this door. I'm relieved. I'm not just known for my late fees in this town. I'm the face of GE around here. People have seen me in the newspaper, they've seen me on channel 12, they've seen me at one of the intimate gatherings we host to keep letting the city know we're invested in the community. She might have even seen my live interview on Rachel's noontime show today at Percival Lake Park which certainly qualifies me for a sympathetic smile no matter where this woman stands on the issue of Frisbee golf.

Nine hours ago, right next to Percival Lake in a section of the park that's designated Meditation Meadow, I stood squinting in the sunlight in front of a microphone that Rachel held with her mittened hand. I was under the impression that I was here to tout this wonderful park we resurrected from polluted land and a polluted lake, and to remind this community that this is the New GE and we're giving back this area that is almost in the same pristine condition when GE moved in here over a hundred years ago. I'd done this at least a dozen times on Rachel's show in the last five years as we made more and more progress toward this summer's upcoming grand opening.

But today, clad in her fleeciest earmuffs, Rachel—the only reporter in town who knows how to report one of our press releases, mother of my daughter's best friend, a person whom I consider a friend—asked me a gotcha question on live TV with leaked information about the planned Frisbee golf course being axed from the park plans, something we were not going to announce for at least another month. I was so surprised I stammered in my answer, I who have never stumbled even with gotcha questions about PCBs on the grounds of Allengate Elementary or when the last hundred manufacturing jobs were finally cut. And before I even got a chance to get a hold of myself, which I was about a second away from doing, the first Frisbee hit Rachel in the back of the head. Then I was hit, then Gus the cameraman. Then dozens upon dozens of Frisbees came flying at us so that all we could do was huddle on the ground with only our winter jackets for protection as we were pummeled—Gus's camera on its side still trained on us, rolling live television.

And then things took an even more unexpected turn. In a lull, Rachel shot to her feet and charged at the masked attackers with such speed and intensity, even in the face of renewed enemy fire (the profanity pouring from her mouth was a marvel in itself as she batted down the Frisbees that came at her), that the Frisbee perpetrators had no choice but to scatter. Rachel nabbed one poor soul at the lake's edge, where she revealed how incredibly strong she is and how unafraid she is to kick a guy where it counts. The guy was stooped over and groaning when she finished the job by pushing him into the lake. The stunner had nothing to do with Rachel chucking her ear-muffs at the guy struggling in the water or the fact that this was the first known person to take a dip in the lake in over six decades: the same Frisbee attacker who ended up in the water was none other than Mayor Dugus!

So yes, I deserve a smile from this librarian for all that she might have known happened to me today and I deserve an even bigger smile for all the things that she doesn't know happened after I pulled the shaking but still-Frisbee-wielding Mayor Dugus from the ice-cold water. But really, I know her smile has everything to do with the very generous gift that GE made a couple years ago to this very library to support its remodeling of the local history room. I might have handed the door-sized check to this very woman. Though I normally hesitate to use my position as leverage, I'll be able to cash this in tonight and search the library for my daughter who has to be in there.

"You're Karen's husband, aren't you?" she asks. "Dave, is it?"

I nod even though my name is Doug.

Dave is apparently the password, though, because she opens the door. Instead of inviting me in, she steps out and pulls the handle to check that the latch has caught. "Okey-dokey," she says to herself and then turns to me: "How is she?"

"Right now she'd be pretty upset about her missing daughter." There's no need to mention that she's 2000 miles away in Tempe and probably thinks her kids are all tucked in.

"Don't worry," she says after a moment of contemplation, a moment of assessing me. Her eyes rest on my right foot longer than would be considered polite even if it is wrapped and knotted in a stained and worn dishtowel. My sock and shoe, and Rachel's clothes are among the several minor casualties, not of the live interview that went wrong (at least not directly) but that playdate earlier this evening and in particular a Scrabble game that took an odd turn.

At this point, I'm sure I'm still smiling though. I'm sure I'm being reasonable, the qualified air of a worried dad who's had a hell of a day but knows he has it all under control, except maybe for the frostbite on his foot which he hadn't noticed until the helpful librarian, best friend to his wife, noted it. "She's not in the library. I check everything myself since that incident with the Erdact boy. . ."

She might have been telling me all about the Erdact boy or all the places daughters might disappear to in Pontoosuc, or perhaps it is actually a story about my wife shelving books when she was in junior high, something about disappearing carts full of books to be put back in the stacks, but it is the rhythm and the hopeful tone when my wife's name first came out of her mouth, the confidence that she has a place in my wife's life, that makes this woman very familiar to me. Her words are just like the ones I hear from the women that my wife has come into contact over the years, especially in her latest job of flying around the country starting stores, chains, franchises. Reach out and touch someone has marked these hirelings' collective imagination. Even though they knew my wife for barely a week or two and even though many have not seen her for years or ever heard back from her, even though they have been hired because they will work hard for low pay (though my wife will never see it this way), they send Xmas cards, send photos of children and grandchildren, call, and always demand that she get with the times and get on Facebook, what are you trying to hide?

I now note that the librarian is no longer talking. Instead there is ringing, a phone ringing. I follow her eyes to my hand, which I have in the air over my head, both of them up as if I'm half-heartedly surrendering. I don't know how long I've had them up there. It's been a rough day. One hand is glowing, shining down on the librarian, ringing—it's my phone. She points it out in a helpful librarian way as she sounds out the word for me.

"Where are you kidnapped to?" I say into the phone.

"Dad," Jess answers. This is not good.

"Where are you?"

Her pause. Her lie-is-coming pause. Already that second I begin to see Jess's past hijinks with nostalgia—the Valentine's Day Heist, the Home Ec Salt Incident, the Pontoosuc Mall Amendment, and last fall's Great Phone Flap. Tonight my thirteen-year-old is going pro.

I know exactly what I should do: help her out, deflect her coming lie by telling her that I'm already at the library to signal to her that that would not be a good choice of stories. The thing is, she knows perfectly well where I am because in her call twenty minutes ago she told me to come to the library quick, but this won't stop her.

"I'm still at the library," she says, her voice climbs as if tackling steep stairs and then balances on a cloud on that final syllable, and I almost cave—the poor kid can't even muster herself to believe her own lie. She must really be in a jam.

"I'll be right there," I say. I hang up before she can. Dad the victor! I raise my arms above my head again. With Jess, I have so few victories.

"You've found her." The librarian smiles, misreading my celebration, and heads right to the minivan. First, she taps the passenger window and then she knocks on the damn thing as if it's a castle door. I see Rachel's head tilt and tilt again, maybe a sound of a groan. "Oh," the librarian says, expecting my wife perhaps, though my wife has very short hair. Then the librarian looks in back, her nose drawing closer to the glass. The middle window rolls down. I was really hoping Tina was asleep. "Hi Tina," she says. "Oh, hi Burty. I barely recognized you without your hair."

Great, the librarian seems to be on intimate terms with a good part of my family.

I hear a small voice, Tina's: "We cut off our hair because we're sympathizing with minks to perpetuate the wrongs on them."

The minks! I should have known.

"Oh, really, well that's one way to make yourself heard, I suppose. Though to be honest I think written words have the greatest power."

"I don't like writing," Tina says.

"You have to spell," Burty adds.

The librarian moves in close to the car again to see if it holds any other surprises and steps back and turns to me, her face close to mine, still cheery (I might have an internship for this woman if she needs another career): "It's been quite a day for protests," she says.

Believe me, I know.

"Tell that wonderful wife of yours that Mary Beth says hello." She swallows and then puts her mittened hand on my arm, just lightly, hardly a touch: "Take care of Rachel. She's our top fundraiser. Without her the library would close at five! And she gets us so much good press with those Monday segments. Of course after what happened today. . ."

She pauses here to see if I know what happened today on Rachel's show. I have no idea how Mary Beth recognized me tonight in the snow and the dark but didn't recognize me on TV with my name on the screen and Rachel's microphone jammed near my lips when the Frisbees started to fly. But I nod solemnly to show her I support Rachel too and she has been a great supporter of the New GE unlike the Berkshire *Beagle*'s young hotshot, Nathan Shaffeur. Therefore Mary Beth and I are in harmony.

"She's tough that way just like your wife."

I am staring into Mary Beth's eyes, her hand no longer on my arm. Her pupils are wide, incurious—apparently this is the stuff of a librarian's usual day. There is an apricot silkiness to her wrinkles and one eye seems to be in imminent jeopardy from the brow above. I realize that she's taken off her glasses and must now be regarding me as a blur. I wish I could see her in the same way. My phone rings.

"Jessica."

"Jesus fucking Christ!" she hisses.

"Is this my daughter I'm talking to? The one that watches her language?"

Mary Beth mouths, "Good night," as she flashes me a mitten thumbs up and heads toward her car.

"Calm down," my daughter tells me in a whisper.

"Why are you whispering, Jessica?"

She starts to cry. "Stop calling me Jessica."

"I want to know where you are, J-E-S-S. I want to come get you."

"I don't know."

"Whose parents drove you?"

She hangs up. Forgive me, but damn my daughter. I almost drop the phone into the trashcan, jump in the car, and head to the Boys and Girls Club to pick up Rudd at hockey. Cross her right off my list. If anyone asks me where my middle child is, I will deny her existence. I will go home and cut her out of photographs. I will burn her birth certificate. Deny and deny until even my wife won't be sure she's given birth to her.

Mary Beth cranks her car once and then again, and then once more without the engine starting and then pops her head out of the car door out of concern for me. I signal to her with a cheery smile that it is all fine, everything is all fine, no worries, I was mistaken: There is no daughter.

The phone rings.

"I'm on Jones Street."

"What the hell are you doing there?" I flash to the exposé in the paper last summer that included photographs of drug deals going down in the middle of the street, how Jones has become a hub between Springfield, Albany, and New York City. I've lived in this town for most of my life and I haven't ever been on Jones Street except for a couple important errands.

"Dad!"

"OK, OK. What number? At least give me a number."

"You know my number."

I curse cell phones and their lack of lines to reel in my daughter.

"House number! What house number?"

"Don't yell." There is a long pause. "There. 255."

"Jessica? Stay put."

An audible pout.

"Jesus. J-e-s-s." I say this as I watch Mary Beth coming back toward me, stepping carefully on the boot prints she had just made on the way to her car.

"257. Hurry."

"Stay put!"

Mary Beth halts mid-step. At least someone's listening.

2

I left the librarian with my jumper cables and AAA card. Come to think of it, I might have pressed my whole wallet into her hand. But none of that matters, I'm on the way to rescue my daughter. Windshield wipers swat the snow as I hurdle towards Jones Street. Cars spin out to my right and left, but I've got the minivan firmly under control. My crossed fingers stick straight up off the steering wheel at ten and two. I was a kid who crossed his fingers a lot—not to get me out of a white lie but to wish for luck, a bad habit I didn't break until a couple years into my marriage. I've got several good reasons to have my fingers crossed tonight, but all the same I uncross them and hold the steering wheel with my full grip. Rachel has stopped her groaning and Tina and Burty behind me are unusually quiet; if they are still awake, I know they are stewing in the worry of impending punishment for cutting off all their hair. I have not said a word about it, and they are old enough to know this means minks or no minks the error of their ways is grave indeed. But for me the situation is completely under control—Jess will be in the car momentarily, Rachel will sober up, and children's hair grows exponentially fast (though not fast enough for my wife to never know). Everything is fixable.

Navigating any crisis is a lot like driving in the snow and sometimes you have to do the counterintuitive thing like steer into a skid. So tonight I'm full of the counterintuitive, like wrapping the naked mother of my daughter's best friend (not to mention my all important news outlet) in an vintage Aquaman blanket and lugging her and two sleepy, buzz-cut, mink-protesting children into the minivan. Steer into a skid, which is exactly what I do as I pull onto Jones Street. The children shriek with delight and when the tires find traction millimeters from the curb, my passengers applaud and whoop and yell, "Do it again! Please!"— the conscious ones that is. There is nothing like the sound of delighted children, so I forgive them a little for their hair. Unfortunately during the skid Rachel's body slips from beneath the shoulder belt and droops over the center consul onto me. One of her refrigerator magnet clips pops off, opening the blanket and revealing her breasts. As I get back in my lane, I manage to prop her in the seat again and cover her using the shoulder belt for a fastener and there instead of breasts is Aquaman and his sea creature friends, much better driving companions.

"Mama?" Burty asks pathetically.

"Shhh," I say. "She's still sleeping."

When I finally see a house number, it's 290. There's no way I'm doing a lap around the block so I slow down, and with cars behind me and cars coming at me I begin my favorite of all turns, the three-point turn. I can still hear the accolades of my license tester, a state trooper, who thought he'd give a kid a bit of fun on another snowy day and have me do it on the steep incline of Summer Street, with a stick shift. The trooper was pleasantly disappointed. He might have even said I had a gift. But tonight my magic is running thin, and as I try to maneuver into the turn the street is narrower than I realized and slicker than I thought. So I'm in the middle of a 21-point turn as the headlights mount on either side of me. The street packed with parked cars doesn't help either. And mind you I still have my eyes peeled for my daughter who is nowhere in sight. Here we go again.

I'm wasting time on this turn. My daughter is out there, needing rescue. I'm out the door. I wave at the cars letting them know that this is a temporary situation and they wave back by honking. One horn lays it on and doesn't come off. I do the international sign for there's nothing that can be done so everyone's going to have to live with it. It's not the greatest move I've made. The middle finger is never good PR. Windows start coming down and a lot of creative cursing begins. Car doors start opening.

I'm scanning the parked cars, the sidewalk. "Jess!" I call into the buzz. "Jess?" A couple guys get out of their car and stand in the wedge of the door.

"You OK man?" one of them asks. He can't keep his eye off my wrapped foot as he steps out from behind the door.

"You need a push?" the other asks.

A little girl comes out from the car and hugs one of the men's thighs. "Daddy, come on."

Out here, the horns honking, the headlights' sandwich glare, the pulsing of my hazard lights, the snow coming out of the orange city-lit sky, right smack dab in the worst neighborhood in the county, and we're just a bunch of dads trying to get our kids home. I head straight for the guy to shake his hand. Maybe we can meet for lunch or have a playdate because it is seriously time for Tina to find a new friend. The next thing I know I'm curled into a ball on the snowy pavement, gasping for air because the guy dropped me with one punch to the gut.

As my breath returns, more people stand around me. Someone says, "Another fucking dope fiend" or something like that. "How do we keep these creeps out of our neighborhood?" another asks. "Guy's so high he put a rag on his foot." I'm unable to defend myself.

Then I hear a familiar voice: "Dad? Dad?" And there standing over me is Jess, shivering. Her hair is flattened and caked with snow. I haven't seen her hair wet in years. But at least she's managed to keep her hair tonight.

"You drove right by me," she says looking down at me, still in the fetal position.

And all I can muster when I finally climb to my knees is: "Where's your jacket? Where's your books? What house were you in? Where?"

"I'm so fucking sick of where."

"Don't swear," I groan, but in the power of her voice I'm glad to hear she's just fine. She storms toward the minivan. She won't want to sit next to me so at least Rachel won't fall on her if she opens that door. My guess is confirmed when I hear the door slide open and a long long pause. Really I have absolutely no idea how her mind will process it all. Finally the door slides closed. She didn't even seem to wonder why I was on the ground. This is a hopeful note for me—she might be so far into her own problems she won't notice mine.

Someone helps me to my feet, the guy who punched me.

"Did she have alcohol on her breath? Were her pupils dilated?" I look at the crowd. "Teenagers," I say finally.

And there's a unified laugh of agreement. The dad claps me on the shoulder and apologizes. He thought I was about to tackle him. I've got my PR back. I feel like handing out cigars. "Being a dad, right? That's how you end up with a dishtowel on your foot in the middle of the snowstorm. You'll never believe my other daughter cut off all her hair tonight. Six years old. It's quite a night. Not to mention Frisbee golf." There's a couple of nods, people are headed back to their cars, the little girl tugs on her dad's jacket, one guy gives me a card for Alexander's Boxing Academy. I thank him and slide it into my pocket. It's a storm, people have got to get home, me included. My phone rings. I bring it right to my ear because I know it's Jess calling right there from the back-seat to complain that it's been "like an hour" and she's wondering if I'm coming "this year."

"I'm OK. Don't worry," I say, crunching across the snow in the glare of all the headlights from the cars I'm blocking.

"Doug?" My wife's voice is my second gut punch in five minutes.

"Oh! I thought you were Jess." I'm stretching for my breath again as I put my hand on the door handle.

"Doug?"

"You can't believe the night I'm having. But I've got it all covered. Everyone's almost in bed."

"Oh good. I was worried they might be asleep already. I couldn't call earlier." She pauses. "Wait, why would Jess call? You sound out of breath."

By not climbing into my car, I've apparently broken the last bit of patience I've been afforded. The horns start blaring again and this time I give them all a thumbs up.

"It's quite a storm tonight. A complete surprise. Did you catch what happened to me today yet?"

"Are those car horns?" Everything sounds normal in her voice, but I can't help thinking about the text she sent yesterday, just one word: "Things." That's it. The previous text from the day before was about poster board for Tina's project on minks. *Things*? Was it the first indication of a crisis? Every free moment I checked to see if she sent a follow-up text that would indicate that she sent this one by accident: "Things are great. Just wanted to let you know." "Things are so wonderful between us. We're so lucky! Love you!" "Things I want to do to you when I get you alone." But no correction, not any other texts, not even an email since then. Dammit, why couldn't the one word she sent be *PCBs* or *spill* or *SuperFund* or *layoffs*, something simple, even a surprise question about Frisbee golf. But *Things*, as innocent as it probably is, inexplicably hit me just like a word that my wife never speaks anymore, *Africa*, which is not so innocent and has been hunting me for seventeen years.

"Must be a bad connection," I reply. "I better go see what it's all about. Love you."

16

"Just let me say good night, I. . .Doug?" I power the phone down. She'll completely understand.

As I climb into the van, I can almost hear the phone ringing at home, my wife's voice on the answering machine, repeating my name. It is all going to be a funny story. Really it is, I know.

"Jess, give me that phone." I reach back. I'm surprised she has squeezed herself into the second row of seats, next to Tina and Burty in their booster seats and not her normal position all the way in the third row, as far away as possible from dad. I have to take this as a good sign. Family unity is required at these moments and instinctually Jess senses that. "Your phone privileges are revoked." If she had superpowers she'd have melted me, but she doesn't and she passes up the phone and I power it down. Rudd keeps his phone off because he thinks it will give us all cancer so my wife won't learn that he is still at hockey practice. And we are just minutes from bed. All I have to do is pick him up.

"This is fucked."

"Don't swear!"

Suddenly Burty and Tina are saying "fuck, fuck, fuck" like they are playing duck, duck, goose.

"Shut up!" Jess yells. After that there's a lot of silence except some unclassifiable sounds from Rachel and sobs from Jess. I get the van moving out of this neighborhood.

A couple minutes pass, maybe it's a couple of seconds, but I can't help it, I have to ask Jess in a polite, non-confrontational manner, what happened tonight: "So, Jess, how was your night? How was the library?" There's no response except for the windshield wipers. "Were you with a boy?" Nothing. At a red light I adjust the rearview mirror. Her head's down and all I see is her wet, snow-caked hair. She's shaking. My daughter is miserable and cold and I'm thinking some pretty awful things about her. We used to be pals and I know thirteen is the awkward age. I keep staring in the mirror waiting for her eyes to meet mine there, waiting for Full-moon Jess to return, wanting to rumble. But now her face is in her hands and the light turns green and I have to drive.

"Are you OK?" Tina asks her.

I marvel at the question.

"Jessica, answer your sister." I take a turn onto Lake Street, which is the straightest line to Rudd. "Are you OK?"

"No, I'm not OK." She starts crying harder. "Stop calling me Jessica."

At the next light it occurs to me, there are reasonable explanations. Reasonable explanations, not just for the Jess situation, but for everything that has gone wrong today. I'm guilty of making snap judgments. Of course, I don't exactly know what the reasonable explanations are yet, but I'm sure they are out there. In time, probably after a good night's sleep, the reasonable explanations will manifest themselves. As we pass Park Square and my mother-in-law's fabric store (Tina yells out, "Nancy's store!"), I could have pointed out the library a few blocks down the other way and I could have made a comment about the exactness of its location. But I don't. As we near Melville where Rudd's hockey practice is, I say aloud, "Everything's fine." Jess lets out a puff. Jess is back. I brought her back. I crank the steering wheel and don't lose traction in the turn. I am calm and positive.

3

I'm in fact expecting Rudd to not even be here. The kid is sensible and when no car arrived for him I'm sure he risked cancer for thirty seconds and called Nancy, who lives close by, at least that is the agreed upon plan for something like this. My first indication that he did not make any call is his giant hockey bag on the sidewalk. Its handles are draped over each other, and the bag is dusted with snow. When I stop in front of it, Rudd steps from the doorway. He leans on his goalie stick and scans the minivan as if it's a long train. The assistant coach Ernie Something steps out after him. With the car running, I tug the emergency brake and look at my feet. I untie the dishtowel and slide my shoe and sock off the other foot. I get out, barefoot in the storm. I lift the back, which I have to hold up with both hands because the hydraulics are shot. I'm too tired to explain, especially when I have my hands over my head, but I'm smiling to show everyone that there are reasonable explanations. Ernie Something, a squat, pugnacious guy who still wears his varsity jacket twenty years after the fact, shakes his head as Rudd heaves his bag and stick next to my briefcase, and I let the door slam down.

"Is there anything wrong?" I ask Ernie, and I swear it is in a soft and tired tone, completely non-confrontational; it is a genuine question looking for a reasonable explanation. I don't even step up on the curb, keeping us at an equal height. I ask it again, understanding that some of these hockey types have taken a few blows to the head. To be honest, I was expecting some slaps on the back and maybe even a high five from Ernie for my part in rebuffing the Frisbee attack, for surely if there's an antithesis to hockey it is Frisbee golf. Maybe fewer people watch Rachel's show than I thought.

"Nothing's wrong. I've just been out here for an hour with your son in the snow. No answer at home, no messages. He refused to even let me call your cell phone, didn't want to give you cancer."

Rudd has one hand on the passenger door handle. The streetlights catch the dots of melted snow on his glasses. I want to ask him why he didn't call Nancy, but I let it go because that's what fathers have to do sometimes, let things go—no one else will. In exchange, I'd like him to let go of the door because if he opens it, Rachel will fall out.

"Why didn't you drive him home?"

Ernie Something looks at me, his square jaw slanted. "If you get separated you stay put. He wouldn't budge."

I give Rudd a nod. The difference between your own children can bring you to your knees.

"Not bad advice unless there's nobody looking for you," Ernie finishes. His round cheeks unwind like ram horns into his nub of a chin. He leans toward me and makes some bloodhound sniffing noises. It is probably just nearsightedness and a sinus ailment. I almost want to point to my bare feet just to see what this guy will do with that information. He has his hands in the pockets of his varsity jacket, and he gestures up and forward with both of them so I can see the hair on his belly. Before he could get his hands out of his pockets I could get in one good punch and maybe a few kicks. It would probably feel really good, especially since I've been on the other end of it too many times today, but I know better.

"Come on, Dad, let's go." Rudd's always the voice of reason. I've got kids to get tucked in. My instinct is to put my hand out and let Ernie shake the hell out of it, crunch my fingers, show what kind of man he is, let him think he won the battle. Without offering my hand, without a word, I head back to the other side of the car and hear Rudd thank Ernie.

"We had a good talk anyway," Ernie says to my son as he slaps him on the shoulder.

I shudder to think what he has told my son: explorations under teenage skirts, how hockey used to be a real sport before they cleaned it up and gave it a lot of sissy rules, his team record keg stand. To men like Ernie, if you didn't check your way through women, sports, and beer, you weren't a man. I'll debrief Rudd tomorrow.

Right when I get into the seat, Rudd opens the passenger door. I completely forgot. Another refrigerator magnet clip has come undone, and this time, Rachel's bare leg, almost her whole thigh is on display. His eyes bulge. He palms his glasses, just like he does whenever some sort of confrontation is inevitable—a habit he's had since he first started wearing them when he was Tina's age. Luckily Rachel doesn't fall out. He closes the door right away—good boy—and slides the back door open and climbs over the seat, not waiting for his sister to move it forward. Jess doesn't complain. And when he's back there he doesn't say one thing about being late, about Rachel's thigh, about Tina's hair. "My mom's sleeping," Burty tells him. "We're singing a fuck song about minks," Tina says. I have to take a breath. Jess and Rudd should be cracking up about this, but there's not a peep from them. Rudd's belt clicks as I reclip the blanket around Rachel who seems to be regaining consciousness.

Now, at least, my three children are collected—everything will be fine. Before I pull away, I know what I have to do.

"Navigator ready?" I ask.

"Check," Rudd replies without a pause from the back, through his teeth—but he replies.

"Bombardier and machine gunner ready?"

"Check," Tina giggles. At least she seems in good enough mood.

"Bombardier and machine gunner ready?" I ask again, my hands at ten and two, my eyes straight ahead, fixed on the road.

"Check," Tina says, this time without the giggle.

"Bombardier? Can you read me?"

A pause. "Check," Tina says in a huffy voice she tries to pass off as Jess's.

"Jess, let's hear you imitate your voice."

Silence.

"Jess?" I couldn't find her in the rearview. I do see Rudd in back and he has yet to put his glasses back on.

I remind myself that my wife, my kids, Rachel, we will all look back at this night down the road and laugh and laugh. It is the funniest thing in the world. It is full of reasonable explanations.

"What about me?" Burty pipes up. "What do I get to say? Who am I?"

I want to tell him he's Turdy-Burty, the name the other kids call him at school. But he's Tina's best friend and Rachel's son and I just have to make do.

"This isn't your game," Tina tells it to him straight, which of course makes him cry. So he's crying and Rachel starts groaning and sounds as if she's asking where she is, all while my family is quiet.

I put the car in drive and start down the road. I won't be surprised if oxygen masks drop down from the ceiling.

Then Tina asks, her voice so, so small: "Aren't you going to say 'Prepare for take off'?"

"Prepare for take off."

"You can do better than that, Dad," Tina says as we make the turn onto First.

Tina's tenacity to the script should give me strength, but it just isn't in me to try again. The lights stretch down First, all blinking yellow one after the other. Something's telling me I should heed their warning.

"Prepare for take off!" I say, suddenly, letting my voice boom. Tina's overjoyed. The snow is coming down still, the streets are slick, but I'm headed home with my three kids, where I'll call a cab for Rachel and Burty. There's nothing to heed. I'm fine. We're all fine.

4

And that's exactly what I'm still telling myself, one minute from the house, when blue lights start spinning in my rearview, and just as I'm trying to process this new piece of information, Rachel springs up and groans, "Oh no, oh God" and locks her hands over her mouth as she starts retching.

It is, of course, moments like these that define you. I could cave in right now and start bellyaching, but when it all falls apart I'm at my best. That's my job. First things first. I get my finger on the power switch and Rachel's window slides down and she's still pretty out of it so with my other hand I push her close to the window, the cold air will do us all good.

"Police, Dad, police," Rudd calls up to me, his glasses back on his face. "Pull over!"

"We're busted! We're busted!" Burty starts screaming. "I'm going to jail!" (Again you can see why kids call him Turdy Burty.)

"Good," Tina says. "We'll know how the minks live in captivity."

Rachel starts vomiting out the window or at least I hope it's out the window.

"Gross," Jess says.

I've got things so under control that I'm even mapping out when I'll be able to hose down the side of the car.

But these blue lights. These strobing headlights.

"Pull over, Dad," Rudd insists.

Rachel is still heaving up all the wine she drank at her house. I'm doing some quick calculations from the last glass I had. I move to the right and slow down just a little to see if the car will pass but instead the lights draw closer.

"Mama," Burty calls out, "Tina made me do it."

"Mama's fine," Rachel says from out the window before she starts up with another round.

"We have to understand the minks, Burty," Tina says, her voice crestfallen.

"What are these people even doing in the car?" Jess says to no one. "Fuck."

Burty and Tina drop their fears and desires and resume their "fuck, fuck, fuck" repetition as I make another mental note to address this word before school tomorrow.

In the flashing blue that fills our minivan, I'm not 100% sure, but I'm pretty sure Jess risks getting vomit on her by rolling down the window and I'm pretty sure she drops something out? Is it drugs she's dumping before we get pulled over?

"I'm going to start barfing soon," Jess says.

"I'm so so sorry," Rachel manages.

As all this is happening, of course I'm still thinking about the wine. I've been in this situation before, the drinking and driving and the blue lights, absent the naked woman and the cacophony of kids; and it was almost as innocent that time as it is now. I'm not driving dangerously below the speed limit, I'm not weaving, I'm not straddling either the yellow line or the white line (though I can't really see them under the snow), I'm not making turns in a wide radius, I'm not signaling inconsistently, I'm not hitting the brakes repeatedly. If I hit the brakes, this guy will plow into me anyway. Police or no police, tailgating is dangerous, especially in slippery conditions. Why in the world am I getting pulled over? I've heard of cases where fake police officers have done terrible things to unsuspecting people.

Rachel's still apologizing when she can, Jess is silently stewing, Tina and Burty are a perfect skipping record of *fucks*, and Rudd keeps insisting I pull over. But I decide I'm just going to get my family home. When I'm in the driveway I'll deal with whatever is going on. Just a quarter mile away, just by this construction at the corner and we'll be there. I mean really how responsible should we be for those things behind us? Doesn't our real responsibility reside with what's ahead?

And that's just when we go into a spin. And there we are floating, anti-gravity, carnival ride without the fun. When we're backwards on the second spin, the rear wheel sticks so we jolt into gravity so that the spinning police car can smash us in that sick sound of crushing metal which catches up to the children's screams as we begin to spin again the opposite direction—the inside of the minivan becomes all windshield, spliced by blue light until the pipes that line the road for the sewer project a mere three blocks from our house—three blocks!—loom in all their concreteness like a planet, disappear, and then loom larger for an instant before a final jolting crush of metal howls through my teeth and sucks the air out of the night.

When I peel my face from the airbag, I find Rachel looking as alert as she was when I first came to pick up Tina at her house a few hours ago and about as naked as she was about an hour ago, Tina crying out for her mother, Burty still blubbering about jail and every other word the f-word, Jess holding her nose as blood squeezes between her fingers, Rudd wheezing—his arms extend forward like sleepwalker's. My feet are freezing and I'm going to get everyone home, so I try the ignition. The car groans once and then nothing. The hood is pushed up like an ice jam. Fifteen years and not one accident.

I'm pretty sure I'm in shock because I'm thinking about my feet, there on the gritty floor and pedals. I might just keep going with the bare foot thing: work, stores, I might never wear shoes again. Everything's a bit blurry. Maybe the airbag hit me too hard but I make an effort to stop focusing on my bare feet and focus on my children. There is a police officer knocking on my window. Some of my children are already out of the car. I try to roll the window down but nothing happens. I try to gesture that there's nothing that can be done. He opens the car door. I step out. The sounds of multiple sirens from multiple directions fill the air. People come out of their houses wearing coats over their robes, the neighbors and passersby asking questions of each other, distributing aid, and all looking at me with horrific, maddened faces. Jess with someone holding a hat to her nose, as she moans, "My nose, my nose." Her angry eyes still able to lock onto me.

I want to tend to my children, run to them, but they are everywhere. The previous Sunday evening, Tina and I laughed our heads off as we sprinted through these giant pipes with our flashlights—the pipes that the city thought they could lay before winter. Sunday's play of flashlights and shadows twisted together with this night's circlings of blue and now red lights. The smoky breath of firefighters, police officers, and EMTs—enough of them for a five-alarm blaze—the line of headlights extending out both ways along the street where traffic is backing up, the minivan dented into the pipe, and the cruiser on the other side of the street with the bumper hanging off. If I could stop everyone for a moment, if everyone could take a collective breath, then I could do something. I just want everything to stop.

"This is your last warning. Please sit back in your car. License and registration please!"

Is this guy crazy?

Where *is* Rachel? There, I see her in the lights. The blanket wrapped tight around her again, but now as if she's chosen this to wear tonight. She's clasping it closed with one hand and it's cinched around the waist with a bungee cord. She's talking in front of a teenager who's filming with his phone.

When the clocks don't turn back, when time doesn't stop, you can never guess what you'll do. I'd like to report that I take control of the scene, put this officer in his place, administer aid to my children, and keep everyone calm merely by my strong presence. Instead I'm still thinking about my feet. And there in the snow at my feet is the dishtowel and I now recognize it. It's Tina's security blanket, her *nah*. It disappeared the summer before kindergarten and here it is. It is a blessing. It is the solution for at least one problem. And then I have it in my hand. That's when I realize officers, a whole troop of them are headed my way—officers who all look as if they need a little more meditation in their lives. The spectators (because what else can I call them?) are pointing at me. Rachel is still talking to the camera phone in dramatic TV reporter fashion. Rudd has his breath back and is in a heated discussion with someone as he tends to Jess. I hear Burty's voice, "You'll never take me alive," and then spot a firefighter chasing him around the cruiser. "I'm Aquaman. Fuck, fuck."

The same cop is in my face, making ridiculous commands. But inspired by Burty, I push by him, push by all these people. Can't a guy just bring a security blanket to his daughter, her favorite thing in the world up until it "disappeared" to help her through this small crisis? Can't a dad see how that daughter is doing? What do Breathalyzers matter? They are a terribly unreliable! Why are you worried about my language? Yes, I'm refusing it. Don't you realize my children are bleeding and Tina is missing her *nah*? Someone works at my wrists, tugging them behind me and locking a handcuff on one. With my free hand I swirl her security blanket. Tina sits on the back bumper of an ambulance, I barely recognize her with her stubbled head. She's talking to an EMT who is smiling. Without her long bangs to block them, her eyes are startling as she turns her head toward me—exact replicas of her mother's, the same unreadable gaze my wife gives me when I most need to be able to read her thoughts.

I pull my wrist free and start snapping the blanket and re-twirling it. I snap here and there and here again. I'm almost through the line when one of the officers lets out a babyish squeal. Then I'm tackled. The blanket is torn from my hand. A sour taste sticks in my mouth as I am sandwiched on the snowy pavement. Unable to lift my chin any longer as the police shout threats, pin their knees to my back, and squeeze my wrists into handcuffs, I rest my cheek on the icy snow right in the middle of a tire track, which is already gritty with salt. And I hear Rachel's voice over all this, "Yes, now the police have apprehended the suspect."

5

Eleven hours later I'm headed home in a cab. I'd like to extend my thanks to the following people:

1) The shift commander, Ray Roy, who had not been at the accident and who I hope is not the exception to the rule as far as police officers go. At first glance he looked to be a frustrated state trooper wannabe, but behind his aviator-style glasses and in his earnestness and age (way over thirty years of service) I could soon see he got into policing for all the right reasons. The way he called me "son" was a comfort. He let me call my mother-in-law, Nancy, right when I got to the station so she could get to the hospital STAT. He let me call my wife twice, and he let me know the kids were all fine and headed home with their grandmother. He even checked in with Nancy himself a couple times. He also completely understood why I didn't have a license on me or my wallet and he was quick to give me the number of a bail bonds company that didn't need any money up front just in case I wanted to get out of jail right away and not wait for the judge the next day.

2) My mother-in-law, Nancy Wiesse, who heard that her grandchildren were at the hospital and her son-in-law was in jail, and simply said, "Oh boy."

3) Officers Murphy, Ricki, and Escobar fresh from the "kill" at the scene of the accident—still having a laugh about the squeal one of their colleagues named Johansen let out when I supposedly assaulted him with Tina's wet, spiraled *nah*, which is nothing more than an enshrined dishtowel, and who, I guess, made a token trip to the hospital. Each time they introduced me to a new officer they laughed their heads off again about Johansen. Their sense of humor reminded me that even at the most serious times in our lives someone is having fun. Telling me to say "Cheeseburger" for the mug shot. Running out of paper towels to wipe my inked fingers. Not taking away my tie thereby keeping my "options open." And finally easing the awkwardness with my fellow inmates as I entered the cell by announcing with trumpet sounds provided by Escobar: "Introducing the bozo with pink shoes." (Again, I must go back to Ray Roy and thank him for the pink Reeboks which were the only thing he could find in the unclaimed bin but much better than the sandals otherwise offered. But mostly I thank him for leaking that I was in for assaulting an officer, which increased my stock significantly and even made me a bit of a hero that night. Apparently this Johansen fellow isn't well liked in the criminal world.)

4) All my fellow inmates in the tank. The inebriated murmurers, the post-vomiting unconscious, the sobbing penitents, the glowering-restraining-order exs, and the one really angry gentleman who was pencil thin and who they had to remove from the cell shortly after my arrival (it seemed the word *bozo* made him uneasy). But I would like to thank four men in particular who, though I never did get their names, were able

to pull themselves together from a terrible conglomeration of odors and states of disorientation into more or less intact, thinking human beings and real sympathizers with a down-on-his-luck dad in pink sneakers who'd had a day for the record books.

5) The crew down at the *Beagle*, who made no mention of the accident in the newspaper. (Ray Roy gave me the rundown of all the morning's accident coverage before he finished his shift.) Whatever their reasons— deadline, sympathy for an ex-employee, tip of the hat to my PR machine, guilt about their usual anti-GE everything, or as I would like to believe, finding the facts of the case suspicious—they gave me the precious gift of time, the most important commodity in the realm of PR. Also to Rachel's station KNNK 12, who, this morning, reported only a minor accident on Greylock with no serious injuries though one person was arrested. No names mentioned, no mugshot put on display, no footage of Rachel on the scene wrapped in an Aquaman blanket. Officer Roy was impressed by the reports about the mayor's Frisbee attack and my involvement in it. He completely understood that I didn't want to "take a gander" at the photo of me at Percival Lake Park and he even said if he and the other officers knew I was involved in the mayor's dip, last night could have gone much much differently (apparently the police and the mayor are giving each other the silent treatment). I do have to say the rest of the morning as I was processed and released I was treated with dignity and kindness and even one heartfelt comment that I didn't look half bad in pink.

6) And, of course, most of all, I'd like to thank my beautiful and under-standing wife, Karen, for really being there for the kids when it counted most by somehow making it from Arizona to Massachusetts by five in the morning, including an hour's worth of slushy driving from Albany to Pontoosuc. For doing her best in understanding the reasons why I

failed to mention the previous night that I was calling from jail. For her valiant attempt at understanding the moral high ground I took by refusing to leave prison. And finally for her wise words (over the phone) encouraging me to not wait until the late morning arraignment (where I am quite sure I could have resolved the whole matter) and get home instead. Urging me to get out of jail and come home, something I was not at all sure she would want me to do, was an extremely large vote of confidence, and much appreciated.

7) And finally my cab driver, who I could tell would be a friend even through the windshield as I waved him my way in the slanted morning sun that offered just a little warmth.

"Twelve-forty-seven Greylock," I tell him, digging for the seat belt, "and step on it."

The sunlight makes him squint as he looks back at me, and I give him the best smile I can muster. He's a big man with a gargantuan neck. He's in his fifties or early sixties and wears a driver's cap snugged down over his forehead. It doesn't look like he has much hair. The chances are pretty good that in my ripped jacket, my tie, my ink-stained fingers, my scuffed pants with their barely noticeable salt stains, and my pink Reeboks, I look more like a beat-down public defender with a flare for sensible shoes than an accused felon with his bail contract in his pocket.

But he looks like someone who would certainly ferry me home safely, and even provide an ear of the common man, a focus group of sorts, for the beginning of my post-accident "Everything's OK" campaign.

We pull from the curb and away from the clean bricks of the police station. "Mr. Jensen," I say, having checked his name on the laminated photo ID. I wait a moment for him to say to call him Vince. "Your cab is the Ritz compared to the back of a cruiser."

His eyes meet mine in the rearview mirror and then he palms the steering wheel and we head onto North. A tough focus group will tell you how it is.

We pass by soaped store windows, three tired people with condensation rising from their mouths at a bus stop, a Don't Walk sign warning no one, and a tattered banner, "Opening Soon," drooped over the place I used to buy Big Block Hershey Bars when I was twelve. We pass another closed storefront. The same landlord owns most of this block and if we are unable to get into our offices for GE for some reason, I have set up a running agreement with him that we'll be able to use his empty office space as a temporary headquarters. I'm a person who makes contingencies, no matter how unlikely—I have files upon files of them at work. But I have no plan for coming home from jail.

As I look at these buildings and people and empty parking spaces, I remind myself that if I could make this city look good as I once did when I worked at the Pontoosuc Tourism Bureau, and if just yesterday I could lead our team in a response where in just a few hours we were able to draw a line through the word *crisis* to something as complicated as a mayor-involved Frisbee attack along with a forced acknowledgment that the Frisbee course was now out of the plans for Percival Lake Park—even with the disruptions of our boss Jason the Kid who wanted to consult "his friend" down at the EPA(!) and who since he took the job has called PCBs PCPs, it certainly should be no problem making my wife see the upside of a wrecked minivan, a night in jail, a revoked license, an upcoming court date, and a some slightly banged up kids.

Only a few hours ago my wife was more than two-thirds of the way across the country and now she is less than two miles away. I'm sure a lot of people in my situation would be pretty upset about how technology strips away buffer zones, strips away the time they need to collect themselves. I, on the other hand, am minutes away from my wife and family

34

and confirmation of our love. I'm eager to heal any wounds. The faster you deal with a problem, the faster it goes away. If, that is, there is a problem at all.

"Has this town ever heard of timed lights?" I ask. We are hitting every one.

"This town," he responds, "this town only stops for Frisbees."

I laugh, I'm in. "Frisbee hats," I say, "Frisbee steering wheels, Frisbee wheels."

I wait for his response. I know he's laughing behind his tough exterior.

At the next stoplight I say, "I refused a Breathalyzer."

"Those things are horribly unreliable," he said.

"That's just what I told them."

"One of my best friends, three beers! Three beers! and they nabbed him."

I can't be happier. After a shaky start, we are now friends. Full disclosure is the way to go. I feel so confident, in fact, I pull out my brand new temporary license and hold it over the seat and he takes his eyes off the red light to look at it. He gives a good hardy nod. He knows the damn thing is only effective for 15 days, until my registry hearing.

"There's more," I say.

"There always is."

"Assault and battery, resisting arrest."

He's quiet.

I take note of this for my campaign. He's wearing a driver's cap. I stopped talking about driving. When you talk to people who are wearing driving caps you talk about driving, the line of communication flows smoothly—you change subjects and the conversation falls apart. I vow to practice this logic from now on. I will talk to lawyers only about laws, police officers only about enforcement, mechanics only about cars, bosses only about bossing, and wives. . .

"Don't turn here," I blurt.

His head snaps around and his gray chin sticks out just enough to show he's puzzled by anyone who won't take the most direct route.

"Go up to the other end. The construction is terrible."

"Your dime."

"See those pipes down there? They should be in the ground where they're safe."

"Some moron crashed there last night."

The vehicles that come at us are caked with salt, the color of which is almost the same as Vincent Jensen's stubble. It is very likely he used to work for GE, *the* GE, but he's found his way into a job that seems to suit him even if he makes wrong assumptions about people and events he does not know the facts about. You're lucky if you can prepare people for bad news in advance—particularly your wife. Based on our phone conversation that morning and of course our years together, I quickly determine a wide range of Karen's possible reaction scenarios, no matter how gruesome and unlikely:

Scenario 1: Wife will give me a big hug, feel terrible for my night behind bars, rail against the injustices that occurred. See me as I truly am: a victim of circumstances beyond my control.

Scenario 2: She will consider me a drunk, no good father who has endangered the lives of her children, assaulted an officer, resisted arrest, and who failed to mention to his wife that he was calling from jail.

Scenario 3: All of Scenario 2 but add Jess's missing hours, picking up Rudd late, Tina's hair, and whatever the kids might have said about Rachel being in the car. And possibly Ernie Something leaving a message wondering if we arrived home safely. The librarian leaving a message about my wallet and wondering if I had any luck locating my daughter? Rachel leaving a message apologizing for her behavior? I better be ready for it.

Scenario 4: Scenarios 2 and 3 plus all the things I'd ever done wrong in Karen's eyes in the last eighteen years and even adding, for good measure, the things I did wrong before we even met. Keyword: *Things*.

I am a guy with a BA from UMASS, two disastrous years as a "reporter" for the *Beagle*, six quiet, happy years working for the Pontoosuc Tourism Bureau, and eight years of experience at the corporate world of GE. I love my wife. I love my kids. I landed in a job I'm pretty good at. I am 100% satisfied with my life. I attained all my goals. I'm not making any excuses, but who wouldn't put his hopes in the best-case scenario? Plus, there is a precedent, a beautiful precedent.

Up ahead of us is Tooley's Hunting Shoppe with the giant trophy of a buck mounted to the wall above the parking lot. The buck's head is turned slightly—the damn thing is dignified.

A few minutes later, Mr. Jensen puts on his blinker early as we pass a small park near our house where the kids and I have had good times and there is the seesaw that Tina loves above all else (except perhaps her mother and maybe now minks), a seesaw that just might be the only remaining true seesaw in America. Then there's our neighbor's dog, Gazook, barking as we pass. According to his owners, Nick and Naomi, he barks at me and me alone. So believe me, I'm happy to find out he also barks at taxis.

"Is that your dog?" Mr. Jensen asks, deadpan. "Never have I seen a dog bark at a person *inside* a moving car." And there it is: in this world there's always someone willing to strip you of even your smallest comforts.

"That dog right there," I say. "That dog, Gazook, and I are best buds. Nick, his owner, said he'd never seen Gazook take to anyone like he takes to me. Plus, in the dog world barking can be a sign of affection."

Mr. Jensen's eyes greet me one last time in the rearview. Right then I vow I'll never again use the rearview mirror to let Jess know exactly how I'm feeling.

"You sure you don't want one more lap?"

"No," I tell him. "No."

With the chatter of the turn signal, we ease into the snow-covered driveway and there's my wife's white Pontiac, salt-stained from the drive from the airport, not pulled all the way up the driveway but parked as if the minivan were in its usual spot in front of it. My poor minivan, sitting in a fenced lot somewhere, impounded and most likely totaled, smashed into paperwork of pink duplicates that are folded in my pocket with all the other duplicates of the law enforcement system.

"Your neighbors are quiet but grave folk," he says.

I don't understand, our neighbors are everything but. I then realize he's talking about St. Joseph's cemetery across the street.

This guy is a talking machine. I tell him to hang on for a second and run up the front steps to get the cash I had Karen leave for me. I grab the twenty out of the mailbox and give it to him through his window and tell him to keep the change. He looks at it as if he might return it to me, as if he's been honored by ferrying me home.

"I wish you luck in all your endeavors," he says, pinching the brim of his cap with the same hand he holds the money in.

I'm astounded, blown away. A guy like Vincent Jensen does not wish anyone luck unless he truly means it. I must have gotten through to him in some way during our short time together. I made my case without ever having to make it. Of course, I don't need luck. Luck is for the unprepared. But it is just the confidence boost I need. I could get my side out there and it could have a good effect. I give him a wave as he backs out and goes safely on his way toward the sewer pipes some definitely-not-a-moron hit last night. The cab's plume of exhaust hangs in the middle of the street until another car, going the other direction, shoots through it.

Gazook's barking subsides—he lives two doors down from us. "Good boy," I think as I turn toward our house. Somewhere along the line barking got turned into a negative, when really it's a lot like applause. Even if Mr. Jensen is right and Gazook was barking at just me (which I doubt), I'm glad he barked; just like I'm glad for the Radisons' pile of ever-changing cars next door, glad for the tinkling from the Windchimers' wind chimes on the other side of us, glad that the garbage cans at the end of our driveway are still knocked over, glad a piece of aluminum siding still droops to the right of Rudd's bedroom window. Here is our home. Nothing has changed in the twenty-four hours I was away, not even the minivan's oil spots, which have burned through the snow right in front of the Pontiac. As my eyes sweep over our house that we'd been renting for so long—seventeen years—a small house that contains so much, I head down the driveway to the back door. The twenty bucks she left out for me was a huge vote of confidence too. I invest everything in Scenario One. The kids will rally behind her, and our family will be pulled even closer together.

6

In the kitchen, I yell, "Hello," and not one person in my family comes to greet me. Two coffee-stained mugs are pushed to the center of our round kitchen table. The chairs are pushed away as if whoever was sitting in them ejected like a Pop-Tart out of a toaster. One seat has a rip in its vinyl exposing the yellow foam. "Hello?" I call out. "Hello." Then more softly: "Anyone home?"

There is brown water in the coffeepot. I switch off the orange light. I pluck a lone yellow leaf from the plant that hangs above the sink. It and the cactus in the dining room are the only two plants that can survive my wife's absences. The death of all the other plants we've had in the last few years has nothing, absolutely nothing to do with my ability to be a dad. It has nothing whatsoever to do with my being a spokesperson for a company that doesn't have the best track record with the environment—in the past—but that is now doing all it can within reason to rectify these past errors as demonstrated with all our hard work on Percival Lake Park. Maybe if I can get Tina to love plants like she loves the seesaw and now apparently loves minks we can populate the house again simply by providing Tina with a watering can. I close the cabinet door and listen. Still no family.

"I'm thirsty even after all that bread and water," I call. I pour a glass of water and drink it halfway down—my mom always gave me a glass of water to fix small problems and I have to say it still works. "We have kids? Where are they? How are they?"

The kitchen is clean. "Look at this kitchen! Sorry it was a mess. It's not usually that bad when you're gone." The house is silent behind the swinging door, which has closer genetic ties to cardboard than wood. I mean, normally, I can hear the TV loud and clear through it, and some-times I can even hear the thermostat in the living room click on. But this morning the one thing I'm not hearing is a family running to dad.

I put my glass into the sink, and then thinking better of it, I put it straight into the dishwasher. I have pink sneakers on. I recross the kitchen to the back door and the piles of shoes and boots that have accumulated and I'm about to take them off and bury them deep in the mix when I realize they will be the perfect icebreaker. I can already see my family cracking up about them. Using a paper towel I wipe the wet marks I tracked on the tile and scrub the soles, plucking a tack from the left one. My shirt is tucked in. I fix my pesky belt buckle. I straighten my tie. I put my phone and Jess's phone in our cell phone drawer. Sure, her phone beckons me, the mysteries of last night are probably captured right there. I stare it down and close the drawer. There are reasonable explanations. As a final touch, I stick a strip of duct tape over the tear in the vinyl seat—something I'd been meaning to do for a few weeks, and with both the kitchen and me repaired successfully I head through the swinging door for the dining room.

"Hey, where're the kids?" My wife is not in the dining room. "Did you send them to school after all?" The *Beagle*'s comics page is spread open on the table next to a plate with crumbs. I roll up the paper and put it under my arm. Another plate holds open *Vogue* to a page with a close-up of a woman's face. The radiators clink and clank. I hear voices as I continue past the happy family photos, the phone with too many messages, and the cactus spread along the mantled half-wall that separates the dining room from the living room.

In the living room the TV is flat black and the VCR blinks twelve. All four sections of the sofa are pulled together and a blanket is embedded between the cushions along with one of the pillows. I wonder who slept there. I pick the remote control off the floor and put it on the coffee table next to a half-eaten slice of toast, another magazine folded back to a woman's face, and my wife's gray suit-jacket—which doesn't have one salt stain from being brutalized by the police.

At the doorway to the basement I finally solve the mystery of my family's whereabouts: the electric buzz of Rudd's trains. Tina giggles, followed by the soft murmur of my wife's voice. My family is in the basement. They aren't sobbing uncontrollably on the floor, they aren't burning effigies, but they aren't giving their father three cheers either. It is morning, and since school was out of the question, my family decided to gather around Rudd's train set. That's a good sign. Halfway down the stairs, I grip the railing and lower myself onto a step, the newspaper in a roll under my arm.

My wife squats next to the shorn Tina on the opposite side of the trains from Rudd, who stands at his usual position in front of the control panel. She is still in her business clothes, a lavender blouse and the suit-jacket's matching skirt. Her thickest wool socks are pulled over the feet of her pantyhose. Her clothes are as wrinkled as mine.

"Looks like you just spent the night in jail," I say as I flip my tie over my shoulder.

"You look like you spent all night on a plane," she responds, without turning to me, not surprised by my sudden presence or my pink sneakers. She seems in good enough spirits. Even though no one rushes to hug me, Scenario One looks good.

Tina, her hair truly gone except for stubble, is still in her mother's good graces. She keeps sneaking peeks so I give her a wave. This is the first time I've seen her hair with clear eyes and under direct light. When you see a little girl with buzzed hair there's only one thing you think, but for Tina, there's more the air of a Navy Seal than of a child with cancer. Her pink sweatshirt and her blue sweatpants are part of her "all clear" ensemble, which she wears when she's getting better from an illness or when she's no longer upset about not getting her way or any time she wants to show that everything has returned to A-OK. She's glowing, basking in the week-early return of her mother. Stubble-headed but glowing, she knows how to see the positive.

Rudd's train set consists of two large pieces of plywood shaped into an L and held up by a warped, netless Ping-Pong table I bought for five dollars at a yard sale two weeks before he was born—I thought we'd be playing together in no time. In the seven years he's been working on the trains, he has created mountains, tunnels, bridges, towns, lakes, rivers, piers—you name it. It's pretty amazing—the eighth wonder of the world. Rudd doesn't look up at me. He did get the best view of Rachel last night. His face is pale, though, no burning cheeks and he didn't slam his glasses down as soon as he heard me. He's in his usual outfit—his standard gray collared shirt along with his standard pants full of pockets and his extra long wallet chain looping along his thigh. Rudd and I usually get along pretty well. We aren't out there passing pigskin around, we never had much luck playing ping-pong, but we are still a team. Really with Rudd everything revolves around his trains and now, starting this winter, hockey too.

At his command center his posture is alert and forward just as it is when he's at the net. Everywhere else he falls into his slouch. It's hard to believe this kid is fast becoming a hockey star—I don't think he even knows it. He's had a meteoric rise this season from being discovered in street hockey during gym, to JV, and finally last month varsity when the goalie tore a ligament and the backup got caught with beer. The county championships are less than a week away. People at work talk about him. I hear his name mentioned at the grocery store. There are absurd rumors that there will be a scout at the game. I doubt anyone knows he still plays with trains. I bet even wonderful Ernie Something would subject Rudd to merciless barbs. With his short hair and wire-rim glasses Rudd still looks more like an engineer than a jock. After his first varsity game, stunned, I asked how he had blocked every shot. He told me that when the puck comes at him he sees it in slow motion. I focus on the sign atop the highest mountain, Less Alpo, (which used to be a volcano I helped him make): *LOOK OUT*. How long has that been there?

Whatever his thoughts are about his father's night in jail and his eyeful of Rachel, I can tell this morning that he is not willing to be the voice of reason.

"Funny thing happened on my way home from the office," I say, lifting a leg to wiggle my shoe. This is hopeful, this is script, these are words that hang in the air, fishhooks with the most wondrous bait; if my wife will only take them, I'd only have to worry about reeling her in.

She does not bite. Nobody bites—not Tina, not Rudd. Someone always bites. There's plenty on everyone's mind, I understand. So I wiggle both feet. Nothing. I wiggle both again and add, "Boy, these new sneakers are fast!" Nothing except a look from Tina that she just doesn't get it.

Tina's head jumps back and forth trying to watch where the engines and the cars are going and where they've been at the same time. Rudd runs one train at full speed on the long straightaway out of the tunnel as another does the mountain run in the opposite direction. I rub the back of my neck, spot the ink stains on my fingers and quickly hide my hand again. Time to change the subject.

"Where's Jess?"

"She's sleeping," my wife answers, a strong hint of protectiveness in her voice, which throws me off.

"How's she feeling?"

"Bad."

"She got a nose job," Tina blurts. Karen squeezes Tina's arm and Tina asks, "What?"

How could my kids have been in an ambulance last night?

"I did better than Jess. I got a just-in-case X-Ray." Tina says X-Ray as if it were an exotic bird. "I saw my skull. Pretty cool. I'm growing into it. That's what all those cracks are. Nothing to worry about. Be sure to tell Nancy again that there's nothing to worry about. The doctor said I had a perfect skull. He'd never seen one so perfect."

"I believe it. I wish I'd seen it. No sledding today, huh?"

"Nope. Snow conditions are poor to real bad."

"What about hair conditions?"

"Daaaad," she draws it out and scratches that perfect skull and then pumps her fist in the air. "Solid dairy!"

I have to work pretty hard not to laugh. I have no idea what she is saying but I pump my fist too, "Solid dairy!" But the way my wife is now looking at me I can see I'm taking the fall for Tina's hair. Something I should be held accountable for. I take full responsibility. Of course Tina's first-grade teacher, Ms. Lowendorf, holds some of the blame for helping radicalize her in the plight of the mink, as well as the school system's new initiative: *Inform Yourself, Inform Others, Activate!*—so in the last month my daughter has learned about minks (random animals were assigned to each student), taught her parents, siblings, and classmates about them, and now seems to be on the Activate! portion of her lesson (apparently Burty has decided not to Activate! his "boring" grizzly bears and is now Activated! for the mink cause).

Rudd finally glances up to the level of my sneakers but he drops his eyes right away. Completely understandable, he has to keep his concentration on the trains, which are eating up the tracks.

"How are you doing?" I ask.

"Fine," he says. His body sways.

"You should see his bruise." Tina is the wound statistician.

45

"I can't wait. It's not going to stop you from playing is it?"

Rudd shakes his head slowly.

My wife's eyes shoot to him, full of motherly concern.

"That's a relief." Then I take a breath. "How's Mom?" I ask.

"She's doing OK," Tina says, her passion forgotten as she waits for the next train to emerge from the tunnel. My wife kisses Tina's head. "Maybe a little grumpy."

I smile broadly at my wife, *whose kid is this?* Her eyes have yet to level on mine. But we are at an awkward angle. If she's truly mad, she'd blast me with a look.

"How's Dad?" I ask.

"Take your jacket off, stay awhile," Tina says from our home-from-work script and then adds: "I like your picture in the paper again. Do you think I can get my picture in the paper for saving minks?"

"Do I look confident? Any hair out of place?" I ask her, continuing a script she's given me which I'm more than grateful for. My wife keeps her attention on the trains though.

"You should have let the Frisbee player keep swimming," Tina says definitively. "Mayors rule the city. Is that why you looked scared? Did the picture taker forget to say *cheese*?"

I try to explain that it's more complicated than that.

"Rachel's smiling. She doesn't forget. I hope we don't get her stomach bug."

"It was a rough day yesterday. One for the record books but everything's so much better today. Mom's home!"

Tina gives her mom a big squeeze and Karen sends a smile my way, but again her eyes don't come anywhere near me. Maybe she's already seeing the humor in it all.

The silver passenger train comes out of a tunnel and Tina follows it with her finger. Rudd flips switches and adjusts the speed of his three engines. Dad comes home, train world doesn't grind to a halt. Great.

"I just saw a place over at the corner of Crane," I say to Karen to keep the positive going. "I think they're having an open house Saturday. Should we blitz it? We haven't gone on one for a while. I've been keeping my eyes peeled for that doesn't-have-to-be perfect house." This time she shrugs—it's not on the top list of neighborhoods we want to live in. "Thanks for the cash. Cabs are great," I say, redirecting. "We should start taking them all the time."

"You might have to."

"Ha!" She's being funny this morning. This is even better than Scenario One! The furnace kicks on, vibrating the stairs. I study my wife's hair. The sun out West during her last two trips has been enough to bring it into its summer amber. She is letting it grow longer than it has been since she left for Africa seventeen years ago, and I'm still trying to figure out if her longer and longer hair is just good news or really good news. Of course, in light of Tina's hair, I'm not sure what to think. As for the smile my wife is wearing, it may fool the kids, but I'm an expert. The slightly heavier lines around her mouth, deeper and tenser, show what a hard night she had, how worried she'd been about the kids and me. I can see that our family's main job will be trying to alleviate those worries, to show her that, sure, it was a perilous situation but it's all over, everything is free to go back to normal.

"Jason called," she says.

There's no way I'm calling work today—if the poor kid knew I was arrested last night his head would explode with his mix of panic and inertia. "What did you tell him?"

She ponders this a little too long, glances at the newspaper under my arm, and then says, "I took your cue."

There's bite in that last remark and I completely deserve it. I wasn't honest with her last night about my exact location a couple of times.

"Touché," I say so that I acknowledge the gravity of my mistakes without bringing the kids in too much. "I hope you understand." I imagine Rita and Sally from the office appearing at the top of the stairs with paperwork full of data. What did my wife tell the kids? What had they told her? What exactly happened after I was carted away? Did Rachel talk to them? What did my wife know? I need some percentages, some hard numbers, color-coded maps. So does she understand?

"I understand," she says, but she sighs it out, a whisper sigh. If she'd just glare at me, at least I'd have a better read of this situation.

My knees crack as I stand up. Rudd races two trains side-by-side before one veers toward Less Alpo, Styrofoam Ridge, Painted River, and Swan Lake, and the other circles and switches toward Cardboard Harbor, Redneck Ville, and Ye Olde City and eventually wends itself back to Less Alpo. A crossing signal sounds as the third engine emerges from a tunnel, Rudd blows the train's horn, and on the outskirts of Milo's Meadow I note two matchbox cars bumped together.

"Solid dairy," I say again, pumping both fists in the air.

Tina follows suit and then says, shouts, "Save the minks!"

"Solidarity!" Karen says firmly. I'm miffed. My wife's eyes lock onto my feet. "Solid dairy is solidarity." Her voice is a little harsh. Rudd's glasses are off his face and on the control panel. His face, my barometer, has moved to lobster red. What happened?

"Oh!" I say. Scenario One?

"Solid dairy," Tina says. "That's what I've been saying."

"I'm going to check on how solidarity is treating your sister."

Tina explains that Jess doesn't care about minks.

"I don't think she wants to talk to you right now," Karen says.

"That's a surprise," I say. She can't take her eyes off my sneakers all of the sudden and it's as if she keeps finding new things she doesn't like about them. Maybe I should have buried them. When I step onto the landing Tina's voice follows me, "Later Gator."

"Awhile crocodile," I call down, thankful.

I wait at the doorway to hear Karen excuse herself from the trains so she can make sure Daddy's doing OK, but instead I hear Tina say, "Before the crash and before Dad beat up the police, Rachel and Dad had a great time skating on Burty's floors. We need to get those floors. But then Rachel got really sleepy. That must have been the start of her stomach bug." I'm tempted to go back down and try to gage all the reactions since no one responds, but it is best to keep moving forward. I dilly-dally in the living room for a few minutes, fully expecting Karen to make her way up the stairs. I'm sure she's going to want to chat. I'm giving her every opportunity. Occasionally she likes to let "things" stew and when the kids are asleep she'll—, well, I still have a good feeling about Scenario One. When there's no sign of her, I head upstairs.

7

I put the newspaper on our bed, and in my top bureau drawer full of keepsakes that have no better place to go—the rocks, leaves, acorns, and crayon drawings of fatherhood, I stuff the paperwork of imprisonment, bail, and the minivan impoundment—the flimsy layers and faded ink. I also study the card from Alexander's Boxing Academy before I place it in the drawer too. I change into my sweats and pull on some socks. I don't think a pair of socks has ever felt so good. I should probably haul the sneakers to the garbage, but I keep them, way back in the closet, under shoes I never wear anymore and a couple of shirts and pants that aren't worth the trouble to rehang. I do a loop of the room with my tie in my hand, wondering what to do with the small wine stain. At first I put it in the drawer next to the paperwork, but then think better of it and hang it on the rack with the other ties. After some consideration I put the tie on the dry-cleaning pile—hey, I have nothing to hide. On the bed, the sheet is tucked and folded neatly but the blankets are askew. I can't tell if Karen slept at all—she needs solid sleep more than *solid dairy*, which could explain her mood. I sit down on the bed and unfold the newspaper to see what Tina meant about looking scared.

Before I open the paper, I'm confident about what the headline will read: "MAYOR LEADS VICIOUS FRISBEE ATTACK!"

The actual headline makes me put the paper down and after a moment bring it back to my eyes just to give it a chance to change to something else—it does not: "GE AXES DISC GOLF." This is unbelievable, completely unbelievable. I'd take a photo of me being handcuffed over this! And that might as well be the photo they ran! The photo under the headline looked as if Rachel and I were trying to hoist the writhing ski mask-wearing mayor off the banking and into the lake. I did look scared and why shouldn't I be? Rachel, having just kicked him in the balls, was trying to throw him into a lake that although was not yet iced over had to be pretty close to freezing—there, at the moment, seemed like the possibility of imminent death for the Frisbee attacker and murder charges for Rachel. Of course at the time I was not happy with either of them, but still, I was able to take the high ground even if to anyone looking at the photo it does look like I'm participating as Ray Roy suggested this morning. How Jason the Kid managed to hold himself together enough to get off the phone with his mom and try to contact me this morning shows that I might have underestimated my boss.

The actual article about the cancellation of the course hacks and misrepresents my statement so badly that it even seems to suggest there's some cover-up involved. The purity and tactfulness of my original statement I can still recite word for word: *We here at GE have a great respect for the environment and particularly the natural beauty of Western Massachusetts. We are citizens here and we want what is best, especially in respect to our own children, the future stakeholders in this community. We are eager to unveil Percival Lake restored to its former beauty, as well as the accompanying park with its trails, meadows, woodlands, playground, skateboard park, basketball and tennis courts, outdoor concert venue, and other amenities. It certainly will be a crown jewel for Pontoosuc. But after many meetings and many hours of discussions with all the stakeholders, we have decided that Frisbee golf, while a vital sport to our area, would be inappropriate for Percival Lake Park. The park is intended primarily as a return to nature. In regards to the other amenities, they are situated on the street sides of the park and thus do little to impinge on the natural element it is designed to enhance. But because of Frisbee golf's nature it would crisscross the whole park including hiking trails and slicing right through the meditation meadow. While we completely support Mayor Dugus's vision, the course goes against Percival Lake Park's charter statement and the original vision we as a community set out for it five years ago. GE is in the process of aiding in the search for a new location for the course to help Mayor Dugus follow his dream of making Pontoosuc a golfing destination. GE has been a responsible partner and we have our eyes on the future as demonstrated by this park that we are giving back to the community.*

The only positive I can see in this is that the article misses so badly the real news, it reveals to any sensible reader how much the *Beagle* hates, yes, hates, GE. KNNK loves the mayor and the *Beagle* hates us. I'm surprised and not surprised that the byline reveals Nathan Shaffeur, their young reporter who always sees the bad side and just wants to show everyone that he's on his way to the *New York Times*. I just feel sorry that Shaffeur has endangered his career with this article. He's way too smart to have fallen for the mayor's story and yet here in his second article in a box next to the cancellation of the golf course: "Mayor Leads Practical Joke for a Cause on Leap Day." Frisbees pounding into the innocent? Real life bruises on real life bodies? A practical joke? A cause? This article reminds the reader that exactly four years ago Mayor Dugus, starting his first term, vowed to use Leap Day as a stunt to call attention to a single issue that he will tackle during his term. So four years ago he and his mayoral team raided a city council meeting with Frisbees to announce his ambition to turn Pontoosuc into the Frisbee golf world capital. The mayor seems to like throwing Frisbees at people. We should all be thankful that he didn't decide to do archery!

The newspaper does not serve as the confidence boost I need before seeing Jessica, but the mindset demonstrated was a perfect warm-up for what I might expect from my daughter.

Jessica is not even close to sleeping and doesn't seem to be feeling "bad" at all. She's in her closet, singing in a high nasally voice, ". . .your tender touch. Oh, oh. Why leave? Why leave? Oh, oh. All I want. . ." Although I can listen to her sing all day, if she planned to be a pop star I'm afraid she's going to have to learn how to lip-sync. Clothes are being launched from the closet to the percussion of the scraping hangers. "You're chipper," I say, pretending to knock on her open door—a real rarity of late. More clothes are spread in piles on her bed.

"You getting out of Dodge?" I ask, smiling. She keeps singing. "Hot date?" I've been using this line with her for years. It used to make her blush. Still she's singing, ignoring me. So I decide to take the first move toward reconciliation: "Jess, I just wanted to say I'm sorry for my part in our misunderstanding last night and I hope. . ."

A foot rises and drops and then Jess backs out of the closet. She stops with her back still toward me and I see she's listening to her iPod. She isn't giving me the silent treatment. She hasn't even heard me. She reaches into the closet again and pulls out a dress. She's wearing a snug black turtleneck I never saw her wear before, and the dress she has draped over her arm is her mother's. A dress years old, a summer dress, light and frowzy, blue and short, short. The kind of dress I can remember my wife laughing in, threatening to fall out of as her shoulders hunched forward just as she pulled me into an awkward dance move at someone's wedding. I'm deciding whether or not to question her about it, most likely going to let it slide for the time being, when she turns to face me.

Bandages wrap her nose and the tape extends to her cheekbones. She says something about jail but it doesn't register. The splint gives a linear aspect to her nose, as if she's one of Tina's popsicle stick contraptions. What I can see of her face is entirely swollen, green and yellowed. Everything that Officer Johansen got last night he deserved. I can't help it, I take a step back. Jess doesn't seem to mind. Somewhere under the bandages and bruising, I swear she even takes on a bemused look. But I am happy to report that upon further examination the bandages and the bruising are not as bad as they first seem. Her hair is as it always is, coiffed to perfection. Some kids collect stamps, some Barbie Dolls, my daughter collects styling gels, straighteners, and sprays. She has a milk crate she hauls in and out of the bathroom with her. I once caught her fixing her hair *before* she took a shower.

She fiddles with her iPod, pausing the song, just as she always does when I come into her room—not to make communication easier, but in a way she might close a diary to keep me from seeing what's in it. "Anything wrong?" she asks, hands on her hips, her mother's dress bunched at her wrist.

I dare another two steps into her domain and garnering no warning, risk one more into the center. I do a quick fatherly scan of her teen idol posters full of squinty heartthrobs and same-age female idols (a lot of exposed belly and breasts jutted forward as if to let the world know this girl was not to be messed with), her open bureaus, her pink bookshelf that's full of stuffed animals and old dolls, the piles of clothing on the bed, the magazines all flipped open to women's faces. She stands before me. If we both reach out our arms, our fingers will touch. Maybe it is the black turtleneck that makes her seem more solid, older. Her bare feet are firmly planted on the rug between her bed and the closet. The shoulder straps of my wife's dress touch the floor as my daughter continues to gaze at me, waiting for an answer. *Anything wrong?* My first post-accident test? I can hug her just for this show of strength (though I wouldn't dare to actually try). Why can't she ever admit she's vulnerable? Even her tears last night had more hostility in them than anything else.

But right then I'm happy for her strength. I think she might even have courage. Most girls would be worried about their noses, crying about their ruined lives, and here is my daughter planning who knows what, but she's planning.

"How's your schnozzle?" I ask, bravely venturing my whole family's happiness on this question.

"Great."

There's no sarcasm in her voice. That fact stuns me. This is the most amazing answer ever. Perfect. "Great," I echo.

"Nancy said I looked just like models do after a nose job."

"What a great way to look at it. It didn't occur to me, but that's just it." I like my mother-in-law even more. I don't know what else to say. This is the longest conversation I've had with my daughter for six months. She folds the dress and puts it on her bed and covers it with a sweater.

"I told mom everything."

"Really?" I'm stunned again.

"Yes."

"That's good, Jess. I'm glad. The truth's best."

"I thought you'd think so."

"So you talked everything out with her? Everything?"

"You bet." I recognize my own intonations in these two words, and that makes me happy. She looks up at me, even the whites of her eyes seem a little bruised.

So it is all out there, Jess being lost in not-the-best neighborhood, Dad down in the snow in the middle of the road after a fistfight, Rachel vomiting out the window. It's only relief I feel.

"The library?"

"Yep."

I trace her voice for sarcasm again, and again find her pure. My daughter has explained everything to my wife; there must be reasonable explanations already in the air and that's why everyone is so neutral; there is nothing to be glad about and nothing to be mad about as far as Jess's missing hours. It's all out there. "Well, you know you can always talk to me," I say as she nods in response. "Good. Now don't work too hard. You don't want to overdo it."

"OK, Dad," she says.

Good advice for a great daughter. I think I will take it too. I wash off the events of the night in the shower (I am sure the blast of cold water from someone turning on the faucet in the kitchen is purely an accident—I didn't place the plastic cup over the faucet). I dry off, feeling pretty good. Go to prison, take a shower, good as new. I should call work, I should see how KNNK is handling everything, if the *Beagle* has posted any corrections on its website yet, but I don't. I roll into the dip on my wife's side of the bed and listen to my daughter's singing. My family. Everything's OK.

8

I wake up to the smell of burnt soup and the sound of my wife opening and closing her bureau drawers. Our neighbor's wind chimes
reach symphonic levels. The sunlight appears and disappears as if it
is shining through the windows of a passing subway. Apparently, both
the clouds and my wife are in a hurry. I yawn and stretch.

"Glad you could get some rest," she says. She's in her underwear. As
if my wife has some inkling of my thoughts, she wraps her coffee-stained
robe around her, cinches the belt tight, and doesn't let go: "Can you
make sure the house doesn't burn down for fifteen minutes?"

"Be happy to," I say with a sleepy smile. I'm smart enough not to give
my wife a hard time about her shower estimate—it will be thirty minutes
minimum. "What about smolders? Would smolders be OK?"

And finally—I'm relieved—it happens: she looks me in the eye. In
the category of my wife's looks, I believe with all my heart the one she
gives me would cause a grizzly at a salmon run to drop its catch. Even
though I don't stand a chance, I meet the challenge, propped on my
elbows, as any good husband would. So after holding out for close to
a new personal record, I say: "I know you're upset. You've been up all
night. Stuck in airports and planes. You've had a scare. Your husband

spent a night unjustly in jail. He has charges pending. He could very well do time. A policeman put your family's lives in danger and your husband has to pay the consequences."

"You were drunk driving with our kids!"

"I refused a Breathalyzer. That doesn't—"

"For the second time!" Her knuckles whitened as they gripped the ends of her belt.

I don't understand her hostility. Has she forgotten? Then it is up to me to remind her: "But you, you—"

"I what?"

"You understood."

"I was pregnant and you were fired and I hadn't been up all night and you didn't have our kids in the car."

I've gone for Scenario One during other times in our lives together when I probably shouldn't have, like when I picked her up in the airport after Africa, when I had to rush Rudd to the hospital after he brought down the Christmas tree by trying to scale it, when I was fired from that job at the Pontoosuc Tourism Bureau, when she told me she was pregnant with Tina, when Jess was suspended from school because she misapplied some advice I gave her about boys, all without success. I'm just hoping for the best, aiming too high—that's where we should aim, right?

"I wasn't drunk this time."

"So you were last time?"

"That's not what I meant."

"I want to believe you weren't."

She watches me struggle for something to close this conversation on a better track than we're on.

"I think," she says, "you're supposed to say Breathalyzers are—"

I'm ecstatic! Here's the script and just like Vincent Jensen I now have my opportunity to show our unity: "—terribly unreliable." I hold my arms out to her, waiting for an embrace. We're on the same wavelength.

58

"I feel like airplane food." She rubs her nose with her palm and blasts her fingers through the hair. "Can I trust you just keep an eye on the kids while I'm in the shower, without getting arrested or anyone else shaving their head."

"Trust," I say, "I'm the pillar." I keep my arms out because maybe it will convince her.

"Jess at the library." She says this more as a retort, which throws me off.

The floorboards creak in the hallway and there's a light knock at our door. My wife lets go of her belt and opens the door, closing it behind her but before it closes completely she asks Tina what she's doing with all those magazines.

"Are you mad at Dad?" I hear.

My wife says something I can't quite make out but does sound closer to *no* than *yes*.

"You've been popular," she says in nearly a whisper as she comes back in the room and heads to where her carry-on now blocks the closet door.

I'm encouraged by the normality of her tone as if one wife went out the door and another came back in. She points to my phone like it is a discarded Band-Aid.

"The phone has been ringing for you all morning. Sam and Jason. Sam was crying I think." She bends over her bag and starts to dig through it, pulling out her brush and shampoo. Her carry-on seems to be her only luggage. She's looking for something. "Dammit."

"Hey, maybe it's in your other bags. Are they still in the car? I'd be happy to go get them." I offer both my hands again to show they are free and willing to help. My wife's eyes fall on my stained fingers. I see now why she didn't rush to embrace me when I held my arms out to her.

"This is all I brought." Her hand rushes up the side of the bag as she attempts to launch the zipper into outer space. "Rachel called too," she says, her belt loosens and her robe hangs open as she walks by with her shampoo and soap in her hands: "You can listen to the message yourself." My wife didn't have to, but she got our landline phone from her bureau and brought it to me, which again, I find encouraging. She doesn't stay at my side. She heads right for the bathroom, somehow leaving a question mark in her place.

The bathroom door closes and locks. I hit the message replay skipping all the messages until I get to Rachel: "We have to talk about what's going on. Can you get a statement about the protests by noon? Sam and Jason both seem, well, baffled. They didn't seem to know about the accident and I left it at that. It sounds like the kids are OK, that nose looked bad though. I'm not even going into Burty's hair. I promised myself I'd keep this just to business." There's a long pause. "I'm not sure if I have more questions about what's going on right now at the park or about what happened last night." She pauses again and sighs. It sounds strange out of her, more like a broken whistle. Did Karen listen to this whole message? "For Christ sakes your sock was in the bookshelf and your shoe was in the guest toilet with a corkscrew and corks stuffed in it." Another pause, I can't imagine she's feeling very good. I'm not feeling very good right now. "I can't imagine you want it back." Her pauses are killing me. I hope for at least that sigh again but there's nothing. "You need to get me that statement." No goodbye.

I look at the time. I've missed Rachel's noon show completely. Yesterday Karen sent me the text, "Things." The room goes from shadow to light, shadow to light. I don't blink, I don't rustle the sheets, I don't do anything. I don't even bother to breathe. What I do is unceremoniously, reluctantly, cross off Scenario One.

9

At this point, I could have rolled into a ball and pulled the blanket over my head and hid out all day. I do let myself lick my wounds for one minute. I time it. Then I'm back in action. Downstairs, I'm dressed for the Arctic. It's the exact opposite from last night: It's daylight, all my kids are home and accounted for, I have no minivan, my feet are in winter boots, I'm made of twelve layers, and the only naked woman around is my wife and she's in the shower where you're supposed to be naked. I put the blue cup over the faucet in the kitchen so no one blasts her. Before I head outside to work on the house, I take a listen to Rudd and the buzz of his trains. All OK down there. Jess is flipping through every magazine we have and thinking about the possibilities. She's seeing the good side to a smashed nose. And, even better, Tina is curled up with her. Something I barely see. Jess wears barbed wire where Tina is concerned and it hurts Tina at the soul-level. But right now she's as happy as can be. Jess doesn't even have her phone in her hand.

Back in the kitchen, I open the cell phone drawer where we are all supposed to deposit our phones when we come into the house. I don't look at any of the messages from Jason, Alexis, Sam, or even from Rachel, but I send a text to Sam telling him I can't make it in and reassuring him he can handle whatever is on tap. He can't, but one vote of confidence will do him good. I also send a text to Rachel to ask if I could get on air tomorrow in the safety of her studio to address the BS in the paper (I keep it simple between us because there's nothing happening between us that's not simple). My phone is now safely off and I put it back in the drawer next to Jess's.

Something looks wrong about her phone though. I realize it's the simple fact that it's off. Also that it is in the drawer at all. It is a requirement but if Dad and Mom aren't around the phone finds its master. It spent the night alongside my phone in an envelope in a locker at the police station and apparently it has gone untouched today. This makes me a little worried. Maybe she just thought it was lost? It's my parental responsibility to check that phone. I make sure the coast is clear and I step into the pantry. Twenty-two messages from Sarah since last night. The ones from last night range from "Wre r u" to "U can't b mad." The ones from today just say in various forms, *please text me*. The message that is most concerning is from someone called The Baker who doesn't seem to be an actual baker. It reads, "yo, frz." This is concerning. Anybody with *The* as any part of his name is trouble (and I don't think I'm going out on a limb by projecting that he is a male). I saw it in a parenting book once: "If anyone with 'the' in his name contacts your daughter, lock her in a room for one year"—or something like that. It was also sent at 3:30 in the morning—maybe he really is a baker.

I'm about to storm into the living room and demand answers, but from the swinging door I see my daughters curled up together, one with no hair and the other with an X of bandages over her nose, and I remember the time a couple years ago when Jess put her leg in front of a beagle that was going for Tina's face. Every time Jess has let us down since then, which is plenty, I have to remember that moment when her leg was mauled to save her sister. It is a spectacular set of scars. The type of scar you never want to fade. Plus, I remind myself that she has already shown that same courage by revealing everything to her mother, which means tonight after the kids are asleep I'll be fully apprised of the events during some great one-on-one time with my wife. I delete the message from The Baker and turn her phone off too and stick it back in the drawer. None of my business.

"I'll be outside fixing the house if anyone needs me," I announce as I pull down my Patriots hat as far as it will go over my ears.

Up the ladder, two stories high, I'm fixing the loose piece of siding outside of Rudd's window. After less than a minute, I hear barking, and there coming up the driveway is Gazook with his red leash trailing behind him. He's a dog that always looks like he's slipping on ice. In an instant, his front paws are up on the rungs, and he's barking his lungs out and shaking the hell out of it. Nick and Naomi sprint around the corner of the house and Nick continues toward Gazook as Naomi stops. Gazook will listen to anyone only if there are a sizeable number of biscuits as part of the bargain. Nick pulls on Gazook's collar to little avail and thankfully steadies the ladder with the other hand as Naomi runs back to the house for a bigger box of biscuits.

"Sorry, man," Nick yells up.

I joke that Gazook must have installed siding in his former life, but Nick can barely hear me over the barking and wind. Nick and Naomi are good kids and it's too bad they don't live right next to us. They're just starting out. Nick wants to talk about microbrewed beers and Naomi is in what she calls a "serious yarn phase." They are nothing like my wife and me when we first moved here seventeen years ago, but whenever I see them holding hands as they walk Gazook or laughing together in their car as they wait for an opening in traffic, I can't help thinking back. But Gazook is another matter.

Naomi's here to the rescue and Gazook agrees to the number of treats offered and the three of them head back up the driveway, all apologies and waves in their yarned mittens, scarves, and hats.

"We're pregnant," Nick yells back suddenly, his voice carried to me by the wind, and Naomi gives him that look that it isn't time to tell the neighbors, but then smiles up at me to show they're still a unified force even if he just messed up.

I know that this is the type of news that requires one to get down from the ladder but if I don't overreact it makes Nick's slip not such a big deal—plus, if I go down I know I won't come back up and I'm looking to capture my own unified force again. "Great news!" I call down. "Karen will be delighted."

Naomi loops her arm through Nick's as Gazook leads the way. Nick shoots a look up at me and hangs back for a second and I know that look too—it is not thankfulness for how I covered his slip but the look of having a future suddenly spelled out and defined right in front of you but no matter how you try to see it you can't. My gloves are too thick for the OK sign so I give him the thumbs up. I'm not sure he sees it before Gazook and Naomi pull him around the corner of the house. I'll grab a beer with him soon, maybe just a coffee, and we'll talk about everything else but being a dad and he'll understand that what he's in for is wonderful, maddening, and terrifying—and he'll love it!

After about ten minutes of work, one piece of aluminum siding is now lying in the snow below the ladder and another one is hanging in front of the dining room window. The good news is that the one I came up to fix is now straight and secure. Maybe I'll tell Nick about my dad— give him an example. When I was a kid he would spend a lot of time on the ladder. Then sometimes he'd just sit on the roof. When I'm up the ladder, now I sort of understand. Dads just need to be up high. Today it almost feels like I'm on Everest. The wind's gusting and it's super cold and from where I stand I can see the tinkle of a stream behind our house and the treed hill that rises steeply, and the other direction, across the street, there's the cemetery and beyond the gray trees, some pines and the distant hills. I close my eyes and listen to the non-contemplative clang of wind chimes next door, the sounds of raised voices coming from our other neighbors (the Radissons we call them because there are new faces and new cars almost every day), the rush of passing cars, and somewhere in the distance a construction vehicle's beeping. I feel good. I'm above it all. I'm getting some things done. It would almost be glorious, except I didn't consider that I would be right outside the wall where my wife is still taking a shower.

So here I am just listening to the pressure of the water as it runs through the pipes toward my wife. There behind this wall, I picture the bumps of her spine, the loose carriage of her buttocks, and the press of her forearms tight against her breasts as the water sprays her face, which always lengthens and calms as it receives the water. Between gusts and passing cars, I can even hear the whir of the bathroom fan and once a shampoo bottle slide into the tub. My wife never opens her eyes from the moment she steps into the shower to the moment she reaches for the towel. Before she went to Africa five days and seven hours after we were married, she took five-minute showers. "Water doesn't grow on trees," she'd say. She even turned the water off when she was soaping up. When she came back from Africa—unexpectedly, with no notice and months before she was scheduled to return, a lot of things were different, but the most surprising were these long showers, running a minimum of thirty minutes even with her long hair gone. Today right through this wall, she might just be going for a new record.

I put my gloved hands against the side of the house we've rented all these years: the cheap aluminum siding, the wood, the pink insulation I always hope fills the empty spaces (though I have my doubts every time I open the heating bill), the wallboard, and olive shower tile. All in all, the space separating us is measurable, not much more than a foot. The rungs press into my thighs and shins. The cold's beginning to eat up my fingers and ears. The arches of my feet are starting to cramp. My wife's reddened body in there. The seep and swirl of steam under the heat lamp and the thrumming fan in front of the mirror that won't clear for an hour. I'm right here. She's so close.

"Hello! Hello, up there. Yo, Dave, down here!"

It's Mary Beth, the librarian—she's no Gazook at the base of the ladder. She's even more mummified than last night. Yo? In her mitten, she has my wallet—which clearly she didn't rummage through since she still can't get my name right. She's holding it high above her head, with such urgency that it seems like she's offering me the solution to everything.

When Mary Beth and I go in, the house *actually is* smoldering. Pop-Tarts are on fire in the toaster oven. Tina is crying and screaming in the kitchen doorway that she isn't a boy. Jess taunts her first about giving her a fur jacket for her birthday and how Tina will have to wear it because it's a present and that Mom and Dad will make her wear it; this brings Tina to a level of hysteria I haven't seen in some time and Jess switches back to saying Tina's a boy because she has a boy haircut and everyone is going to make fun of her at school tomorrow. Rudd knocks over Tina in the doorway as he runs to stop the Pop-Tart fire, swearing his head off (I can't help but think last night Ernie gave the team lessons on the best type of curses to hurl at the opponent). I've got the cord in my hand as the flames begin to die down. Rudd looks at me and then Mary Beth and immediately takes off his glasses and leaves them on the counter After trying to help Tina stand up, which she refuses to do, he disappears back down into the basement and his trains and starts pounding with a hammer, blind.

"I won't stay long," Mary Beth says as she unwinds her scarf as I try to fan some of the smoke out of the house by swinging the backdoor. The smoke detector sounds the alarm in the dining room. "Fire. Fire," the canned voice repeats after each piercing blast. In a second I'm up on a chair trying to get the battery out of the detector and that's when my wife bangs down the stairs, dripping wet in her robe. Speechless she takes it all in: Jess, quiet now with her best *not my fault expression*, Tina spilled on the floor in her biggest tantrum since toddlerdom, Mary Beth smiling "Hi Karen" and waving, with one hand as she rubs Tina's back with the other (my wife struggles to recognize this woman squatting next to our daughter but Mary Beth seems oblivious), and finally her eyes land on me just as I pry the battery loose so the only sounds are Rudd hammering and Tina screaming. Between my inked thumb and forefinger I hold the battery out to my wife.

The sound of her stomping back up the stairs silences Rudd's hammer and even Tina's wailing. I consider whether to chase her with Nick and Naomi's news, but that's when the smoke detector starts in the stairwell, which elicits one blunt curse from my wife before the bedroom door slams. Perhaps my wife has been going to hockey practice too.

"Maybe this isn't such a good time," Mary Beth says and puts a book down next to Tina, *Harvesting Hope*. If I do get some coffee with Nick, it might be best to be vague about the details of fatherhood.

Finally, I put a real X through Scenario One.

10

That night Tina is tucked in twice. When I tuck her in, three flashlights light her room; she calls them *torches*. Every outlet in her room and out in the hallway and in our bedroom is used for recharging batteries for her torches. They are her original hobby, one I'm glad to see has yet to be completely taken over by the plight of minks. Her mother brings a new one home from each business trip and she's up to fifteen different states.

"Are you mad at Rudd?" she asks.

"No, of course not."

"Jess?"

I shake my head.

"Mom?"

Again, I shake my head.

"Me?"

"I'll never be mad at you."

"Ever?"

I nod in affirmation, glad that her room is dark enough I don't really see her shorn hair. Her flashlight beam moves away from me.

"Did March come in like a lion or a lamb?" she asks.

She must have waited all evening—I'm the one who's supposed to ask her, a father-daughter tradition. I listen to the wind. I turn off the flashlight at the foot of the bed and the one on her nightstand with the pig lamp, leaving only the one she grips through her blankets. Last night I saw her packed into an ambulance and she must have seen me handcuffed and put in the cruiser. I wonder once the judge exonerates me if we'll receive her blanket, her *nah*, which is currently being held as evidence.

"We'll have to wait and see."

"It's pretty bad out," she says, lifting her chin toward the window.

"But would you really want to commit yourself to the lion? I'm going to be unprecedented here and say: in like a lamb out like a lamb. What do you think?"

"I like lions," she says. "Except when they eat zebras."

"Exactly." I kiss her forehead. "Lambs have never been known to eat zebras."

"Mom says it came in like a bulldozer."

I place my hand over the flashlight, which illuminates my skin pink. She moves the beam to my parched fingers, the ink which I've been scrubbing with paint thinner at various intervals today. Then she snaps off the light and we're in the dark. "Dad," Tina asks as she clicks on her penlight (she keeps it under her pillow) and aims its narrow beam just below my eyes, "Jess said you're going to rot in jail and that you make Mom cry."

I have to think for a second. "Do you remember last year when Ms. Trudy thought at recess you sat in the puddle on purpose and made you sit in the corner. It's just like that. A misunderstanding."

"I did do it on purpose," she says

I pat her leg.

"Jess is a liar," she says. I'm about to defend Jess especially on the level of sisterly love but then Tina keeps going: "I'm going to march like that man in the book Ms. Mary Beth gave me today. I'm going to march for more than 300 miles though. Minks should be marched for."

"It sounds like a plan," I say—the librarian's book was about Cesar Chavez, which in my mind isn't the greatest choice to give a kid that just cut off her hair and the hair of her best friend for a cause. "Can I come?"

She's quiet so I think she drifted off, but then she asks, "Do you think Gazook would eat a mink?"

"The only thing Gazook wants to eat is your dad."

"He's just trying to tell you something."

There's no need to warn her that plans don't always go the way you want because I'm sure she already has doubts about whatever plans started with shaving her head, but I don't want to scare her away from plans because in this world you need them. You need plans and you need backup plans. Earlier that evening my plan involved pizza, a great way of fixing things. Nothing goes wrong when a family is enjoying a pizza. But it went bust right away when the pizza guy delivered the wrong pizzas. I put everything in the power of pizza. And that's not like me at all. I was not in the least bit surprised by my family's resilience, though. I tried to lead by example by utterly enjoying four jalapeño, roasted garlic, and anchovy slices as the rest of my family made their way more carefully through the pizzas, picking off toppings without a single complaint, even from Jess, as we watched TV. Tina controlled the TV tonight (how had she wrestled control from her sister? some recompense for the harsh words that drove her to a tantrum that afternoon? Guilt for giving a six-year-old a skewed perspective of what happened the night before?). *Jeopardy* was our usual show for a pizza night, but she had on some animal documentary about pandas in a zoo that couldn't reproduce. The choice of shows drove Jess (without a complaint!) to the kitchen table where she chose Cheerios over pizza and her collection of magazines over TV and did not open the cell phone drawer once to check her phone. And don't even get me started about how she was still wearing a turtleneck, the same turtle-neck all day long, her own record surpassing the three hours she usually managed before a complete wardrobe adjustment. I know the real reason turtlenecks were invented and it has nothing to do with keeping your neck warm—it's to hide hickeys. If my wife really did know what happened while Jess wasn't at the library, she was acting rather casual about it—but if she could be casual about it, so could I.

Red-cheeked Rudd was the next one to go, driven to his room by the word *inseminate*. So then it was down to Tina, my wife, and me, until the pizza slipped from my wife's hand and plopped face down on her sweatpants; I came to the rescue instantly with a handful of napkins. She just might have said *thanks* under her breath (the closest she came to talking to me since before her shower); once she changed into another set of sweats, she headed for the kitchen because she had a hot date with bottles of Mr. Clean and 409, some rubber gloves, and three rolls of paper towels, apparently cleaning the pantry was on her list of to-dos for the night—her own small fixes? Were we on the same page? We'd work on our own small fixes until they led us to, say, our bedroom door, where we'd meet with our lips?

The next show was about the strange creatures that live in the deepest recesses of our oceans. Tina didn't even notice when I got up. I had my own date with the nail and thumbtack holes in the dining room from a picture hanging gone wrong a few years back, ten years? Outside the dining room window, the siding still hung in a diagonal—if I got up early enough I might be able to tackle that before work. The Spackle I bought for filling holes was completely dried, so I squeezed a tube of Crest into a plastic cup and filled holes, a trick my college roommate taught me. Besides the wind and the underwater sounds from the TV, the only noises were pages being ripped from magazines and the strangled quack of the 409 bottle. Really the evening passed much the same way it did on any other night when we were all home.

So after I finish tucking in Tina, I head right downstairs to my wife. It's time to have it out. Bulldozer? I've got to take the initiative. I hope to find her in the pantry but she's on the sofa with the TV off, waiting for me. Her barrette is gone. Her hair is pushed behind one ear. I am unable to read the expression on her face in a positive way.

"Done with the pantry?" I ask, upbeat.

No response. She has her hands in her pockets. My wife is not a woman who puts her hands in her pockets, especially when she's on the couch.

Having an argument in the pantry makes a lot of sense. Stores of food around you lessens the tension. It conjures chubby-cheeked chipmunks stacking acorns. It conjures all the little jingles or catchphrases tied to every cereal box and every can of soup, and that just adds to the chipmunk warmth that makes the pantry the most positive place in any house. Every argument we ever had in the pantry ended up being a communion of sorts. But the couch. The couch is no good for arguing. I might be the first to actually admit it but couches aren't that comfortable to sit on—then try to hammer out a disagreement or misunderstanding or whatever it is that went wrong between me and my wife today. Impossible. My wife is on the couch and I can think of no good way to get her to the pantry except to drag the couch to it. It's a sectional and I know that even the individual squares are too big to fit through the kitchen doorway but that doesn't stop me from doing some visual measurements. My choices limited, I sit down on the other end of the couch. I have the feeling that's about as close as she will tolerate me. Couch or no couch, now it's time to take the initiative and set us back on course.

"Road trip," I say—we need entire family unity, not just one-on-one. "The Housatonic, this weekend." I let her soak this in for a moment. "Along the way we will take a break at Bash-Bish Falls, we'll bring warm clothes and have a picnic. And there won't even be any crowds. People neglect the possibilities of picnicking in the other three seasons." I could feel myself losing steam because my wife did not show the slightest sign of excitement or recognition of the similarity of another plan we once had during the very foundation of our marriage. I press on: "We'll find a beach and sit on some sand, watch the sun go down. We'll look for the green ray. Haven't you always wanted to see it? What was that French movie we saw in that class you made me take? *Vert* something or other."

My wife sighs and then she finally speaks: "Doug."

That's it.

To be honest, I'm not sure if the rest of her sentence got lost in the crumb-filled crevice between our two cushions, or I cut her short by directly addressing her thought:

"Of course you're worried about how the kids were affected by the accident. You fall off a horse you jump right back on. You don't want them to develop irrational fears. The automobile is a way of life. You can't avoid it. Plus, they seemed pretty fine today. Amazingly fine."

"Doug."

"Remember we've got some pretty tough kids. Troopers. They've got their first accident tucked under their belts. Statistically they're better off."

My wife has given up on my name apparently. She does not respond verbally, but she most definitely responds, though neither her expression nor her body language change. Maybe her hands are in her pockets because she's cold. If wives had closed captioning for the hearing-impaired, the world would be a much better place.

My plan is part containment, part diversion, part Hail Mary, but most of all I want to show my wife that I'm thinking of the future, thinking of positive ways to move the situation forward, and what better way to demonstrate a family's unity than to pack ourselves into the Pontiac and join the great American tradition? Not to mention that road trips are loaded with precedent for our family. Where pizza and small fixes can't succeed, road trips certainly will.

I suspect she's looking for the ink on my fingers, but I have them safely tucked under my thighs. "What I'm talking about is taking advantage of you being home to put this accident behind us with some serious quality family time." It's hard to interest people in the future, to chug our way forward; everyone wants to keep the anchor in the little tiny thing that went wrong. You think you know your wife, you think you know yourself, and that's why the truth is delicate. It's not some slab of concrete the world likes to make it out to be. It's fragile, breakable, a worn-out feather.

We stare at the black flatness of the TV.

I'm not sure how it is with you, but when I'm sitting on a couch in front of the television and all my containment plans seem to have failed, I can't help watching the screen even if it isn't turned on. My wife and I are in perfect agreement about this tactic. We stare at it so long I won't be surprised if one of the bottom-dwelling sea creatures Tina watched on PBS floats by; it would explain the oceanic pressure. If only I had come down early enough to catch her in the pantry, instead of this, we'd be headed upstairs for, at the very least, a serious round of cuddling.

Getting people to think forward is a great way to persuade them emotionally, but it isn't ever going to win over the skeptics. The first thing you do when a long-time relationship is in jeopardy—whether it be with another company, a city, the public as a whole, your wife, whatever—is you prepare your audience by reminding them about the relationship's solid foundation, a foundation that will hold firm no matter what hits it—just like I did in the press release for Percival Lake. True, I had some hints with my plan of a road trip but they were just hints. The main message was about the future. What I need to do now is to jump back to the solid foundations.

"You remember astronomy class?" I ask.

"Jesus, Doug," she says and it's all the more painful because she doesn't move a muscle when she says it, not even her jaw. She doesn't even give me one of her looks. I'd be able to categorize it and at least guess where I stand. I wait for her to fill in the gap, to give me some kind of opening. But she doesn't.

So I stop with the foundation. Maybe I shouldn't have. Those days are solid to me, a firm beginning to a great life together. But tonight my wife isn't interested in the firm roots of our relationship. She wants to stay up to our knees in the marshy territory of one bad night out of so many good ones.

My only choice is to head to the pantry and hope she follows. I step over her legs which are stretched straight. I make sure it's clear that I'm going into the kitchen.

In the pantry I expect to find a complete makeover, I expect sparkle, alphabetization, order that takes into consideration size and frequency of use. I expect to be disoriented just like when the grocery store suddenly shifts every product. Instead what I find is a sparkling floor for two-thirds of the pantry and one shelf completely cleared of its products and its grime, and Mr. Clean upside down in the bucket of grey water and 409 pushed between the cereal boxes. The pantry was a mess but the two hours my wife was in here doesn't explain the fifteen minutes of work.

This pantry is now no place to argue. I hit the eject button but I'm too late. My wife's voice suddenly finds me and I freeze. She must be in the kitchen doorway. She too knows not to come into the pantry. Except I can't quite bring myself to step out.

"How could you do it! How could you do that to her."

"Rachel?"

"No! God! What? How could you let our daughter wait outside the library alone for an hour in a snowstorm, at night?"

Luckily my jaw hits my chest so hard my heart starts to beat again. "She told you that?"

My wife takes this all wrong: "She waited so long that she tried to walk home herself and got lost. What, she wasn't supposed to tell me that?"

I'm dumbfounded. I'm staring at Cocoa Puffs and not getting any crazy character that's coo-coo for Cocoa Puffs, instead I'm seeing diabetes, addiction, and the rise of the cavity. This is bad.

"So you're not going to say anything?" her voice drops.

Then it gets worse. There she is. Her chin up. Her face filling the doorway. Her eyes more scared than mad. Scared like she doesn't know me. She exhales a quick wounded crack of air that snaps me more than if she shut my hand in a waffle iron.

I can't stand it. I push by her. I'm going for the back door but then I imagine coming back to an empty house or one where the locks have been changed. So I take a cue from Rudd's playbook for when conflict is in the air. I head down to his trains in the basement. I sit at his bench and I don't dare turn a thing on. His hammer rests in the middle of the harbor. I try to figure out what the kid was pounding earlier. I listen for my wife until the furnace kicks on.

Even though habit has made "Jess is lying" about the easiest three-word combo there is (it's hard to believe that I almost admonished Tina when she called her sister a liar), even though I have an inkling that almost everything that has gone wrong would suddenly be corrected if I remind my wife of this, and even though I go so far as to picture her laughing as I recount the events of the night before, I'm also very, very aware that if I tell her my side right now, she will be presented with a choice. She will have to believe one or the other. It will be a snap decision. Precedent should make whom to believe a no-brainer. But right now, based on what my wife thinks she knows about last night and what's on the record (I'm thinking in particular about telling her on the phone that I almost had everyone in bed, which wasn't really a lie at the time, and that there was probably a message on the machine from Ernie Something to see if anyone was planning to pick up Rudd anytime soon and not to mention Rachel's message where she felt it was important to cover the location of my sock and my cork-filled shoe in the toilet—Burty's work?—which could be totally misinterpreted if she even listened to the whole thing but. . .), I decided in that moment up in the pantry to not put my wife in a position of having to make a snap decision. Believe me, I know it is essential to get your side out there fast. The public makes up its mind in an instant and if it's not in your favor it takes years to recover, if you recover at all. So as hard as it might be to believe, I didn't correct the misinformation. I didn't get my side out there. If I had told my wife my side of the story and she didn't believe it, I would have been completely crushed.

I dig out the camping mattress and turn on its embedded air pump. I watch the creases unfold. There are some towels in the dryer and after I reheat them for ten minutes I use them as pillow and blanket. I sniff in the mildewed plastic and sigh it out. All tucked in, I remind myself of our solid foundation. That astronomy class: That day I noticed her in the middle of September nineteen years ago when the professor—Dr. Carloff?—handed my wife a softball in the far corner of the front row and ran up the stadium stairs (this was a guy who shouldn't run) way back to me on the opposite side of the room in the last row and gave me a BB to hold up. And in his mad scientist voice and out of breath he said: "The distance from the sun and the Earth, well approximately. Pluto is somewhere around Springfield." You should have seen the way my wife held up that softball. Radiance. I pocketed the BB and still have it today in my drawer. Who cared about the overwhelming scale of our solar system?

For two months I courted her gently even in the face of constant rejection, which was always accompanied by genuine smiles and even sometimes outright laughter at my antics. Rejection or not, I was sure about how the universe really worked and my hypothesis was proven without a doubt when finally a girl who could say no every time I asked her for a date could be waiting at the curb outside her dorm when I drove up at a time I had appointed, a time she never agreed to, and she could open the door and actually get into the car—"Jesus," she said (in a far different way than she said it just now) as she dropped into the passenger seat and made sure all her hair—which flowed down her back in those days—was in the car before she closed the door. Yes, the universe is a small place where things work out.

I jump off the cot and head up two flights of stairs. Of course she'll believe me! How could she not? My wife's already in bed or at least she's in the bedroom. Our door is closed. I put my fingers on the knob. There is silence. She's probably sound asleep. She needs her sleep.

In the bathroom, her pizza-stained sweatpants look like a brain soaking in the sink. The stopper is closed, but the water has drained—another fix for my list. I turn the hot dial and the stream splashes her pants. On the shelf next to the sink, my wife's clear toothbrush has returned to the circular chrome stand with the rest of our toothbrushes—her bristles face away from mine. "We know less about the depths of our own oceans than we do about outer space," the voice-over said in the introduction of Tina's show as the various odd-shaped sea creatures floated by. I turn off the faucet when the sink is full. Then I adjust all the toothbrushes to face each other.

11

What the headline in the newspaper the next morning should read if the world is just and right:

THIRTEEN-YEAR-OLD DAUGHTER
TELLS WHOPPER OF A LIE

Good father keeps it under wraps—to his own detriment

Some snippets from the article:

"I'm so, so incredibly sorry and sad," Jess Merit stated.

"I completely understand why my daughter did this," Mr. Merit confided. "She's thirteen and didn't know what she was doing. If we don't make mistakes, we don't learn. The important thing is that she acted like an adult by coming forward and telling her mother the truth."

"I don't know what came over me," Karen Merit stated. "I should have been suspicious [of Jess's story] but I guess I just wanted to believe the worst. It was a terrible day and I was tired. But there really is no excuse. I feel terrible and hope my husband will be able to forgive me." She adds, "I love you, Doug. I'm so sorry. I've got two words for you: *Road trip.*"

The arraignment scheduled for today was canceled. "This was a travesty of justice," Judge Weingardner stated.

Donna Swartz, head of the Department of Motor Vehicles, said the registry already had plans in the works of honoring Mr. Merit. "We're thinking about a gold framed license plate and we are also floating the idea of waving the expiration date. He would have a license for life." She added: "None of us ever knew how much guts it takes to refuse a Breathalyzer."

"There will be an official investigation," Police Chief Jefferson stated. According to Jefferson, Rudd Merit and Jess Merit, along with many others have given separate statements which "raise serious doubts about official accounts of the accident."

"It doesn't take much to send him flying off the handle," Lacy Johansen stated of her ex-husband, Officer Johansen.

"Oh, Dave was very concerned for his daughter, I remember that," the librarian with the hat and the scarf said of Mr. Merit. "And there was most definitely no daughter waiting for him outside the library. I'm willing to go on the record about that. And I'd like to add that even in that crisis moment he was still able to help a damsel in distress, when my car wouldn't start."

"The guy I dropped with one punch?" said a man who lives on Jones Street who didn't want his name used. "He was one cool dude!"

"I misread him completely," Ernie Something, THS assistant hockey coach, stated. "He was on a rough night. I misinterpreted it. The guy is solid as a puck."

Tina Merit, six, Mr. Merit's youngest, exclaimed, "My daddy would never steer us wrong. And he's even a better driver in the snow than a snow plow."

Nancy Weisse, Mr. Merit's mother-in-law, stated, "We owe everything to him. His clear thinking even under the malicious pressure of police harassment allowed me to get to the hospital right away. Other men would have been consumed with railing against injustice. Doug was just worried about his children. It really is a travesty because he cares so much."

"I had a bad night," Officer Johansen freely admitted. "I see it was not the best night to pull someone over for a license plate light being out. I was probably a little too close given the road conditions. In the end, now I see the guy was just trying to get a security blanket to his daughter. I even said it to the guys after we packed him in the car. I saw the blanket he was carrying. The thing just grazed me but at that point I thought it was nunchuks or something. It was quite a blow for a blanket. . .I mean that guy must work out. But I put two and two together pretty quickly. It was just one of those snowball things. Police work isn't easy."

"Everyone was doing what he or she thought best. I am not blaming anyone," Mr. Merit graciously stated. "If anything, I think we all could learn a lot from these unfortunate events." He repeated once more: "Like I always say: if we don't make mistakes, then we don't learn."

"I'm sorry, Dad," Jess stated, wiping tears from her eyes. "I'm so, so sorry."

Mr. Merit's family gathered around him and gave him a group hug.

Unfortunately, the world the next day seems to be neither just nor right:

1) *The morning news.* When I climb the basement stairs, I'm greeted by my blazer, shirt, underwear, pants and socks hanging on the door-knob, along with my deodorant tucked into the shirt's pocket. On the deodorant, a Post-It note says, "I can't see you right now." The tie is the one from the other night with the wine stains and I know she chose it because it was the first one on the rack, that's all—or did I put it in the dry cleaning pile? Whatever the case, it's easy access not a statement. So I dress there on the top step and it doesn't help that I'm stiff because the

mattress slowly deflated me to the concrete floor, not to mention in the last 48 hours I'd been assaulted by Frisbees, punched, in a car wreck, and tackled by police—not to mention a long night in jail. But you press on. I get dressed and I'm ready for the day to get a lot better, shower and shave or not. My wife went to the trouble of squeezing "right now" onto a Post-It note and that says it all.

Spoons stall as I walk into the kitchen to find Rudd and Nancy gathered around the newspaper. I don't have to see the article to know what they're looking at. But I have a feeling that the account they are reading ignores the five Ws and is lifted verbatim from the poorly written, one-sided police report that itself has a few glaring errors. "We're famous," I say. Tina checks the window for the paparazzi, Rudd, red as hell and his eyeglasses completely missing, has his face almost in his bowl, and as soon as she sees me, Nancy moves to the sink and turns on the faucet full blast. In a few minutes she ushers me out the door and into her Suburban that is painted as if it is bursting through rolls of fabric and along each side it has the name of her store, Fabric of Our Lives, allowing me a minimum of interaction with Tina and Rudd, and not even a sighting of my wife or Jess. I'm out of there before I can look at the paper or go to the bathroom.

2) *Antennas.* The seventeen times Nancy turns off and on the radio as she drives me to work, seventeen times that antenna goes up and then retracts. Each time she turns the radio back on she gives me an apologetic look. Even though she wears fleece and hiking boots there's this mountain she won't climb. I completely understand—it's beyond explanation. I still have the Post-It note crumbled in my hand. *right now.* It shows definite possibilities. Better than *Things.*

3) *Fellow employees.* At work, Alexis, Sally, and Rita, and Brad and

Brooke all PR-smile-ish as if their guffaws ended the moment I enter the door. There on my desk sits a press release:

FOR IMMEDIATE RELEASE

DOUG MERIT GOES UP IN FLAMES:

Coworkers Are Shocked as Long Time PR Practitioner Dies by the Sword (Not by the Frisbee)

Obituary (Pontoosuc): Doug Merit, affectionately known as Merit to his beloved coworkers, went down in a ball of flames today. The world hasn't seen an event like this one since Clinton's double double: didn't inhale and didn't have sex.

Everyone at GE knew Merit would go out with a bang. When your bald spot is in remission for as long as his has been, you're bound to be pushed off the edge. Merit's only regret was that everyone at work had to find out about it from a newspaper.

He worked at GE for eight years. He will be sorely missed, especially for skills at unjamming the photocopier, borrowing staplers, and making the swampy world of PR an ever-constant delight.

Let his epitaph read: "Merit, a contingency no contingency plan could plan."

# # #

Sam Gowers pops his head over the wall that separates our cubicles:

"I'm sorry, Doug. We shouldn't be joking about this. They wouldn't listen to me."

I look him straight in his watery eyes. Sam's been my cubicle neighbor from the beginning. He's one of those guys with a ponytail who has never been younger than thirty-nine. He looks as if he had large pieces of stone floating around in him. His concern is transparent. He has a long track record of the type of dejection PR can do little in the face of—all having to do with his wife.

"You OK?" he asks.

"I'm great."

"Really, man, if you need to talk, just let me know."

Alexis Burgunder suddenly appears at the opening to my cubicle, the spikes in her hair undaunted by anything. She wields yoga moves like she's harnessing her inner-Navy Seal. At one meeting, we lost Terry, our previous boss, to a position called "pigeon." I know she was behind the press release. She takes not being informed a little too personally. And I understand, completely understand, she is on edge. Percival Lake Park is her baby. She could also be a disc golfer. Even Sam could be one? Brad and Brooke, our interns, could also certainly be part of that sport. It is only Sally and Rita who I can for sure cross off the list as the leak to Rachel and the mayor—they've been here longer than any of us in their secretarial roles and their only athletic interest is bingo (though in their retelling of a game it sounds like helmets and padding should be mandatory).

"Asshole." Alexis does say it with a sweet smile though. She steps in, rolls me back in my chair, and lifts the press release so the newspaper's headline is revealed. "I'm guessing you must have been in solitary confinement until just now because there's no way you didn't check your messages, watch the news last night, or see the morning paper, right? Especially with your face splashed all over it. I hope for your sake you have an evil twin."

The whole top of the front page: *Police Clash with Protesters: 13 Disc Golfers Arrested, Two Officers Injured*. The photo shows Percival Lake Park with officers cuffing people in front of an armored vehicle and the ground littered with Frisbees. Then two editorials: *GE Fails Us Again* and *Police Go Too Far*.

"This is fake, right? How did you do this? You've outdone yourself!"

Both Sam and Alexis shake their heads. I'm still not buying it. Alexis goes onto my computer and brings up the same headline and then does a search and there's a whole list of videos showing footage of the police removing the protesters; and even news clips from the Today Show. Also there are videos that capture the attack on Rachel, the cameraman, and me.

"Tear gas?" I ask as I skim the article and quickly flip through the rest of the paper to look at the editorials (unfortunately the one about the police doesn't give my arrest as an example of the police going too far). I note that the car accident report is buried at the bottom of the second section with the headline, "4 Injured, 1 Arrest in Wahconah Accident." And there is the passport-sized mugshot of me but nothing mentions my connection to GE—I actually don't look half bad. But a riot at the park? You avoid the news for one day, one day! Surely someone in my house must have known about this?

My other coworkers are now gathered around. This is impossible.

"But why the hell did you let the police go in?" I ask. "These morons. . ." I inhale the first syllable of the word and exhale the second with a breath that clears my lungs—I now have rebalanced the universe by using the word *moron* correctly and my only regret is that Vincent Jensen is not in the room to see it properly applied. . ."These morons probably would have left once they got their photo-op!"

"They were trespassing," Jason the Kid's voice emerges from the crowd and my coworkers scatter. He's trying to sound like he's got all this, but his ankles are shaky. Terry, our previous boss, stayed cocooned in her office and if anyone knocked on her door she had one response she yelled: "We'll tackle it at the meeting." And meetings we had. The record was five. And the thing is we never once saw her out walking between the cubicles or even in the hallways. Before her career ending injury we took turns watching her door, trying to spot her out among us, but each time we watched for her, it turned out she was already waiting in the conference room. I know one thing for sure about Terry: she would not have called the police over a Frisbee protest. Before Terry, it was Ed, the boss who hired me. He was no go-to-guy either. He was so shell-shocked from his time in the '80s here, you could drive him from the room by just mentioning EPA, SuperFund, or No Nukes. The guy had a serious Twizzler habit. And although by the end of his time with GE it is possible he might have rolled up his sleeves and gone down to Percival Lake Park to throw some punches, he definitely would not have called the police.

And here's Jason summoning me to his office with his ironic finger beckon. My god, this kid!

4) *Jason the Kid.* Remember this is the boss that GE hired, the boss with impressive diplomas on his wall, but who still confuses PCP with PCB in front of the press, and whose ass I pretty much saved a dozen times since he started working here a year ago. The same guy who had the police clear out a bunch of people tossing Frisbees and chanting "Hell no! Discs won't go!" You get the word out there to the press and the golfers look foolish and it helps your cause, but tear gas? An assault vehicle? Batons and shields? A paddy wagon? True that the golfers still don't come out clean, but it calls more attention to us and more attention is never good unless you are putting out something positive. Believe me, I know.

Jason doesn't break down in the privacy of his office and confess the madness of his decision yesterday. He doesn't try to explain why it is actually a good move to make, or try to get us on a conference call with Fairfield where the string of Jimmy Tripoli's curses must be punching a hole in the ozone—as V.P. of Communications he's got that type of power. I bet even Mr. Cranky himself, our beloved CEO, George Alogosh, printed out a map of Pontoosuc so he could spit on it and crinkle it up. I scan Jason's phone to see if it is unplugged because it should be ringing off the hook.

This is what he does instead: He spins his monitor toward me, which displays the website from our local pain in the neck, Guy the Environmental Guy. There's a video clip and a photo. His headline on his blog is The Real Story? The clip is the only one that I have seen that actually captures the truth of the situation from two days ago: My attempt to stop Rachel from throwing the mayor into Percival Lake. At least he's reporting the real story! The other photo is of Percival Lake and then photos of the two bigger lakes in Pontoosuc that are both frozen. He's drawn a red circle and handwritten words NOT FROZEN? In his post he says he's been keeping an eye on Percival Lake for some time and in the last ten years it has frozen before the other two lakes but this year it still doesn't show any signs of freezing when the other lakes have been frozen for a month. He reminds everyone that this very lake caught fire in the '70s and it was a dumping ground for just about everything GE wanted to get rid of conveniently. He reminds his dear readers that Percival Lake then "dumps" into the Housatonic River which he—as always—exaggerates as a completely destroyed river, polluted to the gills. The one that our "committed friend" GE comes in with "some rakes and a little sand" to solve the problem. "Does the unfrozen lake show that something is up with the 'New' GE? Forget disc golf and remember the real reason why GE is evil."

Looking back over the whole post again, I see he posits that perhaps this is the reason that Doug Merit, GE spokesman, is trying to stop the reporter from throwing the masked mayor into the lake? He's analyzing the audio currently because he's pretty sure he hears me mention the words *pollution* and a *death sentence* and *dangerous*. Then there's a photo of me helping the hysterical mayor out of the lake and Guy said he can hear in the video that the mayor's asking me if he's going to die and there's a clear clip of me telling him to take a hot shower right away…"decontamination?" He promises to have more on this soon. Then unsurprisingly he has a footnote asking if anyone saw that "this same Doug Merit was later arrested for DUI and causing an accident? Is there some connection? It sounds like something big is happening." Guy once again demonstrates his inability to get the facts right and his wild accusations are clearly just that. Who reads his blog anyway? Plus the water is close to freezing, of course it is dangerous and a death sentence, and as far as I know a great way to warm up is a hot shower. This seems just fine. Clearly taken out of context, nothing to do with pollution. I mean it is a little strange that the lake isn't frozen but there's been some sewage breaks from the city in the past and maybe this has happened again.

Then Jason says, "You shouldn't have gotten involved."

"What was I supposed to do, let the mayor drown?"

"Did you know it was him?"

"No, but what. . ."

Jason cuts me off: "I just wish you had stayed out of it. We've been making too much of a big deal out of this park." There's a long pause and he might just be texting under his desk, probably his mom. Then this kid looks at me and says, "What do you know about the lake?"

"What?"

He's not looking for history—he knows that outside of Alexis there is no other employee but me who knows more about it. He narrows his eyes and seems to be trying to make his jaw into an actual jaw—the kid must have binge-watched Dirty Harry movies.

"Is there something I should know?" I ask.

He's stuck. Did he just slip up? Say too much? As of two days ago he didn't know why Fairfield decided to nix the golf. He opens his desk drawer and maybe he's going for a .44 Magnum but more likely he's getting a lollipop out of his drawer to make amends. Instead he hands me binoculars. I stare at them because who the hell keeps binoculars in his office? It's not exactly good bird watching here. He taps on the glass and tells me to look. At the front entrance on the brown grass between the parking stripes and the sidewalk right there is a girl with green hair pacing just outside the gate. I'm trying to zoom in and it looks like she's wearing a burlap bag over a winter jacket—sackcloth? Jason explains that she showed up about an hour ago. A sign strapped to her has the word ASSASSINS sprawled as if done by red finger paint. I hope she's referring to the Frisbee attack. What a fucking day! I ask Jason if he's called the police on her yet and he tries to give me a look. I almost have to laugh. I'll sign him up for a few lessons with my wife.

I put the binoculars on the windowsill. "What about at the park? Have any protesters returned?"

"Not yet. The mayor called for a day of peace and reflection."

"What's the plan?" I'll admit right here that I have no contingency in place for something like this, any of this.

"I think we'll be OK," he says as he falls back into his chair in a slouch.

That's it! It's clear that he knows nothing more than I do about the lake or anything else that might be going on at Fairfield. I'm about to lay into him and open his eyes to what shit we are in when he switches gears and to my surprise builds me up, saying how my absence yesterday really enforced something he already knew: I was an essential team player. There he is circling me with praise so that I start wondering if I'm getting promoted to Fairfield, until he pulls the rug out by "asking" me to take a more "behind the scenes" position at work given the two unfortunate incidents that landed me in the news until "things cooled down" (what is it with *things*?) "because we in PR are news brokers not breakers." He's so proud of himself for this last bit. Did I mention that he isn't much older than Rudd? He's got degrees galore hanging on his wall, he's the cream of the crop, but in the face of all hell breaking loose he crumbled.

"That's fine," I tell him. "I completely understand." I see what's been going on: he's so focused on demoting me that he's missing everything else. I try to act angry as I pull open his door. I'm glad to help him feel like he's made a manly decision. Everybody needs a bit of an ego boost— especially when they are in some deep shit. I know though that as soon as I leave his office he will put in a call to his mom even as he adds me to his resume: demoted favorite employee: makes hard decisions.

When I'm just out the door both my middle fingers safely tucked in my pockets, Jason's voice follows me: "Go down and talk to that girl and see what's up."

5) *Girl with Green Hair.* I send Brad and Brooke down to talk to her since they are closer to her age and my track record over the last few days with teenagers is less than stellar. They came back and say she never made eye contact or said a word. They said she was "sort of acting like a zombie." This seems good enough. Maybe she's unbalanced or high. She's no threat. If anything she's probably another victim of the school system's Activate! agenda. She'll get her points for doing it and she'll wrap it up. Just in case I search to see if there's an actual truancy officer anymore and there is! I bookmark it. I then send Brad and Brooke on a mission for good coffee and treats for the whole office, on me. The pizza didn't work last night with my family, but when Brad and Brooke return, the office buzzes with coffee, donuts, and laughter. I get slaps on the back. Even Jason comes out for a cruller after he promotes poor Sam to my position. I shrug to show him how easy it is to regain unity. Brad and Brooke also give us the latest news from the lake: there's two TV news vans outside the park but no protesters. Maybe Jason is right,

maybe we'll be OK. We take turns with the binoculars watching the girl with green hair picketing—but its better described as pacing. Hopefully the stations won't get wind of her before she packs up and gets back to school in time for lunch.

6) *Rachel.* All my calls go straight to her voicemail and by the time I have to leave for my arraignment she has yet to call back; ditto for the ten texts I send her—each on the half hour. At Burty and Tina's play-date, I might not have given her great advice about getting the video coverage of the Frisbee attack and her actions out there—I just didn't realize how crazy she looked. It's already one of the links on the Weather Channel's website (although some website called "You Go Girl" has been promoting the clip of the kick to the mayor's balls).

7) *Arraignments.* That afternoon, if I thought work was a bit out of whack it only served to prepare me for the arraignment, a farce:

110A: OPERATING RECKLESSLY 2 c. 90 s. 24(2)(a)

111A: OPER UND INFL OF LIQ No 2,3,4 c. 90 s. 24(1)(a)(1) Mandatory/subsequent penalties

A&B: ASSAULT AND BATTERY 3 c. 265 s. 13A

A&B PO: A&B ON POLICE OFFICER 3 c. 265 s. 13D

FL OBEY PO: FAILURE TO OBEY POLICE OFFICER 1 c. 268 s. 24

MV OP LIQ: OPER UNDER INFLUENCE LIQUOR 2,3,4 c. 90 s.24(1)(a)(1)Mandatory/subsequent penalties

MV OP NEG: OPER NEGLIGENTLY 2 c. 90 s. 24(2)(a)

MV OP RECKLESS: OPERATING RECKLESSLY 2 c. 90 s. 24(2)(a)

ID VIOL IDENTIFICATION VIOLATION No 1 c. 90 s. 8H Fine only

LIC POSS 1. c. 90 s. 11

PO INTF: INTERFERING WI POLICE OFFICER 3 c. 179 s. 5

PROF: PROFANITY No 1 c. 272 s. 36A Fine only

As the charges are read, I keep my cool. And when Dayton Shelby, my esteemed lawyer, utters those fine words, "Not guilty," it is the only time I can bring myself to like the guy, really justifying his $200 an hour. Not guilty. I turn around to get a look at my wife to make sure she understands the importance of these two words, but she has her eyes on her lap. She came at least. Nobody forced her to come. Even if my wife didn't react to them, those two words are enough to lift me above Judge Weingardner's bitter streak and the assistant D.A. Denise DeMonico's relentless political ambition (she is obviously developing a solid platform by stomping on the head of the little guy). It is enough to lift me above this whole day. My release on my own recognizance is upheld, the court date will be set later, and they move on to the next arraignment.

I stand up, victorious, and turn to my wife to get a victory hug. She's already headed toward the door. Down the length of her left calf, a run split her stocking. I guess "right now" hasn't ended yet. I want to go after her, but Dayton Shelby sticks some papers in my face to sign and he wants to know what I "made" of the newspaper article. Which one?

8) *Melanie whatever-her-name-is.* That night after an awkward meal where Tina was the only one doing the talking about the buzz her hair caused at school and where apparently during lunch she used the attention to Activate! by making an impassioned plea for students to band together for the sake of minks. The note her teacher sent home told a slightly different story (apparently there's a time and a place to Activate! and one who is Activating! should not hold down another student and pull at her hair with a plastic knife to demonstrate the skinning technique), but Tina saved dinner for everyone even if she was a little murky on the details, and let me tell you how hard it is not to glare at Jess. Afterwards my wife disappears into the pantry again to spruce it up so we could finally clear the air in there. I just happen into the kitchen for

a banana and hear her voice. I freeze because I think Jess is in the pantry with her, confessing. But I'm wrong:

"I know it's not going to be easy to get six months off. What else can I do? Once his temporary license runs out in a few days he won't be able to drive. I told you just let it alone. I can't believe he's out there—Walt doesn't do surprise drop ins. It's terrible timing. No, Melanie, I'm not going to answer that. It's between us. This is going to put a lot of weight on your shoulders. No, I'm not saying you can't handle it. That's not true, he does understand the big part you play. He doesn't think I do this alone. That's not how it works. He's going to take you to dinner? There? No, there's nothing wrong with that but. . .Wait a minute, you can't say that." There's a long, long pause. "I'm sorry Melanie. There's just a lot on the plate right now. Don't mention any of this to him. Please. I know, I know. If I make that tight connection in Chicago I'll be there by three."

I'm tempted to storm into the pantry to tell her that she can't possibly leave tomorrow. But I suspect the pantry is still in its terrible state. I slip back into the dining room and pick up the book about Chavez the librarian dropped off for Tina. After the school knife incident, I should probably have her reread this book, but I know it won't tell the full story, that it will make people like me seem like we're bad. As of 5:15 this evening the girl with green hair was still pacing with her sign. I waved to her on my way out and I swear I saw her flinch as if she had to stop herself from waving back. Assassins?

9) *Jess.* Did I mention Jess yet? Flashing her bandage as if it is a prize? Did I mention turtlenecks day two, apparently the new middle school fashion? Did I mention several times when I had a semi-private moment to approach her that she'd simply vanish and then magically appear by her mother's side? The phone is her constant companion again and I wouldn't mind checking out some of her latest texts and contacts but our cell phone drawer is empty 24/7 now, except for Rudd's. I am

all smiles around her though. If I show any sign of anger, she's going to stick to her guns even more. So I'm going to besiege her with pleasantries and she'll eventually fold. She has to.

I'll jump in front of a bus for my children, Jess included. I'll climb a mountain in Nepal to find a cure if she comes down with a rare disease. I'll empty my back account if she needs to get out of some jam. I just want to make that clear.

10) *My wife flying back to Arizona*. Tonight after a shower that might rival one of my wife's, I hop right into bed first. If she can't be this close she's welcome to head for a sofa or the deflated mattress next to Rudd's trains. She gets into bed though! Sits down at the edge and just lowers herself sideways as if she's lying down on a tightrope, straightens out her legs—doesn't even get under the covers. But she does get into bed. I try to muster a *good night*, a *I love you*. After a long while, her phone lights up the room and soon enough I get a text message from her: "I have to go back tomorrow." I keep responding OK to the quick bits she explains about work that I already know from overhearing her conversation. She doesn't go into great detail. She never says it but I now can see that she's worried about her own job and worried about mine. Something must be going on. It's work that's been bothering her, not me.

From early on, Karen was destined for the business world even if she didn't originally want it. By the time she was eighteen she was written up in a fabric trade rag for changes in inventory management and pricing that allowed Nancy's store to knock Sew-Fro and Jo-Ann Fabrics out of town. "David and Goliath," it said. "Teen Innovator," they called her. "Part-Time Wunderkind." Throughout high school she worked at her mother's store after school, and she continued to work there during the summers up to her junior year at UMASS. But she was a political science major, not business. One competing company offered to send her to any business school she wished if she would commit to them. She told them no before they even got out a complete sentence. She hated the store, which was just about making money. She claimed all her innovations stemmed from boredom. Her only driving force was that her potential pleased her father, a man who had known hard work on the transformer lines of GE. He had framed the article for her and it still hangs behind the counter at Nancy's store.

We graduated from college and eloped and then she went to Africa, all in two weeks. She came back from Africa early—I'm still not completely sure why, though I'm pretty sure it was because she needed me. We had a rough patch, then she was pregnant with Rudd, we were overjoyed, then her father died as no-nonsense men like him die, a massive heart attack, dead before he hit the ground next to his barbecue. We of course used his name for our son, Rudolph, which by the time he could hop on one leg I had been able to transform into Rudd. Rudd was a charm and after Jess was born, my wife needed to work part-time at a woman's clothing store called Fashionable Fit. Then she worked full time, and then in a snap of her fingers, she had helped the owner open two more in the county. Next, she got a bigger job for Talbots where she turned around a store that she later discovered was on the chopping block. They began sending her to other floundering stores around the country. Then Tina surprised us both and job prospects changed. But her record and efficiency were not forgotten and a call out of the blue from a headhunter put my wife back on whatever track she was on. So two years after Tina was born she started her current job, for a consulting agency that specialized in starting retail stores. She managed many things but her biggest task was getting the employees in place. She didn't go into behind-the-scenes politics, international relations, government, the UN, NGOs, the plans she used to keep me up with when she got back from the graduate-level classes Professor Finley let her sit in on when we were undergraduates. I don't know what happened. She went to Africa to feed the hungry and only lasted a few months and then decided she'd help corporations save their stock prices instead of saving the world. But who am I to judge?

Look, I don't blame her for having this job at all—or hiring these women who try to stay in contact with her. She says she loves what she does. I didn't even have a single inkling what I would do for my career when we were in college, but I did know that *Things* work out for the best. And *Things* have worked out. Sure, when she's gone, life is more complicated and we miss her, but, after all, she will be home for a week or two between trips. In these intervals she spends some serious quality time with us. When these days are all added up and distributed, the time she spends with the kids is probably equal to that of any hardworking mother. The only difference is that on many nights she isn't there sleeping in the next room.

We are all happy when we are doing what we want to do: my wife jetting around the country accumulating frequent flyer miles and starting stores, Rudd working on his trains and stopping pucks, Jess lying about her father and dreaming about her nose, and Tina, just being sweet, wise, and a bit-over-the-top. And me? Well, me doing what I do.

Maybe I'm reading too deeply into the light from my wife's screen after ten, twenty minutes pass without a new message, but I can hear her wanting to ask if she can trust me, wanting to ask if Nancy should move in to "help out" while she's away, but she leaves this all unsaid, untexted, and I can only read this as encouraging. She knows I am perfectly capable of taking care of my children as I have done pretty much successfully for the last five years. I turn off my phone and mimic her position on my side of the bed so if some aesthetic guru just happened into our room he'd be awed by the unity and symmetry of our positions. Her screen light is still on when I close my eyes. It's just work, I repeat until I'm asleep. It's just work.

12

The next morning Nancy drops my wife at the Albany Airport. I'm not even worried that she didn't get the chance to say good-bye. I drive the kids to school just fine—apparently I'm just as good a driver with my temporary license as I am with my real one, which I'm sure will be restored to me within a week. Rudd is mobbed by other students as soon as he's out of the car; he won't admit it, but clearly he loves being the center of attention—who knows if he can keep on his scoreless streak for the county championships but it's good to see him popular when he's never had real friends before. Jess doesn't want to talk to me and I don't need to talk to her or her bandage—since I have yet to confront her about her story—she's clearly confused because her cause and effect expectation has been blown out of the water. She doesn't think she has gotten away with anything and she knows what she should do, and this all is clearly weighing on her because she is try-ing to hide it by seeming excited to go to school. Turtleneck day three! The mothers at Tina's school are impressed that I'm totally supportive of self-expression in my child; I have a feeling though that the strains in their smiles and nods indicate they wouldn't have the same courage if their children Activated!, so they'd take their daughters out of school or buy a wig. I let my kid be who she wants to be, even if it's a sympathizer of minks (though I do remind her not to try any dramatic demonstrations today). She's also pretty sad that her mom's gone away again.

Right when I woke up this morning and confirmed my wife had departed—I'm sure she didn't want to wake me up, which was kind of her, I checked the paper and the TV and it looked like GE and Frisbee golf were off the menu. I was about to switch off the TV when the promo for Rachel's Local Lowdown at Lunch came on. It showed several images of the portion of GE that is shuttered, a PCB sign, and of me extending my arm to help the mayor out of the lake. And then Rachel in a blue sweater at her table asking everyone to join her at noon when she'll "get to the heart of what is at the heart of the protests against GE" by talking to an "insider," a "respected environmentalist," "a voice from the youth," and Mayor Dugus. "Hear it here first." If this were any other local noon-cast it would be no big deal, but Rachel is a respected voice in our community and has the number one viewership of any local lunchtime show in a comparable market in the nation—I'm sure that's why they keep passing her up for the nightly news anchor. The other issue is that we are on the radar of the national news outlets, scanning for any other juicy tidbits that they can blow out of proportion—a little scuffle over Frisbee golf should in no way be national news and in no way should it lead to greater scrutiny of GE or for that matter me. The thing is that she has always been fair to our side, so I'm in shock that we don't have a representative on the show. Is she now the adversary like Nathan Shaffeur and my former bosses at the *Beagle*? I text her a bunch of question marks. But by the time I'm done dropping off the kids and pull into work there's no response. Maybe she's changed her number.

I scan the front gate carefully again and at least there's some good news this morning. It is confirmed by my very own eyes that the girl with green hair is not here. Upstairs, I step into Jason's office to express my exasperation about Rachel only to discover Jason declined to put a representative on the show. When he sees my incomprehension, his eyes turn to Sam's cubicle where his ponytail sticks out from the entrance— he must be leaning back in his chair. "This all comes back to you," Jason says. I tell him to put me on and he says he can't. There's no way. I picture Sam nodding and agreeing as the protesters each state their view. The camera focusing in on his total agreement. I can hear him say, "GE told me to say. . ." Perhaps Jason made a good decision. Still in his doorway, I don't even bother to try to embarrass him by asking why he didn't volunteer himself. I'm sure after the last time he said PCPs instead of PCBs when I was out with strep Fairfield decided he was not to make any more appearances. The good news is that Rachel has offered us the whole show tomorrow and we have the rest of the day to prepare Sam. Until broadcast time, the main focus of our office chatter is about who this "insider" is. Several of my colleagues (well, Alexis mostly) keep looking at me as if I should know. As we get closer to noon we keep track of each other. Anyone look like they are getting ready to leave? I'm actually watching Sam the closest.

But by the time of our meeting to watch Rachel's show, everyone is accounted for. I think it has all finally hit Jason—he's changed his shirt twice by airtime. It's good to see he now knows he's weathering the biggest crisis of his career, a crisis made of his own poor decision-making. I'm not that worried though. First, even though we're not represented, I'm sure Rachel will ask the hard questions. No matter what's going on with her not responding to my messages, Rachel is fair and pretty much on our side—why would that change? Second, this insider can't be too much inside, probably someone who worked here as a janitor thirty years ago—on second thought that might not be so good, it was former truck drivers who spilled the beans about all the clean fill dumping— clean fill that wasn't all that clean. But, hey, nobody back then knew anything about PCBs and really it's still a bit up in the air how bad they actually are. Brad and Brooke set up the big screen TV to channel 12.

We bring our lunches into the conference room but no one's eating, except Brad.

Rachel starts the newscast with the standard recap of the events of the last few days and touches a little too much on GE's history with the environment and Pontoosuc for my taste, but she does have to seem like she is well balanced in her report—all of what she says is true but none of it is pertinent to the current situation. When she comes back from the first commercial there's a photomontage of GE in its glory days when it employed the whole town, to a shot of the decline: broken windows, hunched over workers leaving the complex for the last time when the transformer unit was shut down, the sections that had been demolished, the image of the unfrozen lake juxtaposed between images of the other two lakes that are frozen, followed by a gigantic question mark and then the chemical formation of PCBs, then shots of diggers dredging, and picket signs being raised…whoever is responsible for this (some art student intern most likely) clearly should be fired and I'll bring it up next time I speak to Rachel. Those images alone have us pretty worried and Jason is about to go change his shirt again. But here she is live, "reporting from the frontlines of the protest to find out what has caused our town to be so up in arms" (again the exaggeration is a little much since there were really only about two dozen protesters—but that is part of our sensationalistic system and I can forgive Rachel that).

Rachel is sitting at her round table with her four guests. There's the girl with green hair and she's still wearing her sackcloth and ASSASSINS sign—what is Rachel thinking? There's Guy the Environmental Guy— what the hell is Rachel thinking? Nathan Shaffeur uses him all the time for "expert" opinion, but Rachel should know that he's basically a militant activist. The mayor who is usually pumped and ready to take over the show doesn't look well at all. He's sweaty and pale. Then there's the guest I don't recognize. The camera zooms on her first. She looks vaguely familiar and we learn why because she's one of the trustees who

100

is guiding the "vision" of Percival Lake Park for the local community—
the "insider." After we dredged some of the hot spots and then capped
the lakebed in our clean up of Percival Lake, we decided to turn the lake
and the accompanying land into this park with all its amenities and then
donate it back to the city. It was a PR coup. It cost a lot of money but it
was a perfect way to unveil the New GE and with the worldwide good
press even Fairfield came around to the idea that they so far hadn't quite
swallowed completely and even gave us a boost in money for more amenities and the greenest parking lot in the world. The trustees are there
to make sure we do what is best for the community. We exchanged letters with the trustees in a game of constant revision over the last couple
years: *we think fourteen shrubs would be ideal in this area, we think the
slats on the benches are too close*, things like that. We've been completely
accommodating to all their "suggestions": *native plantings*? Of course!
Woodland areas? Yes! *Meadow/reflection area*? Why not!

When Alexis says, "Hey, that's the beaver lady," right away all of us
in the know relax. She couldn't be a better choice of "insider." I haven't
met her in person but she's one of those people you see in the paper all
the time at check-handing-over ceremonies who is neither receiving the
check nor giving the check but just in the photo. She's not exactly suited
to live television with her severely pulled hair, wooly suit jacket, and her
tendency to make her points by leaning toward the camera and opening
one eye wide.

She actually compliments GE quite a bit in the first few minutes
of the conversation about how we really worked hard to get it right
and mentioned Alexis by name, which prompts cheers in the conference room. She then laments that it is really too bad GE caved to the
"other" interests and allowed the park to not be fully restored to its
former woodland grandeur before GE came to town (more than a hundred years ago!!!) and she was very much against adding anything to
the park that was not there before GE came and implying that a skate-

board park and basketball courts and the such would taint the park with the rabble that accompanies these types of "hangouts." "We all saw the other day the menace of those Frisbee throwers," she says leaning into the table and that eye of hers bulging with exclamations. She then complains about most of the trails being paved "which is just not natural." Apparently the disabled are in her definition of rabble.

Alexis stands up and puts her finger on the trustee's head on the screen and says, "Wait for it, wait for it!" and the trustee as if on cue takes a big breath and begins: "But what has most horrified me is the lack of respect to beavers, not just by GE but by this whole community. Every since we had that so-called 'beaver fever' scare three decades ago beavers have yet to find the respect they once had and I still believe this respect should be shown by making the park and this lake more beaver friendly." Rachel's a complete professional but she's obviously been sideswiped by this. She tries to cover by staring at her notes, sweeping them for any mention of beaver and then evening the edges by banging the stack on the table. Who can blame her? Beavers smack dab in the middle of a city and bordered by industrial buildings of all manner, busy roads, rough neighborhoods…a perfect place for beavers? We won't even have to bring any of this up because it is so obvious. Rachel has not been at her best these last few days and she's not vetted her guests well. I make a note to have Alexis check the other trustees to see if this lady has gone rogue.

The trustee holds up a piece of paper. "Here's an example right here of how much the beaver is disrespected in this town. Here's a copy of an email from the GE spokesman Doug Merit who won't condescend to come onto this show today and hear us out in person. Stuck in his GE high tower." I wait for Rachel to stand up for me, but she doesn't. At least some of my coworkers boo. Then the trustee reads my old email: "'I don't think Ward and June would let Beave swim here' followed by one of those winking what-do-you-call-thems."

My coworkers clap. Jason turns toward me, but his gaze is over my head as if he's seeing a dunce cap there. Alexis feels the heat of my stare which she shrugs off, always innocent as charged. Between this quote and Guy the Environ"mental" Guy's accusation about me trying to stop the mayor from falling into the lake for another reason besides hypothermia, I now see that the only way I'm going to be able to keep my job safe is a Polar Bear Club skinny dip accompanied by a dozen beavers as I simultaneously drink from a jug full of lake water. Luckily the trustee follows my email with several others from the game warden to a beaver expert over at UMASS expressing pretty much the same sentiment. I mean really anyone with common sense is going to understand it would be a bad move to stick beavers in the place to watch them get run over by cars and chop down telephone poles.

Rachel looks a little woozy as she heads to commercial. I suppress my wish that it goes better with the rest of her guests. I also think of putting in an anonymous call to her husband to tell him to consider clearing out the wine cellar because if this keeps up she's headed for a night to rival the night of Scrabble and the accident—and that would not be good. Some of my colleagues voice that Rachel didn't hit her with any hard questions that pointed to some of the ridiculous accusations. True, she did a lot of nodding when the camera panned to her, but I defend Rachel: she knew that that lady was full of crap; it would be cruel to try to bounce the plank she was already walking off. The nodding was an affirmation that she had put a crazy woman on her show, that's all. The woman did quote every expert that beavers just didn't belong there.

It takes me a second or two to tune in after the commercials because I have a flash of worry that in fifty years if I don't steer through Tina's mink issues exactly right she might be on live TV making herself look like a kook.

The next person is Guy. You can see Rachel is relieved to be on to a new guest who must be of sounder mind. Uh-oh, Rachel, I think.

So does Guy start in about the lake not freezing over? No! He starts in about beavers. He says that in his personal opinion that behind corporations, and human beings, beavers are the worst environmental offenders: "Just like their human brethren they change the environment to suit their needs and force their will on nature." The Trustee's livid!

"You take that back," she says—off camera. Guy laughs. The camera falls back on Rachel who for a split-second looks worse than she did the other night passed out and wet in the blanket in the minivan. But she shows her stuff by recovering quickly: "Enough with the beavers. I'll have you both on soon so we can talk about beavers but today we're talking about the protests. Please, Guy, can you elaborate what you think is going on here at GE?"

The camera returns to him. He immediately blows us all away by saying Percival Lake is the least of our problems, "It would better serve the community as a parking lot." That "the system is f'ed" (he catches himself at the last minute) and "these companies need to do some massive owning up to the monsters they have turned loose because of their blind greed. The Housatonic River is a PCB but the 'success' of cleaning a few miles of this piss poor river is just a ruse to make us think the whole river system is clean. Then they still try to save money by fighting the right thing to do, dredging the whole damn thing and getting the pollutants out of the bed. But they try to scare us that dredging will ruin the river and just pouring some sand to contain the pollutants is the best thing for the environment and the people—we see how well that worked for Percival Lake. The money they put into this stupid park would have gone a long way in cleaning the river the right way. Everyone wants these short term goodies when that lake is probably going to keep spawning three-eyed fish for a hundred years just like that spokesman for GE has been hinting at."

Rachel is trying to break in now to this tirade—I'm sure to say that this is not what the spokesman from GE has been saying at all. He then goes on to what he calls his "very modest proposal" that "corporations being a person, and thus having a soul, are morally obligated to use 50 percent of their GDP to do what they know is right and pay back the only real shareholder we should be trying to please, Mother Earth! And shows like this, no offense, even our little puny newspaper, being fed free and easy PR statements so they don't have to hire reporters anymore to fill pages; until this systematic backrub ends, including all those pseudo environmentalists out there"—his head turns to the Trustee— "who talk about these things but still drive big cars and live in manses" (yes, he uses the word "manses") "that could and should house at least fifty people instead is devoted to the comfort of two. . .Until people start putting the air they breathe, the water they drink, and the plant life and animal life and to really put the cellular level on equal footing with their own, we are just going to be talking about nothing on shows like this one, no offense, Mrs. St. John, of course."

As they go to break, the camera pans over everyone but Rachel. The girl with green hair is as expressionless as her sign. The mayor looks like he's about to lay his head on the table. The Trustee is busy with her phone, probably penning nasty comments on Guy's blog. I do feel for Rachel, I really do. Jason makes the command to order pizza and cupcakes. This is the best PR we've had in years and we have nothing to do with it—it's much better that we're not there. Maybe the Kid knows what he's doing after all. Guy has just basically ridiculed every viewer watching and dismissed the value of the lake and the park. I'm floating in my chair—though, again, I'm not sure how I've suddenly got this reputation as a Percival Lake protester in my own right.

Now it is the green-haired girl's turn. From Rachel we find out that her name is Cleo with a Polish last name that rolls off Rachel's tongue. She goes to Rudd's school. She is red-faced, whether out of nervousness or out of total embarrassment for her more adult protesters it is not clear. Rachel's hair has come a bit undone and again I'm wondering if I should put in that anonymous call to her husband (lucky for me there's no playdates scheduled for this afternoon!—though an image of my wife driving frantically with a passed out naked Rachel does cross my mind—it would be a perfect script if she could live through what I lived through!—though it probably would not have come down to that Scrabble game, which seemed harmless at the time—but the image doesn't matter because, I remind myself, Karen is probably almost in Arizona by now). The break has done Rachel some good even if I can see she's hurting on the "cellular level." She's got to salvage her show and she's pinning all her hopes on this girl with green hair whose dad clearly lets her express herself too. When Rachel asks what her sign means and why she is wearing a sackcloth, the girl does not respond. Rachel asks again, but nothing. The girl is a zombie and then she looks right into the camera and she has the saddest eyes. She pulls her sign up and puts it in front of her face. ASSASSINS. This is great. "But Cleo," Rachel pleads, "right before you came on you were speaking so eloquently about all this." The girl does not have stage fright, the silence is her MO, a stage act.

The camera switches to Mayor Dugus. He's not smiling. This is a guy that can work a room. To his credit he goes to every single event in town and then somehow becomes the center of attention. I'm really surprised so far that he's had so much restraint. I would have expected him to break into the beaver lady's comment about "other interests" or even chirp in when Guy talked about just capping the lake and river-beds which Dugus fully supported. "Let's move on," he said a couple years ago. Even with the girl with green hair I expected him to turn on his fatherly side and make some joke to crack a smile. Maybe he's come down with something. Maybe he's just remorseful for his behavior the other day.

"Well, Mayor," Rachel prompts him and I know she wouldn't be surprised if he suddenly took off his face and revealed that he was an alien from some Frisbee-loving solar system.

"First off, I want to extend my deepest apologies to you and Mr.

Merit, who I assumed would be here today. My behavior was childish. After my near-death experience. . ." He pauses waiting for Rachel to extend her apology but she doesn't say anything, probably too stunned as I am that he's turned his moment in the water to a near-death event. "This near-death experience has affected me and I know now that it is silly of me to try to bring light with my antics to this city I love so much. But I just wanted to do the best I can do and I really believed, believed with all my heart that if we had this disc course we could really turn things around. Call me crazy, call me a disc golf fanatic, something has to be done. A little lightheartedness can go a long way but I was wrong. So…" and he reaches into his jacket as if he's reaching for a holstered gun and somehow pulls out a golden Frisbee. "Instead of antics I bring gifts!" He hands the golden disc to Rachel who grips it, and then with a sleight of hand he pulls out three more, giving them to the rest of the guests. The girl with green hair is still holding the ASSASSINS sign in front of her so he hangs the golden disc from the edge of her sign. "Thanks to Disc Delights International every citizen of this town will receive a golden Frisbee and we'll be a city unified under one big golden disc!" Here's the mayor I know. He stands up and from under the table he pulls out a gigantic bag of Frisbees, throwing them through the studio this way and that. They fly everywhere. He's not whipping them like the other day. Just tosses, though you can still hear the occasional crash of something being toppled. It doesn't matter, Rachel is crouched beside the table—PTSD—the original attack was traumatic and even at my safe remove I'm getting flashbacks. For the record, today, the mayor is more like a fairy tossing fairy powder as he's saying "one for you, one for you, one for you" as if he's sending them right into people's homes. I wait for Rachel to come out of her protective mode and back into her angry mode by flying through the air to tackle him but when the camera returns to her she's now upright assessing the Frisbee in her hand as if it's poor Yorick. The credits start rolling as the camera pans over the guests one more time, the beaver lady laying into Guy, the girl with her sign still in front of her face with the Frisbee like a artistic beret off to the side, and the Mayor with a seemingly endless supply still flinging his golden Frisbees.

When Jason hits the power, we are still staring at the TV.

"What was that?" Alexis asks.

There's no way to answer when the mayor has gone mad. Though I'm about to say that maybe there is something in the water. Wisely I hold my tongue.

"What that was," Jason says with a confidence I've seldom seen in him, "was the best thing that could ever happen. Prepare for incoming pizza and cupcakes!"

I hear Brad asking Brooke about how they'll be able to get their Frisbees.

I text Rachel, "Tough day. Not as bad as it seems." Then a little later: "You got the scoop. Mayor's gone nuts."

13

Over the next hour Alexis talked with three of the trustees who are livid about the beaver lady's performance. A scientist from UMASS that I contacted on my own assured me that PCBs would not prevent a body of water from freezing over, which is a relief— sort of. And Sam took a call from Rachel's assistant to confirm that he was on the show tomorrow. "Did she say anything else? Anything about me?" I ask. "Nothing," Sam says, already wiping his brow. So now our job this afternoon is prepping Sam. Jason and Alexis are running him through the TV talking points while Sally and Rita keep printing out new things for him to memorize that we all agreed on. Sam requests (begs really) that I give him some feedback, but I don't want him to be nervous and don't want to interfere with his own style; the whole office is watching him and there's no other choice but to make myself scarce. It's his big day coming up. I don't need to be in the way.

So I head for archives down on the first floor. I'm as glad as the next guy that this crisis is practically over, and I'm really hoping Sam can do a good job up against Rachel tomorrow.

In a world gone digital, there's nothing like boxes of file folders that you can leaf through. I usually prop the door open with the wedge to cut through the mustiness, but today I let the door close behind me. It almost feels like our basement. The wheeze of the heater isn't far from the sound of Rudd's trains.

I browse a bit, and then I pull out a couple boxes I stumbled upon with Rita and Sally when we were organizing everything we had about Percival Lake. These boxes contain some of my best stuff. I make a comfortable seat out of some other boxes and start flipping through the folders. There is nothing, nothing in this world, like being able to quantify your success. My releases involving the brownfields initiative, my statement dealing with the front-page rumors that GE was leaving town, my quote when they discovered a load of PCBs in the Allen Heights Elementary (I was the perfect spokesperson since Jess attended the school at the time—the boys in Fairfield loved me). And here, here's my coup d'etat. A kid named Ralph Constantine and his dog, GE (that was his name, no kidding—you cannot think of every contingency), found a hole in the fence that surrounded Percival Lake at the time, and Ralph threw a stick in the water and GE jumped in after it. The action was repeated several times before concerned motorists pulled over and yelled at the kid about the pollution. The paper was called. The photographer made it in time to get a photo of a vet, who happened to be driving home from work, examining the wet dog along the bank as someone carried gallons of spring water from a nearby convenience store to wash the dog—and in the background on the other side of the lake stood the brick buildings and green tanks of GE. Ralph provided the quote of the century, "I'm sure he's OK. He drinks from the toilet." Because of my contingency plan we had the paperwork ready and we were able to show how clean the water in Percival Lake had gotten. Not that it was ready to be opened to the public yet but it ended up putting a positive spin on the lake the city likes to hold up as a symbol of everything wrong with GE, even though it hasn't caught fire in a few decades. Both GE and GE came out fine—not even a welt or a blister or a change in the consistency of his poop. There was even a follow-up photo of GE licking the hell out of my face as I handed him a "I LUV PERCIVAL LAKE WATER" T-Shirt and Ralph a "GE LUVS PERCIVAL LAKE" T-shirt along with the copyright waiver OK-ing the fact that he named his dog GE. Our positive buzz went nationwide—the three of us and Ralph's mom were even on a national morning show, thanks to Rachel. There was even talk of moving me to Fairfield.

But on this Thursday afternoon at two o'clock, four years later, I never get a chance to relive all the successes because apparently if you are in pursuit of any kind of good, bad is right there to block your way. The door to the archives opens. I see through the shelving that it's Jason the Kid. He's on his phone and his voice is cracking: "PCX? Are you kidding me? A box in here? All of here? PCX? Hold on." He puts his phone against his shoulder. "Is someone in here?"

Please don't ask me why, but what I do is curl up on the boxes—it's actually pretty comfortable—and start making light snoring sounds. Possums have nothing on me.

"Let me call you back." I hear footsteps coming my way and Jason is above me. "Jesus, Merit. What are you frigging doing? Napping?"

I jump up. And make a play of unrumpling myself as Jason is shaking his head in disbelief. I'm now even lower down in his esteem: drunk driver, chemical-lake-admitter, and now on-the-job-napper. Soon I'll be recommended for custodial service. I start to say something about a rough week, but he's not listening anyway. "What's this?" he asks at first suspicious and then relieved as he starts leafing through the stories about the dog in the Lake. "I heard about this. You were on top of your game then." He turns his little kid eyes to me, and maybe I have Jason all wrong, maybe he's not so helpless as he seems even if he fucks up pretty badly. There are pinpricks in those eyes.

"Did you come to find me?" I ask.

His pinpricks disappear. I've stumped the poor kid. If he has any future in PR he better be quicker on his feet than this. I feel bad about it, really I do, so I'm just as relieved as he is when his phone rings again.

He walks off toward the door as I rearrange the boxes. "Fine. Nothing. No just an employee in here. No. Nothing. Of course not." The door opens and his voice is cracking all over the place again and then the door shuts with a slam. I'm alone. Employee? He's just protecting my identity, covering for a guy who was pretending to be asleep on the job to help his boss keep a closed circle on whatever new crisis is now unfolding—I did him a favor and he doesn't have the slightest clue. I'm the first person ready to jump into any crisis, no matter how daunting, but this week is not the week for it. I scan the room, the shelves of boxes, the piles. PCX? I lie back down on the boxes and close my eyes.

When I return upstairs, Alexis tells me the joke about the PR man, the priest, and the parrot ("Get it? It's the parrot in the confessional!"). Becky has a photoshopped copy of the trustee surrounded by adoring beavers, and Jason, poor Jason, is pacing behind his office door with the phone stuck to his ear, waiting for a discreet moment to slip down to archives again. I salute him through the window as I pass just to keep him on his toes. If he had bothered to ask I could have told him he wouldn't find anything down there.

"What a mood," Sam says as I pass his cubicle. I don't take his bait.

I lean back in my chair and review some notes in my pad to pry my mind from everything when I notice Sam peering over the top of the partition. He's shaking his head.

"It makes me sick," he says in a low voice. "These excuses to avoid the right thing. Why can't we do it right?"

"We have done it right. You're about to wrap this up."

"Honesty. The truth." Sam's eyebrows rise dramatically. He actually believes it. "When a kid sees the truth and we don't, we're all in trouble."

"Guy? You're on his side?"

"The girl, she. . ."

"Assassins?"

"We all are, aren't we? Jamie warned me when I signed up for this. Complicity is just like pulling a trigger. Blood on our hands."

"Look, Lady Macbeth, Rachel's just going to walk you through it. She'll hold your hand. You don't have to freak out. If you end up having to talk to Nathan after this, as you probably will, he's tougher but there's nothing to crack open. We can only work with what we know. That is our honesty, that is our truth."

"Of all people I thought you'd understand." He drops out of sight.

My cell is buried under some papers and I see I have two texts. One from my wife and one from Rachel. I have a good feeling about both.

"It isn't done," Sam says, popping over the partition just enough to see his eyes and forehead. "I know it's not done." Then just as suddenly he's back on his side and his keyboard is going, but just one key repeatedly.

I've never seen Sam so worked up. It has to be about something else.

"Sam, everything OK? How's Jamie?" There's no response. It's me over the top of the cubicle wall now. I redirect: "You're not upset about taking my job. I'm fine with it. Really fine. It will be a relief to keep my bald spot behind the scenes for a little while."

He doesn't laugh but just keeps tapping with his eyes closed. "I'm at a motel, Doug. Living at a motel."

I think about my wife, I think about Jess's truth, I think about my own truth, I think about PCX, and I think about the protests finally being behind us. All I am asking for is that one morsel from this tough week be placed on the done pile, one tiny bit.

"Sam," I say, hoping to put a smile on his face, "why don't we just call for a town hall-style meeting. That would open it up. That will surely fix everything."

Sam's head cocks just like Gazook does when he's finished barking at me. He should be cracking up on the floor at even the idea of a town-hall meeting. "Huh," he repeats as his chair swivels and keeps swiveling.

Suddenly I see the future very clearly. Sam is going to screw up everything tomorrow and he's going to be fired and perhaps Fairfield will fire us all. I am on my feet again and stand in the entrance of his cubicle. I'm halfway to picking him up by his collar and screaming into his face, but I see him sitting on the bed at the motel room, hugging a pillow as he watches a movie on Lifetime. "Shit, Sam." I have to take a deep breath. "It's over. They all fizzled themselves out today. Savor the small victory. Hold onto to it as hard as you can. Prioritize." His elbows are on the desk; I'm not sure if I've ever seen him so excited. "Finish this, Sam. For Christ's sakes, finish it. It's just a game, all a game, and then you go home to what really matters. You'll be able to concentrate on what's most important."

Now he's standing up and you know what he does? He gives me a bear hug. I'm wishing for the Sam of a few seconds ago, eyes closed, tapping away at the spacebar. He won't let go. This is the kind of hug I haven't had for a long time, since I was a teenager and my dad would grab me randomly and hold onto me for too long. "Don't you worry, Merit," he says *to me*. "You're going to be OK. You're going to get through this."

Alexis yells from down the corridor for us to get a room. Sam blows her a kiss with his middle finger...who is this guy? Maybe he's been drinking the lake water.

"Will you just take this," he says in a whisper, producing a card between his fingers as a magician would. "I meant to give it to you yesterday. It's our therapist. We should have started sooner. Marriage trouble, it's like cancer. You've got to zap it before it spreads. Even the best cars need a tune-up. Catch things before it's too late." He pushes it into my hand and closes my fingers around it. "It's like cancer, Doug, like cancer. Right when you think you have it licked.
. ." He loses his words in shaking his head as his ponytail whips violently, loosening more strands of hair, which he doesn't push away from his face.

"Sam. . ." But I never finish this thought—I'm so turned around. I don't even know what's about to drop from my tongue: the letters PCX, or how he really needs to understand that he and Jamie might just be better without each other, or that he better start getting his resume together, or perhaps even I'm going to come clean that Karen and I are off our game just a little bit this week (though I wouldn't want to rub in how we might not be super great this week but we're still pretty great— plus, again, I have some pretty big hopes from that text blinking on my phone that might just bring us back to super great if I could just wrap up this conversation with Sam!).

I'm good at reading people, and at the very least I know I can read Sam, so when he lifts his eyes to meet mine, his lumpy, sincere Abominable Snowman smile sends me right back to my seat. I hold the card in both my hands. *Regina Samsonetti* is followed by about three dozen initials. Beneath her name in quotes is the phrase: *a new way to get along.* I try to rip the card but I can't do it. It won't rip. I'm about to flip it into the trash but think better of it and toss it into the scatter of papers at the back corner of my desk. I keep it because I admire the damn thing for not ripping. I need to replace my card with this brand. I stare at the blank screen in front of me for a few moments. I understand now that Sam cares about the truth because it will be coming out of his mouth, it will be tied to his name. "Sam," I say through the cubicle wall, "finish it."

"Make an appointment with Regina," he responds.

No one really wants the truth.

14

The text from my wife *is* full of good news, we *are* super great, no therapist necessary. That's why this evening I'm at the Albany Airport in search for the prime parking spot. My wife is returning from Arizona not a week later but the very same day she left. In fact, she only made it as far as Chicago. She's made a monumental decision but didn't give any details. It's not hard to guess though: she decided to come home *and* she asked that I come pick her up. This very morning there was every indication that from her perspective even being in the car with me for a moment would result in self-immolation (whose, I'm not sure). Now I'm her designated driver for an hour's long ride back from the airport!

My wife, Karen, is back! The one that is positive about *Things*! The one that knows whether her husband had or had not left his daughter in the cold and snow outside the library for hours (which he certainly did not!). *And* whether she harbors any suspicion about the other events that night, they are clearly not on the radar of IMPORTANCE. Who needs the truth! Karen and I are beyond the truth!

There was, however, one aspect of her text that gave me some pause. She asked specifically that I pick her up alone. She had even gone so far as to already arrange with Nancy to watch the kids. And then even more curious, she ended the text with "no surprises." This flew in the face of everything I had ever known about picking her up at the airport.

Tomorrow, Sam will screw up. In the coming weeks, GE inevitably will disregard our small office's humble opinion (if I'm even brought into the loop, which I'm not sure I even want to be in—but chances are Jason will have to seek out my opinion even if he's not supposed to) and make some monumentally poor decisions. There will be repercussions, far-reaching ones. Smack dab in this growing snowball, I've got this chance not to screw up with my wife. So just moments after I received the text and as Jason prowled for PCX files downstairs (good luck with that) and Sam typed wildly, with all fingers on board, I understood what I had to do. I called Nancy. I was taking the kids with me to pick up Karen. Of course I was sure. Why wouldn't I be sure? Nancy paused. I could see her in her fabric store, in her fleece vest, her jeans. She's taken to sitting on the front counter next to the cash register, aloft; business has been on the decline. It was a long pause and I didn't fill it because I was sure she would make the same calculations as I did. And sure enough: "You know what's best," she said. Exactly!

The only wrench manifested itself in the text I received from Rachel. She needed me to pick up Burty from school when I got Tina. It would mean the world to her. I agreed. She didn't need to explain. I completely understood. I was happy to do her a favor. Burty would be the perfect distraction for Tina who otherwise would be so excited about her mother's return that by the time we actually got there she'd be a blubbering wreck, which would be a terrible welcome home for Mom. Burty did his job well—except when it was time for Rachel to come get him at our place, there was no Rachel. No response on her phone. Stacy, the receptionist, said she wasn't in the building and then hung up when she usually chatted me up. No response at home. I even called the hospital but Dr. St. John was in the middle of surgery and couldn't be bothered by a missing wife and a son who had nowhere to go. Nancy stepped in to save the day, but Burty would have nothing to do with her.

And so here I am scoping for the prime spot at the airport with my three children and Burty. To accommodate the extra passenger (the minivan has received its last rites and in the terrible mechanism of insurance it is far from clear what form its resurrected soul will try to take) we had to borrow Nancy's Suburban, so we're bursting through rolls of fabric. And the whole drive Tina and Burty were all whispers and Jess and Rudd all earphones and the Suburban loud even with the radio turned off. It was quietly agreed that the front seat would be left empty in anticipation of Mom. Frankly I was happy with the whispering, Tina and Burty can sound a bit like a couple on their way to a silver anniversary. I remind myself that I have to put more of an effort in finding Tina other friends, preferably ones who believed in reasonable animal rights, such as the right for their Magic Ponies to have all the accessories they deserved.

And then I can only take it as a sign when a Subaru's backup lights magically appear, a parking spot that is for sure the best spot in the airport. My blinker instantly claims it. The spot ends up being a bit tight for the Suburban. Who needs doors? Like a school bus fire drill we have the best time on the obstacle course to the back hatch. No problem. Burty loves it so much I let him climb back in and jump over the rows of seats again. I've never seen the kid happier. Tina joins him. Rudd is showing his mastery by not suggesting we should have found a wider spot and Jess enjoys the fact that her Dad isn't perfect in every way. Karen will start cracking up as soon as she sees this, pulling me to her side, so happy I'm still me. It's win-win all the way around. All Jess has to do is confess to her lie on the drive home and everything will be back to normal.

The arrivals area that's right across the street from our parking spot is lit like a stadium. I spot my wife as soon as Burty and Tina jump out the hatch a second time. The evening rush of travelers pass her every which way as she stands with her bag behind her. I wanted to be there at the gate, one big happy family waiting as she deplaned, but getting Burty into the car took a while, plus when did flights start arriving on time? Even though we're right here bursting through fabric, she hasn't spotted us because her head is turned toward the incoming traffic. Our late arrival is fortunate, though, because there's a play from our playbook that we haven't used for a couple years, a great plan B—so great it should have been my plan A.

I herd the kids behind a row of cars and cross the street to the drop-off area without her seeing us. We regroup behind an empty porter stand, and it's time for my pep talk.

"Three," I coach, showing my fingers, "I love you very much and never forget it. Two, there will be no need to spoil mom's homecoming with any mention of flashlights." I peer at Tina until she gives me a nod. "One, we are going to take advantage of your mother coming home early by being the best big happy family we can be. OK, now the usual plan. I know we're a bit rusty, so I'll review."

I turn to Tina first: "You're the scout. Your mission should you choose to accept it, is to sneak up behind mom and give her a big hug. Then you, Jess, then Rudd. Then finally me. We'll surround your mom in hugs!" I pause until everyone nods. Maybe not everyone's heart is completely in it, but they are playing the game. I can even take some solace as Jess and Rudd cast a glance at each other. I'm all for bonding even if it's at my expense. I smile at both of them to show I'm oblivious of their inner dissent. "Everyone ready? On three. Hut, hut, hut."

"Doug," Burty's tiny voice, halting us all, "What about me?" In the few days since the accident, Tina's hair has filled in and it almost suits her. It's hard to imagine her with long hair again, but poor Burty looks like he's losing a fight with some hair-eating disease, which reminds me that I'm not showing parental responsibility because after a quick survey, none of them are wearing a hat or gloves but at least most of them have on jackets. I contemplate going back to the car to check for winter gear, but I don't know how long my wife has been waiting.

"Big job, Burty, the biggest. You're riding caboose with me. You're job is not to let anyone see you. You're Invisible Man."

"I'm Aquaman?"

Tina pulls him behind me.

"Ow!"

Tina knows how to stick to the script even if I don't endorse physical contact to get the point across. And we're on our way again.

My wife is wearing a fleece vest which is zipped down even in the cold. Her red sweatshirt has an arched *Tempe* stamped in purple on it. She is wearing blue jeans, and her beat up tennis sneakers are bright compared to the multitude of dark shoes that pass her on either side. She usually didn't assume this casual outfit until she had been home for at least a full day—it certainly is not what she wore this morning—maybe it should give me pause, but I think it's great…we're all in our casual, non-winter best.

She jumps when Tina hugs her from behind. But after her, things go wrong. Jess heads way over by the sliding doors, which do not know whether to stay open or to close. I try to hiss that she's off target. Rudd, confused by his sister's actions, looks back at me, but sees something on TV inside the concourse and his eyes stay fixed there. The automated voice from above reminds us all not to leave our cars unattended, loading and unloading.

Tina carried out the first part of the plan flawlessly but now she's asking over and over again as she bounces into her mother the one thing I told her to not ask: "Where's my Arizona torch? Where's my Arizona torch?"

"Surprise!" I yell from fifteen feet away and the throngs halt for a moment. Everyone, it seems, is eager for a surprise—everyone, that is, except my wife, whose eyes narrow as they map a course from Tina, to Rudd, to Jess, and finally to me, where those eyes land hard. In the San Andreas Fault of all relationships this is the look that sends you sliding into the sea.

A few months ago, between Thanksgiving and Christmas. It was on December 5th, or something around there, maybe. We were at the mall, on a bench with bags, the two of us, Karen and me. Rudd and Jess were on the loose. Not more than ten feet in front of us, Tina crouched on a bright blue elephant on one of those mini merry-go-rounds that she was too big to be riding. The glee she had even in those slow circles made me proud. Meanwhile my wife, the mother of the girl who was having the time of her life, was telling me in a calm voice, telling me as we stared forward surrounded by bags of loot, telling me something. Really I only half listened as I engineered different bodily contortions that would allow me to join Tina in her glee. I had quarters in my pockets and big plans. And suddenly words from my wife registered. Had she really just said it? It couldn't be, but it was unmistakable: "I don't love you anymore."

On a bench in a mall, twenty days until Christmas, our daughter spinning and laughing and waving at us, I knew not to look at Karen. It was the mall on a Saturday in the middle of shopping season in the most stressful time of year. She just got the call the night before that she was needed back in Columbus. Basically, what I'm saying is that in this type of situation none of us are in our right minds. Even though my whole body went weak, I was able to stand and hobble to Tina. I'd been sitting too long. She frowned when she saw me but on her next trip around I mustered a smile, I flashed quarters. The first quarter wouldn't go into the slot and it jingled and rolled until a passerby slapped it flat with her foot and kept walking. I got the other quarters in and Tina in cramped bliss spun and spun on a little elephant with wild eyes as the electronic tin of organ music ground out of a saltshaker speaker.

I glanced back only once, worried perhaps Karen would be gone, but there she was still on the bench with bags, her eyes on her shoes stretched before her. The quizzical look she gave those striped sneakers (the same ones she wore now at the airport), as if she were surprised that these shoes were as good as they were, that they had defied her expectations of them. I knew that look from way back in our relationship. And I turned to Tina who maybe was bored by now but knew she had to ride out the quarters. And soon enough my wife and the bags were next to me, along with Jess and Rudd who both goaded their sister in baby voices. My wife's profile, chin up, the eye I could see, unreadable. A swallow crawled down her neck before she turned to me, and said, "Let's get out of here." So there we were a family midway to Christmas, headed for the car. I relaxed right away. Nobody, nobody should be held accountable for words they use in a mall at the height of Christmas season, nobody.

Now outside an airport under the crushing gaze of my wife, with those words she spoke at the mall spiraling in my ears, I realize for the second time in this rotten week I'm in a situation that will be the fodder of future laughter. *Remember how you came with the kids to the airport, I was soooooo pissed. But not as pissed when I thought you left Jess outside the library.* We would laugh, my wife and I. Our joint laughter is so clear I feel like right now I can hold it in front of me on this crisp night even as some jet momentarily tests its engine, hold it up against those mall words, against *Things*.

The problem is, though, there is no fast-forward. I'm here. She's here. There's nothing to laugh about. And then this voice comes to me, not quite clear, but I can pick out "I forgive you." It's an angelic moment, something I've never felt before, a supreme sense of *OK*. I figure an aneurysm has just burst in an important part of my brain, and who could blame it? It would be a great way of fast forwarding. Unfortunately all the cog teeth connect again and the angelic voice is actually Burty screaming "Aquaman!" as he charges right by me toward the terminal door where Jess and Rudd lost their way only moments ago.

His fist is in the air as he sprints by my wife and Tina. Burty must have been using telemetry to communicate with Tina because instead of her eyes locking onto Burty, they land on something ahead of him, just through the sliding glass door that's open wide. She almost knocks over her mother she pushes off so hard. "Solid dairy!" she yells. In an instant I join them in my own sprint and battle cry, "Get back here!" Rudd and Jess take their eyes off the TV. Just at the door Burty is on a collision course with a big guy. I shout but too late. Burty hits the guy at full speed. He has a ferret on his shoulder, two ferrets. Burty bounces off the guy's thigh and then Tina bounces off the other one, both of them dropping back to the mat. Burty's in tears instantly and as the guy lifts him back on his feet he collapses to the ground again. Then he reaches down for Tina who says, "Mink killer," as she grabs a fistful of the guy's hair and tries to swat the ferrets off him with the other. "Run," she is telling them. "Run." One ferret is on the ground and off among the stalled feet of the airport goers and the other one snaps its jaws onto Tina's hand just as I arrive. The guy stuffs the ferret back into its case in one expert swoop, as his eyes search the ground for the other one. At the same time he surveys Burty and then Tina's hand which pops with blood as she sits on the ground looking at it, stunned. "Julie-Anne," he calls. I'm about to swoop up Tina and staunch the bleeding and begin a serious round of apologies and organizing a ferret search and figuring out a noncombative way to find out if the ferrets are caught up with their shots, when both the guy and me find ourselves swamped by TSA agents.

No explaining, not even from the ferret guy works. He's almost as worried about his ferret as I am about my kids. The uniforms surround us and instantly hurl so many commands at once there's no telling what we're supposed to do. The ferret guy gives up on words and points through the gaps between the uniforms to the kids, to Tina, before his arms are forced behind him. And in that moment just before my arms are taken from me, I too find myself trying to point her way. As I'm cuffed for the second time in a week for no reason, as the ferret guy curses understandably because a moment ago he was just a guy with his ferrets heading for his car, I catch a glimpse of the TV that Jess and Rudd stopped to watch. There, Rachel reports in a snowstorm, wrapped in Burty's Aquaman blanket. My wife's scarf is wrapped around her neck (a detail I don't remember), the purple and red one that I gave her as an anniversary present way back; and there is Burty running circles with an officer behind him (the kid that's videoing this moving away from Rachel to zero in on Burty's cartoon antics). There is Tina sitting on the bumper of the ambulance. There is Rudd holding a hat on Jess's nose. There I am filling the whole screen with no shoes, swinging Tina's blanket wildly at the cops. Suddenly a palm is over the front of the camera, Rachel's, as she swings the kid's phone back to her. The kid then must try to hold the phone high so it can peer between her scarf and blanket to see her breasts but she is having none of it and reaches for the phone again and she's such a pro she's able to judge where the camera outlines her face. There at the bottom of the screen is the YouTube icon. Then there are the two anchors who are laughing and shaking their heads in the small talk before the show closes out. I can faintly hear or perhaps in a moment like this I have a natural ability to read lips: "Our colleague at our sister station over in Pontoosuc certainly goes all out to report a story. First the Frisbees, then the Mayor's other stunt on her show today and now this comes out." They laugh. I now understand Rachel's disappearance. And still just inside the sliding door as passengers gawk and move on, there's my wife holding Tina who is not crying but looking at her bloody hand in that same inquisitive way that her mother was looking at her shoes in the mall that day. Next to them Burty is running from the law again in a perfect reprise from TV as a single TSA tries to figure out what to do with him. "Free the minks! Free the minks!" he's yelling. But Tina's not joining him. Jess and Rudd are right near their mom, and all of their eyes are on the TV and not on their dad, again in cuffs. Rachel filling the screen in a still, that scarf.

15

My wife insists on driving home. As she eases the Suburban from my prime parking spot, I keep the kids corralled to the side and, really, if you take a look around a lot of cars are parked pretty close together. My wife's reaction to the parking spot didn't quite line up with my forecast and it didn't help that she bumped a knee or elbow or head climbing over the seats. Beside me, Tina can't keep her eyes off her wrapped hand. I wonder if she is showing early signs of rabies. Her hand only needed a Band-Aid—we were told it was just a warning bite, a "back-off, my friend, bite," but under her jacket it's wrapped to the elbow in gauze and I'm not sure why since I was in detention. And now for accounting purposes I have one daughter in a new bright bandage and the other with a not so bright bandage still over her nose. At this rate, Rudd should be feeling pretty nervous. Since I've emerged from detention, Jess and Rudd have the haunted stare of kids who just caught their parents doggy style—if only that were the case, if it were only that simple.

When Karen successfully slides the car out of its slot, I see that we have been a victim of parking lot rage: a large dent from what must have been repeated bashes of a car door, the fabric paint job is peeling.

I already can see Nancy's no problem smile tomorrow when I return the car. Both Jess and Rudd eye the dent and only Rudd has the sense to keep quiet about it.

"You wrecked Nancy's car too!" Jess says.

It's just essentially a ding, but I'm not going to argue with Jess right now.

The night as a whole isn't quite sticking to plan.

But as we pile in the boring way, through doors, I know the wounds to our family are just like the ones to this car: external, cosmetic, insured. What I have going for me is that we are in here for the next hour, and our family history is all about wonderful, even glorious moments in the car.

I'd had a minivan since college when my parents decided after a few months with it that they were not the type. I don't think I even changed the oil or vacuumed it for a year before I met Karen. The check engine light had been on for several months. I was just a kid. But after our first date I saw that the minivan had to survive. In the next decade I did everything I could, risked bankruptcy by only bringing it to the dealer and doing everything they suggested each time, but still it only lasted ten years. Kip the service manager patted my shoulder on that grim day and told me it was time to let go. I walked home to quietly mourn the loss of that car and all its history and to practice how I was going to break this news to my family (no Tina yet but she might have been on the way). Would I be able to get behind a wheel of another vehicle?

When I reached the corner of the dealership, right there in front of me the minivan, the same color, almost brand new. As I stood before the vehicle, ready to drop to my knees before its sparkling presence, a sales guy materialized next to me and told me straight off a lady who was not the minivan type just traded it in for a Z28. I do not believe in fate but when I encounter it, who am I to ignore it? I came home that day and the kids were all fooled (before they got into the car and saw the clean interior), and my wife could appreciate what I had saved even if I'd gone ahead and bought the car without any notice and the sales guy had me pegged so I paid way too much. Can you put a price on such things? Could you put a price on all the experiences we'd had inside?

And what experiences! Though we've had two minivans there's only been one and I'm not the only one that sees it that way. On our first date I couldn't find a parking space. We circled and circled Northampton in the minivan until she ordered me—laughing, but definitely nervous laughing—into the new parking garage. "I'll pay for it," she said as she slapped a five on the dash, "to prevent us from running out of gas on the way home." Then she turned to me as I pulled into the garage, turned to me in that way I could tell she, just in the car ride so far, started to like me: "Are you that type of guy?" she asked. "They died out in the fifties, you know. Maybe you watch too many *Happy Days* reruns." So when we parked and we got out and she locked her door, I told her how I never locked the car even if I had valuables in it because *you just had to trust the world.* She nodded, too stunned to respond verbally—it was the first time I really impressed her. I knew she had me pigeonholed and I was showing her that there was more to me than she thought. (It was worth every item that was stolen over the years.) She turned around as we waited for the elevator and took one long look at the minivan. "By the way, have you ever heard of a car that doesn't guzzle gas? I mean thank God it isn't a big van. A big van wouldn't have surprised me, but did you sleep through the Crisis? Is your last name Exxon? And what kind of guy has a minivan in college? Do you have a family I should know about?" She bumped me with her elbow. I had never been happier in my whole life.

Six months later, the minivan broke down on top of Windsor Mountain on our first trip home to meet each other's parents. We were from the same town but different high schools. It was stunning that we had probably passed right by each other, been at the same sports events, maybe when we were even younger we'd played in the lakes during the summer—splashing water on each other. While I looked under the hood, my wife started hitchhiking. I think we were in a middle of a fight. When a pickup stopped, she turned and ran back to me laughing, her skirt outlining her legs and her hair out behind her, as the guy in a baseball cap leaned out the window to see where she'd gone.

When it wouldn't start in the winter before we were married, did we go around looking for a jump? Did we call a tow truck? Did we call a friend to drive us to class? No, we made love in broad daylight behind the frosted glass.

Or after Jess was born. That's when it really saved everything. We could never get Jess to sleep, and worse, she cried as if everything we did to soothe her caused her great pain. We didn't know what to do. Rudd was the best baby anyone could expect. Other new parents would ask our advice. They wanted to know our secret. Nancy was astounded: "I didn't think you two had it in you." But we were the ones making the desperate calls after Jess's birth. With Rudd so easygoing, we quickly realized we hadn't learned any tricks. We couldn't get her to sleep, ever. We were beginning to go crazy. And my wife's postpartum depression made everything more difficult. If Rudd's birth had pulled my wife out of a depression that had hung heavy with her since returning from Africa—not to mention the death of her father, Jess put her right back. And believe me I wanted to help my wife, try to be in her world, but I couldn't reach her. I didn't know how.

"When you did that," my mother said, "we would take you in the car and drive, drive, drive. It worked every time. Of course in those days I just held you in my arms."

"Where to, James?" It was our catchphrase to utopia for years. The minivan made it all possible and I refuse now to ever envision it differently from these times as it waits somewhere to be stripped of its few valuable parts and crushed in some metal heap in some oil and antifreeze soaked field. I mean as soon as all the doors were closed, before I even started the engine, our world was completely different. We were a different family, the real one. Jess quieted almost immediately, Rudd traced his finger along the glass, and my wife perked up as she sat in back between them. There was no distance between any of us, all of us looking forward—well, except Jess but her little mirror strapped to the headrest counts as seeing what's coming.

"Where to, James?" I ask as we make our way out of the airport parking lot, but no one answers. Why is it that airports have the straightest runways and the most circuitous roads? Maybe the script only works if you're the driver. Maybe, too, the Suburban couldn't hold up to the minivan's precedent. Certainly when we all piled into my wife's Pontiac on occasions it just wasn't the same.

"James?" Tina asks after some time. "What about the bombardier?"

Good to hear Tina back to her old self.

"Rudd, Jess. Tell your sister."

There is still no answer as my wife reaches for her ticket as we head onto the Thruway. I've been pretty busy the last few days, but there's no excuse for why I'd done so little to find a replacement van.

After the Thruway split, we get on I-90. My wife takes up residence behind a U-haul with a pack of bicycle racers painted on the back. The highway thumps, and before I know it we sweep through the four-lane-wide S-turns which hug downtown Albany like a willowy arm, and plunge beneath the cement clover leaves layered and curled on top of each other. An orange sign warns of construction ahead. "Give Us a Brake." Once we are across the construction-narrowed bridge over the Hudson, another river full of PCBs that we're trying to figure out what to do with—luckily this isn't our office's purview (though there's been some rumors we're going to be folded into the Schenectady office once Percival Lake Park is done—the Schenectady guys certainly could use my help). The cars thin and the road opens ahead of us—wide, freshly paved, and the dotted lines coming at us like video game laser bullets.

"Mom," Jess says.

"Yes?"

Is this going to be the moment? Her confession coming unprompted? The one thing that will erase the entire week. We might have this library business wrapped up by the time we hit exit 11. My next car just might be a Suburban.

"Did you ever do that thing in school where you have to take care of an egg like a baby?"

"I don't recall ever doing it but I've heard about it." My wife says. "They did that in your school? In seventh grade?" She looks into the rearview but there's only darkness.

"If you went through three eggs in an hour? Is that bad?"

It really seems to be weighing on her so I have to wonder why she didn't bring it up earlier this evening with me.

"Jessica, Jess, it depends," I say, already smiling at myself. "Were they over easy, hard boiled, or sunny side up?"

The collective thumbs down is so palpable that I vow to keep my mouth closed unless directly addressed for at least the next ten minutes.

"They are eggs, Jess," my wife says, taking her eyes off the road. "They aren't babies."

"I'm just asking," Jess says too defensive.

"It's no big deal," I say breaking my vow, but it is more important to show our children we're a team.

"You're so harsh," Jess whisper-hisses.

"What?"

But there is no answer and the car stays silent for minutes and I'm about to throw out the whole idea of fixing everything on this ride when Rudd saves the day.

"How was your flight, Mom?" he asks.

Great question.

"Were you next to the lady from Palookie?" Tina chimes in.

The script is beautiful—it more than makes up for the lackluster response to "Where to, James?" We're back.

My wife doesn't respond right away, but finally says, "I flew first class. The flight was full but they bumped me up because of my frequent flier miles."

"Did you get caviar?" I ask.

After my wife doesn't respond, Tina says that caviar is fish eggs and if everyone ate caviar there'd be no more fish.

"Can you drop a fish egg?" I smile but there's another silence of the deathly kind. I recover quickly and save the team: "They're big in Russia," I say. "Perestroika."

Tina repeats the word.

"Perestroika, perestroika," I repeat from my seat where I'm still absolutely sure I'm inching back into my wife's good graces.

"It's a Russian word," Rudd adds.

"That sounds like a Rachel word, doesn't it, Dad?" Tina asks. "How many points would *parrazoika* be in Scrabble if the z were on a triple letter?"

"At least a billion," I offer as I analyze, from the safety of my periphery, my wife's reaction to Rachel's name, the scarf she surely recognized. She lifts her palm to check her speed, and for a moment the green glow of the dash, lights her clenched jaw—though it's pretty much been like that since we surprised her. My jaw is clenched too as I try to close a giant eyelid in my brain over the images I have of Rachel during our Scrabble game.

"Wow!" Tina exclaims. "I thought you could only go as high as a million with Rachel's rules. A billion. You'd definitely spank Rachel with that."

Rabies!

"It's not polite to use Mrs. St. John's first name," my wife says.

"OK," Tina whispers, and then after a pause she adds, "She asked me to."

I know Tina directed this last part to me, waiting for confirmation—but I'm sitting this one out.

"That doesn't matter," my wife replies as she pulls into the left lane when we come upon several slow moving trucks blocking the two right lanes. Once we are past, she studies the rearview and pulls back into the center.

"Why do we call Nancy, Nancy, then?" Tina asks.

What's going on tonight? I cannot answer why my family will not cooperate with the script we have made together on the highways of the past, but you know what? I'm fine with it. I'm more than willing to let it be. All teams are entitled to a bad night. Today has been just one bad day in one bad week. It showed some promise with the protesters flopping on Rachel's show, with my wife's sudden reversal in travel and work plans, but it had all been undercut by PCX and Sam and the difficulty six-year-olds have in distinguishing ferrets from minks. Then the State Troopers and the TSA agents just added to the equation with their trouble distinguishing between an innocent slapstick moment and an actual terrorist threat. But once our stories panned out in our holding rooms and Rudd proved himself a hero by locating the ferret Julie-Ann, all was forgiven. Everyone involved in the incident (with one notable exception) had a good laugh about it—it was one big collision of people trying to do good: me trying to give my wife a proper homecoming, Burty and Tina trying to save minks, G. Willikers Willy trying to give his circus ferrets a little fresh air after being cooped up on a flight, and the TSA agents and troopers thinking they were stopping a threat to the public.

Even Dr. Morgan St. John tried to do some good by offering me and Karen a hundred dollars for our troubles. He appeared on the scene in stunning time considering the distance he covered from when the authorities contacted him with their discovery that Burty was not part of our family, still in his scrubs, still puzzled why his son was with us at the airport and leaping on a man with ferrets, still without word about the whereabouts of his wife, and still probably unaware that his wife is making her second star appearance on YouTube in under a week (with the performances on her show today inevitably being a third hit by tomorrow). He was kind enough to look at Tina's bite wound and tell us it didn't look like she'd need surgery. By his hesitation after our refusal of his hundred dollar bill, it seemed like his mind was racing for some other way to pay us, and so he, of all things, lifted his hand in the air and when I stared up at it he added with his perpetual one-sided smile, "High-five!" So I gave him a high five and then Burty a high five and then he and Burty high-fived the whole family before he jumped into his Porsche (clearing up how he got here so fast and also clearing up that if you want to be an actual terrorist you should just drive a Porsche and wear scrubs and then you can park your car right in front of the terminal and run into the building with no questions asked and your car will still be there forty-five minutes later). That's when he put Burty in the passenger seat with no booster even after I offered to run to our car for one. I suppose if they crash he can administer first aid.

Since we haven't seen any burning cars yet, I picture Burty and his dad pulling into their circle driveway just about now—and I'm glad we're going the speed limit, I'm glad I have more time. The mile markers pass, and as we near our exit, I'm ready with my last card, Rudd. I ask him how he's feeling about the big hockey game on Wednesday—something that is a relatively safe subject.

"OK."

"Just OK?"

"I thought OK was ideal," my wife says, a little too quickly.

"Right, right, of course you're right. Let me rephrase." Turning back to Rudd, I ask, "Do you get nervous? Here it is the end of the season and I don't even know if you get nervous. You don't seem like you do."

"I don't know."

"Does anyone know if Rudd gets nervous? Jess, do you? He *is* your brother."

"He *is* your son," Jess replies—a fine response—I want to keep her larynx as warm as possible.

"Just tell him to leave you alone," my wife says.

"What's wrong with asking him if he gets nervous?"

Another silent moment fills in with tires on pavement, wind whistling, and then the throaty engine of an orange Roadway eighteen wheeler re-passing us on the inside lane.

"No," Rudd says, filling the void left by the tractor trailer (good boy), "I'm nervous until I'm in the net and then, well, then, I'm somewhere else. It's like I'm not even in the game. It's not even hockey."

Jess laughs.

"What?" Rudd asks.

"Nothing."

"At least I'm honest. That's exactly how I feel. I don't make stuff up."

I sit up straight. Does Rudd have the goods on his sister? I'm about to seize this golden opportunity when my wife jumps in first.

"You know," she says, measured in that way that makes the whole family lean toward her, "that's just how I feel when I'm starting a store. The store disappears and even I disappear. It's like…" She doesn't go on.

Car sounds again. We exit 90 and head west on Route 20 through Speed Trap Ville—a town with all its businesses and residences too close to the street and where there's a ten to one ratio of radar guns to townspeople. I remind my wife to watch her speed, which she seems to appreciate because she slows down. No one wants a speeding ticket, though I have a feeling she's slowing down because she somehow doesn't want to risk getting me cuffed and hauled off again. But that's something, isn't it?

As we curve our way out of town, my wife stays to the right on the climbing lane. We still have a good twenty-five miles to go. I look at this road, right now devoid of any other cars—no lights, no houses, just our headlights and some worn lines guiding the way, the rest of the world in shadow. And I shoot back seventeen years to a different history, one that predates three of the passengers in the car and one that the other passenger—the only one whom I want to reach at this moment as she stares into what the headlights illuminate—will resist. "Did we ever tell you," I address the backseats without turning toward them, "about the back roads river honeymoon extravaganza your mother and I planned?"

When you bank everything on one history you can't switch to another. You lose every time. I know better. But it doesn't stop me. I'm desperate to get our family back on track and we only have twenty minutes to go.

"Doug," my wife says. "Please."

I go on with the story, punctuated once more by my wife saying my name and please, but just once. I explain to them how we had planned to take the minivan around the country for two months and hit as many rivers as we could while avoiding the interstate. And as I spoke, the names of rivers rolled off my tongue. The Delaware, the Susquehanna, the Allegheny. Then the long free ride alongside the Ohio to the Mississippi, the U of the Tennessee, the Alabama, the Chattahoochee (a word that causes Tina to scream out in delight). From the Gulf, we couldn't *miss* the Mississippi, then west along the Arkansas to the Rio Grande. The Gila, the Colorado, the Green, the Snake, until we gandered at the Columbia where we would head back east along the Madison, the Missouri. Then there was always the Cheyenne, the North Platte, the Platte. Finally, to the Des Moines and onto the Great Lakes, which after all are just bloated rivers. We'd for sure hit Canada at this point and take the St. Lawrence back to the Hudson. Anyone could map a trip on roads, even their mother admitted my plan didn't lack imagination. "Do you know what your mom said?" I ask. "She said, 'Doug, only you would turn a boat trip into a road trip.'"

My wife takes her eyes off the road for a moment to focus on my left knee.

"Did you really say that, Mom?" Tina asks.

Her eyes move to the road again and then to the sideview mirror. "It was a long time ago."

"Did she really say it, Dad?"

"Did he screw that up too?" Jess asks.

Talk about getting the wind knocked out of you. *He* instead of *Dad* is enough to get me wheezing, then add *screw up*!

"Jess," my wife says, her vocal cords swollen—which is perhaps why it took her so long to respond, "that's an awful thing to say." I can feel Jess shrink. There will be no bonding over bashing Dad.

"Jess was just being funny," I say. "Weren't you?"

My wife swallows and her voice crispens, "You can't plan for everything. Things come up."

There it is again, *Things*. I see it capitalized, underlined, bolded, italicized, and then wrapped in a scarf.

"Dad does," Tina says. "You've got to have a plan. Right?"

"You've got it, kid."

"But what happened?" Rudd asks. "Why didn't you go?"

"Do you want the honor?" I ask, turning to my wife.

"I know, I know, I know," Tina jumps in excitedly. "It must have been Africa. Everything goes back to Africa, isn't that what Rachel says? I mean Mrs. St. John."

It is my turn to look at my wife's right knee and then the simulacrum of my dashboard-lit reflection in the window. Without my training, I might have opened the door and stepped out into the safer world of sturdy, predictable pavement. It would have been the easy choice. But you have to be tenacious. You push forward even if you wind up at the North Pole, alone and with only one slice of stale bread to get you home.

"Let me tell you about a big decision we made when we weren't really much older than you guys. . ." So that night, I push on and explain how I was packing the minivan for our honeymoon extravaganza when their mother came out—the very woman driving this car, the one who didn't look a year older and yet somehow had even gotten more beautiful since then—and told me Professor Finley had just called, the position they had talked about had just opened up and she would have to leave for Africa in four days. I told them how we both knew it wasn't even a choice really, that it was the best thing, an opportunity not to be passed up. "Your mom wanted to make a difference in the world and she did. And that's why we never went on our back roads river honeymoon extravaganza."

When I'm done, the car remains quiet. They don't pummel her with questions about why she went to Africa instead of our honeymoon. I really don't know what I want tonight—do I want to apologize or do I want her to apologize?

"Did you have a plan for that, Dad?" Tina asks finally.

I really wish I could say *yes*.

Then Jess, after a few miles, nails the question with her bandaged-nose voice: "Why didn't you go when you came back?"

I look over at my wife. Finally I say something about making ends meet, about Rudd arriving on the scene. The plastic armrest is rigid as I lean into it. I check the lock. Tina's head settles on Jess's arm and they are sharing Jess's earphones, and because of this I mostly forgive Jess her sealed lips and harsh words. There's a growl that I recognize as Rudd's stomach. My seatbelt cuts into my neck. Out of the corner of my eye, I look at my wife's knuckles on the steering wheel—she has resorted to wiping her cheek against her shoulder.

It takes a long long time to get home—maybe we should look into a Porsche.

Here's what I didn't tell my children: I didn't tell them about the slight give in the minivan's transmission when I leaned into the rear bumper after she told me about Finley's call (I used to be pretty rebellious when it came to the use of the emergency brake). I didn't tell them how their mother used to be crazy for the scent of lilacs and that the scent of lilacs had filled that moment outside our apartment in Pufton Village. I didn't tell them about how she wore grubby blue flip-flops—her toes digging into the rubber soles as only I know her toes could dig. I didn't tell how my wife of only two days was wearing jeans with a hole in one knee and the other thigh showing through the white threads, how she wore my favorite T-shirt of all time, the one with a nuclear symbol with a red circle around it and a line slashing it—the one that clung to her breasts like none of her other shirts. Her hair in a bushy ponytail, her expression twisted by excitement, her thumb pushing into her cheap wedding band. I didn't tell the kids how I cut right to the heart of the matter, as I always do: "Don't women in some tribe over there take multiple husbands?" And you know what? She knew what I was talking about. After her hopeless shrug and sigh, she smiled and pulled me away from the car bumper and held me in one of those hugs where our bodies fit so perfectly that it erased any doubt that we were not supposed to be together. So of course I supported her fully: it was her dream, her big chance at making a difference, a real difference. You might not know it but my wife used to be all about trying to make a difference. I wish I could go back and erase this drive and just tell her this.

But why stop there? Why don't I go all the way back to that hug. Why don't I go back far enough to tell her not to go?

In the kitchen my wife clings to her carry-on as if she's handcuffed to the nuclear codes. Tina sleepily leans into my leg, her wound forgotten (I check her forehead just to be sure she doesn't have a fever). Rudd stares into the great Oz of the open refrigerator. Jess walks right by the blinking answering machine which immediately puts me on alert. I hit the button. "If this is the home of Rudd Merit, can you please have me call him, whoops, I mean have him call me, I think I got the right number"—a girl's voice, Rudd turns red but does not take his eyes off the fridge. Beep. "This is for Rudd Merit again. I, um, um forgot to leave my name, I think, thanks—it's about our project. . .Oh yeah, 250-1588, like the Spanish Armada, except it's not on water it's a landline." There's a long pause and then she continues, "And by the way I totally get your distaste for cell phones. I'm right with you." Beep. A hang up. "It's me again. I just wanted to say you didn't absolutely have to call me tonight. We could talk tomorrow."

A girl for Rudd! Now that's the *real* headline grabber so far today, even if she didn't leave her name. I'm on my way to give the kid a pat on the back when the next message plays:

"Hi Mr. Merit, Doug, it's Rick. Sorry I'm getting back to you so late. You will be able to keep your insurance but your rates are going through the roof. I tried to work the numbers for you but my hands are tied. Come down to the office and we can talk."

Bad news, but I'm all smiles. "Bummer," I tell the machine. At least it shows I'm covering my bases and investigating outcomes of an accident that was in no way my fault. And it is clear that Rick is on my side, just where you want your insurance guy to be.

"Karen, remember us over in El Paso? Well, Judith wanted to tell you her son just got into Rice and she's too shy about her accent to leave a message. She really owes this to you. We miss you and would like an update soon. Please get on Facebook so we can see photos!"

We got one or two of these a week from all over the country. The one thing I don't get is why they don't call her cellphone, but right now, I'm not about to ask. "That's great for Judith," I say without looking up.

Then the final message plays: "Girl baby, I know this is your parents' line but you won't talk to me. I got to talk to you."

The machine beeped. Jess freezes but starts to walk again.

"That's the Baker, isn't it?" I ask.

She shoots a look over her shoulder. The one difference with her mother is that I know exactly what the look says. She stomps up the stairs.

"The Baker?" my wife asks, showing that we can talk about parent things.

"The Baker?" Rudd asks, knowingly, looking up from the hamburger he had stowed in there a few days ago. "The Baker," he repeats, and he takes off his glasses so I know this is serious.

Then Jessica's voice bursts through the ceiling (our house is basically made of cardboard), "At least he doesn't have green hair!"

"Baker, baker, baker man, bake me a cake as fast as you can," Tina jumps in, rising onto her toes. "Bye, bye blackbird, first comes love then comes marriage. Wait I think I messed up. Baker, baker—"

"Patty cake," my wife says, turning to her. "Patty cake!"

And in the way she speaks to Tina I can hear her indictment of me. The Baker is all my fault.

And what's up with her green hair retort?

With that settled, the family disperses—it's super late. We all have to get to bed—except me. In my pants pocket on my phone is a message from Rachel telling me to meet her down at the lake, now. What I should do is call Rick back and see if he's got insurance for this type of thing.

16

The night of the accident, it was just a peck. Even though Rachel was topless, it was part of a game, innocent, innocuous. Earlier that evening before that peck, before the accident, when I arrived to pick up Tina from Rachel's house, I was running a little late so I expected to find Tina getting in her jacket and boots in their high-ceilinged and chandeliered foyer. Tina would be acting like everything weighed 200 pounds and Burty would be crying because he couldn't bear to see Tina go. His only solace was the squeak in the top hinge of the foyer door which he'd be riding for all it was worth by swinging the door in a small but potent arc. But when I entered to Rachel's "It's not locked," there were no children in sight. She was on one of her chairs in the "living area" that is defined by the plushest white rug. I envied Tina and Burty their ability to rip off their socks and shoes and immerse their bare feet in it. The pure whiteness of the rug was a marvel of optimism in a household with a kid. Rachel had one leg lopped over the padded arm and was sitting back, sort of slouching, at least for her. And in her right hand, a wine glass that was about the size of a globe. "Cheers," she said toasting me. "To disc golf and wet mayors and losing it on live TV." She seemed to be taking the disaster in stride. There were plenty of people who would like to drown the mayor, so maybe she'd even increased her stock. She did really lose it though. I toasted her in return with my air glass. This sparked an idea and she leaped up and raced across the football-field of a room and all its different "living areas" until she reached the kitchen on the other end (they have a big house—my wife has never given her opinion of Rachel—she does seem to watch her show though when she's home—but she has noted their house as being extravagant and she hoped it didn't give Tina ideas about the way people lived. Rachel is from "old money" I think my old boss, Ed, explained when I started my job, ". . .as in Sproul Street, as in the Sproul Park, as in. . ." and the list went on). I noted two ice packs on her chair—Frisbees do hurt. From the other end zone she held up a glass and a bottle of wine. "Stay for dinner," she called.

Suddenly both Tina and Burty raced out of a hallway with their double socks. Their favorite activity in the St. Johns' is putting on "slippery socks" and skating around the house. Both pairs of socks were down around their ankles and the sock toes spread and squished limp as the kids jumped to celebrate the idea of dinner. How did these kids get from this frenzy to a couple hours later a monastic rite in sympathy of minks, I might never know. Dinner? I was looking forward to hitting Burger King with Tina until it was time to get Jess at the library and then I'd go back out later to get Rudd at hockey. In a blink, Tina and Burty were at my side. Burty was pulling on my arm and screaming hysterically to stay, stay, stay. Tina just looked up at me in a silent plea as if I was controlling the guillotine. Confronted by the two rhetorics of the first grade, I was pretty much helpless. The full reluctance of my "OK" was drowned out by Tina and Burty's cheer.

Before I knew it I'd lost my shoes, and Rachel, two wine glasses in hand, greeted me in the kitchen, and Tina and Burty were both shouting "socks, socks, socks" as they held up extra pairs for Rachel and me. They disappeared and Rachel told me I better take a drink and handed me my own globular glass. When I took a small sip, to be sociable, the top of the glass was at my forehead. "We're bonded now," Rachel said a bit conspiratorially and with a definitely buzzed wink—but who could blame her for an extra glass of wine after today? I took another small, small sip. "We've crossed the golf disc community. We have to prepare ourselves for battle." She held up her glass again and we toasted. She gave me another wink that seemed to say, stick with me and you'll be safe. It was all funny and frankly a relief after this day so far. She then told me how her stepfather called to ask if she was going to have a security detail to protect her because he was convinced her life was "imperiled," adding after she polished off her glass: "I'm following his advice as you see and taking it very seriously." Before I knew it, I was skating around the house in silky socks on the ice-polished floors with Tina and Burty and Rachel. Honestly we were all laughing so hard I have to say it was the most fun I've had in a long time. If Karen and I ever manage to find our doesn't-have-to-be-perfect house, which should be soon because we've been looking for seventeen years, I will be the biggest proponent for slippery floors. If we had slippery floors in our home the night of the wrong pizza delivery, everything would be different right now.

Both of us panting and still laughing and whatever it was popping and hissing in the oven (I had wrongly pegged Rachel as the microwave type), we stopped in the kitchen and I had another small sip. We reviewed our ridiculous day as Tina and Burty were still testing the Doppler effect as they screamed and skated through the cavernous house—their voices muffled in the rooms and uncorked in the hallways, punctuated on every lap by pounding up and down the stairs. Rachel opened up and said even before the mayor fiasco that she'd been passed up for the evening anchor chair again and she was seriously considering quitting: "He told me, that fucking bucktoothed bastard, that I'm *a noon face*. What's a fucking *noon face*? He inherited the station from his father and basically keeps it floating for the last twenty years with no competition and thinks he's a fucking media mogul. A noon face!" Then he told her this afternoon that they were a strictly pro-Frisbee station and that he'd already reached out to the mayor: "Noon face! What a fucking fuck!" I listened to see if the kids were getting in range of her voice though I did sympathize with her. I really wanted to know where she got the information about the cancellation of the Frisbee course, but I didn't want to cross professional lines. Maybe the mayor set it all up—but still someone had to tell *him*.

She tried to open another bottle but the cork snapped. "My husband refuses to use one of those cork openers where this doesn't happen. It goes against the grain of the wine, he says." She tried another bottle and broke that cork. She held the corkscrew up to me, pleading. She had a cable sweater on, and skinny jeans but the type you sit in the bathtub with. I realized that Rachel's drinking this evening could not be tallied by glasses but by bottles. She was genuinely drunk. I was going to say something about eating some food before the next bottle, but she looked as if she was going to cry. Rapid emotions need damming. I'm that kind of guy. I got out my keychain Swiss Army knife and brushed away her corkscrew. I'm a consummate cork snapper and as a result I've become equally good at removing broken ones. I extracted the cork with minimum residue. And no kidding, simple as that, Rachel perked up. She embraced me and called me her little MacGyver, her hero, the cork surgeon. I felt pretty good about my success.

It was just a thank you hug from a drunk woman. Her reaction times were slowed and I'm sure that's why she held on maybe one moment too long. After the attack we were sort of like war buddies. She stayed close though to fill my glass even though I'd only taken a few sips of the last batch. "What do you think?"

"It's OK. I don't know. It's good. I'm a little behind on all the wine things. Tannins or whatever they are."

Rachel's eyes grew wide and I worried I offended her. "I'm so glad to hear that. Morgan can be a bit of a fake with wine. You should hear him wax about this and that. Cranberries and coffee or some such bullshit. This one you're drinking has a good nose." She actually reached out and touched my nose but this caught her off guard and her hand dropped to my tie and she held it up closer to her face and in her eyes I could see her hope that it was a Father's Day present. She didn't let it go though.

Tina came around the corner and I stepped back so my tie slipped from Rachel's fingers.

"It's Daddy's noose," Tina said.

"Tina!" I responded.

"Life's a noose," Rachel said and raised her glass to her lips and took a gulp. "Jump through it!"

"You sound like my mom," Tina said as Burty pulled her arm to get her to do more skating but Tina's stronger and Burty could barely tilt her body. "When I wanted to stop my dance class after one class," Tina continued—she loved telling stories about her mom, "she told me to memorize what she was about to say: *When you start something you see it through to the end.*"

I was staring at Tina.

"But how are you're supposed to know you're at the end? Then she got mad so I sang a song to make her feel better."

Tina only had one dance lesson.

"That mother of yours is full of good advice. Africa this, Arizona that, something about torches. Starting up all those stores. The travel! Tina, you are simply indefatigable when it comes to your mother. Burty are you that good to Mama?"

Burty stopped pulling on Tina and had no idea what he was asked. "It wasn't me," he ventured. I was staring at Tina but not because she was now going through the good things about Rachel, namely "You're on TV! You live in this house! You're pretty!" What does Tina know about Africa? Why in the world would Rachel have it on top of her list? Did Karen and Rachel hang out more than I thought? Did Rachel know things that I might not even know? But even this didn't prepare me for when Tina said everything comes down to Africa on the way home from the airport.

"After dinner," Tina asked, "Can Burty and me have a meeting?"

"Scrabble, Scrabble, Scrabble, Scrabble, I want to play Scrabble now," Burty sputtered.

I made it clear that we could only stay for dinner even in the face of the collective frown. But as we ate, Jess called to request more library time. Jess, wanting to stay at the library? She was becoming an academic. Of course she could stay. It made sense to remain at Rachel's after dinner to keep the tantrums to a minimum and to prevent a bunch of trips from home to back downtown to get Jess and then back and forth again to get Rudd. This way we could just do one clean sweep.

The St. Johns have a dedicated room for games. A pool table, something called snooker, air hockey, and every board game that has ever been made (Morgan is a collector of games). When Tina said we should play a quick match of "ping pong," Burty gasped in terror and looked left and right and then whispered: "Never ever call it that, remember." Tina blushed. Rachel laughed: "The good doctor only allows the name table tennis in this household." I laughed, but it seemed to me she could be a little hard on the guy.

Something called "Rachel's rules" was in effect. With the kids, anything went with Scrabble. They could spell words the way they wanted and they got originality points for spelling and even more points for creative nonsense words. Burty and Tina were up to a couple million points when Tina declared it was time for her meeting with Burty and they had some serious matters to discuss. Burty complained that he was winning but followed Tina out of the room. I got up to follow but Tina made it clear I was not invited.

Here was Rachel at the Scrabble board and I did really want to stay with Burty and Tina and see what this serious matter was all about. Rachel was already a bit sideways at this point but hiding it pretty well except for hiccups, which made her giggle—this was a much different side of Rachel than I'd ever seen. She took some gulps of wine and scanned the board. I'm no wordsmith but at times I have been called the three-letter-word terminator. In the point tally of the two adults who were playing by the rules, I had a good lead, though I'll admit I had the advantage of sobriety.

I was rearranging my tiles when she put her glass down dramatically on the board scattering the letters. Then she rested her hands on top of mine from across the table. She laughed and shook her head but whatever editor was there had hit the hay. "You know when you're in high school and college and every game you play is a strip game…strip checkers, strip trivial pursuit, strip poker, strip twister, adding real stakes to the game. Bending the rules on the box. I'm tired of those rules." I nodded. Apparently Rachel had a much different group of friends than I did. I think we all jumped into a pool once but with our underwear still on, that's closest I ever came to stripping with a group of people. But I'd understand if Rachel grew up with people trying to get her to take her clothes off.

"Mr. Douglas Merit. I challenge you to a game of strip Scrabble."

I'd like to report that I did the sensible thing: tipped an invisible hat with a bow and dragged Tina out of this house never to return. But I quickly made some calculations. We were both wearing several layers of clothing, including two pairs of socks each. I had on a tie and a blazer. Rachel was wearing a sweater that looked pretty itchy so she certainly had at least three layers under it. We would only be down to autumn wear by the time Tina's meeting adjourned. Plus, I was 100 percent sure that Rachel, even a bit drunk, would come to her senses. And I was 110 percent sure this was some kind of joke/test thing that Rachel put people through and I could already hear her saying when we were both down to just our bare feet and I was hesitating on a more substantial article of clothing that she'd drop from her chair guffawing, "you really thought I was serious? I'm so impressed you were going to keep playing." Not to mention the plain and simple fact that our kids were in the house, and even with my wife we have trouble getting naked with the kids in the house, so just the idea of strip Scrabble was preposterous anyway. As soon as I nodded my assent, she immediately stood up and locked the game room door. A nice touch to make me think she was serious. So I matched her by taking a chair and levering it under the doorknob like they do in movies. Then I slid the tiles off the board and back into the bag. This was one script I could read plainly even though it was my first time.

I lost the first word battle and I took off a silky skating sock, making a production of its stretchy material, and slingshot it over her head, which put her into hysterics. I lost the next one too and took the other sock and then the third so again off with another sock—this time flinging it across the room and maybe even added some bum-dah-dee-dum stripper type music for effect (by the way I flung my sock in some far-away crevice in the room, that's how I lost it!—nothing untoward).

"I'm going to have you naked in about five more words," she told me. I stepped up my game which to be honorable I might not have been playing to the best of my ability. Rachel lost the next word battle. Instead of going for her own silk sock, she pulled off her sweater. She was not wearing layers, but just a blue bra. There went my script. I was stunned and I kept my eyes the best I could on her face and then down on my words. She laughed really hard now. Her smile was quite stunning, and in her eyes it was like she knew the riddle of the universe. Her hiccups had disappeared and maybe the game was doing her some good, sobering her up. Then it dawned on me: Rachel plays hard after all— she did this very day trick me with her surprise revelation on live TV, something I thought I should receive an apology for. But maybe that was just a game to her, that she'd say she was trying to keep me on my toes, keep me in practice, maybe she did it because she knew I'd handle it no problem. It was a way to compliment my abilities. So now the bra there, right there, was just her way to distract me and lose my focus from winning—she thought I was playing seriously so she had to push the joke further and what's really the big deal—I mean if we accompanied Burty and Tina to the pool this summer she'd be wearing about the same thing. And I was proud that she did not succeed in distracting me, I gave her hardly a glance. I won the next round, unfortunately. Off came her bra.

I immediately headed for the door. She blocked me in the gap between air hockey and ping-pong (because right then it certainly wasn't table tennis). With her own spinning eyes she tried to track mine. "Merit," she said, "what's the problem?" I had no idea what she was talking about. I told her she was too drunk and she was going to be embarrassed tomorrow. "It's just a game," she said. Then she kissed me. True she was topless, but it was a game kiss, impish, joking, not serious. There was no passion or insinuation behind it. If we happened to take Tina and Burty to the French Rivera this summer (on the St. Johns' dime) we'd be at the beach just like this and it would be no big deal, right? I was just in the middle of a goofy situation that required goofiness. I gave her a peck on the cheek to show her I wasn't that prudish. I might have even given her butt a slight tap, but again it was in the football spirit and not sexual at all. "Game on!" I said as I sat back down and waited for Rachel to puzzle out her word.

Fifteen minutes couldn't have passed when I surveyed the floor. Rachel was down to a sock and I was in my boxers and my shirt and tie. We were pretty evenly matched at this game but I'd come this far I was not going to lose. Rachel was having a great time giving me grief about my choice to leave my tie on. I laid down my word and Rachel fell off the chair she laughed so hard. Down on the carpet she struggled to take off her sock and when she finally managed to unroll it, she dropped it beside her and stayed flat on her back on the floor. Her laughing stopped. "Oh, Dougie, this has been a blast." She kept staring at the ceiling and then her eyes closed. I took a long listen for Burty and Tina and heard nothing. I thought she might still be joking, playing dead to get out of this situation we now found ourselves in. It was tricky getting a good look at her to see what was up without getting a good look at, well, all over her. But when I went over, it was clear she was out cold. I picked up her jeans and sweater. I kept my eyes off her as best as I could and I really wished that I had had three or four glasses of wine instead of my three or four sips. *Winner*? I laid her jeans on top of her legs and her sweater over her torso, averting my eyes and when necessary squinting my eyes to blur my vision. It was like gluing flat clothes to not such a flat person. But it would keep her warm enough. I tugged on my clothing. As I removed the chair and unlocked the door, I thought about what Burty would do seeing his mom like this. If I tucked in Burty and got him to sleep, what would Morgan do finding his wife like this? If Morgan was in an all night surgery situation, what if the house caught fire? What if Burty got sick in the middle of the night? I left Rachel on her back! I went to her and rolled her onto her side and rearranged her clothes. She had a gigantic bruise on her hip I assume from the Frisbee attack. I called her name, lightly slapped her cheeks, nothing. Cold water. I was on the way back to Rachel with two Dixie cups of cold water when Jess called. Emergency, have to get her right away. I flung the cold water in Rachel's face. Nothing. I now could hear Burty crying somewhere in the house.

I shut the door and ran upstairs to find the kids but they weren't in Burty's room. Burty likes Aquaman. I liked Aquaman too but renounced my childhood fandom when I learned Burty was even more of a fan. But I was now in the midst of a superhero moment. Action was paramount and I did not have the capability to prioritize one emergency over the other. I had to handle them all and I could handle them all. I saw Burty's Aquaman bedspread and I knew what I had to do.

In short order, I had rounded up the kids, using super dad power to ignore that all their hair was now cut off, braved Burty's "itchy, itchy" complaints and bundled them up and stuck them in the minivan. I was still in my super strength when I noted the rate of snowfall and accumulation on my first trip out in a few hours and changed a few of my calculations. Within minutes (most of them in a vain attempt to locate my shoe, which I cannot prove but I'm pretty sure Burty hid in the toilet so Tina could stay at his house indefinitely), I had Rachel bundled in Aquaman and went with the fireman's carry and as I struggled and dropped her once in the snow, I might have questioned why I did not channel Superman instead, even though the snow was coming down at some pretty aquatic levels, a motionless human being is stunningly heavy. For a time I tried to carry her like we were newlyweds but that didn't go well.

With Rachel propped up in the passenger seat, Burty still crying, Tina reminding him that it was good to be crying, my foot shockingly cold in the wet grit of the minivan's floor mat and gas pedal, I worried I might have left their front door open as we pulled out of the driveway and headed to the library to rescue Jess, whose definition of emergency is very loose: a friend looking at her the wrong way, a boy with an arm around another girl, a broken fingernail, an assignment waited too long to complete that was in need of some parental revision. But I knew my job was not to question or doubt but to come to my daughter's aid no matter the stakes of a naked woman, two buzz-headed kids, and one shoeless, sockless foot. Right now I was Super Dad and I had it all covered. I really thought I did. Nobody, nobody would have been able to predict that in just over an hour I'd be handcuffed and in the back of a cruiser.

17

Tonight, though, as I head into Percival Lake Park, I've got some predictions I'm feeling pretty good about. I flick on the blinker of the Suburban, a blinker I hadn't noted before that has some real power—when it is on, you feel like you could turn anywhere.

After this day, after this night, it certainly is not ideal to head out from my family with an excuse that there's an emergency and I've got to head down to the lake, not even a lie really. And in the silence from my wife I got the sense that she was disappointed to lose me *and* she completely understood, work is work. Plus, on the way home I've got to pick up some milk—what better errand in the world is there for dad? If knights were out on their quests nowadays the Holy Grail would certainly be in the form of a gallon of the white stuff. The dangers omnipresent: parking-lot teens hoping for a beer buyer, inexperienced dads trying to make sense of fat percentages sending texts back to their wives or Googling for answers, some pretty sketchy people in canned goods aisle, high markup on the milk, the clerk who is something of a dragon, and if there's a temptation to lead any honest fellow astray it certainly is the rolls of lottery tickets and the columns of candy.

On the homefront there's still important work to do and some inquisition-type questions for Jessica and her bandage. There's also Tina's slight mink issue that probably needs some outlet—kickboxing? But in a few minutes after my meeting with Rachel and after the store for milk, I'll be headed home with a small portion of "problem solved." Solving problems is like coasting down a hill, once I get started there's no stopping me.

I expect to find Rachel's BMW parked outside the temporary chain-link gate that's supposed to keep people out of the park until its official opening day. The gate, slanted open, looks like an elephant leaned on it. The only thing that blocks the way is the yellow police tape from the protest, stuck flat to the pavement. On either side of the gate someone has hung two of the mayor's golden Frisbees with frowny faces drawn on them. The gate was supposed to be repaired today—perhaps ABC Fencing is pro-Frisbee. I ease the Suburban through the opening and roll down the window and grab one of the Frisbees. It actually has some weight to it. A serious Frisbee. The mayor does go all out.

Before I round the corner to the main parking area that is hidden by low shrubs and the old growth "forest," part of me wonders if I'm going to find the KNNK van, Rachel with her mike in a bubble of light. She does have to counter those viral videos with something, and hard reporting would be one way to do it. I'm up for it. I can handle it. But when I see just the BMW slashed across the handicap parking spots, for a split of a split-second I'm not sure if I can handle Rachel. I'm not sure at all what I'm actually taking care of. It is hard to reach reasonable conclusions about people when your brain presents just one single image of them: lying naked on the game room floor. I park the Suburban right between the lines. At the outer reach of my head-lights there she is facing the lake at the edge of the reflection meadow where she sprang her gotcha question on me and where the blasting Frisbees took us down. She has clothes on, well at least a jacket, so

154

that's something to say. There, on the steering wheel, my fingers want to cross, but I will not allow it.

It is warm out tonight for March, much warmer than at the airport, as if Arizona weather is seeking out my wife who did not return to it today. She's back. She chose me and the family. That's what's important. I shut the door, and Frisbee in hand I cross the pathway and cut across the dead grass in the meadow. Rachel's right at the lake's edge, just where the mayor had his "near-death experience." I remind myself that she's having a really tough couple days, maybe tougher than mine. I can see a headline: "Local reporter found drowned in the lake. PR spokesman last person to see her. Police suspicious." I'm pretty sure though that she's not the type to jump out of despair—but what about rejection? I see another headline that I'm not sure what to make of: "News anchor and spokesman arrested, skinny dipping in Percival Lake." It would be at the very least a repudiation of my current image as being too cautious about the lake's contents. And as for my wife: "Take a look at this," I'd say, pointing to the paper as I hand her a cup of coffee. I might even snap a photo of her reaction so I can study it.

Rachel's wearing a pea coat with the collar turned up. Otherwise she looks like she's still in the same outfit from the noon show. I don't know how to describe it exactly but here along the shore of what should probably be called Percival Pond, a small body of water that really should be frozen over, there's a definite vibe coming from Rachel, a vibe that has skinny dipping written all over it. I decide one thing: I will not ask her about the location of my wife's scarf just yet.

"Should we go for a dip?" I ask her instead, both of us facing the lake. It's funny, right? Nip it in the bud.

"No," she says, noting my Frisbee, "I think I've met my quota for naked antics. Plus, I like my water warmer and with a lot less question marks."

155

"Hey, now, it's been cleaned up. I can get you the numbers. We're putting this park next to it. It's safer."

"Don't put on your PR suit. Especially not after those documents you sent today."

"Huh?" All I sent her today was a bunch of texts pleading for her to pick up Burty.

"I don't know how you got your hands on them." She scans the lake, the darkness of the old GE structures on the other side of the water, and then the meadow behind us. "You couldn't have known this all along?" She asks the lake the question but turns to me suddenly. Looks me right in the eye. "Did you?"

"Rachel, I'm in the dark here. I have absolutely no idea what you're talking about. What documents?"

"Of course. " She nods to herself and then slides the Frisbee from my hand and examines it. "No bugs here." She then looks at me, again, right in the eye. "I know you have a lot on the line here. I respect that. But I hope you didn't give them to me. . .for the wrong reasons." Reporters look at you in all different ways. Some just see you as a mouth, take their quote and evaporate. Some look at you like puppy dogs that want a scrap from the table because they are behaving so well. Some, like Nathan Schaffeur, look at you like a wall that they will find a way around and barring that, take a sledgehammer to. Then there's Rachel who probably is not meant to be a reporter at all but perhaps that's why she's so popular. She looks at you like a puzzle piece, with genuine curiosity, about where you might fit in. And right now I can see her looking at me as if she thought she was working on one puzzle only to discover it is completely different.

I again tell Rachel I have no idea about any documents. That I didn't send her anything but texts today about Burty.

"Well, *someone's* given me a flamethrower." She's back to looking at the Frisbee. She flips it around to the frowny face and her face imitates the frown, but she can't hold it. She's smiling, glowing but for some reason trying to keep it undercover. "I'll try not to crisp Sam too badly tomorrow, but I know you wouldn't want to parse around this. I'm going to put the whole thing out there. I'm going to do this right. *Someone* put this in good hands. Really I'm going to do this."

"Rachel, I have no idea what you're talking about. What flame-thrower? What whole thing?"

She faces me again and in the dark I see a moment of panic and then it disappears and she laughs. "You had me for a second."

"But, I—"

"I get it. I get it. It's not you," she says with a smile. "I'm sorry I brought you out here." She changes her grip on the Frisbee and gives it a good toss over the lake. It hangs in the air for a second and then drops with a quiet plop. "Fucking mayor," she says. "Fucking GE."

"Rachel?"

"Dugus's going to be wishing you left him in there."

The Frisbee keeps floating. She's watching it as if she's expecting it to burst into flames. Should I remind her of press neutrality?

"I know that this is going to lead to so much trouble for. . .the person. He's really got guts. This is movie material."

I think she's coming to kiss me and I press my lips together as a block, but no it's a hug she's going to give me, maybe a Sam hug. No. Nothing. She just pats both my arms with her palms like she's trying to clap and my body is blocking her hands, and then puts her hand under my elbow to lift my arm so it meets her hand and she gives me a hardy shake, like she's just given me a diploma.

"And since apparently I dragged you out here for no reason," Rachel says, "I should let you know that I don't want you to worry about what happened with Burty tonight. But I agree with Morgan that maybe Burty needs a break from Tina."

"Burty. . ." but there's no place to begin with that explanation—

Tina's certainly to blame even if she didn't instigate the physical violence. I have to wonder, though, if Morgan really said Burty needed to not associate with the *Merits*. Whatever the case, Rachel's staring at me like she's got it all filled in and I'm coming out the better for it—I'm the hero, I'm Aquaman. "Rachel, I really have no idea what documents you're talking about."

"Yes. I know that," she says. "I've made a gigantic tactical error." Her eyes catch the Frisbee out there floating and then they shift to me once more.

I really do want to correct the record.

She says she's got a lot of preparation to get to for tomorrow. I wave as she heads toward her car—she's practically skipping. Did she blow me a kiss? Whatever it is, I wave again but with both hands. Jesus.

Rachel's headlights launch my shadow across the water and then I'm winding counterclockwise past the floating Frisbee and then there's just her car's engine and the other cars out on the road. The industrial glow that used to light up this part of town is long gone. From where I stand I can't see the row houses and stacked apartments that separate this area from downtown. There's GE across the lake. The shadows of the buildings that aren't torn down, the security lights that dot some concrete here and there, the cylindrical tanks that still have their red lights wrapped on them, and the blinking lights atop the two remaining stacks. The buildings in the dark over there that we can't touch. Hill 48 that we are still allowed, EPA approved, to add PCB dredged soil to even though it's right behind Tina's school. Then, out of sight from here, our offices in the newest building that looks like a fancy red brick plopped down with its own groomed grass and a couple of fountains in a field of cracked concrete.

The lake before me, this pond, is officially clean, the PCBs down to the proper acceptable parts per billion. The lakebed has been capped and sealed. I stare hard at that golden Frisbee and it won't answer anything about the lake's contents, about why it isn't frozen, about Rachel's flamethrower. Is the lake not clean anymore? Was it never clean? It's hard not to think that there must be something up with PCX but the timeline between Jason's flub this afternoon in archives and Rachel's getting a trove of damning information seems unlikely. PCX isn't even supposed to be real.

First we heard cursing from our boss at the time, shell-shocked Ed Beamon. Then what must have been his kicking the side of his filing cabinet. The guy already consumed Tums by the handful, and bit into his Twizzlers like he was biting the head off a snake. After the kicking subsided, he called me in and said he's had it and study these papers and get everyone together for a news conference first thing in the morning. "Sick of it, sick of it." He mumbled as he slammed the door behind me. This was a guy who had seen every kind of crisis and he had a siren going off on top of his head, so I was freaking out. PCX? So far I'd only had to weather a power outage and a false claim about PCBs. I didn't sleep all night, those letters like a neon sign out the window. Why in the hell were we going to have our own little press conference when this was an international-level issue? This was nuclear meltdown status. This was not in our little office's skill set. The shit was going to hit the fan and I, a novice, was supposed to launch it? This could not have been a good PR strategy. The next morning Ed came out of his office and apologized, called off the press conference—it was all just a test—he hadn't seen Fairfield do this in a long time. It was their "stress test." A damage control exercise. We were a great team he said and we showed we were ready for anything. Then he went back to his office. I figured we would do some more follow up on what we had prepared and I waited for a week then asked him to critique some of the releases I'd prepped and asked him more about his strategy which seemed unusual. That's when he said it was a joke—his old friend in Fairfield had made up PCX as a prank and I shouldn't worry about it at all. Just a good ol' funny prank, trying to "get my goat, the asshole." By the end of the year, Ed was moved to Indiana, to a tiny town in a big PCB mess. We heard he quit right when he crossed into Ohio. Pulled into the first town, had the moving company turn around, bought a house and a Dairy Queen franchise. PCX.

Back at the car, the dent really isn't that bad. Under my feet is the green parking lot. It is really green and *green* too. It is "imagination at work." The most environmentally friendly parking lot in the world right now. We have some Academy Award-nominated documentary team going to make a short film about it. Fairfield fought us on it at first but they finally got on board even if it cost a fortune. The stone wall that fronts the park is hand-laid just as the Trustees desired—some guy and his son that are the only two remaining people on the East Coast who know how to still do this old school. The park embraces the past and the future. The lake itself is the past and the future.

Even though we've moved on to "imagination at work" as our modus operandi, we can never escape from the shadow of "we bring good things to life." Except for my issue currently with the word *things*, it is something that's still mostly true. GE did bring good things to life. On paper some of the stuff wasn't that great, but what can you really do about corporate desire to make money? It's like telling a lion not to eat a zebra. There's the jobs that made this town come to life, that brought a good living to families like my wife's. I can see her dad over there across the lake, his metal lunchbox. The guy loved the place. "The GE," they all called it. He was still proud of the place even when he had to drive an hour to Schenectady for the five years when they shut the transformer plant down here and most of his buddies were canned. My wife still remembers riding on his shoulders during family day, where the whole place was opened up and there were electricity displays and gifts and how her dad took her away from the crowd and counted off the numbers that represent each building. PCBs were supposed to be a force for good, to prevent fires. From what I remember about PCX—the test, the joke—it was about a new chemical that could literally eat PCBs but everything had gone wrong and the solution was a bigger catastrophe than the original. That seems to be the problem with trying anything with the intention of doing good: you might do some things that aren't so good on the way to it; you might just mess up on the way to that goal and you really didn't mean to. In the end you've left all these micro-particles, parts per billion, yeah, and parts per million here and there. Some clerical errors, some people keeping secrets about taking an easy way out, making human decisions, misinterpreting advice. But it's those microparticles, those few screw-ups, that's the only thing anyone wants to focus on, no one remembers the good that was your original aim.

From inside the Suburban with the high beams on, I can still glimpse the Frisbee floating, the golden dot. I also see Sam sitting across the table scorched by Rachel's fire. His ponytail still smoking.

It's got to be me! I'm the only one that can fix all this. I'm the one that has to face the firing line.

On the way out, I reach for the other Frisbee.

18

The house is dark and quiet when I arrive with the milk—three gallons of it, the more the merrier, no "Mission Success" banners hung around the kitchen for me. I head down into the basement with the couple boxes of cereal that had my name on it at the store, a perspiring gallon of milk, and a bowl. I put them all down on Rudd's train set as I prep my bed, putting some towels we use as rags under the cot so that by morning when it's flat I'll still be in a cozy nest. There's no sense waking up anyone. I sit down on Rudd's bench and lose myself in the cereal.

After a couple of bowls, it's time to try this contraption. Rudd is currently on his longest period of not playing with his trains. The hammer he was banging is still right in the middle of a forest that looks like it was just visited by a tornado. I'm happy about that girl calling him and happy he might let go of this train set. If the girl did have green hair, as Jess implied, what were the chances of it being the same one as the protester? Green hair just might be trending at his school. Besides, the protester doesn't seem to speak and the girl on the phone did speak. I switch on the power. Rudd's train world lights up.

I turn one of the motor dials and try to spot where the engine is.

I start it on the slowest speed and there it is, its headlight emerging from a tunnel. The control panel is smooth from where he rests his palms. What a world he has created down here. I take the train slowly by a drawbridge that goes over a river, a river that looks wet. The train, carrying a mix of tankers and boxcars, moves through a neighborhood where there are streetlamps that work and house lights that are on. Inside one house a miniature family sits around a table. A railroad crossing gate rises as I start a second train, a passenger train. It climbs the track lifted by girders that gradually rise to a truss bridge that is two tracks wide. The train inches by factories and then it moves right into the surrounding hills. The other train slowly buzzes by the knocked over trees and the hammer. I try to stare down the LOOK OUT sign at the top of Les Alpo.

I reach out to the middle to uncrash the two cars that are smashed together at an intersection. I set them on their non-moving ways in opposite, safe directions. I turn the direction of some pedestrians. I note that I can cast a shadow over the table. I increase the speed of the first train. I watch. I have another bowl of cereal. I put down the bowl in the harbor, and with my hands locked at the thumbs, I make a giant bird shadow flap over the world.

This is what I'm doing as my wife sits down on the stairs, just where I sat the morning after the accident. She's wearing her sweat jacket zipped down and a plain white T-shirt under it and her sweatpants pajama bottoms. The light catches the silver teeth of the zipper. She has her elbows on her knees and one arm levered straight out. The fingers of that arm clamp the mouth of a beer bottle. She looks as if she is threatening to drop it. Her shoulders are hunched and her eyes are on my hands which are still out over the table. I cup them into a little prayer as I pull them back to me. I watch the two trains, tracing for any possibility they might collide.

"We could buy this house right there," I say pointing to the house that has the family in it. "It looks like a nice neighborhood." I take another spoonful of cereal.

"We might have to," she says.

"I'm not sure about the schools though."

Silence, not even a snort. She usually snorts even if she's pissed. I pushed it too far on the way home tonight, I know, and I'm solely responsible for whatever is about to happen. But it *is* important to remember that past.

I start the third engine. Maybe this is a good time to tell her that I didn't leave Jess waiting out at the library. Maybe it is a good time to tell her about my meeting at the lake with Rachel. I take a deep inhale and there is a slight perfume to me, which isn't that big of deal—I just came from an emergency meeting where there would be plenty of colleagues wearing perfume. It also doesn't look like my wife is going to suddenly rush down and give me a hug. I close my eyes for a moment and picture my wife all those years ago leaning on the minivan.

"I haven't told you lately," I say, "how much I love you."

She pulls her nose with her free hand before she takes a swig.

There's emptiness that needs filling so I know that's my cue: "The clerk at the store tonight, talk about giving me the stink eye! Rudd on the dating scene, can you believe that? The Baker, that guy's not from Pillsbury! And Tina with this whole mink thing is really out of control. This whole Percival Lake thing is getting out of control."

"Doug, you never want to talk."

I'm confused.

"Would you just talk to me?"

"I am!"

"You're not."

"We're great together. We're in a blip maybe. But Karen, we're great." I shake all the boxes finding the one with the most in it and begin to pour it into a bowl. I should have spent that last few days making the pantry immaculate in preparation for a moment like this one. We're once again in the wrong place to argue. I should have bought five gallons of milk.

"Put the milk, down," my wife says as if I'm holding a gun.

I put it down on a bunch of cars.

"I quit my job today. There's apparently no policy about husbands fucking up. They wouldn't let me try working from home. I said I would quit. They said that's fine. I quit. I fucking quit. He let me quit."

I'm stunned. I thought this was going to be a fight about us and it's not. In every scenario I ever formulated about her leaving her job I am overwhelmed by happiness, but now I don't know how to react. "Wow."

She put her beer down and zipped up her jacket as if she was launching something into orbit.

"I'm really worried," she says.

"Maybe this will be good for you. You can figure out what you really want to do."

She's staring at her slippers. "I want my job."

"Do that then!"

"He. . .they let me quit."

"You could start other stores. You're in demand. You have connections. Call someone!"

One of the trains must have triggered sounds of a farm. Pigs were oinking, chickens, cows.

"Start a farm!" I shout.

She takes a deep gulp of air. "I think we're done."

"You're right. We should get some shuteye. We can figure out what to do tomorrow."

She stands up. "This is what I mean."

"Tomorrow it'll all be clear."

Her eyes shut and stay shut—as if she's about to start counting while one of the kids hides.

I start with the cereal again.

"Jesus, Doug."

She turns and I watch her slippers slap the corner in the stairs and disappear.

I've got this. I tell myself again. I've got whatever Rachel has in store for us tomorrow. I've got this situation with Karen, though I'm not exactly sure what just happened. I'm on top of this. Right after I have one more bowl I'll know exactly what to do.

Done, her word finally hits me as I grab for the gallon. I fumble it and milk dumps onto the control panel. In my bobbling to stop more spilling I take out a city block and knock over my bowl and cereal spreads everywhere and the bowl smashes on the floor and milk is dripping. There's some sparking sounds and the engines go dead. The whole train world goes dark.

Done.

I picture Sam's scorched body slumped in his motel chair. Motels make me feel sticky after two nights.

I leave the milk dripping as I chase my wife up the stairs. "I know what to do," I call after her.

In our room, where I find her sitting at the end of the bed, I open my top drawer and give her Regina Samsonetti's card, Sam's therapist. I could hug Sam—because of him I have the best contingency plan. I will not let him burn tomorrow. I will make it all right. I'll open it up.

My wife looks at the card, her eyes going through different measures of squinting.

"Alexander's Boxing Academy?"

Shit. The wrong card—this is the one from when I was sucker-punched. Samsonetti's is still on my desk at work.

I try to explain. And Karen nods and nods, her eyes fixed on the card.

But she's on board. We're going to try therapy. I've saved the day.

19

ASSASSINS. I'm greeted by the sign as I head into the parking lot in the Suburban (Nancy lives walking distance from her store and I've still got a dent to take care of). If the girl with green hair would just give me the finger or call me an asshole or just yell the word, say the word! At least put an exclamation mark after the word! But she just holds out the sign with both hands and pivots so the sign turns with me into the lot. That sign, done with a faded marker on rippled cardboard. Add it to her expressionless face, the sackcloth! She must be the most deactivated Activator! in the world.

The parking lot is as large as a grocery store's, but these days it just isn't that full. So even though I'm quite a distance from her, I use the passenger door. As I get out I knock the golden Frisbee onto the floor. It's not like I'm scared of the girl. I just don't want to give her the satisfaction. Plus, it's closer to the dent, which I inspect. It's really just a dent. A few more paint chips come undone when I run my finger over it. It's just a dent and I'm making too big a deal about it, just like this girl. Right after I'm through dusting my hands of this whole mess this afternoon I'm going straight to Nancy's. I move from car to car carefully and I'm about to make the last dash to the glass doors when of all people Nathan Schaffeur pops out of his little Honda and starts coming toward me.

He's in his long winter jacket out of some movie from the forties, long hair, wire glasses. I note right off his hands are empty. I don't think I've ever seen him without his narrow steno pad in one hand and his red flare pen in the other. Who does he think he is anyway with that red ink?

"Do you have a second?" He holds his hand out to me. He's never offered to shake my hand once. This can't be good. He studies me for a second. "I need your help," he says, dropping his hand into his pocket.

"That's Sam's department now."

"Someone's contacted me, from GE."

Oh, great, Rachel's going to be devastated that she doesn't have an exclusive and she's going to think that it's me who shared the information with Schaffeur.

"It's not me."

"About a job."

"What?"

"I don't know what to do."

Were they going to bring him in for Sam's job? Alexis's? And who the hell sits in a parking lot waiting for someone to show up at work?

"Was it Jason?"

"No."

"Who?"

He puffed a plume of condensation. He shrugs. Clearly he's not supposed to say. Clearly it's from Fairfield. Clearly something's afoot. Are they thinking about him for Jason's job? Or maybe to replace me when I get moved into Jason's job?

"The thing is, I know you used to be a reporter. I've got two kids and one's got some issues. My wife thinks I have to jump on it." He has two kids? I'm flabbergasted. We could have had him on our playdates.

He could have been riding around naked with me too. But as far as me being a reporter, either he didn't do his research or he's being nice: I wasn't much of a reporter. The news was too messy. You can't wrap it up. You have to pry. It never ends. The senior calendar and the lunch menus were what I excelled in. I would get the supplied statements from various organizations and Morton, the editor back then, would tell me whether to ask some questions or just run it as is. Then the tourism bureau was heaven, complete heaven but I messed up. Here, it's no tourism bureau, but it's better than the news.

"Does it suck out your soul?" Schaffeur is never one to beat around the bush. "That's what I want to determine. Even if the benefits are better, I want to be able to go home each day and look my wife and my kids in the eye? What will I see when I look in the mirror?"

He's not looking at me but across the parking lot to the girl with green hair. I'm an optimist, I'm aware of this, but even I know that *everything* sucks out your soul. It's the human condition. His naiveté is almost endearing. That of course doesn't stop me from zapping the bastard.

"Is it true that the paper will support the mayor's initiatives no matter what?" I ask. He turns to me disoriented. "Hasn't the newspaper turned a blind eye on the economic value of Frisbee golf? How do you address the allegations that you forget that spokespeople are actual human beings with a job to do? Do you go to a public defender and harass him for representing an accused criminal?"

Schaffeur doesn't try to answer.

"I look my wife and kids in the eye. In that mirror, all I have is thumbs up."

"I'm sorry, I didn't mean to suggest, I was just. . ." He takes a step back.

"Watch Rachel's show this afternoon and you'll get your answer."

He doesn't offer any more apologies and he doesn't try to follow me through the door. He just stands there with his feet planted on the walkway and his hands in his pockets. Stumped.

On the way upstairs, I take them by twos, I'm confident. Do you know what I feel like right now? An expert clock repairman who's inside a giant clock where gears are grinding and springs are popping and I have no idea what I'm getting into, but I know that all I need to do is roll up my sleeves and get to it. I detour to archives and discover it locked. My key doesn't open it. Even odder, when I drop in on Jason to ask about it, he shrugs and agrees that it's odd. He tells me to take a seat. He's got to tell me something. He's playing around on his computer, holding his finger up to me to keep me patient, and I'm pretty sure he's going to show me Rachel's naked reporting in the snowstorm but then his phone rings and he picks it up before it even finishes the first ring.

A voice booms, as if it's been too long confined to the constriction of lines and comes out like water out of a hydrant. Jason is actually holding the phone away from his ear. I'm trying to figure out if I should go or stay. I don't want to hear the word *PCX* again. I don't want to hear the word *Schaffeur* yet either—I don't know if I could work with that guy. Plus, if anyone asks he might not be the best candidate for a job— he already seems pretty leaky to me with his inside info about GE's hiring plans. I hear: "What's that guy you have up there?"

"Sam?" Jason offers.

"Oh hell, not him, Jesus." I wait for Shaffeur to be mentioned. "The guy that saved our asses for the Allengate School thing and turned around all that negative SuperFund shit with that dog? Merkachek? The Frisbee guy? The drinker?"

"Doug Merit," Jason says.

Drinker?

"Yes, that's it. I want him in on this."

"We were actually just going over some ideas," Jason lies. "He's right here."

170

"Put me on speaker." The guy that needs no speaker phone is Jimmy Tripoli, VP in charge of all communications. Jimmy cuts to the chase: "Look," he yells, "it's a gigantic fuckball there with that damn park. The number one rule: leave well enough alone. Totally disregarded by everyone from day one. You don't eat where you crap. Jesus, Pontoosuc should be a wrap for us and now all this shit. I'm coming up there today and you two are going to keep this status quo until I can clean up after you."

Jason says that we *will do*, but I give him a nudge. Jason sighs and then tells about Rachel's show. "Holy cow fuckers," Jimmy says. "Why isn't Merit on this?"

Jason volunteers that he could go on if he thinks it is important enough. Tripoli actually laughs. Jason's eyes plead with me. "Kid, I like you, don't get me wrong and you seem competent, but people don't like you. You go on TV and we're already behind the ball. I don't know what's going on up there but I want you, Doug, on that show today. You're the only one that can handle it."

Jason, poor kid, actually tries to stand up for his decision to put Sam on. I'm impressed he only makes some vague references to "incidents." When nothing is gaining traction, he even tries his "newsmakers" turn of the phrase he evidently is still proud of. Tripoli doesn't say anything. Jason nods to nothing. He turns to me—my stock having increased—as if he needs my consent before he actually verbalizes his nod. I look down at my hands. I don't want to seem too eager, but half of my mission this morning is completed. I'm on with Rachel.

I leave Jason to put in that call to his mom. I too have to use the phone for personal business. I find Regina Samsonetti's card right where I threw it in the corner of my desk behind a stack of paper. I unfold it and don't make the slightest hesitation in placing the call. Samsonetti doesn't have an opening for two weeks, but she definitely sounds like someone I can work with. She gives us two starter assignments each. Maybe her receptionist is out today?

I've still got the phone cradled at my ear even though that call is over. I pick up the family photo on my desk. It is from the one time we went to Cape Cod. We're on Nauset Beach and a German exchange student snapped the shot for us. Jess and I stand arm in arm, with matching sunburns, Rudd looks toward the remnants of his sandcastle, Tina stares skyward at what must have been a seagull or a kite, this was five years ago, and my wife, with a towel wrapped around her waist stretches out in a beach chair in front of all of us except Tina, who's sitting on the blanket with her back against the side of the chair. My wife isn't wearing sunglasses but a baseball cap shades her face. She looks tired but content—almost triumphant. Her arm muscles are noticeably pumped from her surprisingly long swim in the ocean, where I had lost track of her several times. At one point I even identified the nearest lifeguard post and readied myself for the dash, but she appeared far down the beach, walking toward us slowly, stopping occasionally to bang water out of her ears or watch some child run into or away from the water. It was at least two weeks later, in our bed at home, just after we had sex, that she told me she'd been caught in a riptide. For someone who complains that I don't talk to her she has a history of withholding information, including two of her pregnancies, Rudd and Tina. And both times before she revealed the information she had gone through a period of saying we were in trouble. There's a pattern there.

I think of texting Rachel about the change but the element of surprise might be just what I need—she'll be so shocked it's me and we'll just have a pleasant live chat about our kids and their foibles. The viewership will spike and she'll learn she doesn't have to say one thing about GE. I'll be moved immediately to Fairfield where I'm sure Karen will find the perfect job.

I call home and leave a message on the answering machine: "I love you."

I call back: "Don't miss Rachel's show today."

I keep the phone at my ear. I email the news that we do have an appointment and I tell her what the two exercises are. Then I text her the same info. I scribble in my pad. I still have the phone at my ear. I check that my text didn't get stuck in my outbox. She probably started on the exercises instead of replying. I scribble in the pad some more.

No one can find Sam. He was spotted in the building early and his car is still in the lot. I volunteer to find him (I know his hideouts). After I tell him the two pieces of news he'll be the happiest guy in the world.

I go right to the downstairs bathroom. Beneath the one closed stall, Sam's sensible shoes. I stand right outside the door so he can see my own shoes. The door unlocks. His ponytail is off-center, and he swats the loose strands as if he is swarmed by flies. His tie is flipped over his shoulder. Those large pieces of stone that he usually has floating in him have been smashed into a thousand pebbles. He's without a jacket and his belt cuts into his waistline as he stays hunched.

"I have two pieces of good news for you," I say. I tell him about the Samsonetti appointment.

"You have the exercise she gave you to do?"

I nod. Sam is pleased. He looks better already. "It will work for you."

Then I tell him that he's off the hook. They've put me back on Rachel duty today. I expect him to jump up and give me another hug, but instead he swings the door closed.

"You really wanted to do it?"

No answer.

"If it were up to me, I'd keep you on it."

He locks the stall.

I step back, leave it to Sam to get his shoes to look disappointed.

He won't be so sad this afternoon when he's watching as Rachel points her loaded gun and pulls the trigger. Unless he's a masochist he certainly isn't the leaker even with all his talk about "opening it up" yesterday. I take a step closer to the stall so he can see my shoes again. He doesn't say anything. I'm tempted to tell him about what Schaffeur said this morning and then it crosses my mind that all of this is a plan from headquarters to justify closing us down. They could be making a big PR move here by revealing some bad shit and then squelching the furor by putting our office in the pillory and they'd make a big deal of firing us all, and dust their hands: PR disaster done. In comes Nathan Schaffeur to quietly be the lone local rep until the environmental issues are resolved. Maybe Jimmy Tripoli's coming today because he already knows what Rachel's going to say and he's going to close down the office by five o'clock so he can get back for dinner? I laugh at myself for even thinking it.

I shuffle a little closer so my belly is up against the stall and my toes are beneath the door. I wait for a laugh, a "fuck you" or something. Maybe the girl with green hair is Sam's niece or something. Activators who aren't activated. After a minute with no response I head out.

"Take those exercises seriously," he says, just as the bathroom door is closing.

KNNK is a little unimpressive box of a building that sits under a giant antenna and a couple satellite dishes that look capable of transmitting to Pluto. On the way there I got all green lights.

I tell Stacy, the receptionist, Sam isn't coming, and she knows she doesn't need to smile or point to the corridor that leads to the studio. I've done this all before. Rachel's usually live out around town but I've had at least a dozen in-studio interviews with her, not to mention the morning show and the nightly newscast too. The hallway is full of all the personalities that have disseminated the news over the decades—*decimated*? Rachel's face is the last photo in the line.

I'm now sitting at the round table where the four "protesters" sat the day before. Some kid comes in and pats my face, looks at me, pats it some more, asks me if I want to fix my tie, she fixes it for me, pats my face, dusts my shoulders, and then Rachel comes out. Apparently she's not yet aware of the change, but she's a professional, just a slight tic as she looks over at me after she's seated. In the minutes before we air, in the time where we are supposed to be civil to each other and make jokes and talk about our kids, we're silent. The girl comes in and pats my forehead one more time. When the guy with spiral hair and earphones starts the count down with his fingers at five, Rachel mouths "Sorry."

As she reads from her notes that she must have worked on all night, as documents are being posted live on screen with circled words that look like you increase your risk of cancer by trying to pronounce, as people's names flash across the screen and lines and quotes from them are highlighted, as dollar signs mount and fill the screen with numbers, as I imagine my colleagues' jaws dropping in the conference room, of Jason's phone dropping and Jimmy's Tripoli's voice filling the room with curses from the floor as he drives off the side of the highway, I'm even more confident about the outcome of all this. Does it really matter what she's revealing? A circle within circle of double-dealing, questionable money flow, which implicates the mayor when he was a council member. The nods, the handshakes, the small checks, the emails that somehow never got deleted. The path of destruction that we've already ridden and tried to make amends for renewed again in the constant cycle. PCBs have been tattooed on us all and we're always just trying different brands of soap to wash it off. Again, we're shown to be spending a lot of energy and money on making sure the easiest and cheapest clean up of PCBs is the only one that should be considered. I listen for a while and then assume as grave and honest expression as I can. I hold my arms wide on the desk to give the impression that I'm surprised and I am anchored, *and* I am surprised by a lot of what is revealed, surprised that it has happened while I've been here and I am unaware of most of it. *And* I am anchored.

Rachel's documents are damning as hell, but the thing is, except for the bits about the mayor, the audience is as unsurprised as I am. It is one of the benefits of already having your standards of behavior so low. This isn't really "news" in the sense of the word where it gains traction; it is just what everyone already knows and what everyone has come to expect. It is not exactly a surprise that we'd pick the easiest and cheapest method—no one is really surprised by this and not even the underhanded way we handled some elements of it. One percent of the audience is enraged, ready to pen a letter to the editor, vowing to pick up the picket sign, and one percent of those will actually do something. But everyone else thinks "Can you believe this? Again!" and that's it. The only reason they continue to watch is to see me squirm and then at the end of the half hour they turn off the TV and go about their business. They'll read about it and watch it in the coming week and then the cycle will slow and there will be a mention once a week, once a month, on the anniversary of the revelation and that's it. The only letter combination I listen for is PCX and when that doesn't come before the commercial break I figure it's not coming.

Rachel slides a note to me with a thumbs up drawn on it. I'm doing great. When we're back on and the litany continues, and to help me not to smile I start thinking about my therapy homework. Back at the office when I looked at the photo of my family on a day when my wife was nearly lost to a riptide, I was thinking about her answer to the first exercise: *a secret you've never told your spouse that would affect that spouse directly.* But the incidents with Rachel, the real location of Jessica that night, or that I was probably technically drunk the *first* time I was arrested for refusing a Breathalyzer (*not* the night of the accident) are not what come to mind for me (though when I actually write this down I'll probably reveal the drunk driving incident). What I won't write down for this exercise is the answer that I'm pretty sure will correlate with the answer my wife should reveal, but probably won't either. It's an answering machine message I erased sixteen years ago, a couple months after she arrived home from Africa with her short hair and a depression that clung to her like her skin. "Hello there, Konjo. This is the only

176

number I could find for you. I just got back and I'm heading over again in two weeks. I've heard you wanted to talk more. It was all a bit of nasty timing. I think we have some unfinished business. There's an opening in July. I'd really love to see you back here. I'm going to be all over so call me as soon as you can. Konjo, keep those elbows up." As soon as his voice stopped, I hit erase. Then without a moment's hesitation I called the phone company and asked that our number be changed and they changed it and I don't even remember the story I told "Konjo" of why our number changed and it was a time where it might have set her off or it would just be a nodding acceptance, and actually she liked the new number better. It was full of threes. This is before we had cell phones, before we had email addresses, lucky for me. A year later and it all would have played out differently. But I know I saved her, I know I did.

And for the second exercise, a list of positive things about me! That's easy. I've got it all in my head already and there's nothing not to be upfront with here—though I work hard to keep a straight grave face for the TV audience as Rachel continues—if only these documents were the ones appearing on the screen:

> General profile: At 39, Doug Merit has accomplished 100% of his goals. He has a job he's good at, a great wife, and great kids. He works hard to help support his family, gives great advice, makes a damn good quick lasagna, does dishes, refills ice cube trays, buys tons of milk, and gives out as much love as he can give.

> Contributions: Besides donating 100% of his after-taxes salary to the worthy cause of the Merit family fund, he volunteers 100% of his time to the Merit family's economic, social, and cultural health, both locally and nationally.

Record of Innovations: Too numerous to mention, but here are a few (all of the following would have been impossible without his wife and children): Open House Blitzes, "Where to, James?", quick lasagna, cookie consumption, the patented Get Jess Out Of The Bathroom Kamikaze Reversal, the full body swoop and the airplane, the beanbag hop, the middle of the night blanket swap, the expulsion from cha-cha class, the ten tales of the Suburbanian nights, the hose rainbow maker, the fire drill to end all fire drills, the patented "Mom and Dad are doing the taxes" fake out, the moonlit dinner under the basketball hoop, and his most overarching and proud achievement: his family.

Data on Performance: (these numbers speak for themselves) 200,000 miles driven over 8395 days and only lost his license on two occasions. 50,000 hours of work and only fired during one of those hours! (though this number might be about to change depending on my response to Rachel), 7,884,000 minutes of fatherhood and only at most 500 minutes of fair to poor decision-making—that's less than .001 percent of the time. Only a .00002 percent of blips in 531,360,000 seconds of marriage.

Documentation: Years and years of film footage, stock photos, and happy memories, featuring scenes of human competence, warmth, and concern.

At the next break, Rachel slides me a note with a drawing. I think it's an Oscar statuette. I guess even though I'm 100% checked out I'm doing great.

When we're back on for the last segment, Rachel's nailing the coffin shut. It's not far off from the way she looked at me across the Scrabble board. The camera does a close up on me. It is my time.

"You have been very quiet, Mr. Merit. What can you say to address this flood of frankly damning information?" She gives me her best John Stossel stare-down. This is the moment that the world loves most. A spokesperson that doesn't have an answer. When the spokesperson is clearly biased and babbling about some horseshit that everyone and his sister knows is a complete lie, people get angry. But what they love is the deafening silence. The camera capturing the twitching eyes. The hem and haw in slow motion. I understand that Rachel sees in this my perilous position as leaker, spokesperson, and someone who beat her at strip Scrabble and drove her around naked afterwards. But this is my calculated move. It confirms what the audience expects and with that confirmation it will pass out of their minds sooner. It becomes about me. They'll remember me, but nothing else. I see her winding up for another blast. Did she withhold the PCX until now?

Whatever she does have coming, I do have to say something, but the key is to make it as inane as possible while it also hits the mark. Time is running out. But, no, she doesn't mention PCX, just outlines the major elements again.

There are five strategies of image restoration. The first is denial. The second, evading responsibility. The third, reducing the offensiveness. The fourth, corrective action. The last is mortification—when I first was introduced to the term I thought it meant death, which is a great way to resolve a crisis because you're not around anymore to be a part of it. But it just means you confess, seek forgiveness, and hope the public will not judge too harshly—which of course is a painful death in its own way. Crisis after crisis, companies (including my own), people, politicians, and children (including my own) avoid mortification even though it has been proven again and again to actually boost your image in the long run.

Denial just doesn't work, even if it's what everyone has come to expect. Corrective action is great because it has elements of evading responsibility and reducing offensiveness, but I'm in no position to do this. Even if Tripoli was in my place right now, he wouldn't have that type of power. I'm a worker bee and can't offer solutions for upper-management screw-ups. If they want the local office to represent the company, they should probably tell us what the hell they're doing—but by the sound of it, they might not even know what they're doing. So as Rachel continues to play hardball, pressing me for some kind of response, "Surely there must be something that you can say," that type of thing which everyone eats up—I can see it in the spiral-haired director, the TV execs who have been told to be in the studio. I'm giving them what they all want. I'm taking it all in for GE, like a magic sponge *as seen on TV.*

And so what I need to say is that inane deflective remark that will give us more time, that will make us look guilty, but not necessarily too guilty, but also on the verge of repentance and that passes the ball up the ladder—in short I need to make it seem like corrective action is where we're heading: "This information has just come to light and it is new to all of us and we must have time to understand the full implications. If true, this is an issue of immediate importance though. GE wants to move as fast as possible but also to give enough time to investigate." And right here is where I should stop, where Rachel should stop me because time is out. But nobody is cutting to the soap opera. I just keep going, stunned by my own words and by the relish with which I say them, but I know that this is the only solution: "In one month from today, we will host a town-hall meeting in Pontoosuc where George Alogosh himself will be on stage. We, I assure you, will be ready to fully answer and begin addressing what you have outlined here."

Rachel's looking at me in that puzzle piece way again, trying to figure out whether she's being played. "This sounds like a deflection. Surely you can't make this sort of call. We are going to get an announcement later today that you misspoke, won't we?"

"I assure you Ms. St. John, this will happen. I am even in the position to offer you the moderator position for the event."

As soon as the camera's off, Rachel smiles a really big smile, but looks to see if anyone noticed it. Then in front of everyone, she whispers in my ear, "What did you just do, Doug?"

I can tell she wants to give me a sympathetic hug. A slap on the back, but it wouldn't be appropriate. At least I can impress Rachel with something that I actually did. Her bosses swarm in with congrats. I spot the owner who is not bucktoothed at all and he seems just fine that his pro-mayor station has just started a chain that will surely lead to the mayor's resignation. Once I know for sure my legs still work, I make a beeline. As I swing out the door, I look for Jason and Tripoli holding a guillotine, for Alogosh spitting on my face even as my head begins to roll down the street. But there is no crowd, just Lance, one of the cameramen, already smoking a cigarette.

I sit with my hands on the wheel for a few minutes. I study the base of the gigantic antenna and the gigantic satellite dish. My words this instant are spreading over the whole world. "What have I done?" I ask myself in the rearview mirror as I turn the ignition. I just fucking saved the day, that's what.

20

Instead of heading back to the office, instead of checking my phone which seems to vibrate more and more insistently, I burst through fabric just south of town, up Swamp Road, and then left on Hillside, which is aptly named because after a sharp turn it takes you straight up. This road has some historic precedent for me and my wife. Near the top of the hill, a shark face is painted on a rock outcropping, which juts over the road. It is cartoonish but the rock really does look like a shark. It's been there for years but someone repaints it whenever it fades.

"Shark!" my wife would call out when we drove by.

"Jaws has given sharks a bad name," I would say. "They never stop swimming, never. That's something that would make anything irritable. At least chimney swifts get to stop flying at night. That makes a big difference. Swifts aren't irritable. Insects might see them as irritable. What am I talking about?"

"A rock," she'd say.

I crest the hill and after going under some supercharged power lines, the road descends. At the first corner the trees are cleared and there is a dirt pull-off overlooking the valley below. It's a gray day. In the distance the mountains panorama, one big blue rolling cutout. Down below, farmland in patches between wooded areas—or I should say farmland that is now the land of second homes. The Housatonic runs through here in a gray S. The same little tinkle of a river that runs behind our house is much more river-like by this point. In that gray there are the PCBs we've been trying so hard to mitigate. They can be found all the way to Long Island Sound. And all that Rachel really exposed was confirmation of the cloak and dagger system of business where the short term interests of everyone from the local government, to the EPA, to GE were the driver to all the clean-up issues; there was some substantiation of Guy the Environmental Guy's belief that our river was just a chess move in the big game of the Hudson river pollution. But there was no mention of PCX, which I hope very much remains just a forgotten damage control scenario, a joke—though I do recall something about one possible repercussion being the lack of ice on the lake. Why isn't the lake frozen over? In the old days it didn't freeze over because they would dump super-heated water right from the power plant into the lake. But there's no more power plant and no more super-heated water. Maybe I just misheard those letters or it was Jason doing some of his letter transposing.

We would come up to this lookout if time permitted during one of our open house blitzes. We have been going on open house blitzes from even before we were married. Something fun to do on a weekend when we were in college. Imagine how our lives will be whenever or wherever we settled down. Even though our need for a house has grown immensely, what family of five can survive with one bathroom, no walk-in closets, en suites, open concept living, granite counter tops, and stainless steel? How can anyone look for houses for more than seventeen years and not find one? A terrible thing happened to us early on in our open house blitzes; it was not my wife's massive depression upon coming home from Africa, it was not my changing our number so Robb Lamonty could not reach my wife, what happened was that we found a perfect house.

When Karen found out she was pregnant with Rudd, pregnant, we had a mission. Back then we'd scan the newspaper for all the possible open houses we could squeeze in; we'd map the perfect route; and off we'd go. Our open house blitzes took on an air of certainty not just because of the baby but also because my part-time job that I had secured at the paper while she was in Africa just turned into a full-time job and Karen had found a part-time job just weeks before finding out she was pregnant. In our twenty-three-year-old's view, we were rolling in dough. We had no intention of spending our lives in this town where we had grown up, Pontoosuc; we dreamed of Seattle or Portland or maybe Atlanta or even Boston but right when she got back from Africa she was in no shape to move anywhere or have any kind of dream—she was a wreck, we had some tough times. But then the jobs and then the baby and everything looked better. Plus we were just starting things; we'd fly out of this town once we got our feet on the ground a bit more. We were heading places. But first there was the call of family, establishing ourselves. You do this by buying a house, that's what you do. You get equity and a foundation and the ultimate wedding band of shared debt.

Then the terrible thing happened. We found the perfect house over on Oak Street. We knew we'd be in over our heads, but I could take on a second job, my wife could go full time, our parents could help with the baby. We couldn't miss this opportunity, we had to have this house. We filled out our mortgage application, we drove by the house at least twice a day, stalked the thing, made plans. We were so so certain it would be ours. Before we even got word back on our application, some other family bought it with cash. Once you find your perfect house and you don't buy it, you're done. Nothing can ever rival it and even though our open house blitzes continued (it was what we always did and what we'll always do, I hope, even if neither of us has a job; it's something we'll keep doing even if we buy a house). All these years and we never found another house to match it even as our incomes increased. We've seen realtors grow old, quit the business and return, many know us so well that they don't bother to waste a word even if no one else is in the house. Sure, we could find a realtor and look at houses the way everyone else does; sure, we would certainly be snapped up by one of those reality shows that force people to choose a house from just three. But it was our open house blitzes that brought us to our perfect house and it was through this method we would strike gold again.

Early last fall, on what turned out to be our only open house blitz in the last six months, my wife said something stunning as we headed out in the minivan with our carefully choreographed route. She said, "It doesn't have to be perfect anymore."

"Perfect?" I said exhilarated. "Who needs perfect?"

It was a gray day. Karen maintains that these are the best days because you don't get tricked by the sunlight. I don't see it that way but she hinged a lot on this and I go along with it in spirit. But that day, who cared? It didn't have to be perfect. The first house we hit was a Cape with an addition on it in an OK neighborhood in a great school district. Still in the car we synchronized our watches and commenced the stakeout portion of our house hunt. We were parked on the street and we struck our casual poses as if we were waiting for our kids to come out of the house after a play date. We watched a few couples drive up and park in the driveway! And hurry right into the house and hurry right back out. Amateurs! My wife and I exchanged knowing looks that made me wish more home buyers would keep pulling into the driveway so I could keep confirming we were on the exact same wavelength: Exterior forces take their toll just as much as interior ones; we knew that from our own neighbors. The houses were tucked closely together. In the photograph of the house it looked like it was smack in the middle of a hundred acres. I showed my wife and she snorted. "If only we could live in the photographs of houses," she said.

I learned to see the neighborhood and yard with my wife's eyes.

The wonderful trees in their spectacular colors did mean shade in the summer, the possibility of a hammock, the joy of jumping into leaf piles with the kids. But these trees had to be calculated: maples were susceptible to disease: tree trimming, tree cutting, and trees falling come at a considerable price. I noted the near perfect sidewalks for Tina to finally try a bicycle, but also a few houses up, a garbage can was on its side at the curb.

And if this wasn't all bad enough, the whole time we sat in the minivan there had been a constant barking of what could have been two or three small dogs but sounded like ten. This might have been some rare occurrence. We looked at each other: "It doesn't have to be perfect." "Should we go then?" I asked. My wife nodded. I started the car and we got out of there. There's *not perfect* and then there's barking dogs.

The day wasn't going well at all, not even for imperfect. Two other houses, maybe three, they started to blur. But at the last place the stakeout portion passed with flying colors. My wife still seemed skeptical and I reminded her that there's just something about a split-level that gets me every time. It has something to do with the stairs. You go in that front door and you can go up or you can go down. I like that. She shook her head. She was amazed with her husband. Maybe this would be the house. We then went on to try the car door test: We each stood with our hands poised on our respective doors—my wife holding the handle and me holding above the window. No kidding, you can judge a neighborhood by the sound the car door makes when you close it. My wife closed her door and we listened, a nice resonance. I closed mine a little harder, not such a resonance but a finality. Flying colors! That means it was time to check what the sliding door of the minivan sounded like. Again, there was a perfect pitch.

So we were heading up the walk to a house, perhaps a little spooked. This had the most potential in any house we'd seen in years. A couple with their arms interlaced came out the front door. The woman was wearing a long skirt and clogs and her hair was back in a ponytail. The man, clean-cut hair and a chic bit of stubble, had a baby papoosed on his chest. They were all smiles, as if someone had just given them the place for free. They were walking out of a J. Crew catalog. They were still picturing how it would be when they owned a house—mapping out their lives, just picturing themselves in a place and around it, picturing themselves in various happy poses in the rooms. Sunday mornings in bed with the smell of coffee, Saturday nights staying in by the fire, even vacuuming—when you're their age vacuuming has romantic potential. They missed the rotted trim at the corner of one window, the decade old paint job, the open seams in the decorative brick. They weren't thinking about schools and taxes, all the possible invisible infestations, the length of walkway and the wide driveway to shovel. My wife didn't gush at the baby as you could see the couple was used to. They did seem likable—they might be Nick and Naomi's best friends.

I caught the man's eye to see if he had what it takes to keep it all together. He nodded and smiled as he passed. Just like Nick with the news of their baby, this guy couldn't fathom what he was entering into. But I silently wished him and his family luck.

When they were out of earshot, my wife asked me if that couple reminded me of anyone.

"Who them? No one I'd want to know."

My wife smiled, tight-lipped and joyous, and then said: "You almost want to take a hold of them and tell them *be careful, watch your step.*"

And you know what, we stood at the door of that house and neither of us could get ourselves to go any further. When another couple came up behind us, they asked us if it was locked. We didn't answer but jogged, really jogged, down the walkway and zipped into the minivan where we stretched across the divided seats and kissed and kept kissing. "We should head to the lookout!" I suggested. "No way," my wife laughed as she brushed her lips against her sleeve. Instead of the lookout we headed to pick up the pizzas for the kids.

"I think we dodged a bullet," she said when we were almost home.

About a month later we had our moment at the mall when we were watching Tina on the too small merry-go-round.

So here I am at the lookout. I've never been up here without my wife.

"Hey," I say into my phone, "you'll never guess where I am right now."

"Jail," my wife says.

"Ouch," I say, admiring her joke, even if it is a bit at my expense.

A bunch of blue jays fill in the gap for a minute. I honk the horn and they move on.

"Nancy would like. . ."

"Ask her how much she wants for it. I like bursting through fabric when I drive."

I can actually hear her trying not to laugh.

"We might all be working for her soon," she finally says.

"You saw the show?"

"Jesus, Doug, are you really a part of this?"

"You haven't guessed where I am yet?"

"Even if you were aware of all this, it was awful of Rachel to corner you like that again. Did you know?"

She's defending me! "Guess where I am?"

In the pause, I can feel her cogs turning. Did she want to drop the talk about work and follow my lead?

Even though she hasn't returned any of my messages from this morning, I can tell just the idea of therapy has got her back, closer to my side.

"Come on." Calls keep coming in but I don't even look who they're from. I've got the phone tight to my ear.

"Why is this a guessing game, Doug? What's the big deal about your location?"

"I'll give you a clue. It's the one place where *you* got into trouble with the police."

"Doug, I. . .oh. What're you doing there?"

"Not sure actually. But I'm here."

"You OK?"

"I made an executive decision."

I know my wife was thinking *but you're not an executive*! But what she says instead: "Why can't you just admit everything is a mess? Surely Rachel was right that you can't possibly do a town-hall meeting. People I've never heard of have been calling since the show. What are you doing?"

"Remember that night in the minivan when we were up here after one of our open house blitzes. We were both OK."

Again, she has a decision to keep talking about the town-hall meeting or follow my train of thought, and she follows me into the past: "The good old days when we presented a united front for the police."

"You mean a naked front for the police?" I laugh and she laughs and I laugh because she really is on my side. "I remember your panties on the emergency brake. I remember flinging your bra into the back. I remember your hands under my shirt. I remember the minivan, the wonder of vehicles, may it rest in peace, great for making love in. But I'm still not convinced it was the police that night. I mean that was orgasmic, flashlights, voices of authority, the glowing badges of victory."

"Do you remember what I told them?"

She was on top of me in the passenger seat. This was after Rudd and Jess but before Tina. We hadn't heard the cruiser pull up. There was the flashlight, the rap on the window, and one of the officers asked, "Ma'am, you all right?" while the other one leaned over the hood, trying to get a good look at her ass.

"*I'm better than all right,*" the words came to me out of the blue.

"That's what you said."

"I still can't believe I said that. But, God, what a question to ask someone when her skirt is up around her ears."

I change to speakerphone because I need both hands on the wheel even though I'm parked. How are we here in this conversation? I'm going to have to find a really good gift for Sam—just the idea of therapy works wonders. Maybe we'll never even have to go.

"You'll never guess what I'm drinking right now?" she asks.

A guessing game? I love it. "Tequila?"

"A Yoo-hoo!"

This silences me. That drink is her number one pregnancy craving.

"Doug, I know what you're thinking. I just saw it when I was getting gas and I thought why not? That's it, drowning my woes in Yoo-hoo."

I can't help doing some quick calculating. I hear her take a sip.

"Stop, Doug. I can hear you thinking it."

There's a pause, a long pause. More missed calls come in. The blue jays have returned. I honk my horn again.

"I just want to feel that way again, sometimes," she says. What just happened to her excited Yoo-hoo voice?

"Pregnant?"

"*Better than all right*. I haven't felt that way in a long time."

You know those magic tables that fold up and keep folding up until they are practically gone?—that's how my insides feel. In fact that doesn't do justice to what her comment does to me. That guy under the falling safe, that's me.

"Don't you want it better than just OK?" she asks me. I can see her twist-tie frown of knowingness, of knowing me.

I only know what I am not trying to say. There are only spoken words and written words and planned words and buzzwords.

"I talked to our therapist today. We have an appointment."

"*Our* therapist. . ."

"We have exercises. I sent them to you. I've already done mine."

I hear her rinse out the Yoo-hoo bottle and clink it into recycling.

I hang up. I wait for her to call back. She doesn't.

I have a photograph of both Rudd's and Jess's first steps in that top drawer of mine (OK, really their third or fourth or fifth steps—it takes time to grab the camera)—I hadn't been present for Tina's (my wife decided not to capture those for posterity). I agree those first steps, captured on film or not, are pretty important, but really the most momentous steps we take in our lives are our missteps, especially those missteps that are full of good intentions, the missteps we take toward resolution. These are the steps that define us.

I feel one thing at the core of my being: my wife and I will be up here again soon and we'll be better than all right.

I text her again the two exercises she's supposed to do just in case she didn't get the earlier ones. I hang out a little while longer for her reply. I can't help but to go back to the fun we've had here. I can't help to think of her naked. We needed an open house blitz, and fast, but I'll need to set it up just right. We'll stand at another door, but this time we're going in.

21

"Here's an idea for you," I tell Nancy, who is sitting up high on her store's front counter even though there are several customers milling around. She's keeping the store cold enough for people to want to buy their own fleece material to wrap themselves in as they shop. "Why don't you hire your daughter?"

"Did she put you up to this? Is this why she was here for four hours this morning giving instructions? I smell a rebellion afoot? She just quit her job. I don't like hiring quitters."

I'm trying to read Nancy here and I'm getting the sense that she feels a little conflicted.

"Also, I'm worried about her character. If I quit a job you'd see me lounging around the house for at least one day, but who's waiting for me this morning at this door when I came a little late because I had to *walk* in the cold this morning. She's tapping her watch. *This is no way to run a business.* Passing it off as a joke, but I know it's not. Also I have a report of my car being seen late in the night around Percival Lake vicinity which caused me some problems since I told this certain person I planned to stay in for the evening. And now I find out there's such a sticky web of lies every spider in town is stuck to it, including my own dear son-in-law."

I'm trying to break in, there's a customer ready to make a purchase but Nancy doesn't stop.

"And nostalgia. I won't have any nostalgic employees. Do you know the very first thing that wife of yours did? Did she start brewing coffee, check the till, start vacuuming, indulge her mother in a little chitchat? No, she takes down that article about her." Nancy points a thumb behind her—it's the article about the wunderkind high school student whose ideas made her mother's store cutting edge and a force to reckon with even in the height of downtown stores closing. "Takes it down and I'm not kidding she practically cradles it in her arms and dusts it like she's washing a newborn's face."

Seeing the customer, Nancy swings to the other side of the counter where there's a stepstool. Back on her feet, she chats with the customer about GE and the mayor and their web of lies. And the woman actually says, "Well, at least Rachel stuck it to that ass today." Nancy winks at me, but I'm fine—that's my job, but clearly she's missed the takeaway from my interview: optimism and excitement for airing everything out, getting down to the bottom of things at the town-hall meeting. Also I'd really like Nancy to stop with the *web of lies* thing.

"Good-bye," the customer says, even to me, not even a second glance. I'm just a guy in the store, not an ass on TV from two hours ago.

We both watch the customer wait behind her car for an opening in the traffic so she can get in without her door being taken off—if she got mowed down right now I'd still be the first one to run to her aid. When she's safely in her car, I turn to Nancy and I'm pretty sure she'll tell me some reassuring counter-opinion about my not being an ass.

"What you should be asking me is if my daughter will keep me on in *her* store!"

I decide not to enter this game. I've got my own issues.

"Flowers," I tell Nancy. "Where's the best flowers in town?"

Apparently giving me the name of the store is not enough. In about a minute, she's shooed out the remaining customer who's holding a whole roll of fabric, assuring her that she can pay for it next time. She's got a sign already prepared that she suctions to the door. "Out on an ERRAND. Wait at your own RISK." (Maybe my wife might be able to help Nancy.) When we get to her Suburban, which I parked in back, she goes right to the driver's side—she's repossessing her car. I'll try to break the news about the dent as soon as I get an opening.

"Do you know Rudolph only bought me flowers once, all those years of marriage. Twenty-three years and one bouquet of daisies, not even roses, and they weren't for any special occasion or even to make up. It was pretty suspicious." Nancy takes her eyes off the road and smiles at me to let me know, that my flowers surely won't be suspicious.

"Maybe he was just suddenly inspired."

She laughs, "I forgot that you never really got to know him."

Believe me, the couple hours I spent in his garage were enough. After he finally got laid off from the Schenectady plant, he kept working wherever he could: bagging groceries, mall security, but no way was he going to work at his wife's store! He died while Karen was pregnant with Rudd and it was a blow. As Nancy has repeatedly told me, Karen shared a special bond with her dad. And hence our son Rudolph Burl Merit. The night he was born as he and Karen slept in the hospital room, as I stared at diapers, it suddenly came to me, one of those gifts of terror and exhaustion. I found some hospital stationary (now lost) where I drew a map of Rudd's name: Rudolph Burl to Rudy by two, Rudy to Rudd before kindergarten. The name just came to me and it fits him to a T—I still see it as my defining act in his life—I can't top it. And even my wife eventually made the jump from Rudy to Rudd.

My father-in-law died sixteen years ago. Nancy has been a widow that long. I can't help thinking about who spotted her car last night—is she seeing someone?

"Do you ever think about seeing someone else?" I ask, though I understood completely her devotion to her husband.

"I know I have been accused of loving him only after he was gone. But if she thinks *you* can be difficult she couldn't have survived Rudolph for five minutes." She hesitates knowing she said something she wasn't supposed to and maybe she saw my confusion—me difficult? We were now parked at the florist. She checked the mirror and picked at her hair. I'm not saying anything about Nancy's driving but it might have been the first time she checked her mirror. When she's done, she gives me a sly smile and reaches over and pats my knee: "We see what we want to see, I guess. We can't control how other people see us."

"That's my job!" The golden Frisbee is at my feet and I can't help pushing down on it hard with my shoes.

"Oh, yes, of course." Nancy says, seeing the Frisbee. "Then you already know."

"About the show today, I really—"

She stops me with her palm. She doesn't want to hear about any of it.

She then just stares through the windshield as if she's giving me the option to not take the flower route. But flowers are the way to go. As soon as I open my door, Nancy follows suit.

Inside, I pick up my two-dozen roses as Nancy speaks to the only other customer. When she sees the roses she rushes over to me.

"This is for you." I push one bunch toward her, hoping to work in something about the dent.

"How kind." She gives me a winning smile. "But these," she says taking the other bunch out of my hand.

"But she loves roses. I've always gotten her roses."

Ignoring me, she walks back to the refrigerated flowers and calls the florist over, "Emily, emergency." They consult. At one point the florist eyes me as if I am some rare aphid she's found under a leaf.

I swear to god I hear Nancy whisper, "Their problem is that they're both only children." To which Emily nods gravely. Why do florists wear aprons?

Emily disappears into the backroom as Nancy tells me of Emily's rare talent of hitting just the right note. *What note?* I want to ask. When Emily returns, she carries a bouquet of flowers that hadn't been seen since the last royal wedding. Oranges that aren't quite orange, reds not quite red, yellows not quite yellow, purple not quite purple and down through the rainbow. They have names I forget as soon as I hear them.

"You got the Amazon back there?"

Emily cocks her head as she hands them to me. She has blonde hair about the same length as my wife's, but she is maybe five years younger.

"If these flowers went on to commit some crime," I add, "I wouldn't be able to identify them in a lineup."

Her head cocks further and her bangs slide, revealing a mole just below her temple. "Are these compliments? Nance, tell this guy he has to work on his compliments. Flowers don't work if people don't know how to compliment."

"It will work wonders," Nancy says as I gape at the numbers on the cash register.

"Is there some kind of guarantee?" I ask as I put the cash back in my wallet and hand over my card.

"What kind of guarantee would you like?" Emily asks, a mischievous smile.

I give it a lot of thought since Emily seems interested in my answer and Nancy is momentarily involved with another customer and I hear another reference to web of lies: "They'll make everything better than OK."

She cocks her head the opposite direction this time.

"What about world peace?" I ask. "Can you do that?"

"That I can do."

"Isn't she sharp?" Nancy asks with a wink when she joins us again. "Now, Nance knows how to compliment."

Nancy sticks her nose into her roses: "These smell like heaven."

"You can't stop this woman," Emily replies.

Back at our house, Nancy keeps hold of the wheel, the roses in her lap. Karen's bouquet is belted in the back seat. The Pontiac's gone. Of course, it's already time to get the kids. Nancy reminds me that tonight's Rudd's big hockey game. Of course I don't need reminding. But she asks if I'm going. "Why wouldn't I?" "Oh, I was just wondering." That's it. Even if everyone thinks I'm an ass, I'm still going to the game. I'm certainly not going to hide because I'm trying to fix everything. I drop off the flowers on the kitchen table. I decide they need no note. I look in the recycling and confirm there's not one but two Yoo-hoos in there.

Nancy drives me to work, or tries to. The green hair ASSASSINS girl is no longer alone. There is a swarm of people. They all have similar signs. They're all wearing sackcloth! Nancy says, "That's one mystery solved." She explains that a couple of kids came in and bought her out of that type of fabric. The protesters block the driveway. On the other side of the ASSASSINS is another smaller crew but more vocal. Their signs say things like, *No PCBs for Frisbees*. They must be too scared to be close to Percival Lake. I give Nancy directions to the other entrance. As we drive by, I think I see Rudd in a sackcloth and strain to look back. He wouldn't do that. He should be in his mother's car by now, coming home to rest for the big game tonight—plus protesting is not Rudd's style.

As I step out of the car, without broaching the dent, Nancy rolls down the window.

"Doug. She jumps into what she's afraid of. You know that by now, don't you?"

I'm puzzled but I nod.

"I'm starting to notice that Jess does the same thing."

Now I'm really puzzled. The only thing Jess doesn't do is set the record straight. From where Nancy is sitting she does a panoramic scan of the buildings that surround this lot.

"I haven't been back in here for a long time." She points to Building 57, the doozy. "So many years going in and out of there. How did he do it? Do you know he used to wash off his arms every day in a barrel of PCBs along with his two friends? Not one bit of cancer. But who knows, maybe if he'd lived longer. . ." She starts to roll up the window and stops midway. "Those daisies he brought me were yellow. He didn't say a word, but just held them out to me. Neither of us knew what to do. We never knew what we were doing and then he was gone." Her eyes lock on a place just above my head. "Well, I've got a store to run," she says. "I wouldn't want my daughter to think I'm slacking." Then she adds, "I'll see you newlyweds at the game."

I'm still nodding as she pulls away.

The moment when Rudolph dropped dead in his backyard, I was there watching a fish fillet he held in tongs over the barbecue on a hot day in August as he explained how to properly barbecue. Then the fish and the tongs disappeared, the fish's charred skin left on the rack and Rudolph disappeared too...they were all down in the grass: the tongs, the fish, and Rudolph, neatly displayed as if they had been laid out. And I got the feeling that his last thought was "My daughter's never going to have barbecue done right again." We had no idea what to do. We just stood there. It was just clear he was dead. I kneeled and touched his chest and it was only then that Nancy ran into the house and Karen dropped down on him sobbing. Even though the doctor said he was dead before he hit the ground, a week later I took my first CPR class and have renewed every year. Nobody knows that I'm certified, not even my wife. In the big scheme of things it's my only true subterfuge. I've never had to resuscitate anyone. I'm not an ass.

The shouts of the protesters float around from the front of the building. I forgot that I'm most likely going to be fired. I probably should have asked Nancy to idle a minute, while I clear my desk into a box. I take a deep breath. I could use a couple rescue breaths myself right now. I remind myself that I know what I'm doing.

22

In the office, the panic has been stuffed in filing cabinets and under keyboards. There's no satirical PR statement from Alexis. Brad and Brooke do a little rubbernecking, but who can blame them? They all have on their best PR smiles over the vibration of chattering teeth. After the initial onslaught of sympathy and backslapping, everyone keeps their distance. Sam passes my cubicle and makes a big deal about fanning himself with the papers he's carrying—not even eye contact.

Jimmy Tripoli's voice emanating from Jason the Kid's office is more like birdshot than cannon blast. I can't tell if it's enraged or enthusiastic.

It's not long before I'm called in. As I head toward the door, Brad asks if he can switch to my desk after I clear out, Alexis holds a cocked finger to her head and looks genuinely concerned, Sam is typing away at something madly, and Brooke tries to look professional even though she is excited to be part of her first beheading. Sally and Rita are nowhere to be seen, probably updating their resumes. I'd like to think kind thoughts about my coworkers, but it feels more like that kid's book where the animals convince a friendly rabbit to chat with the super hungry and scrawny lion so their own asses will be saved.

And there is Jason shrunk in his clothes as if Tripoli has been sucking him like a lollipop and put the original wrapper back on just before I came in. Tripoli does not wear a cowboy hat or cowboy boots but if you close your eyes that's exactly what you see. He is a brow wiper, a nose tweaker, and a man that grabs his own thighs hard as if he is keeping himself from jumping through the roof. He's in Jason's seat behind the desk and he points to the empty chair next to the Kid. He explains that I'm like Bartok, the Beatles, Led Zeppelin, I'm cutting edge. He lets it be known that Mr. CEO, Alogosh himself, actually said over the phone: "The brightest idea in PR this century." He goes on that it isn't exactly the cap he had in mind in our chat this morning, but he can see the genius in it in light of the ugly information from that "pretty lady." Tripoli finally lets go of his thighs long enough to stand up and he sidesteps between the desk and the wall and slaps me on the back, hard. And his smile shifts for a split second and there's murder in his eyes which gives me some pause, but it switches right back to gushing brilliance and I'm thinking that I nailed this one—he's just trying to control his jealousy. It is a bold and brilliant strategy! I've just stamped my ticket to Fairfield and Karen isn't going to have to worry anymore about not having a job. The kids are going to private school. Tina will have her very own rescued mink farm. We are out of this place, a place that both of us never thought we'd actually live in—I mean who lives in the place they grew up? I'm to be paraded, I'm to be celebrated. And then he looks at us both. "Boys," he says, "enough of this ego grooming. Priority number one is to plug up this leak, now." There is a very small circle in Fairfield that knew about this and an even smaller circle here, he gives Jason the dirty glance and the kid shrinks another size—he's one of those Shrinky Dink toys that you stick in the oven.

He sends Jason out to his new office in the conference room and then shuts the door. He pulls the chair that Jason had been in close to me so that our knees are touching. He's holding his thighs even harder now and from his face it looks just like he is still giving me compliments, anyone looking in would be jealous about the praise it seems like I'm getting, but what Tripoli actually says is this:

"I just wanted you to know that you haven't gotten away with anything. We know it's you. And don't even try to tell me it's not. But we have to go through with this whole thing and we have to be especially nice to you and even when it is all over even though we could get rid of you with this DUI and assault charges, we'll keep you around a little longer, but then you are going to be gone. Why am I telling you this? I was supposed to keep playing the game with you, but you've made my goddamn life so miserable I'm not going to allow you even a minute of thinking that you got us."

He's slapping my back as he guides me through the door—again, a little too hard. He's laughing like we're both in on the best joke. "Here he is," he announces to the office, "the man who will save GE!" And the whole office breaks into applause.

I hitch a ride from Sam to get home. He actually offered, the only thing he said to me so far this afternoon. There's a security guard now at the exit and ostensibly it is for our protection from the protesters. But if that's the case someone should have a chat with him because he pats us down and checks our bags and then our IDs. But he's a good guy. He sees that I'm Rudd's father. He was on the hockey team for THS too, a few years back. According to him, Rudd's going to be in the NHL. Out into the night the protesters' chants aren't quite as loud as earlier. I'm a little more worried about Sam because when he opened his briefcase for the guard there was only a sandwich in it. But now I'm truly worried about him as I try to figure out why he's heading to a brand new red Camaro. A few days ago he had a Pinto-like car and now he's driving a red Camaro? He has the keys to prove it. I still don't believe it even as we drive away. And no matter how much I know I'm profoundly fucked, all I can do is keep thinking that Sam, Sam Gowers is driving a bright red Camaro—how can I feel sorry for myself when Sam's ten-thousand times worse off than me?

Sam is a wild driver. He shoots off the line as soon as the light goes green and gets to 38mph in about a second and then tones it down right to 36. When he's gunning it off the line, he gets this look, and I wish he's just showing off but there's something that his quick start internally pleases—his smile is so internal it's a bit creepy and Sam for all his woes is just not a creepy guy.

I have to ask it again: "Sam, give me the report, how are you doing?"

"I'm adjusting," he says. "I've been looking at some apartments. You know anything about Lincoln Heights? I hear it's pretty nice."

We chat about different apartment complexes.

"Buying this car has made her so pissed," Sam says, a little scared. "It's the exact same one she always wanted. But if she wants to get a lawyer I can certainly get a car."

I nod as he takes the corner a little too fast, especially now that a steady rain is falling. There's no way I'm going to bring up therapy again. Frankly, I'm thinking I should cancel the appointment.

"That's where I am," Sam says. He then apologizes for not being able to make the game tonight which I say is fine—why in the world would he come anyway? "You know," he says, "we've led these parallel lives, starting at GE at the same time, when you were pregnant with Tina we had that miscarriage and now here we are after these years—we have opened it up."

"Yes, it's amazing."

"Something good is going to come of all this. You'll see. Something good will come from this. It has to."

He pulls into the Windchimers' driveway but I don't say anything.

"You know who I was thinking about when I was watching you and Rachel?"

"I have no idea."

"Ed! Do you remember that guy? Hardcore. He used to ride your ass so bad. Then he just disappears. What did he do? Open a Ben and Jerry's outside of Nashville or something? I feel like he's the only boss that really got me. He even sent a card. It's one of my biggest regrets, losing touch with him."

"Huh."

"If I didn't need this job, I'd. . .well. . .you know. Maybe we'll really open it up. Maybe the culture will change."

He idles in the Windchimers' driveway and twists his hands on the steering wheel as if he's revving a motorcycle, as we just shake our heads together for a minute or two and I think it does him some good.

"Life," he says.

"Life," I reply.

23

And after a quick bite, I'm in the passenger seat of another car, the Pontiac with my wife and Tina. Jess along with her bandaged nose and sealed lips has gone to her hockey hideout at Sarah's house—I guess they are back on good terms. At the stoplight at First and Tyler, I look at my wife. The red shadows of the raindrops bead her face and round her eyes, while the shadow of the constantly passing blades washes her cheek and chin clean. It is really only sprinkling, and a mid-range interval selection would be sufficient for the wipers.

She actually seems like she's in a good mood—not quite the Yoo-hoo good mood in the first part of our phone conversation, but pretty close to it. She didn't say anything about how excited she was to get her two exercises done, and she didn't say anything about the flowers, though she did put them in another vase and move them to the mantle between the dining room and the living room. Better than all right?

Tina is quiet behind me. She doesn't have a band-aid over the ferret bite anymore. The bite looks like dots she drew to make a face on her fist. Tina is usually perfect for these moments because she knows how to stick to the script.

"Give me the latest on minks?" I ask, ready for ten minutes to be filled easily.

"Minks jinx."

I turn around and she's in her booster seat, looking at the rain on her window. Her seatbelt is twisted like a Chinese paper yoyo along her shoulder and waist.

"What new plans do you have, then? What's your next move?"

There's a long pause.

"Jess said I'm going to turn into a ferret when the moon gets full." She stops, then adds quietly: "I don't believe her."

Both my wife and I counter this. Here we are, a team.

"I didn't want to hit that man. Does that mean I'm bad like Daddy?"

Who needs an ejection seat? Tina just popped me right through the roof.

My wife explains that what she did was out of good intentions. She was trying to protect an animal. "You didn't try to use words first. You have to use your words. You never try to hurt anyone."

"Words hurt," Tina replies.

No kidding! My wife just skipped the whole bad Daddy thing. But when she flashes me a look I find myself searching for times words have hurt her.

It's agreed that the windshield wipers should have a few moments of input on this whole situation.

"Burty's dad gave him a hundred dollars all in one." Tina's here to save the day—a total reversal. I could kiss her. "He showed it to me and then put it on Ms. Lowendorf's desk. Then she asked us about plural words that end in *y*. He raised his hand. He's not good at plurals. He said his mother knows something that nobody else knows." Tina seems to be perking up. "And every time she asked the class something he raised his hand and said it again. And then he kept raising his hand but she never called on him."

Windshield wipers.

"Burty's hardly ever right," she says. "That's why I like him."

"He's right this time," I say.

My wife reaches over and pats my knee, no kidding. She's expressing sympathy for a day of tough PR. There's no way I'm telling her about Tripoli's plan for me. Plus, there's no reason to. The town-hall meeting will be so amazing that it will be Tripoli that goes because of his short-sightedness. You deal with a problem head-on, right?

"I've been thinking," Tina pauses. This means that we're in for it. "Do you know how we read that book today at the library about that dog that lost its collar? I've been thinking that Gazook is just like a mink, but much nicer and he's not harvested, but he's in jail too just like minks but instead of taking his fur they take his licks and his freedom."

Tina does have a plan! We have to get ahead of this or we might have a kid attacking Nick and Naomi, we might have a kid attacking every dog walker we meet. My wife tells her how much Nick and Naomi love Gazook. How much he loves them. I tell her he's man's best friend. She comes back by asking why does he have a collar? Why is he left out-side with a rope on? Why does he get locked in the house all day? We again respond to all this with perfectly reasonable explanations.

"Then why don't we have a dog?"

I can't help admire the Escher logic. Jess is allergic, we remind her—it's not a true allergy but ever since she saved Tina that one time and got that bad bite she is scared to death of even the most harmless pup.

"I want a free-range dog," she says to herself.

The blinker is a relief as we arrive at Melville Street. As my wife brakes and waits for a car to splash by, I remind her that this lot is always full: "Our best bet is my super-extra double secret spot behind…"

"There will be a spot," she says, and she is right. Being a passenger all of the time is going to take some getting used to.

With the rain tumbling down, Tina splashes the sidewalk ahead of us. We call after her but she doesn't respond. She pries open the door to the Boys and Girls Club herself. We pick up our pace but then we see through the door that she's with Nancy all the way at the top of the steps. My wife has her hand on the door but doesn't pull it.

"I think this dog thing is a passing phase," I say. "Her mind trying to get over her disappointment with minks. But that's Tina for you." I pull the other door open for her.

"Doug, I just wanted to. . ."

A woman already shaking her umbrella steps between us through the door and does a double take. "Oh. My. God! Is that really you?" she asks my wife in near-to-a-scream. All I see is her black hair, which pivots on her head as if it is spring-loaded. She pulls my wife inside and I stay long enough to wipe my feet. "Remember me? Jill Dart, you hired me at the Talbots over at Crossgates Mall? Oh my God that must have been ten years ago? You saved my life. It's really you! I'm over to see my nephew play."

I give them space to reminisce. At the top of the stairs, a banner hangs: Pontoosuc County Championships. At the end of the lobby the double doors to the rink are open and the icy light pours through them as a pimply teenaged boy sits on a stool while he rips tickets and scratches his ear. Skates scrape the ice, but the sound is muffled here in the chatter of the lobby. The various groups of kids each with either the red and white of the Greylock team or the green and gold of the THS team move as if each individual group is glued together. The hockey parents are strategizing, fathers arguing about defense and offense and the way the refs will call the game, mothers chatting about post-game celebrations. One mother mentions a new Italian restaurant and another in a quiet voice says, "We're going to slaughter them." There are bets made, scores guessed at, children lauded. Rudd's name keeps popping up. A circle of girls wearing red and white giggle as they check out the forbidden fruit in the room: the boys in gold and green.

I check back with my wife. She's made it to the top of the stairs and looks as if she's trying to escape but the woman grips her elbow. I'm trying to eavesdrop now but a gold-and-green group squeezes between us and I distinctly hear Rudd's name mentioned—a girl's voice—and I am so proud I'm about to introduce myself. But there are no introductions because Ernie Something and Nancy and Tina are suddenly standing in front of me. He, like most of the team (except Rudd), has shaved THS into the side of his hair. I admire his enthusiasm and pity him too. He looks worried, probably about the way he treated me the night of the accident. I put my hand out because I'm genuinely glad to see him. I don't hold grudges.

"Where's Rudd?" he asks, scanning the room. "He headed to the lockers?"

"He's here, with you? He stayed at school to have the team dinner."

"No he didn't." He looks at his watch. There's twenty minutes to the game.

"I told you," Tina says.

"Yes," Nancy responds, "but it is good to check anyway."

"Is he kidnapped like Jess was last week?"

"Jess was not kidnapped," I say.

Ernie is looking back and forth. "So where's Rudd?"

"Rudd's not here?" my wife says as she finally breaks with the woman whose voice follows her with the command that she has to promise to stop by and see the whole gang—"we still meet once a month and all of us that you put in that store have become so successful."

"Where is he?" I ask.

Ernie says he's going to check with the other players. My wife and I call Rudd's number even though we know we're calling the kitchen drawer. I dial the house and when the answering machine picks up I ask if he's there. Then I check the messages on the machine to see if he's called home.

Ernie's back and reports that Corey Bolby says he thought he saw him heading toward the library after school.

My wife's eyes meet mine: 1) Rudd has never disappeared or been late in his life. 2) Can I help it that the library seems to be some mystical point of convergence for missing kids?

"Is he on Jones Street then if he's not kidnapped?" Tina asks, but how the hell did she remember that? To my wife, it is a non sequitur.

Suddenly, I know exactly where Rudd is. I go into contingency mode. I put my rain jacket hood back on, but my wife is already in her own contingency mode as she brings the phone to her ear. "Yes, Mary Beth? Are you working tonight? Have you seen my son?" My head does some racing: from no acknowledgment on the day Mary Beth came over to return my wallet to calling her that fast? Tina did say they were at the library today. It didn't occur to me. "Thank you. And you'll let me know? Yes, I'll send a photo so you can ask."

"She hasn't seen him, but she's going to look and call back."

"Great. You stay here and I'm going to drive around. Maybe he's headed here on First or Tyler or North. I'll go up and down and I have another idea. You should call Myerson's Hobby just in case he's losing himself in trains." My wife knows this is ridiculous but she starts looking up the number and I'm heading down the stairs to the door when Jess and her bandaged nose come in. Sarah is actually dragging Jess behind her. Both are wearing tan trench coats I'd never seen before. The jackets are adult sized, so instead of looking like two girl strippers they look more like it's Halloween and they're going as junior Inspector Clouseau. Neither looks happy—and why would they—both have avowed their everlasting hate for hockey all season long.

"What's wrong?" Jess asks.

I suppress my surprise and go right by them without a word. I love her dearly but I don't love how she's been acting.

"What?" I hear her say after me. As if she doesn't know.

Here I am again, two of my three kids accounted for: *vu jà dé?*

Bernie, Sarah's dad, is in his car right at the curb, the hazards blinking. He is getting out but sees me and jumps back in and rolls down the passenger window. He stretches over the seat as he starts easing the car forward so I have to walk alongside as he talks. His cologne stings my nose from here. He's got to go to work, so could I drive Sarah home after the game? Sure thing. He's relieved and a second later he's headed down the street with his hazards still on. Why can't everything be as simple?

24

I wish I were bursting through fabric in Nancy's Suburban but I'm not bursting through anything in the Pontiac. My father-in-law was loyal to Pontiac and his daughter has stayed true as well. I pass Rudd's school and then a few blocks later I wave at the library and its bright lights as I drive right by. Mary Beth is somewhere in there doing the same thing I'm doing. Believe me I'm tempted to go in and say hello and see what she has to say about my record on child tending and what she and my wife might have chatted about this afternoon. But here's my chance. Find a lost child, save my wife from worry, save the county championships. My image will be restored. I'll be the type of hero whose wife has to reassess her quibbles. That's all they are, quibbles. I've got this one.

There are a lot of cars on the road for a rainy evening and soon enough the lights of the active part of GE greet me. I'm guessing that what I'll see under the orange lamps will be a pile of signs and some litter, and on the curb a soaking wet Rudd trying to make a girl with green hair feel better about the lackadaisical nature of their high school class-mates. If it isn't that best-case scenario, I picture a protest divided into cliques. The scene won't be much different than outside the hockey rink.

Groups of kids that are concerned with the other groups of kids. There will be the dopes soaked in T-shirts and backward baseball caps trying to hide their oncoming hypothermia. There'll be the hoodie crowd, again soaked. There'll be the prepared crowd with parkas and small hibachi. The clown-car umbrella crowd, mostly girls, dressed poorly for the conditions and five under an umbrella lit with cell phones—they'll be the cheeriest. The protesters aren't really here to protest. They are just regular kids who all got roped into one girl with green hair's Activate! assignment and they'll be just looking for an excuse to leave: some sirens, some dad that's going to tell them it's time to go home now. They were hoping to have an excused absence for Activating!, but they probably realized they were just helping green hair get her points, so they left.

As I park across the street I spot the KNNK van, and there's the camera spotlighting Rachel with dozens of dozens of people behind her. It seems to be the teenage crowd. The older PCB protesters know enough to get out of the rain. I can already see the eleven o'clock news, *prodigy goalie and son of the GE spokesperson, skips county championships to protest his father: Father's plan for moving to Fairfield squashed.* She's got the confidence of a hurricane reporter as the rain comes down. She's got the right. She was on national news tonight, explaining her evidence, refusing to talk about her source, and explaining what she'll think will happen at the town-hall meeting. She even got to joke about the viral videos, which is the best kind of PR. And now she's still at it with this group of defiant teenagers. Why not milk it for everything it's worth? I certainly can see why Rudd would join them. I myself might have been susceptible to a girl with green hair in high school. I pull my hood so my face is in the shadows. It's time to fetch the boy. When I find him I'm going to haul him to the game, but I do understand his choice.

The teenagers are standing in the rain in perfect rows, holding electric candles (made by GE?). There's at least forty of them. They have the sackcloth material wrapped around them, and most of them have a question mark painted on their foreheads. Their faces full of actual sorrow. It's eerie. I walk along the rows searching the faces for my son. If it weren't for Rachel and the TV van here, I'd feel like I was in a time warp to a pagan ritual. Someone hands me a candle and a sackcloth and directs me to the back in a whisper. "What's happening?" I ask. "Shhhh!" the girl responds. By the time I get to the back, someone calls out "one minute."

No sign of Rudd though, which is a relief but also a problem. There's no saving the day.

Then it strikes me. These kids have it all wrong. They all should be enjoying their lives. Worry about if your team is going to win the game tonight. Worry about that guy or girl is going to like you. Worry about passing that chemistry test tomorrow. Be kids for Christ sakes! What's wrong with you all! Go watch your team play! I get a quick image of them marching behind me to the game. I'll save their lives.

There's a flutter up front. The cameraman is up on a step stool. Green hair can speak. She's arguing with Rachel about something. I hear, "This isn't for the media, this is for the world. Please stop." Rachel ignores her and stands in front of the group and says to the camera, "Let's watch." The girl says, "I won't be co-opted." And her intensity radiates. She's trying to decide whether to be co-opted, cancel whatever in the world is about to happen, or push the cameraman off the step-stool. She falls into the open spot in front of the line and from somewhere a bell chimes.

I'm still scanning for Rudd but pause near the KNNK van as one by one the kids extinguish their lights until we are in only a dark glow of street lamps. It gives me a quick chill. And the kids just keep standing there in the dark. If they are not cheering at the hockey game, they should be cheering their successful choreography.

I remember how in high school there was a rumor that kissing wasn't allowed in the halls anymore and we the students walked out. I wasn't at the head of the crowd but I walked out once I calculated that the number of students that had already left made getting in trouble doubtful. Some of the more enthusiastic types hit the downtown and smashed windows at Burger King and turned a car over and set it on fire. The next day we were in the national news. The principal came over the intercom, his voice mournful, stating all the things that made sense to protest, but a rumor about kissing with all the problems in the world? He was wrong, wasn't he? If we don't protest about love, where are we?

I turn to head out—I've lost track of the mission. I've got to get back to the car and check out the library, start calling hospitals and the police. Rachel takes my arm suddenly and ducks me behind the van. I drop the fabric and candle.

She's holding me by both arms like she's going to start shaking some sense into me. But under her hood, her eyes are wide. It's just like in a movie where the woman looks at the hero with total wonder and total devotion.

"You haven't seen Rudd?"

"Rudd? No, the only thing I've seen is the new stuff you sent after the interview. I'm not complaining but why didn't you send me this first?"

I will only think about Rudd. "Rudd's missing!"

"Peanuts," she says. "Everything else is just peanuts."

"Rudd?"

"You are amazing how you're orchestrating this. And I—"

"It's not me."

Then I'm only thinking about Rudd as there's a crinkling of wet rain jackets and hooded-heads, and before I know it, Rachel and I are holding each other close. I'm not sure why she's holding me like this, but I'm holding on to her because sometimes you just have to anchor on to something, or you just might fall right off the Earth. Then there's a kiss. A peck, really. A transactional peck. Then one more.

"Mrs. St. John," a familiar voice behind her. "I want to urge you to not use the tape of tonight's requiem. We did not want. . ."

Rachel turns and there's Rudd staring right at me, right there at the front bumper of the van, his rain dripped glasses right smack on his face. And to boot, he's got a black eye. He is here. The fabric is still over his shoulder and the unlit candle is in his hand. I wait for him to snap the glasses from his face, to blur this scene, but there they are, his eyes in their 20-20 rain-bleared vision, one swollen. I might as well be the puck.

25

In the car together, hurrying to the game, I know the only tactic in this situation is to tell the kid he's letting down his team and they need him. I tell him I'm proud of him though for standing for something and protesting because free speech and making your voice heard is a good quality, and to myself add: even if it's the company that helps pay for his train set and hockey equipment (I'm also thinking of that pro contract that might finally put some food on the table in a few years if both his parents are unemployed).

He nods in the passenger seat like a melting snowman whose head is about to tumble off.

I nod because what else can I do but keep nodding? I'll probably nod in my sleep. I may just nod the rest of my life. Every vein and capillary pulls tight in me as if by some master winch. I wish I could explain.

I get an image of him, twenty-five years from now, stopping by to see his old man. Maybe I'm out on the sofa watching TV and he's visiting with his family and now they are all asleep, he sits next to me. During a commercial our attention is drawn to the kitchen where our wives laugh and he turns to me and says, "Dad, I get it now. I really get it."

But I know the best thing to do and that's what I do: let the kid process it. If I force it on him right now, if I'm defensive, cold, mumbling to myself, he's going to think I'm trying to cover something. But here I am just the same old dad he's ever had. I'm just getting a kid to his spot in goal so his team can win the championships. There's nothing that happened that is a big deal at all. That's just how I'm treating both his decision to miss the game and his black eye. No big deal. He's letting me process these things too. Father like son.

He never does take off his glasses, his cheeks never get super red. Maybe he already sees it as no big deal. Maybe he's only thinking of the anonymous way the girl with green hair said goodbye as we headed to the car: "Thanks for coming." Skipping the county championships for that? Then as soon as I'm parked he's out of the car. "Go get 'em, tiger!" I yell after him, glad he's come to his senses and hurrying to the game.

26

Only the pimply ticket taker and my wife are in the lobby when I make it to the top of the stairs. The game is already started. I hear the buzzer and slapping skates and the calls of the crowd. Karen's look of relief is something I'd give her a hundred bucks for. She tells me Rudd ran right by her, and then asks about his black eye.

I shrug. He's not talking. My wife's relief leaves. She looks me up and down as if she's going to lay this all on me. I'm soaking wet and my jacket is stuck to me.

"Why didn't you let me know?"

"Sorry. I was rushing to get him here."

"Where was he? What happened? Who punched him?"

My first instinct is to tell her he was at the library. The story works so well for Jess so why shouldn't it work for me, but I'm happy to report I told her the complete truth. He seemed to be protesting against GE. I thought I saw him when Nancy dropped me off, but I shook it off as impossible. It wasn't. I have no idea about his eye—we didn't get to address it.

She doesn't seem surprised. As if he's been a part of the protests from the start and she knew all about it. Maybe I'll never get her idea of a reasonable explanation down. Maybe if I added that Rachel was kissing me when Rudd found us she'd take it in the same way as something that was of course reasonable. No further explanation needed.

"We've got quite a cheering section," she says, walking by the pimply kid with a nod. I slick back my hair and follow her. "Ticket, please," the kid says. Karen doesn't wait for me as I finally find the ticket in the fifth pocket that I check. The kid looks at the drip that falls on his hand.

A roar goes up just as I come in. It's not for me, however. The THS defenders are checked one by one and two Greylock red and whites, 02 and 15, head right for the net, exchange the puck between them—two cats toying with a mouse. The fake, the pass, the fake, the pass, the shot! Deflected! The coach's son is not as bad as everyone says. From where I stand I locate Tina on the very highest row. She's sitting right next to Burty! Did Rachel play some kind of magic trick? Tina has her arm around him and seems to be telling him something very involved. He's got a bill—the hundred dollar one?—spread out between his hands. I find my wife again as she sits down in a place next to Nancy. Right next to her, wearing the enemy colors is Morgan St. John. He's putting down his arms and he says something to Nancy and my wife and they both smile. Someone puts a hand on my shoulder and I jump, "Excuse me." I'm blocking the aisle. There's a mini-line behind me. I apologize and step aside. I'm not quite ready to join the cheering section. Then I see Jess on the other side of the rink.

She's lost her trench coat and she's standing next to a boy. He has on THS colors—high school!—and has a buzz cut. He's got a bandage on his chin. What in the world? A girl with a bandage on her nose and a boy with a bandage on his chin! There is another cheer and I turn in time to see two players sprawling on the ice. Sarah, who I suddenly remember being asked to take responsibility for, is not with Jess. I scan the rows for a tiny brown-haired, bad-postured girl. I don't see her. Perhaps Jess hasn't had Sarah over since before the accident because she's afraid that I would get a chance to question her about that night and she, being the good girl that she is, might spill the beans. Well, here's my opportunity.

I head out into the corridor to another resounding set of cheers. With my shoes sloshing, I check all the corridors and stairwells until I find Sarah on the steps outside the darkened basketball courts in a quiet area past the restrooms. She's crying. Her trench coat is off her shoulders and Jess's coat covers her lap. When she sees me, she pushes her hair back and drops her face into her arms again. I sit down next to her.

Sarah and Jess haven't been friends for that long, but I'm happy with Sarah. She's a mellowing influence. What she doesn't have in brains, she more than makes up for with a kind heart. It is the kindness that I hope will rub off on Jess. She's obviously distraught because Jess refuses to see that she shouldn't be involved with a kid like that.

"You OK?" I ask.

"She's messing up everything. I love him. I love him," she says into her arm, followed by a big sniff. "He's here to see me."

"Does this have to do with the library last week?"

Sarah stops mid-sob and lifts her head. Her forehead is red, her eyes are pink, and snot hangs from her nose. I realize that under her trench coat she's wearing that flowsy, skimpy blue dress that Jess had in her room the day after the accident—my wife's dress. It's far too big for her. "I don't know anything about it. I wasn't there. Really. I don't know anything. Nothing at all."

"Sarah," I ask, "have you ever heard the line 'Me thinks she doth protest too much'?" I can't tell you how pleased I am to use the only line of Shakespeare I know besides "To be or not to be," "Get thee to a nunnery," and "Toil and spoil and boil" or something like that, thanks to my eleventh grade teacher and the lines we had to remember. "That's Shakespeare and if he were here he would say you're hiding something."

At this point Sarah gets pretty flustered—the name Shakespeare and some pretty insightful questioning from your best friend's dad can do that

221

to a thirteen year old. She runs her palms down the dress as if to pull it over her bent knees and toward her ankles. But even in the face of a dad and Shakespeare she hesitates, seems to be reviewing some options, which I admire, she doesn't want to hurt her friend with the truth.

A muffled cheer, a distant gulp of breath, and then an even louder cheer.

"She left with a boy."

"The Baker?"

Sarah cocks her head, her eyes seem as if they want to go in two different directions, and it's obvious that this is a name that is not supposed to be common knowledge.

"He called," I inform her, "for Jess."

"He called?" Her body stiffens. "He wouldn't do that."

"Right after that night on Jones Street. And again last night."

She swears and then covers her mouth.

"Is that who she's with right now?"

She nods in slow motion and then puts her head back on her arm. She begins to cry again with renewed vigor.

"Stay right here. Don't move," I tell her. "And don't ruin my wife's dress."

She gasps. Now it is Jess's and the Baker's turn to gasp.

As I trot toward the rink, the buzzer sounds the end of the first period. The pimply kid makes me show him my ticket stub. The scoreboard shows zero-zero. The teams clear the ice and the walls are pulled back and the Zamboni starts to make its rounds. I see Rudd cross the rink in full gear to the bench with his teammates. None of them look at him. Most people are stretching their legs and hitting the concession. When I find Jess, the boy is gone and instead she's standing next to Nancy, who is tugging at her silk scarf.

"Nice hair," Jess and her bandaged nose greet me.

"Where is he?" I ask.

222

"Who?"

"You know who."

"Rudd?"

"Nancy, did you get to meet him?"

Nancy raises her hands in a plea: "Anyone else want some coffee? or a soda?"

As Nancy escapes toward the concession, Jess tries to get away too. But I block her path. Some joker in the opponent's getup looks our way and I bring Jess over to a section that has emptied.

"Who was that?"

"It's something called a boy. You spell it b-o—"

"Was that the Baker?"

"The Baker?"

"Don't lie anymore."

"What?"

"Sarah told me everything about the night at the library."

No response. Nothing. Her expression is as blank as her bandage.

"Jess, what did you do?"

"What did I do?" She just needs warming up: Jess's eyes are now burning holes into my toes. I feel the burn. That's why I know I'm right.

"Where is she?"

"You can't keep running from this. You can't blame Sarah. She's only trying to help."

"Rudd disappears for five minutes and everyone goes crazy." She reaches into her jacket and pinches at her shirt under her arm. "You've got me, Dad. You caught me. Rudd's got me. Everyone knows who I was with and what happened. So can I go now?"

"What happened?"

"We baked"

"Jessica."

"Jess!"

223

"Where is he, Jess?"

"Dad, I was just. . .really, I. . ."

"Where is he?"

"Are you going to punch him too?"

"I just might," I say.

"Fine! Right there." She points. I follow her finger to her mother. My wife waves an everything-OK-over-there wave and I wave back and everything's fine. Jill Dart has found her and seems to still be talking. When I turn, Jess is gone. I fell for the oldest trick in the book.

I watch her speed out the door, brushing past Nancy and her coffee. A few red and whites and gold and greens point toward Jess as she runs. The world is all about sides. Nancy turns her head to watch her go and then to me. I shrug, Nancy points after her, I nod, and Nancy does a one-eighty and disappears back into the corridor. My wife across the ice checks her phone as the woman keeps talking to her.

I turn and there's Morgan an arm's length away from me. This perpetual half smile is even too much for me. When he's got his hands in your guts, is he smiling like that too?

"I'm so glad we don't have a girl," he says, drinking from a bottle of water they don't sell here; by the name of it, they don't sell in the U.S. I can't help looking at Burty still high up next to Tina with the hundred dollars stretched between his hands.

"They broke the mold with those two," he says following my eyes. "What happened to just being a kid?"

"I was just thinking the same thing."

"Your girl, the one with the bandage? If I had a girl I'd want her just like that."

Do I have to be worried about this guy and my daughter now?

"You didn't see it?"

"What?"

"That guy she was with before you came over. She was giving him an earful. The poor kid slinked away. It was better than the game. She was letting him have it. You don't have to worry about her. A tough cookie."

I'm trying to recalculate the night at the library with this new information, but Morgan won't let me do it.

"I wouldn't mind another kid. But Rachel says no way."

He looks at me.

"You guys are done, right?"

"Done?" Rachel and I just seem to be getting started.

"With kids? Anymore on the way?"

"Ohhhh!" I say, considering the Yoo-hoos my wife drank this afternoon, thinking about her being better than all right. I am really about to answer when he starts up again.

"Two I could handle. Three, you're outnumbered. I know that. . ."

Again, I'm about to respond, but he keeps on talking about families and size and somehow diverts to bicycle riding and asking me if I want to go on a ride with him when the weather gets better and I might have nodded yes even though I don't have a bicycle and really all I can concentrate on is his water which he drinks pathologically often and I'm not even thinking about that so much but trying to figure out how the water could be chemically altered to look clearer than water even through a bottle. If his eyes ever met mine he'd see my conscience is as clear as his water.

"I hope you don't take what Rachel did to you today personally?" he says. "I mean. I hope it doesn't affect the kids."

Again, I'm about to speak as he takes another drink.

"That's why I brought Burty here tonight because Rachel seemed to think they shouldn't play together anymore. So when Burty said Tina's brother was playing in the big game tonight I knew we had to come. I want to send a message that there's work and there's friendship. And what she revealed today is important to our community, but I do feel for you man. I wouldn't want to be you."

On the other side of the rink, still on the top bleacher, Tina's laughing and Burty's trying not to laugh but the bill is shaking. I wouldn't put it past Burty to have glued it to his fingers.

Morgan is staring at me even as he sips from his water. I just don't know what to do about this guy whose wife's lips were on mine within the last thirty minutes.

So I do the only sensible thing I can to put a stop to this conversation. I root through my pocket and just as he polishes off his water I hand him Regina Samsonetti's card. It seems to be even waterproof. He's staring at it and I don't know what he makes of it, his expression didn't change and maybe he's got people handing him business cards all day and he thought this was me giving him a number so we could go ride. Maybe he needs one of those scopes to see what's right in front of him. And finally I bow out because the game is just beginning again and I should go sit next to my wife. Morgan follows.

"Everything OK over there?" my wife asks. Jill Dart must have returned to her seat.

"Just trying to play diplomat. Jess and Sarah got into some sort of fight."

"That boy?"

"Not sure."

"She let him have it."

"I heard. They going to put Rudd in?" I ask.

"Yep," she says.

"You all caught up with your old friend?"

My wife turns to me and gives a twinge of a smile as she shakes her head. "I still can't place her."

"Well, you certainly have fans out there, a lot of them."

Morgan doesn't sit down when he comes back. He said Rachel just texted him and they should head home. His half-smile is gone when Burty won't budge from his seat. Morgan actually has to drag him away from Tina. Once they're down the steps, Morgan tells him something and Burty stands right up and he doesn't even wave to Tina one last time. I swear the kid is almost skipping. Morgan can't help it that it is hard to like surgeons and hard to like people with Porsches and hard to like people who hydrate with fancy water, and hard to like a parent who bribes his kid. He just happens to be all four—I mean you have to feel for the guy. It must not be easy for someone like him to have a son like Burty—I'd probably resort to bribery too.

Tina doesn't look happy up high. I wave her down but she does that full-body shake she's been doing since she's been a year old. People settle down around us. My wife pats my thigh and leaves her hand on it. I put my hand on top of hers. We watch as the red and whites take it right up the ice and shoot. Rudd deflects it and now it seems as if there's twenty people behind the net. I worry for Rudd. That his head might not be in the game. But my worries are misplaced as he catches a puck that deflects from a pile of blades and ricochets off some padded knee.

"How do you think he got Burty to do a 180?"

"Ferrari when he's sixteen," my wife replies too fast, smiles and takes her hand off my thigh so she can slip her arm through mine and pull me a bit closer.

My head begins to swim with all the possibilities. This jovial spirit is not in my reaction scenarios. I'm not sure what to do: "I better go get Jess."

"She's fine," my wife says, holding me in place. "Nancy knows what to do. I gave her a lot of practice." Rudd skates far out of the goal to say something to the defender and she stares at the empty goal for a moment.

"Jess wasn't exactly telling the truth about the library," I say. I'm proud of myself. I've done it.

"I know. I haven't *quite forgiven* you for that yet."

"You know?" I'm a little bummed. This is my big moment.

"You drive me nuts, Doug?" she says after our team gets close to the goal and makes nothing of it but a shot that goes wide—the crowd howls. "I don't know why in the world you didn't say anything. Mary Beth was telling me about how worried you were, how she hadn't seen Jess at all, how you were trying to call her and she kept hanging up. Why would you let her lie to me and not tell me!" She swallows. "You of all people let this get blown out of proportion. Why in the world would you cover for Jess?"

I'm speechless. All I can do is a slow motion nod and gaze at the lines and circles on the ice. Somehow that safe that's been falling my way the last couple of days stops in midair. It refuses to fall. There's no indication that Mary Beth said anything about Rachel being in the car. After all this, I still don't know if my wife has a full picture of the car that night. I vow to never turn in another book late.

"I should have believed in you more." She squeezes my hand.

"No, I've been handling this poorly."

"You're freezing." She takes my hand and lays it on her thigh and covers it with her hand. This makes me even more speechless. "You have to admit, you don't make it easy."

"It was really terrible that night, I couldn't find her," I say. "I just wanted her to fix things on her own. I don't know what I was thinking."

My wife soaks this in and squeezes my wrist and nods.

I nod too and take a deep breath and then take a quick glimpse of her belly—which reveals nothing under her jacket—before returning my eyes to hers: "The boy she was with, I think he was a part of it."

"I don't know how we're ever going to get the truth out of her." She moves her hand from my wrist to my hand. I stare at her two wedding bands—the cheap one when we eloped and the pricier one when we could afford it—she still hasn't quite forgiven me for tossing out my original. The thing that has been between us is suddenly lifted and we're back to what we were.

Rudd plays that night better than he has ever played. Usually he's a statue in the net, only making the save at what seems like that last possible second with the bare minimum of movement—reaching out with his glove, dropping to his knees, or slanting his stick in the smallest degree. But tonight he's physical; he's all over the place. He moves his body this way and that, so it seems as if he's going to split in half, but always at the last minute some elastic force snaps him back into one piece. He certainly takes after his old man.

Nancy appears with Jess behind her. I spot Sarah with her head down in the corridor just outside the rink, still trying to make my wife's dress longer, her trench coat unbuttoned and falling off her shoulders. Jess zooms right past us and sits up top with Tina, who is delighted. Nancy tells us that she's going to drive Sarah home and she hopes she'll make it back for the end. My wife asks some questions about the fight, but Nancy doesn't know much or at least doesn't reveal much. My wife looks back at Jess and Tina as she thanks her mother. My wife's eyes lock onto Jess's just long enough for her to know the jig is up. And do you know what Jess does in response? She pulls Tina into her in a sideways hug and tickles her underarms. Tina is even more delighted. On Jess's face there's a beaming smile. I'm about to get up but my wife puts her hand on my knee. "It's Rudd's night," she says.

Rudd is awesome and Rudd's team is terrible. You don't even have to watch the game to see how badly Rudd's team is doing—you can just tell from how red Ernie's and Coach Bernard's faces are, how raspy their voices by the third period. The coaches are chewing out the players one by one as they come off their waves and then turning around and giving them desperate pep talks before they are sent back out. The wings are arguing with the defense, the star center, Corey Bolby who is on a free ride to Dartmouth, is spending all his time trying to do everyone's but Rudd's job. A two-man team. Pucks keep flying at my son like birds into a jet engine and he's stopping every one of them. But the inevitable is bound to happen and finally it does. The score is a ricochet off a team-mate's skate. It is impossible to block, even though Rudd gets damn close to getting his stick on it. 0-1. The other side of the rink is buzzing.

Still 0-1, as the third period winds down, the discord on our team rises to a pitch as the left wing, Arnold Fibich, checks his own teammate, defender Junior Herbert, while the puck is out of play and then proceeds to lay into him. The refs don't know what to do. My wife is still holding me close, no discord here. Coach Bernard sends another wave in and Fibich and Herbert go at it in the box. My wife covers her mouth. The Greylock spectators begin to boo. Our side is dead quiet. Coach Bernard looks to be a candidate for pulmonary thrombosis. Ernie has his hands behind his neck as if he's stuck in the middle of a standing sit-up. It's taking all his willpower not to jump in and try to fix the game himself.

And then not two minutes later, the impossible happens. Rudd clears the puck to Bolby, who takes it up the ice as if he's skating between cardboard figures. Before anyone can react, his stick is drawn back. Slapshot! The puck nests in the upper right-hand side of the net for a split-second before it drops and the little blue siren blares. Our half of the bleachers goes wild. Even my wife leaps into the air. Tied! Discord or not there are two minutes left and our team is on a roll—well, Rudd and Bolby at least.

And when there doesn't seem to be anything else that could top Bolby's beautiful goal, with 1:12 left on the clock, the Greylock red and whites have a breakaway and the THS defenders are smoked again, and 02 and 15 are teaming it with the same passes and fakes they'd been showing off all night. The puck looks as if it is going to the left corner but instead drops onto the ice right in front of Rudd, who has blocked something like sixty shots so far, forcing him to readjust his own trajectory and he comes down too late with both knees. This time the red siren blares behind Rudd and my stomach drops and I feel the weight of loss. Cheers and moans balance the scales. My wife and I look at each other, maybe a moment of disappointment in our son, which is just an unavoidable gut response, and then a merged sympathy for him.

"You almost got it," I'm pretty sure I hear Jess yell.

But more surprises. A late whistle. A ref waving his arms. A conference. A screaming coach. Boos from the red and whites. An offside call. The goal is invalid. We still have a chance! Heckles and jeers. I hear the father in front of me say, "Bad call, but we'll take it."

"Was he offside?" My wife asks.

"He must have been," I answer.

"Something doesn't feel right," she observes as Rudd skates across the ice to talk to the ref. "What's he doing?"

"I'm sure he's complimenting the ref on his good call."

Number 15, Gregory Leiper, the one who has been called offside, is now with the ref and gesticulating wildly at Rudd as the ref keeps shaking his head. Rudd still has his mask down but I can tell he's talking. The ref points back at the goal. A bunch of Rudd's teammates try to pull Rudd away from the ref. My wife looks at me and I shrug. I have no idea. Leiper keeps shaking his head. Blowing into his whistle a final warning, the ref sends the players back to their positions. The point is removed from the scoreboard and I cheer along with the rest of my fellow gold and greens. What the ref says goes.

Luckily for that one ref's homelife and business (I believe he's a mortician), it's the next shot with ten seconds to go that is the one that no one will forget. THS is actually keeping the puck down in Greylock territory, finally pulling themselves together like the team they can be. But Leiper gets it again and I see him actually look up at the clock as if to confirm the countdown chant from our side that is rocking the rink: "Ten, nine, eight. . ." His shot looks to be one of those half-hearted attempts, blind and without any hope as it slides at a turtle's pace across the ice. It looks so hopeless that half the crowd is already headed to the concession stand to prepare for overtime. I don't know why none of the defenders try to stop it, maybe it is the pure hopelessness of the shot that makes both teams ignore it. The puck continues on toward Rudd who is staring at it so hard I swear I can see his eyes through those tiny slots in his mask. The puck comes nearer and Rudd is standing there, straight up and down, not in the goalie hunch. The puck gets closer and Rudd still doesn't move (is he back to his old delayed ways?). He is showing some bravado, no problem, showing how good he is, how confident he is that he can stop this dud of a puck. It gets closer and closer and Rudd does not move, and he still does not move, does not put down his stick, as the puck slides by his skate and across the line into the net and the red siren lights up just as the buzzer sounds. Rudd's teammates, who are so confident in the shot's outcome that they are pumping their fists and skating into each other, excited to prove themselves in overtime, but nobody else in the arena, for more than a few seconds, nobody, nobody cheers or moans or moves or whispers, not even Gregory Leiper.

Of all that happened tonight, that is what I will remember most, that for a moment there is no sound at all—that moment of potential, a place with no explanation. I stay in that moment for a long time, longer than slow motion. I stay there before the squeeze of my wife's hand and her words that hung in the air, "What did he do?"; before the cackle, the disbelief, the half-cheers, the jeers; before the Greylock bench clears and piles atop Gregory Leiper; and before the THS bench all look at each other for explanations as their teammates on the ice fall to their backs and put their gloved hands over their faces. Rudd standing there taller than he has ever stood before, watching the trail of the puck just as if it were one of his trains that had just disappeared around a bend, and it is only in the replay that I notice Rudd's mask is flipped back, I see his black eye, I see the glitter of the lights reflected in his glasses. This boy whose name I had transformed on the day of his birth does not seem horrified or miserable at the goal he had let slip by.

As his teammates with angry cries skate toward him, he breaks from whatever stupor he's in and flips down his mask and assumes his goalie position as if his teammates are all pucks—Bolby, his stick up, leading the charge.

27

You should have seen my wife the next morning in the darkness of our bedroom. Her body is wrapped in the blankets that tuck perfectly beneath her chin. Her body so soft and relaxed. One arm hides under the blankets and the other arm—bare from her T-shirt sleeve—bent delicately at her side, her palm and its tangle of lines facing up, her fingers curled. The blankets outlining her breasts, the outward curve of her hips, down to the smooth stones of her knees. I'm pretty sure she never put on her panties or pajama bottoms after we finished last night and it leaves me wishing I'd checked before getting out of bed. I know not to mess with a good thing. Her toes rise at the end of the bed like two serene peaks. But her eyelids, you'd have to see them up close— like two gentle purses lightly clasped by her lashes. The conches of her ears are half absorbed in her pillow. Her forehead, calm and curved and unwrinkled. Her dark hair pushed back, streaming out from the pillow in the odd strands of sleep. The rise and round of her nose. Her lips slightly parted, locked in a whisper of breath.

I track two fingers gently, gently across each thick eyebrow, down along her cheek, graze the ridges of her ears, glide beneath her smooth jawline to her chin, across those lips, so lightly, then just barely skim my fingers along the tip of her nose, which has always brought (and I hope will always bring) a small smile to her sleeping lips; then I lean over her, careful not to bump her body or shake the bed. I'm pushing my luck and know I should just hit the bathroom before work, but I can't restrain myself—I lay my lips onto hers, just lightly, just for a pause of her warm breath (I'm holding mine), and those lips respond and hold me there an extra moment. . .That's a start to a good day, that's your wife giving you a new beginning.

Weather is everything. I'm no meteorologist, but I can wake up knowing the barometric pressure is just right. And this morning as I tiptoe toward the bathroom, having just kissed, having made love last night (sure, it was a bit awkward but we were back in the saddle—that is what's important), I know there are new adventures ahead of me, new adventures for our family, and everything is going to be all right, better than all right. "Even though summer and fall are our main draws," my boss used to say from behind his desk at the Pontoosuc Tourism Bureau, "spring is what we should aim for." He didn't have to tell me that, I already knew.

The people at Dial soap should have been filming me in the shower—all lather and energy. After I suit up, Tina is leaning against the wall at the top of the stairs. She's wearing her green pajamas. I pretend I don't see her as I approach and just as I'm about to pass her I swoop her up in a giant bear hug and then put her back down. If you could hold the perfect barometric pressure in your arms, it would be a lot like holding Tina.

"How you doing, pal?" I ask in a whisper as I readjust my tie. "Razzamatazzle?"

"Razzamatazzle." Her pajama toes are pointed at each other. "Do you know what the saddest sound in the world is?"

A joke. What a perfect time for a joke. "No clue."

"A chained dog howling at the moon."

I don't get it, but I laugh anyway and give her a little punch in the arm. "That's a good one."

She gives me a punch back, but kisses her hand first.

As I start down the stairs, she acts as if she's headed to the bathroom, but when she thinks I'm not watching, she sneaks across the hall to our bedroom. I don't understand why she thinks it has to be a secret, but I don't mind. I get a picture of my wife scooting on her pajama bottoms as Tina makes her way under the covers. It's a great way for my wife to wake up: kiss from the hubby and a snuggle from the youngest.

In the kitchen, which is dark except for the stove light, Rudd's up extra early, a shadow at the table. He spoons cereal into his mouth.

"How you doing, kid?"

"All right."

"Wonderful. Should I shed some light on the situation?" When the overhead light comes on, to my relief, Rudd doesn't look mad or depressed or scared or even angelic—not even a mythic figure in front of a net, he just looks like a groggy teenager before school. Throw the county championships? No problem! Piled on by your angry teammates so your slip-sliding assistant coach along with your slip-sliding parents, and a smattering of the opposing team try to rescue you? No problem! Catch your dad kissing a TV reporter? Kissing who?

Next to the coffeemaker there's a glass jar with construction paper taped to it. I'm sure it wasn't there last night. I pick it up and spin it to read the word written in thin capital letters: TRUSTFUND. My heart sinks for one-tenth of a second because I think this is a message from Rudd and that maybe there is a problem, but just as quickly my heart lifts because I'm a hundred percent sure that it is Jess's writing on the jar. I put it down just the way I found it. When I dump yesterday's coffee grounds in the garbage can, there's a strong scent and a strong color of spaghetti sauce. Jess came down in the middle of the night, cleared out a brand new jar of sauce and wrote this? That's incredible. I don't know

236

what it means but I know it's a leap for her—she's reaching out. She's taking the first step. Amazing.

After I get the coffee going, I sit opposite Rudd and pour my cereal and reach across the table to empty the box into Rudd's bowl. He waves away the milk carton I tilt in his direction. Instead he stirs the dry flakes into the milk already in his bowl. The coffee maker gasps and I take two mugs out of the cabinet, what the heck! I pour Rudd a little coffee and place it in front of him.

"You want milk with that?" I ask as I admire his black eye. I don't need to ask about it. He probably had some other bruises too. I do try to connect his black eye with the Baker's bandage. I wonder if his strange behavior yesterday wasn't so much for the green-haired girl but some brotherly response to save his sister.

"I don't know," Rudd says, a bit stunned. He watches as I put milk and sugar in mine.

"I'll just have it plain." He takes a sip as if it is his first alcoholic beverage and puts the mug down right away.

"Did you burn your tongue?"

"No."

We're just two guys eating breakfast at the break of day. There's a couple of things, miscues, we witnessed last night, but we've moved on. I'm picturing us going out to take care of animals in a barn or jacking up a tractor. I'm almost done with my cereal when Rudd looks over at me: "Dad?"

I take a deep breath and nod. Here it comes. I misread our morning, but I'm ready for it.

"I was wondering. . .I was wondering if—" He looks me right in the eye and I can't think of the last time we looked at each other this way. He's a strong kid and I do my best to show my own strength in my eyes. Ask away kid, I try to tell him, I can handle anything from kisses to ASSASSINS.

237

He drops his eyes and studies the milk in his bowl. He shakes his head to himself.

"Don't be shy. Ask me."

"Dad, I was wondering about, wondering about. . .chest hair. I—"

I almost jump out of my chair to hug the boy. My family is amazing. If we were rubber balls we Merits would have a whole lot of bounce.

"Chest hair," I tell him (I am still the father, I still have advice and guidance to give), "chest hair is a great idea, but someone didn't see it all the way through. Because if you have chest hair then you have hair on your back, and if there is one place you and the women who will love you don't want you to have hair is on your back or for that matter your backside. Smoothness, Rudd, smoothness is key. The men with chest hair just try to fool themselves that it is better and more masculine. It's a pitch. They're trying to cover up about their back hair. You can't be one-sided—you have to look all the way around an issue." I check Rudd's face. He is interested in what I'm saying but he also looks concerned, the expression he gets when he can't figure out why one of his railroad track switches is malfunctioning. I'm not too sure about the state of Rudd's body hair (he never did show me his bruises from the accident). I'd bought him an electric razor a year ago and showed him how to wield it, but within the month he had sent his mother for disposable razors and cream. I scan his forearms where his sleeves are pushed up, but no fur. I check around his shirt collar and don't see any hair there. Just in case, I add: "Hey, maybe I'm a bit sour grapes. I know for a fact that hair works for some women. A real turn on. So no matter if you have a hairy body or not, there's someone out there for you no matter what. That's the good news. I mean look at me and your mother, we found each other, we worked against the odds."

Rudd doesn't even turn red. He gets it that I'm telling him what he saw last night was nothing. He's also clearly getting that I don't know what exactly he did last night but I'm super proud of him anyway. He gulps down the rest of the coffee he hasn't touched since his first sip and from the gleam in his eyes I can tell I've hit the right note with my son. He is dazzled and delighted and relieved. He knows we remain one happy family.

With my raincoat folded over my wrist, my umbrella snugly secure under my arm, my briefcase in one hand and my extra cup of joe in the other, I'm out the door. I'm brimming. Above me the clouds are clearing and the sky is brightening on all sides. The tension between the high- and low-pressure systems has dissolved, leaving the air cleansed and brilliantly new. The image of my wife in bed this morning, the way she smiled when I touched her nose, and the way her lips felt on mine—but it isn't just my wife. I communed with Tina and I gave my son some food for thought without embarrassing him. My only regret is that I didn't run into Jess—I don't know what might have happened but it would've been great. As it was, I put a dollar in the TRUSTFUND jar, why not? I can picture the split second of bliss on her face when she sees her jar has money in it—sometimes that is all it takes to get a positive ball rolling. I breathe in the gorgeous air. I wrap the umbrella in my raincoat and leave both on the back step along with the newspaper—I don't even need to look at the headlines: Heartbreaking last second loss. GE Town-Hall Meeting Called. Mayor Under Pressure. Candle Kids. And splashed on the whole top of the split page: Family Pulls Together!

I cross the street before I reach Gazook, let the dog rest. But he's up, staring through the fence at me. He doesn't bark. The first time ever. I give him a hardy wave. I must be exuding positivity even on the dog whistle frequency. Under the streetlamps and along the damp sidewalk, I whistle all the way past the cemetery as the occasional car headlight streams my shadow along the stone wall. Down the road the playground is empty. I'm tempted to go over and shift the balance of the seesaw by bringing the side that is on the ground up into the air, but I don't want to miss my bus. I also note that with the better weather Tina and I need to hightail it down here and have some fun. Maybe instead of Burty and Rachel, we can play with Gazook here. We could bring a Frisbee or tennis ball.

The bus. I don't know why I've never done this before. I am free from the automobile. The registry and the courts can't take it away from me because I'd beaten them to the punch. Maybe inspired by Rudd last night, I dropped my temporary license in the trash. For me there would be no more shortcuts, no more tight parking spots, no more sitting behind the steering wheel, no more quick decisions at yellow lights, no more awkward moments at four-way stops, no more possibilities of the police ramming into me, no more heading up to Jones Street and driving slowly by the houses that offered no clues to what Jess had been doing that night.

I stop for a moment and watch the slouched drones driving their cars to work. Poor bastards. This is a big opportunity for my life to slow down. In fact, for our whole family's life to slow down, particularly my wife's. She won't have to try to cram everything in anymore. And in an effort to keep my wife's new life as simple as possible, I truly look forward to taking the bus to work this morning and every morning after, whether it will continue to be GE or, worst-case scenario Seven-Eleven or Target—if Jimmy Tripoli is to be believed. I'd be happy either way. Although I'd just be getting ready to hit the snooze button in my old schedule, I'm now able to number myself among the conscientious users of public transportation. I'm doing my part. I'm ready. I take five quarters from my pocket and squeeze them in my hand.

On the bus, looking through my own reflection, I fantasize that I'll see my whole family at the front door of our house cheering me on, but instead I see that our house has been the victim of a toilet-papering so substantial that I spend the rest of the ride trying to figure out how I didn't notice as I walked right through it.

28

If I liked worms I'd have my choice of them at work. The parking lots are nearly empty. The protesters have cleared out of the front entrance. There's an eighteen-wheeler backed up to the rear entrance. Maybe I would have to share the worms: two guys with dollies are clanking files down the stairs. Then there's a new guard who checks my ID and my briefcase and when I ask him if we're moving our offices and then wonder aloud if "our files are going for a little drive," the poor guy gives me a genuinely puzzled look. When he finally gets to bed and wakes up before the night shift, I hope he'll have a "morning" like my own.

I pass by the archives and the room is nearly empty. I must be wearing body armor today because the toilet papering and the archives removal don't even dent my mood. Plus once I get upstairs I've got competition. I have to up my game. Ted the Guatemalan custodian is vacuuming around the cubicles as if he's doing the Macarena. His smile outshines mine, but he has gold teeth. I don't want to get in the way of the second happiest guy in the world, so I head into the quiet of conference room B.

Jimmy Tripoli is sitting in there, leaning back in one of the padded chairs, his feet up on the sill that extends the length of the room. He's in his shirtsleeves and stocking feet. The knot in his tie is so stretched that he could slip it right over his head. His hand is in a bag of popcorn. He's asleep. Catching a guy like Tripoli sleeping feels indecent. He's just an innocent puffball. I should snap a picture of him and pass it around the office, put it on the Web. But I'm not that kind of guy. I look out the long rectangle of a window, out at what's left of GE. Almost the opposite view from the lake the other night. I still don't know why we ordered the cancellation of the Frisbee golf especially now that GE seems to have been one of the main supporters of the mayor's passion. What new information could Rachel possibly have? As I back out of the room, Tripoli resettles and the chair complains.

At my desk is a stack of quarterlies. Research? I pop over Sam's cubicle wall and there's his stack in the middle of all the photos of his wife. I suspected the photos would be all face down, but there they are still in full display. In another cubicle and another and another, piles of quarterlies. We're steeping ourselves in the company's books? Profit and loss? How is this going to help us prepare for the town-hall meeting?

Instead of sitting at my desk, I empty trashcans for Ted. He's delighted! I'm feeling better already. I'm back on track. I stop Ted and gesture to the vacuum. It is a heavy vacuum, metal, the weight of it is stunning, vacuuming with a stick attached to a boulder, who knew they actually still made vacuums with a bag that droops from the handle and fills with air. I get into the groove of it and I even raise one arm like I'm riding a bucking bronco. Ted is amazed that I've mastered this machine so quickly. When I hear clapping, I look up and there's Jimmy Tripoli, a shadow with the bright sun behind him. He looks like he's coated with smoke. He's the one that's clapping, his elbow pinches the bag of popcorn at his side.

"Good to see you're thinking about the future," he yells over the noise.

I smile because he's right. Maybe not the bathrooms, but this, the vacuuming, I've got it covered. I keep vacuuming. I outlast Tripoli who watches me for a while but disappears into his office when I show him I'm unflappable. He can think what he wants but it's not me. It is so tempting to just drop those three letter in front of him. PCX. But it would only confirm his belief that I'm the trouble. A trail of popcorn follows him to his office. Really? Ted's smile doesn't last as long as mine. I vacuum the popcorn trail, leaving a few kernels at his door. On second thought, I can do the bathroom. I can do anything. I vacuum up those last kernels without even banging against the door. No problem.

29

And really, as the days go by, *no problem* characterizes almost everything; and really *things* are *better than OK*:

1) Sure both Rudd and I are fielding some death threats, but it turns out that Nancy has a boyfriend, a police officer, none other than my favorite cop, Ray Roy. There's nothing he can do about the threats and the nightly TPing, but he does promise to have a patrol car check us out regularly. At school Rudd uses the bathroom in the office for his own protection. And really the death threats are suffocated by the amount of girls calling him. It's dumbfounding and inspiring. Black eye? We didn't ask. Boys will be boys, right? Of course he's taking the most reasonable course of action by retreating to his trains once more and stunningly has never asked what apocalypse had visited his miniature world. He just rolled up his sleeves and got to work. He's taking after his father.

2) Jess is doing her duty as the stereotypical teenager. When Karen and I confronted her, she seemed to gather herself up behind her bandaged nose—a bandage the doctor says could be taken off by now. I believe her exact quote was: "Pick on someone your own size." But what can

we do? You can't force the truth out of someone; and knowing Jess she might have already convinced herself that she was telling the truth! Her TRUSTFUND jar defies logic by the day as it is stuffed with more and more cash—as if her complete silence conjures dollar bills (and how in the world does she resist emptying the jar?).

3) As for Tina, much to my relief, she has a new best friend. Gazook. It should be a Norman Rockwell painting, those two sitting at our back step side by side. Tina lifting the flap of his ear to whisper and in reply Gazook licking her face. Nick and Naomi pay her a premium, the going rate for babysitters, but she won't take the money (they give it to me to put in her piggy bank). She hasn't said a word about going to Burty's house or Burty having a playdate over here.

4) As for me, my official license revocation was a sham and unnecessary, and as I told the board, I had already torn up my license and didn't plan to drive in the near future. It was an eloquent speech, clearly causing some members to question their decision, but I was going to see my plan through. Also I showed that I know how to compromise and do what is best for my family. My plea-bargain for oodles of community service hours on reduced charges was best for everyone even though I certainly feel we would have won in front of a jury. I look good in dayglo orange, I like vests, and when it starts in a month, I'm sure I will find immense satisfaction in keeping the roadsides clean. Not to mention the cool tools you get to use.

5) At work, the whole office flips through the quarterlies all day with no clear plan and no clear explanation. None of us are doing logistics for the town-hall meeting, none of us are given any more information other than what we could glean from recordings of Rachel's broadcast and the news reports that followed, and none of us feel like we are going

to have a job the day after the town-hall meeting. I have daily one-on-one time with Tripoli. I can say with certainty that my office mates look upon these meetings with suspicion. Jason the Kid, unconsulted in his conference room office, has that feel of the boy who thinks he has the nicest soccer ball in the neighborhood but can't get anyone to play. What are my colleagues missing? Me sitting in a chair as Tripoli paces back and forth reciting baseball statistics. I can't even tell anyone because who would believe me? There's one thing for sure: the guy does know a lot about baseball.

6) Rachel is still making her rounds on national news venues and hasn't released any new information, and as I predicted the news story on our side of things has deflated. The town-hall meeting has taken the heat off us. It also has helped that Mayor Dugus has gone missing—the speculation of what happened to him grips the community. Nobody has seen him since Rachel's revelations. Even his Frisbee golf team who was confident he'd reappear for the tournament in Syracuse last weekend soon reported that he did not show up—his first ever missed tournament in a decade.

7) There are no green-haired girls with ASSASSINS signs, and the PCB crowd can only muster a few people a couple times a week to picket, even as Guy the Environmental Guy writes scathing posts on his blog. But are their fiery comments condemning GE after each of his posts? No! The only comments he gets are threats from the worldwide beaver-loving community—the Trustee is not alone.

8) And the only real form of protest that's directly affecting me is the nightly TPing of our house. And even that is no problem. It has become an aspect of my marriage that is *better than OK*. After the first few days of outrage and calls to Ray Roy and looking up surveillance camera

246

prices, Karen and I have settled in to a nightly ritual, a date night of sorts. We pull the sofa sections close to the front windows, close enough that we can rest our feet on the sill. We cover ourselves with a blanket and she'll tell me about her day at Nancy's store and speculate about her mom all hot and heavy with Ray Roy (I'm surprised she's not more protective of her father's memory, but, hey, we're all moving on around here!). When she asks, I am honest as I can be about the preparations for the town-hall meeting without going into details about how my coworkers seem to hate me or about the contents of my daily briefing with Tripoli, which she is maybe a bit too excited about and calls a real opportunity; and the thing is, it is an opportunity because when this one town-hall meeting defines the New GE and reverberates worldwide, my future will be assured—(or worst case scenario I can parlay my new baseball knowledge into a career change).

As we sit there, we polish off two or three Yoo-hoos a night. Our next dentist appointments will be filled with cavities, but drinking them together—as we once did during her pregnancies—as we watch for vindictive teenagers armed with toilet paper is honestly the high point of each day and arguably all these nights together are becoming the high point of my life so far. Each night we'd grow quiet and then head to bed thinking they've finally got bored of it, only to find in the morning that they have struck again. But for the last three nights my wife has fallen asleep right here on the sofa, my arm around her. Tonight as she started to drift off she told me that she'd been talking to Regina Samsonetti on the phone and that she thinks that the first session should be with the whole family. I nod in agreement. The way *things* have been, we'll go through the door and Samsonetti will turn us right around and say, "Give me a family with real problems."

Tonight, just as with the two previous ones, with my wife sleeping next to me at our sofa command post, I watch as five to seven teenagers, who I do not recognize and who seem to be different from the ones the night before, go about their work of TPing. They are just showing another way of Activating!, doing their homework. The stealth they demonstrate, the sheer joy of transgression, the power of their silent throws are all something to behold as I run my fingers through my wife's hair and take the last swigs from my Yoo-hoo.

30

Family therapy's scheduled for 1:12—unorthodox but according to my wife (who seems to be more of an expert on her than Sam), at least Regina Samsonetti is someone who "thinks outside *the line*." At work, I tell everyone, even Sam, that I'm stepping out for a teacher conference about my daughter. In the corporate world therapy is publicly applauded and privately condemned, I'm sure, so with my job already on its last thread until the meeting I can't take any chances. On my way out, Jimmy Tripoli seems in too good a mood and he says, "Merit, I have to give you credit" and instead of telling me what for he guffaws and slaps me on the back so anyone watching would think we are best buddies—just what I need for the next hour, a red tattoo of Jimmy's palm print. My smile is bursting.

In the parking lot, my wife is already waiting in the Pontiac. Now with therapy soon to be crossed off, the family will be free and clear. I really get a sense that this is going to be a drive-by session. My wife has told her how good things are and just wants to parade us in front of her to show her it's true. I'm encouraged too because she picked me up first even though I'm closest to the therapist's office. After I snap my seatbelt,

I see right away, as her feet work the clutch and gas, she has on her blue slingbacks. This is the first time I've seen her without sneakers since she quit her job—and considering our history with those sneakers, it's exciting to see them gone.

As we loop through the neighborhoods of Capes close to her mother's, along Allendale, heading toward my shortcut to Benedict and Tina's school, my wife stops at a four-way stop and keeps letting cars go by, waving them on until we get a beep from behind. Karen steps on the gas and we plow through.

When we pick up Tina, there are four-leaf clovers markered on the back of each hand. She's still crazy for St. Patty's Day even though it's gone by. I have mixed feelings about a six-year-old worrying about luck. "Nice clovers," Karen says.

When we pull up to the back of THS, we catch Rudd with his face pretty close to a green-haired girl's face. My wife almost hits the car in front of us. They are sitting next to each other on the cement steps leading up to the door, and she has her palm on his knee. She does a quick awkward wave, pushes off his knee, and runs up the stairs, pausing with the door open to watch Rudd head to the car. She is certainly the ASSASSINS sign holder. Does she even realize who Rudd is? Does she draw the line between personal life and business? The clear devotion in her eyes stops my worry that Rudd is just part of some bigger protest plan.

"Don't give him a hard time," my wife says right when Rudd's hand connects with the door handle.

"Who me?" I'll fill her in on the details later about ASSASSINS.

Rudd's cheeks are burning through various shades of red by the time he swings into the seat after his backpack and immediately musses Tina's hair, which she appreciates.

"How'dey folks," Rudd says, giving his own PR smile. His glasses are cockeyed. There's not even a hint of his black eye anymore.

"She really likes St. Patty's Day," Tina observes, showing the clovers on the back of her hands to Rudd as she points to the girl.

I don't say it aloud but really, this family, our family, needs therapy? Com'on!

At North Middle School, my wife and I wait outside the office for the vice-principal to locate Jess. My wife keeps checking her watch. We're going to be late. The receptionist informs us that Jess has been found. Found? There has been some sort of incident. It certainly looks as if there has been some sort of incident as Jess and the vice principal come down the locker-filled corridor toward us. Mr. Banister is holding something in his hands. I believe I hear my wife gasp as Jess comes into better view—I know *I* gasp.

Jess is wearing jean shorts that might as well have been a bikini and a cut off shirt that exposes a wide swathe of her midriff. The sleeves are haphazardly scissored off along with the triangle of material that now exposes a plunging neckline—her shirt is barely covering her bra. Her bandaged nose is about the only thing on her that is covered. My wife let Jess go to school like this? The school let Jess go to school like this?

My wife's jaw is dropped and forward. She has a very emotive chin. I just wish it is this easy to figure out what it is emoting all the time. Meanwhile her eyes pierce Jess's heart, which isn't very hard to do since it is almost in full view: "She didn't leave looking like this."

Mr. Banister carries what I identify as Jess's sweater, two pant legs, and sections of cloth that matched Jess's top and outweighed it. When he is close enough, he hands these bits of clothing to me, and out of his back pocket pulls a pair of scissors with a broken blade, which I immediately identify as ours.

"Would you like to come right to my office?" he asks, poking the scissor handles my way. He is one of those balding men who are all ears. But the ears aren't for listening apparently as I struggle to make it clear that we can't have a conference right now because we are going to family

251

therapy. He's also talking about suspension and I try to reiterate that we're going to therapy and that's going to give our family a clean bill of health so suspension is completely not necessary. I look to my wife for help, but she is so consumed with anger right now that I stop everything and give a little blessing of thanks that I'm not the focus of this anger. I'm not sure if Mr. Banister and I are on the same wavelength, but we do seem to have come to some agreement. Maybe after therapy I'll call the school secretary and find out what it actually is.

As we head down the hall, I can't decide if Jess looks triumphant or dejected. It is a good thing that one way of demonstrating strong parent disapproval and disappointment is by pretending the child does not exist. As we pass by the lockers, I try to spot mine from my three years here. I still remember the combination: 14-28-14—back in a time when combinations were easy.

In the car, Rudd and Tina don't say a word, not a peep, which illustrates the gravity of the moment—not a barb, not a question, just stunned silence. I follow their cue. After I stick the scissors into the glove compartment, I fling the sweater over my shoulder so Jess can put it on once she realizes we aren't living in Miami. But Jess doesn't go for the sweater. She tries to hide her shivering, her goose bumps as my wife turns the heater on full blast—an action which surprises me because I'm sure the best strategy is to try to chill her into putting on some clothes. I wonder if my wife will make a pit stop at the house, but she turns left back toward downtown. Even if the Sunbird's turbocharged and every light is green we will be late.

I discover that the therapist's office is in the same building as the DMV—I thought it was just nearby, not in the same place where I had my hearing (*hearing* being ironic) where my six-month revocation was upheld—you even have to do paperwork and stand in line to get your license taken away. Regina Samsonetti must have some business sense to place her office upstairs at the DMV—she is sure to have a constant supply of patients. The DMV is a department that needs much better PR (I make a note of this as a possible opportunity in my future: "Take it from me, I know what the DMV was like, so I'm here to introduce the new DMV"). I already had my line ready for after therapy: "At least it was better than waiting in line at the DMV." We'll be on the floor laughing.

When my wife pulls into a space, I wouldn't be surprised if the therapist is taking notes from her fourth-floor window: *1:28 family pulls into parking lot sixteen minutes late. Scantily clad daughter with bandaged nose gets out of the car last as father holds door open for her and is not acknowledged or thanked. Wife goes up to husband and removes sweater from his shoulder and ties it around her waist. Family walks toward building respectful of one another's personal space.*

The people we pass on our way into the building look as if they have just failed their driver's exam. Some of the men seem to cheer up when they see my daughter, and I show considerable restraint not to get myself arrested for a real assault. Let the world leer while it can, not one bit of my daughter's skin will see daylight again until she's thirty-five. As a family we skip the elevator and look for the stairs—a family that exercises together is a family that's just fine. We pass a custodian who stops whistling (I check quickly to make sure Ted hasn't found a new job). It's not Ted. The slap of the mop sounds like sobs.

After we regroup at the top of the stairs, we find the foggy glass door with Samsonetti's name on it, followed by her alphabet of abbreviations, which I know erase every worry I have that this person is qualified to help our family. Yelling is coming through the door. My wife and I exchange looks, two people who don't know what they got themselves into, not just now but seventeen years ago. What *had* we been thinking? What *had* we gotten ourselves into? Sometimes you have to go all the way back and ask these sorts of questions. I bet it's a good way to prepare for the therapist.

The raised voices continue. I guess we aren't that late. Samsonetti doesn't run a tight ship. No receptionist, no coffee, no comfy waiting room with magazines. Just the dimly lit corridor, which smells as if someone is mixing chemicals and experimenting on mice, with two slatted benches on either side of the door; the benches look as if they were stolen from Park Square. This is what I get for listening to Sam. Tina and my wife sit on one bench and Rudd and I on the other, while Jess practices various stances of naked impatience.

The voices behind the door crescendo. Tina looks at the clovers on her hands. Rudd pinches his right ear. Jess hugs herself, digging her hands into each armpit. Then everything is quiet behind the door. The sudden silence is three times as ominous as the yelling. I start to hum "Oh Suzanna" until my wife's eyes cut me off. Humming can have a calming influence in an awkward situation, it's a proven fact. But I'm accommodating. The world is all about accommodation, that was one thing I'm becoming more sure of. Plus I'm even more sure Regina Samsonetti will take one look at us and send us away so she can deal with these families with real issues.

When the yelling family emerges, everyone is all smiles. Almost as if they are acting. They are the snapshot of a perfect family. Dad has a fatherly heft and a serene glow, mom has her arm around one of the teenaged boys, who has his hair cut like Rudd's and who is wearing a jacket with the name of an exclusive private school in the next town over. The teenaged daughter looks like Brook Shields except for her pierced nose and bad girl bangs which screen her eyes, but god dammit, even she looks as happy as if someone just offered her Kool-Aid and cookies on a perfect summer's evening. *Wow*, we are supposed to think, what wonders this therapist is capable of. I know that smiling family will be all frowns as soon as they're out of sight. Therapists offer discounts for such things. Not to mention the fact that nobody likes to show that they are wasting money. I try to see if they go for the stairs or risk getting stuck on the elevator together, but we are called in.

I don't trust, never have trusted, nor will I ever trust a person in a poncho with a Ralph Lauren insignia. OK, this is the first one that I've ever seen but why she's wearing a poncho I can't understand. She has pink faded jeans and clogs that look like they were drawn up by the Department of Defense. She also wears expensive glasses that I'm willing to bet are not corrective. Poncho? Maybe she didn't have arms? There's one thing that is clear though: She looks as if she thinks she has seen every problem and knows every solution. She thinks she knows our future. She's maybe fifty years old, she has gray strands in her hair, and she has thin lips and a tiny nose. Her voice is welcoming, the kind that invites strangers into her home so she can cook them.

The room is a light pink with cheery clusters of color on every wall. There are no chairs. I'm astounded. "Why no chairs?" I ask by way of an introduction.

"It's easier to hide our body language when we sit. We hide a lot of ourselves when we sit. It is also an indication of being hunkered down, unmoving, not willing to move. On our feet we are ready to confront anything, make decisions, react."

That's right, I think, I'm hunkered down. In this world if you're not hunkered down, where are you? And why the hell is she telling me about body language? First, she's wearing a poncho that so far has hidden her arms and hands. Second, how am I going to exhibit natural body language now that I know that's what she's watching for? Maybe it's all a trick, reverse psychology. She's going to study the effect of mentioning body language on our body language. Jess, of course, has it made—body language is the only thing she's wearing. I look for dolls with pins in them, look for newt eyes, menacing straw brooms, electric shock machines, but all I find are crayons and construction paper, colored blocks, shelves filled with stuff, bright, unidentifiable stuff. In one corner padded headgear and poles with Nerf padding on either end balance on each other. Not one goddamn chair—even at the cluttered desk. This is what I get for listening to Sam.

After a round of introductions, Samsonetti claps her hands once and takes a large piece of construction paper and casually tears it into five pieces (she does have arms!). She has us form a circle around her. Tacitly everyone agrees the therapist needs a lot of room and we gradually widen the perimeter of our circle. Each of us will get a piece of paper and our choice of crayon from a single box. We are to draw whatever's in our heads, not to think about it, just draw. The therapist is good; she has not even given Jess's outfit a second look, has not even cocked her head at Jess's bandage and the grime of it. She does get a pretty good look at it as she hands each of us the paper and crayon because she has to stand in front of Jess for about five minutes with the crayon box and paper held out to her—which, I calculate, earns the therapist about twenty bucks. My wife, who is directly across from Jess and about three feet from me, is livid and wants to intervene. It's probably a strike against her for not being patient, but on the other hand maybe it's a strike against me for standing back and letting come what may. Jess finally relents, taking the paper and the crayon in one of those fast-slow motion moments, like when a Venus's-flytrap snags a bug and you're the bug. Without looking at the box she pulls a crayon and fists it, keeping the color hidden. I'm the last to pick and I can't decide. Tina and Rudd both have green, which isn't a real surprise but I can't see my wife's color. I'm taking too long and unlike Jess I am reprimanded: "Just pick a color and hand it back." Panicked, I go for yellow. A good color. I display it proudly to my family. I'm sure in that choice alone I erase most of the strikes I have racked up thus far. The only thing that is clear is that she's not just going to send us home, but certainly after she sees what we draw, she will.

We spread around the room. She tells us to draw wherever we feel most comfortable. Jess stays put near the door, Rudd goes over and puts his paper on the windowsill, and Tina plops down right where she is, crosses her legs Indian-style, and spreads her paper out on the floor in front of her like a pro. My wife turns to the closest wall and I go to the one opposite—the only other clear spot. What if four of us happen to be located pretty close to the corners of the room? The room did resemble a boxing ring more than it resembled anything else, except perhaps Romper Room. But I'm sure there are all sorts of strikes against me for my location. I'd like to explain that I am only over here for practical reasons, so I can best carry out this assignment without straining my back and neck.

It is not easy drawing on a wall, not easy drawing whatever comes to mind. Tina's having no problem filling the page. Jess isn't doing anything—she really is practically naked. Rudd is thoughtfully stalled, my wife is stalled, and I'm told by the whispering poncho-wearing therapist to keep my eyes on my own piece of paper. Thank you, but I graduated from the second grade a few years ago. I hold my tongue. Another strike. I'm battling the rapids upstream and losing. I gulp for breath, wipe my brow, and draw a sailboat on a calm day.

Done, Tina proudly walks over to Samsonetti and hands her the drawing. Jess has yet to make a move.

"Just whatever is in your head, even if that means scribbling," Samsonetti prods. "Scribbling's fine."

I'm pretty proud of my sailboat and decide to take advantage of our extra time. I draw a yellow house next to the body of yellow water, which holds the sailboat, a hill behind it, the sun shining gloriously in the sky, and five smiling faces in each of the windows, and stick hands that are waving. It isn't just for show. As soon as I came up with the idea I'm lost in it, and when I'm done everyone is staring at me. I guess there's a little of the artist's spirit in me. OK, it's not exactly museum-worthy, but it has feeling. It is only after I'm through that I regret doing a lake instead of a river or why not remove us from all possibility of chemical taint and go with the ocean? But this is quibbling. I can't help but to admire it. I hope we get it back at the end.

The therapist doesn't seem too disappointed with Jess's inaction. My wife has that body language of the big fish about to eat the little fish.

The strap around her heel has slipped, and I notice that both her heels have Band-Aids on them. Why are her heels full of Band-Aids? In fact, why is she wearing these type of shoes when it is still pretty cold out?

On the strikeout list, I have to be doing better than Jess. And my wife's behavior toward Jess has to be ringing some alarms and the Band-Aids on her heels and her shoe choice must be putting some asterisks in there I'm sure.

"We are here to get things out. Not to restrain ourselves," Samsonetti intones, surely addressing my wife.

And to my surprise my wife speaks: "I'm angry at Jess for not participating. And I'm even angrier that she did this to herself at school. And the bandage on her nose, why won't she take it off?"

"Good," the therapist says, turning right to Jess.

My wife is a pro. I'm going to say I'm jealous my wife is a natural at therapy, but when you're down you don't want to take any chances. By the end of the hour if things aren't looking great for me, I can call in the firepower if it comes to that.

"Jess, what are you feeling right now?" the therapist asks.

Ah, a thirteen-year-old's dead silence. There is nothing like it in the world. If there's an analogy to the quiet chaos out there in the universe, this is it.

"Jess," I say before I know I'm speaking, "answer the question." Strike, strike, and strike.

"Silence," Samsonetti says, "is a perfectly valid response."

I snicker. I can't help it. Strike or no strike, Regina Samsonetti might know a thing or two about therapy, but she doesn't know anything about PR. She turns toward me I'm sure to ask me to explain my snicker, and I'm ready to blast her with my own knowledge about silence, but Jess interrupts.

"This sucks," she says to the floor—a perfectly valid expression and I agree with her wholeheartedly. I stop my head in mid-nod and make it look like I'm just loosening my neck, and opening myself to hear my family.

"Why does this suck?" Samsonetti asks without being condescending. "Are you just saying that or do you really believe it?"

Jess falls into her clam imitation again. I check the rest of my family. Tina's obviously terrified and keeps looking toward her mother and me. Standing there, the poor thing, she has her legs wrapped around each other as if she's holding it in. Rudd's practically out the window. My wife's anger disappears and now she's back to deflated, her shoulders slump forward. I scratch my head. It occurs to me that the yelling family might have been just performing. That is what she wants us to do: She wants us to perform for her, and the closer to the textbook we perform the happier she will be, the better our report will be. The smiles from the family were actually the relief that they had passed the test. I think of ways of forming a quick family huddle, and I make a note to practice the shotgun formation for just such occasions: Tina up the middle acting hysterical, Rudd lash out with the full force of your tongue, Jess start crying and apologizing, wife do the button hook to explain why you have on two too many occasions said you don't love me yet here you've been snuggled up against me each night. I'll fake the punt, and as a team we'll haul ass into the end zone and go for some ice cream. I'm about to start yelling randomly when Samsonetti determines that we've hit a wall and collects our sketches and crayons.

I'm hoping for some recognition for my drawing, even just a smile, but the drawings are taken away, probably to be brought to some lab to be analyzed under a microscope—the drawing itself not being important, but the crayon movement revealing the essence of each of our personalities. What would mine reveal? *Presses his crayon too hard and can't draw a straight line to save his life = a caring father who's got all his bases covered.*

The next exercise should be ridiculously easy. Once she explains it to us, I raise my hand to go first, but I guess she plays by the same rules as Chinese checkers, which is perfect with me—I know Tina will do it right. The exercise is to group family members spatially. She is down on her knees explaining the drill to Tina. I believe after Tina's arrangement of the family there is a pretty good chance the therapist will send us home.

Tina nods her slow, weighty nods. She takes it all very seriously. Samsonetti backs up and her poncho and pink jeans allow her to camouflage herself. Tina steps forward and stops. I can see her four-leaf clovers smudged on the back of her hands. Dad, I think, go to Dad, a great place to start. Tina goes over to Rudd by the window and pulls him a quarter of the way into the room so he's about five feet from me. My wife's face droops, her lips part. Me next. But she turns to Jess, grabs her hand, and pulls, but Jess isn't budging. Tina brown-eyes her sister and Jess relents, her body moving like a zombie behind Tina as they cross the room toward Rudd. (*Therapy turned my daughter into a zombie*, our family's ready for the *National Enquirer*.) Tina pulls her toward Rudd and passes him by, thinks about it for a second and brings her back like a good girl and places Rudd and Jess side by side, pushes them in together so their right and left arms are touching. Rudd is taller than his sister, but not by much. They look as if someone has made them go to the prom together. Rudd's going for the red face world record, so far twenty minutes and counting. I don't know why, but Jess breaks from her zombie state and looks shocked to find herself so close to her brother. Her hair seems to have flattened. She looks like the child she is. My daughter's standing there skinnier than I pictured her, barely clad, and I bet a millions bucks she wants to put on every piece of clothing from her closet. When Jess and Rudd unstick their arms, Tina is there to push them back together.

Me, Tina, me! Tina creeps toward her mother. Apparently Samsonetti keeps the room warm as hell for some purpose, and my ears are itching. I knuckle them without success. Tina has seen *The Titanic*, she knows *women and children first,* she repeated it for a week—that is all she's doing (Of course she has her own version: *animals first, then children and women*). I switch the foot I have my weight on. I'm still about five feet from Rudd and Jess. And ten feet from my wife. My wife puts out her hand and Tina grabs her wrist and moves her a foot forward. Tina lets go of her mother's arm, but her mother keeps the arm out as if she expects Tina to keep moving her. I'm not sure what Tina's doing, but I'm still sure that this is a prelude for her pushing us all together. I watch my wife's arm finally return to her side, hanging there as if it has been stretched. When her eyes measure the ten feet between her and Rudd and Jess, my first thought is that she expects to be even farther away.

As Tina comes to me she looks as if she has just stabbed her mom. Her buzzed hair. The little mark left on her hand by the ferret, now covered in a smudge of green—the clovers exploded on her hands. When she grabs my wrist, her hand's cold, and I can feel the numbness she must feel in her body, the act of self-removal, the protections from the horrible act this therapist is making us do here. No wonder my daughter is guiding me to my wife's side of the room, away from Jess and Rudd. No wonder she doesn't push me into her mother as I hope she will. I try to guide her but she keeps going. Tina has made a triangle: my wife and I formed the base and Rudd and Jess the tip. Where will Tina go? Will she stay by my side?

Tina weaves and wobbles around each of us, circling and moving away, finally landing with her sister and brother, where she pushes face first into them and wraps her arms around each of their backs. Her shoulders and head shake as both Rudd and Jess absently put their free hands on her back.

Regina Samsonetti is delighted. "Very good Tina, now Jess—"

"I don't think Tina's done," I say.

She turns toward me with a complacent smile.

"Tina, tell the nice therapist how you aren't finished yet. How you're taking a hug break."

Tina doesn't budge. Regina Samsonetti has scared her.

"Tina"

"Please," Samsonetti says.

I get angry. I can see that my wife wants to give Tina more time too and I wait for her to speak up, but the therapist won't have it: "Jess, your turn."

"I'm going next," I say.

"Doug, cool it," my wife says.

Then I see it all very clearly. I can't bring my family together. I can force them all into the middle of the room but I can't keep them there. I can't do it. I can't hold us together. I turn to my wife.

"Why do you want to leave?" I say it aloud—I'm amazed. I don't stop: "Throw seventeen years out? Why do you have to put our children through this? Why do you think you have been placed where you are?"

She looks at our children and at Regina Samsonetti, who can't hide her surprise, and back to me. Hey, I can express myself.

"What do you want it to be about?" Karen replies. "Would you rather have it be about something? Is it easier than it being about us? Like why you were driving around with Rachel naked and slamming your brakes in the snow when the police are asking you to pull over? Driving drunk with our kids in the car? A clear crisis you can point to so you can go about fixing it? Instead of the wall that's between us?"

Samsonetti's jaw's cocked, as if she's trying hard to keep her eyes from rolling like fruit on a slot machine (talk about body language!); she doesn't know what to do and neither do I—I'm tempted to hide under her poncho. But I push on.

"What about Africa then?" I ask.

"It always comes down to that for you, doesn't it?"

"OK then. What about your job? What happened to your dream of. . ." But she doesn't hear this part.

"Wad Sherife, Sudan, not Africa. . .You know what, Doug? Do you really know what? You're wrong, you are wrong for wanting to know, *now*."

That one word, *now*, nearly drops me to my knees. The rubber band I'd been aiming snaps back at me. There is silence and then there is silence. Pins drop, molecules collide. My children opposite us, in this pink room, Samsonetti holding up her palms to both of us like a police officer in the middle of two cars that are failing to yield—her poncho now a perfect half-circle.

"You," Karen says, "only understand it one way."

I shake my head. I won't say his name, I will not drop that bomb, I will not let her know that I know. I never will say his name and then what do I do: "Wad Sherife? Really? Why don't you try Robb Lamonty?"

My wife's head cocks. There is no way I could know his name, and then she shakes her head hard, really hard as if she's trying to get water out of her ear. Could she possibly yearn for another life, one spent with Robb Lamonty?

Regina Samsonetti is saying something. "The kids, the kids." She's trying to get us into the hallway or the kids into the hallway. The scene is messier than the car accident. Why am I the one down on the canvas, KO'd, when I delivered the knockout blow? If only a horde of police officers would break through the door and tackle me! I'm seriously considering dialing 911.

"We keep doing the same things," my wife says taking a deep breath. "I keep doing the same things and you. . .and I just. . ." She took a deep breath and I know something is about to come, something I should at least make an effort to block by covering my ears, something maybe I should just jump out this fourth-floor window before I hear—I have about the same chance of survival.

"I slept with Walt," she says. My mind is racing because I don't know who the hell he is. "Why are you making me say this all here, why am I saying this?" She looks in the direction of the kids as if just realizing they are still here and then covers her face with both hands. "Why don't you just let go?"

"Please, you two, please."

"I slept with Rachel," I lie. "So we're even. We're fine."

"Oh my god, Doug! Oh my fucking god!"

And my heart reverses its cave-in. She's mad. She still must love me.

"You. . ." I start

"You just. . ." she starts at the same time.

But we never get a chance to finish because Jess launches. The kids, the kids, what did we just do? Rudd and Tina struggle to keep their balance so fast does she break away from them. In the ten-foot sprint in the Olympics my daughter would have won the gold. My wife, the word *just* still on her lips, reaches for Jess as she passes, but there's nothing of her to hold onto. She's out the door in a blur. She slams the door behind her, walls shake. We all stare after her, waiting for glass to break. My wife covers her face in her hands again.

"OK," the therapist says as she sidesteps in front of the door. "That's an excellent starting place for us to begin when you two come back on your own, maybe first thing in the morning?"—she's talking as if our daughter has not just bolted—"but right now, please, let's continue. Rudd, you're next."

"What?" I cry.

As Samsonetti turns to me, my wife makes a move for the door but Samsonetti steps in front of her and actually grabs her wrist, which must be an action that would get her disbarred from whatever association all those abbreviations after her name stand for. The full weight and sharpness of my wife's look finally lands on someone whose name isn't Doug.

"You can't chase her," she says. I have to give her credit for holding up so well under the look. "If you chase her now you'll always be chasing her. She has to come back on her own." Then she turns to me as if I've done wrong. "Just like on an airplane you have to put your oxygen mask on first."

My wife is looking at Rudd and Tina and the door. "I'm so sorry you two, I'm so sorry, we are just all. . ." but she can't finish. She's sobbing. Tina holds tighter to Rudd. My wife can't even stand. She's down on the floor now.

Here I am, only trying to save my family from this diabolical experiment. I'm trying to be a textbook. I've only expressed what I'm feeling. And what do I get for it? Something from my wife that I never saw coming. Something I have no contingency plan for. If we can chase after Jess we'd be together. That is all I want. But we are hostages in this space. Is this lady nuts? Hasn't she done enough damage? I will strangle Sam.

"Why would she come back to this?" I ask.

"You have to let her find that out on her own. When you pull, she's going to pull the other way. Now maybe if I can just have a moment with the parents."

Samsonetti's neck twists as she watches Rudd slide behind her. My wife too watches Rudd go by. He makes the save of his life with his long stretch out the door, which he leaves open (his voice of reason has obviously not been damaged). My wife goes from sobs to a sprinter's stance in an instant and then is out the door. I look at Tina, who's rubbing the back of her hand red, and I feel pretty bad for leaving her in the therapist's clutches, but I have no choice.

"—believe—" I hear as I slam the door behind me to see a family, not unlike us, all sitting on the benches; their terror is palpable. "Exercise therapy," I smile the biggest smile I can muster (because no one should feel as terrified as I do right at this moment) and then I light down the corridor after my wife.

She's a shadow in the bubbled sunlight coming in from the window at the end of the hall. Then lit by the same sunlight as she repeatedly presses the elevator button, she glows. And it is in that moment that I forget all about Jess and Rudd. I'm chasing only my wife. She steps into the elevator and the doors close before I can get to them. I'm down the stairs a flight at a time.

Out of breath, I find my wife outside amid the group of dejected looking people. Am I in the middle of a protest? Is this a vigilante group that's headed to put Regina Samsonetti out of business? As I watch my wife, I hear the voices within the group. No protest. It seems the computer system is down. A crowd of smoking dejection. Did anyone see a scantily clad daughter running this way? What about a kid with glasses, a crew cut and pockets in his pants? A few people put in an effort to point in different directions. I stay put as my wife yo-yos every which way: pauses at the car, stops and feels for her purse and her keys but they are upstairs with Samsonetti. She comes back toward me, passes me, heads the other direction, only to stop and come back again. She has already stripped the sweater from her waist and she holds it in her hand as if offering it to me as if I can squeeze our marriage out of it. Finally, standing right in front of me, my wife, my wife. Who slept with another man. Who doesn't love me like she used to.

I take the sweater and wrap it around her shoulders. I push her bangs from her eyes. I run my fingers along her ear and down her neck and onto her shoulder. I check once more in all directions but I don't see Rudd or Jess. I pull my wife close. I put my arms around her and rub her back and repeat "OK." Holding on is important. She doesn't pull away either. But she's a statue. "OK, OK, OK, OK." I can feel Tina looking down from four stories. She is probably chewing jellybeans or sucking on a lollipop while the therapist jots notes: *2:02 daughter rockets, brother follows (to help? or to run?) husband and wife break through. I'm damn good.*

I wish. Because what my wife—the whole of her trembling—what she keeps repeating in a whisper that manages to slice through my OKs: "Fuck, fuck, fuck, fuck."

31

The hardest thing in the world is *not* letting go of the past, it is *not* the recognition that your wife doesn't love you, *not* that she slept with someone, *not* the poor performance in front of your kids; the hardest thing in the world is putting a good face on *things* for a six-year-old.

When we pack our only child into the car after telling Samsonetti that, *sure we would be there bright and early* (the one lie my wife and I could agree on), I know I'm not going back to work and Tina's not going back to school. Tina can't hide that therapy has replaced the helium that usually fills her with five hundred pounds of sand. Her mother takes a long look at each of poor Tina's chaffed and cloverless hands and kisses them. When she's in her booster, I give her chin a pinch and say "Rumpelstiltskin." When there's not even a "Dad-that's-lame-I'm-not-four-anymore" smile, I know the situation is serious. I give it one more try: "Solid dairy!" and I pump my fist. Nothing. This is bad. My wife is in no shape to cheer her, so action is needed. "The playground," I suggest. "The seesaw playground! Who's game?" Tina lights up like her Clipper 3000 flashlight. Seeing Tina's reaction, my wife nods wearily or maybe warily. At least I know how to turn the tide for half of my current family.

"Will Burty be there?"

"We'll pick up Gazook and see if he can seesaw."

Tina lights up again. I can handle it all. Change of clothes and snacks at home first and then fun at the park. Tina's a great first step for disaster recovery. Step two? I have no idea.

At home, we get word from Nancy that Jess ran the ten blocks to her store and now that she has some fabric on her body she's feeling pretty good. She's even learning the cash register and really interested in patterns, "cuts straight lines like a natural. Didn't get that from her mother!" "And oh yes," Nancy adds, "she said there was no way she was going home and asked if she could stay with me, forever." Without consulting my wife, I give my consent—I could use a break from the bandage and any thought about what she did in class that day or not at the library weeks ago; not to mention how Rudd and Jess might never look at us in quite the same way—God knows I'm having trouble looking at my wife at all. Nancy's need not to know what happened is stunning and I doubt Jess filled her in on the details or if Jess even fully understands what she heard. Though at the end of the call Nancy reveals that she now knows the origins of the dent in her door and may not be on speaking terms with me for a few days as well. That's fine, I tell her, all fine. And she laughs a my-boyfriend-is-a-police-officer laugh, which just confirms that she's unaware of her daughter's actions.

We don't have word from Rudd, but I'd like to think that after he saw his sister going into Nancy's store he headed to Myerson's Hobby, but I know where he probably is. My wife wants to stay by the phone, but I convince her Rudd is fine. I don't mention how getting consoling kisses and hugs from a certain girl trying to make him feel better about his cheating parents is a great way, well, to get kisses and hugs. He's fine, better off than any of us. They are probably testing out some new protest chants between smooches. At least someone can profit. Really, once we get Tina playing in the playground, all three kids will be saying to each other, "therapy was awful but what a great afternoon!" I envy them that luxury.

We have to fight the wind as we open the gate to get Gazook. No one seems to have told the wind that it's April. Naomi and her little pregnant belly peek from behind their front door. Nick's away on business and she's been terribly sick. "I'm so glad. Poor Gazook has been going crazy today. I'm either in bed or the bathroom. This kid better behave when he comes out!" We look at her belly which she points to with an accusing finger. Gazook pushes by her and into the yard. He gives us the once over but there's something in the corner he has to investigate first. He doesn't bark at me, continuing a trend.

"Do you have any theories why Gazook stopped barking at me?" I ask Tina as my cheater wife chitchats with Naomi. I don't know what they are saying but I'm surprised how my wife can sound positive, almost happy.

Tina sighs heavily as if she's told me a hundred times. She has her neon green fun sunglasses on and her parka. She finally relents: "Because he's told you everything."

"But what did he tell me?"

"How am I supposed to know?"

"Do you think it was important?"

"What do you think?"

An eighteen-wheeler downshifts into the corner and startles Gazook out of his reverie in the corner of the yard. For a moment, Tina and I have to lean into the wind to stay upright.

"Everyone's mad at each other. I'm mad too," Tina says with a smile, trying to make some calculations and charts from therapy and everything else she knows. What I see in her sunglasses is that she knows there's no answer, no way to respond. Sometimes it's better to just let the words sit out there until the wind carries them off. I give her shoulder a squeeze that says everything gets complicated and then it gets simple again. Gazook proves this by not barking at me as he stumbles toward us, his tail wagging so fast that he can barely walk. He slobbers his thanks on Tina's face, pushing her sunglasses up to her forehead. She laughs and hugs Gazook and runs her finger between the collar and his neck and then quickly loosens his collar a notch. How does she know how to do this? "Dogs never get mad," she says, as if it is her own answer to everything that happened today.

I check myself at telling her about that dog that Jess saved her from. But maybe Tina's right in her own way. Dogs may be the ultimate spokespeople.

My phone goes off. It's Sam, of course, the ultimate therapy spokesperson, and someone who I will strangle next time I see. Does Regina call him to consult? I dismiss it. He leaves a message.

"How many Gazooks are left in the wild?" I ask, sliding my phone into my pocket as I latch Gazook's leash and explain that it is for his safety to head off Tina's request that Gazook be free on our walk.

"None. Gazook's in captivity."

My wife has finished with Naomi and she hears this last statement. We look at each other for the first time since therapy, we're parents still, we produced this kid, we have to look at each other sometimes. Maybe everything isn't so bad. Maybe I even saw an "I'm sorry" in her eyes.

While we wait for Gazook to finish sniffing the sidewalk side of the fence, my phone buzzes again. I want to throw the phone and see what the wind can do with it. Gazook pulls with the strength of a whole sled team.

At the park, holding Gazook (or trying to hold Gazook) as he strains against the leash, I watch Tina and my wife seesaw. She loves Gazook but even he can't hold up to the seesaw with her mom. Park and recreation departments all around the country have taken the seesaw away from playgrounds, at least real seesaws that give you maximum height and the trust for the kid on the other side to not just walk away when you're up there. Somehow this seesaw has been forgotten. I've been on it myself with Tina, with Jess, with Rudd. I've been on it with Rachel just once when Burty and Tina insisted on a playground playdate and she saw the seesaw and had to try it out...first with both kids on the end and then with me. She said she should do a report on this lone seesaw, something she had thought had gone extinct, and I told her there was no way this should be brought to the attention of anyone. Maybe we should throw out all the plans for Percival Lake Park. Do a seesaw park, the only one in the world. The mayor would like that—if he ever appears again. This seesaw right here, I've been on it with my wife before we had kids. In the middle of the night, drunk, and ecstatic we played a game where we had to keep balanced as we moved closer to the middle, scooting, contorting our bodies, we made it surprisingly far before she couldn't distribute her weight enough to keep me horizontal and she slid the rest of the way across the fulcrum and met me with her lips. Then we both fell off. And we lay in that grass which was thicker and better taken care of. Just lying there on our backs staring up at the stars and the moon and a few gauze strips of clouds. I forgot all about that night until now. I wonder if she remembers.

But I'm not going there. I'm not jumping into the past. There's a future ahead of me. The sun is bright but it isn't giving off much heat. It's not helping spring along, concentrating on making some other place warm. Here there's just that March chill, that March wind. There's no way to tell April that it's not March. And there on the seesaw my wife and daughter go up and down. The wind whips my wife's hair and has no effect on Tina's—my wife, back in the comfort of her sneakers and new jeans, the hood of her jacket slung on her back. Tina's pink parka makes her thick. Her purple pants are high-riders, exposing her pale shins where her socks have sunk to her ankles. It's a shame she won't fit into them much longer because she likes them so much. She's absolutely delighted. I watch Tina, I register the moment and keep registering it, stacking it on top of images of hotel rooms and flung sheets and Warren or William or Winslow or whatever his stupid fuck face is called, on top of my wife.

Finally Gazook's gasping on the strained leash convinces me to break park rules. I let Gazook free, the leash dragging behind him as he swoops by the seesaw and dashes to the far edge to sniff and do his business where brush hides the cemetery fence. My wife pauses in a squat, and perched up high, Tina looks triumphant. The weight of the world has been lifted from her on this seesaw as she first watches Gazook zoom by and then as she takes off her sunglasses and closes her eyes and tilts her chin to catch the sun. And in that moment, it is if my wife has come alive in her. Her hair the same length now as my wife's when she came back from Africa. It's like understanding something for the first time. Something that's still good to hold onto.

Tina squirms off the seesaw and drops before my wife can lower her. She and Gazook sprint and chase and tag and roll. I wipe the wetness from my eyes that can't quite muster its way out. The wind. My wife remains squatted on the seesaw staring at the raised end. I'm thankful, very thankful she doesn't come stand next to me, that she doesn't feel compelled to fill me in on details.

32

That night we are in bed, and the being on a bed together confirms that Einstein only needed a tape measure, a queen-sized mattress, and a pajama-clad couple to contemplate the most mysterious part of the universe.

33

In the morning, Rudd is up and at'em with me. He's got coins in his pocket and his backpack slung over one shoulder. He's not talking to me, but I get it. I completely understand. And I'm almost moved to tears as he follows me out. We might not be talking up a storm but we're a team. We make our way through the web of toilet paper, two days' worth. If the perpetrators saw how nonplussed we are about it, they'd come and pick it up themselves. We walk together to the bus stop, but he can't quite keep up with my pace. I figure he's getting to school early to study for a big exam or maybe to avoid someone; or even just trying to get some good one-on-one time with the old man; or maybe just to show me that he's in my corner. He didn't get in last night until after dinner and he went straight down to his train tracks and then straight up to bed a couple hours later. On the bus, I sit on the window side of a bench. He goes right past me and sits in the back row. Unless the few other people on the bus take a good look at us, they'd never know we're father and son.

When we near his school, he doesn't pull the signal so I do it for him. The bus stops, the doors open, but he's still sitting there. The bus driver looks at me in her big mirror. I tell Rudd that this is the stop, you know that big building right out the window? I even gesture with my finger. Our eyes meet. The other riders look at us and then don't. The bus doors close. We are moving again.

I see what's going on. We are involved in a father-son game of chicken. He really wants to hash things out and by riding the bus and by skipping his stop he's put the ball back in my court. My stop is coming up but I don't make a move for the signal. There's the bell and I glance back in time to see his arm coming back down. Touché. The bus stops, the doors open, and I stay put. Check. I show him I'm man enough for a needed collision. I can put it all on the line. I can hear him coming up the aisle to me and I prepare for him to sit next to me and we will ride around town for as long as it takes to hash it all out. I'll be honest with him. He's old enough to start understanding that love is hard work with some major doses of trial and error. It's not that different from a hockey game. I glance in time to see him going out the middle door and there on the sidewalk is the green-haired girl in her sackcloth and sign. She's already holding out an extra sackcloth and sign for Rudd. The bus driver eyes me in the mirror and holds the door open for about thirty seconds even though I don't make a move. As the doors shut and the bus pulls away, green hair and my son hold up their signs in unison and nobody else on the bus notices.

I've got a key for the padlock to Percival Lake Park on my key-chain. The fence has been repaired for a couple of weeks. Sam's probably already in the office wanting to tell me something about a new therapist, on top of all my coworkers hating me and Tripoli calling me to his office for another session. I'm not all that eager to get to work. If we have gone out of our way to put in a meditation meadow, I'm going to plant myself right smack in the middle of it and put it to use. God knows I need it.

I transfer to another bus and after a short wait and a shorter ride, I'm at the park.

The green parking lot actually feels soft walking on it and at the very end of the lot there's a couple port-a-potties for when there's construction going on. We are still ironing out the bathroom facility issues with the Trustees. We just want to tap into the city's pipes, they want a composting bathroom that uses rainwater or something like that. They don't understand that this parking lot exhausted all our resources. From the little I get from Tripoli, I have to even wonder if they are planning on canceling the whole park. It might be just this lot that people come to admire. I hear the whistling first and locate the sound from the port-a-potties and I figure it's some homeless guy who's taken to the park and its facilities. I'm about fifty feet away when the door opens, and I have my fingers on 911 ready to nab a trespasser. A guy in all camouflage comes out. It's Mayor Dugus. I'd rather be facing my two ASSASSINS right now.

"You found me," he yells with a wave.

"I wasn't looking."

"You are a member of a pretty big club then." He's got a Frisbee in his glove. The guy really is dedicated to his sport—he brings a Frisbee into the bathroom with him. It's not one of the golden ones. "I was only playing at night but for a week I've been playing in broad daylight and no one's noticed. I'm even guilty of looking in the direction of city hall and wishing fire and sirens and chaos. But from the park at least everything seems to be still smooth and running and not really needing a mayor. I am sorry about not being at the ribbon cutting for the new bakery over on Lincoln." He's got a ski cap on and a ski parka and thick winter workpants and duck boots. It's not that cold this morning. His face has thinned out. He doesn't look that great and I can smell him from here. He looks like he has his own reality show. "One thing I know is that if you live outside you just never warm up, never. I'm thinking about incorporating a warming hut on some of the courses so the homeless will have a place to go." He looks around and he sighs and then asks for my forgiveness because he's not talked to anyone in twelve days and his cell phone battery died a week ago because the solar charger doesn't work. Finally he adds: "The person who should be looking for me is my ex-wife. I'm really having some bad luck."

He comes up to me and holds out the Frisbee.

"I'm not responsible for this," I tell him."

"Yeah," he says. He leans the Frisbee into my sternum.

"I'm not responsible for this." I bat it away and my gesture goes beyond the park and beyond GE. Out toward the universe.

"I never said you were." But he's looking at me as if I'm the guilty one.

It's then I realize that I'm dreaming. Of course, that explains it. That didn't happen with Rudd this morning, right? I didn't find the mayor at the park? That's ridiculous as our conversation is right now and the load of crap he's sending my way! I'm dreaming. I'm going to wake up any second and feel immense relief. Maybe therapy, maybe this all has just been a dream. Maybe the mayor knocked me cold that day on Rachel's show and like Dorothy I've just been in a strange land for a time and I'm going to come out just fine. My wife is in Arizona. I'm going to give a proper text back about *Things* and no way will I let Jess go to the library and no way am I going over to Rachel's.

"Now come have a Powerbar and we'll play a round. I forgot the satisfaction of using trees as holes. It brings me back and given me some ideas for a new course. The fresh air is something and we'll get ourselves out of this mess. You and me. Come on and I'll fit you with a Frisbee."

He turns, but I'm not following him. Who's this guy insinuating that I'm responsible when he's hiding out. I tell him this.

"I'm not hiding. I'm occupying."

"Nobody knows you're here."

"You do."

"Pshhhh."

"You think you can just be a little cog, strike that, a little tooth on a cog and keep going around. I know you. I've been around. You think that's just the right spot. You laugh at people like me with our big ideas. But you don't even begin to understand any of the machine you're a part of. You think I'm just a one note disc golf, but there's much more at work here. Much more. And if you just stay instead of walking away I can tell you because you need to know. The shit is going to hit the fan Monday at the town-hall meeting."

He's lost it. The poor guy's completely lost it. I expect him to keep talking. I expect him to chuck the Frisbee at me. As I walk away, I almost turn back just to tell him that this is going to work. It is going to work. Everything is going to be fixed, or almost everything. I lock the gate. Through the tree trunks, I can just see him. He's standing there, hugging his Frisbee. Lost it—if he ever had it. I hoof it all the way back to the office. Dream or no dream, I'm on solid ground. Maybe I'll even start eschewing public transportation.

34

As soon as I get to my desk, I stare down the phone telling me to call the cops on the mayor. Instead, I just go about being that tooth on a cog, which isn't that easy to be right now. By lunch, I'm thinking about getting the two protesters some food from the vending machine but this is work and they are the enemy. I don't know what my wife did this morning when the school called checking on Rudd's absence, but she must have been home or they would have called here next. Did she know? Why wouldn't she check with me? Jason the Kid keeps tabs on the two protesters with his binoculars, sometimes mentioning that the new one looks familiar. Sam is a little too quiet on his side of the cubicle. When I move out and about in the office, Alexis, who has always given me the finger as a joke, continues to scratch her chin with her middle finger, or to point to some word with it, or to punch numbers into the photocopier with it. It seems to have turned into a thing so I even notice Brad and Brooke doing it. With this atmosphere, I wouldn't mind sitting in Jimmy's office and hearing some old baseball statistics, but he's out for the day—probably with some secret PR team preparing for Monday. All afternoon I feel like jumping on my desk and telling them how everyone's got it wrong. All afternoon I don't. Town-hall meeting? What town-hall meeting? For someone who came up with the idea, I have no idea what's happening on Monday at ten o'clock. I'm not sure if I'm even invited. It's going to be at the community college's theater that can hold a thousand people, half of whom will be students from around the city as part of an Activate! activity—all three of my children will be there and I don't even know if I will be there. The mayor was originally scheduled to be part of it, but since no one but me has found him yet, it will be Rachel and Alogosh. And that's all we know. Rachel hasn't even been in contact with me. When I'm back in my chair, I see one of my legal pads has "Lift me up" written on it. I flip through and there's nothing. Then I see the folder beneath it. Sam! There's no fucking way I'm opening it up. I slide it into another folder and drop it over the avalanche of papers in the corner.

I flip through one of the quarterlies on my desk. My wife slept with some guy. In the surprise of it, I can't remember if she said she loved him. I'm not sure which is worse. Right in the middle of the thought I get a call from the principal of Jess's school who tells me she's no longer suspended. They found her essay on Activating! against bullying and it was an impressive statement and her actions though misread at the time clearly were a statement about bullying and she certainly will get an A on the assignment with a subtraction from not having a teacher check her plan first. She's quite a girl, he says. Activate! This put me right back on the side of a dream, how could it not be?

Sam finally catches me and asks, "What do you think?"

I tell it to him straight. He needs a new therapist.

As I head out for the day, my two ASSASSINS are already gone. I'll have to encourage Rudd to aim for a stronger work ethic. After the bus, I head up our driveway. There's no TP and no Pontiac. Our garbage can is on its side in the backyard with a wagging dog tail sticking out of the end. It's extra full and there's a dog in it and I go from a fast walk to a very slow walk when I see it's Gazook's tail and there's Tina sitting at the back step watching and smiling.

I hurl words like "halt" "shoo" "sit" at Gazook but he's not paying attention. I don't really want to grab his collar because until just recently he had an issue with me and pulling him away from delicious trash might push him from barking and jumping to biting and mauling. Tina runs to me and pulls me to the steps and sits me down next to her. "He's free range." So I guess it's telling of my current state that I just sit there and watch. After a few minutes, I point out that he could get sick from something he shouldn't eat. "No, he can't." I'm not in the mood to argue with Tina and her stubborn logic. Plus it's clear that this is one way she's trying to recover from therapy. "I put the biscuits in there," she says. "He's controlled by the biscuits and he's got to learn to think for himself."

And really I have to laugh. I pinch myself just for show because I know that a pinch never wakes you up from the dream.

"I've been experimenting and the biscuit has a much greater hold of him than his collar or leash."

"But he's just going through and getting the biscuits!"

"Well, that's the part I'm stuck on because he ate the biscuits fast but he's still going through."

The thing is that even in the weirdest dream ever, you still have to be Dad. I tell her that the dad in me is going to come out soon and start complaining about trash being all over the yard, so I'm going in until that happens. She asks me not to because she has to go to the bathroom really bad and Gazook isn't quite free range enough yet to leave him to "his own devices."

Tina goes in, and so here I am watching Gazook. My wife's not home, Nancy isn't sitting for us. Jess isn't supposed to make her big homecoming until Saturday. So I'm hoping Rudd is somewhere in this house and actually keeping a tab or two on his sister. What's happened to that kid's voice of reason? I remind myself that it is all a dream.

And then Gazook stops his digging. I see his head for the first time as he backs out of the can with a grocery bag in his mouth. It's knotted and full. He traipses over to the center of the yard with his prize and settles with his front two paws on the bag as he starts to gnaw. His eyes are on guard. Gazook looks like he's got an iron gut, but I don't want Tina to lose Gazook privileges when Nick and Naomi find bits of bag and whatever is in there in his vomit or worse when the emergency animal clinic opens his belly to try to save him in the middle of the night. I prepare to wrestle with him, to risk my life, for his good, but I see a biscuit he's missed and we do an amiable trade. He's happy with the biscuit. The bag is gross, coated with drool. It's from Rite-Aid and its handles are knotted, not just once, not twice, not three times, but I count them, five knots. Five knots call for vigilance, for investigation no matter what. If Sam's folder had been knotted like this, I would have opened it.

The bag has no weight. I work on the knots fingernailing and pinching the plastic handles, stretching them. Inside the *first* bag was a second knotted bag and inside that, another. By the third bag I realize there is no need to handle this evidence with delicacy and I tear it open along with the bag that is inside. It is full of dry wads of unused toilet paper, at least a roll's worth, but this isn't the cheap stuff they TP our house with. This is our toilet paper. There are shredded pieces of cardboard packaging. Unrolling the tissues I find something that explains everything, I mean everything.

A pregnancy test! Faded but clear as anything it says YES. My knees pop as I hop into the air. A literal jump for joy. I can't help myself. I have hang time.

This is no damn dream, but beautiful, beautiful reality. I understand my wife's preoccupation, understand her frustration with me, understand every "I can't do this," understand how she never looks at Naomi's belly, or brings up childbirth with her. It explains everything. I should have known all along with the Yoo-hoos. There's one little caveat that puts a slight dent in my excitement, but then right there I let it go, drop it. A blip on her side of things, that's it. It doesn't matter because my marriage isn't over. My marriage has just begun. We're pregnant!

I tie the bag and return it to the garbage minus the prime evidence which I pocket. I run into the house and hug Tina, who looks concerned. Gazook! I forgot all about him. We rush out the back door and there's Gazook, his tongue out, staring at us as if we're part of his experiment. We both let him lick our faces with his garbage tongue. We walk him back to Nick and Naomi's. I give Nick a big hug. I could give him a cigar. We're going to be seeing much more of each other in the future; I can see us with the kids on a autumn afternoon with the game on and his microbrews in our hands and our burp cloth over our shoulders. I could plant a big kiss on Naomi's belly (though of course I don't). Instead, back at home when my wife arrives, I surprise her with a kiss on the lips and a hug. Why not? She even pauses a second before she remembers and pushes by me and disappears upstairs. That pause is remarkable!

While Rudd, Tina, and my wife are sound asleep, I sit at the control panel of Rudd's trains, where I have carefully taped a note: "Sorry, love, Dad." I'm going to take responsibility. I'm going to smash time.

35

It's early Saturday morning and I'm taking responsibility. The bus schedule is different on the weekend so I had to hang out at the stop for a while but it gave me time to review my plans. Now I'm getting off the bus at GE. No protesters. No cars in the parking lot. I figure the secret Fairfield team might meet here since it's the weekend, but maybe they're doing it at the auditorium at the community college. There's no longer a security guard inside, at least today. There are no more secrets here anymore, except what Sam has passed on to me in that folder. All those years ago when Ed showed me the information about PCX, how official all the documents looked put a little asterisk on the whole incident for me. If it really was a prank, the person went all out. It made Alexis's little joke memos look like pre-K. I don't have a plan for what I'll do with the information Sam has in that folder, but I know once I view the contents it will be my responsibility. I'm ready for it, especially if it's PCX that Rachel unveils in her gotcha moment. When Alogosh is stunned into silence, I'll jump onto the stage and save the day and my fourth kid won't have to worry about where dinner is coming from.

The office is empty and I feel like I'm intruding on it. Things haven't exactly been going well with my coworkers but all of us are so ingrained into the walls and cubicles and chairs and keyboards I can feel everyone's presence, as if their shadows are in for the day, and it's not so much that it's haunted by the daily work and interactions but by the quiet. Here's the Cape Cod photo of our family. There's my secret-keeping wife who can only hold on to secrets so long. And there's certainly one secret she's going to tell me this afternoon when we go on our open house extravaganza which she agreed to once I convinced her that we couldn't keep living like this and we really needed to talk in a quiet contained space.

I lean over my tumble of papers in the corner and find the folder Sam hid on my desk. Once I look at its contents there will be no turning back. I steel myself as I open it.

There's a Post-it note on the paper inside: *A little something I've been really wanting to share with you. —Sam*

"Marriage Story" by Sam Gowers

As my mother lay in her hospice bed close to her last breath of air, she said to me, "I have to tell you my marriage story." Her eyes were like two strong blue marbles. I could barely hear her and had to lean in close. She...

I skim down and flip through and skim more. It's nearly fifty pages long, single-spaced.

Marriage is three things. Trust, forgiveness, and. . .

It was on my third date with Jamie that cupid struck his arrow. I still hold that arrow proudly. . .

The despair I felt when. . .

The way an onion is made up of layers and how it makes you cry, that. . .

It was gazpacho we were eating that night. . .

I close the folder. My chair squeaks as I lean back. On the ceiling, every fourth fluorescent rectangle is lit. There's no way to turn them off. They are always on. There's no way to sit in the office in the dark.

"PCX!" I shout, full of relief. I do laps around the office shouting it. I poke my head in both conference rooms, shout it. Each cubicle, shout it. I shout it as I flicker the lights. I shout it into the bathroom. I try Tripoli's office but the door is locked. I put my lips close to the wood and I annunciate the initials. I'm free of it now. I've been absolved. The town-hall-style meeting can proceed and after we finish it up, we'll come back to this office and we'll get Percival Park done and open. I'm even thinking about a beaver exhibit; maybe Guy the Environmental Guy can give guided "spot the pollution" tours; maybe an interactive exhibit of getting pummeled by Frisbees. I'm eager to get back to actual work. Today really might turn out to be one of the best days of my life.

Out in the parking lot as I consider my options for getting home quickly, I spot a police cruiser idling on the far side of the lot. I cut across. It must be Ray Roy. I'll go home in style! I wave. My family woke up this morning and couldn't find me, so they called Nancy, who called her boyfriend to do some detective work. I can't wait to get home and show everyone my note right there on the counter, probably under a cereal box: *Taking care of business.* The cruiser starts to roll toward me, and then the lights start flashing and there's a warning chirp. Ray Roy's a joker. I wave again and then do my own joke by putting my wrists together as if I'm cuffed. Officer Johansen steps out of the car.

"You're that guy," he says.

"You're that guy," I reply.

And it is uncomfortable at first especially because I don't have my ID. But he's not such a bad guy after all. He runs my info through the system. SOP, he says. But somehow we get chitchatting about kids. His daughter goes to the same school as Jess. Then it turns out that both his mom and dad worked here. I bet he idles here when he has some downtime. Like my wife, he probably has fond memories of this place. I offer him a tour, but he declines—"No friggin' way."

How can I not like a guy who says friggin'? Really, at the heart of me, I'm all about making amends. I can change the trajectory of his life—the locker-room jibes he must still weather from the night of the accident, taking out a family in a minivan and then being taken out by a kid's dishtowel security blanket. Just like Rachel was able to recover from some career ending Youtube videos, why not this guy? If he finds the mayor, he'll be a hero down at the station and also in his teenaged daughter's heart. I explain to him about a transient who's been camped out at Percival Lake Park. I show him the key to the gate.

He says *we'll* check it out and opens the passenger door for me. I hop in. I'm on patrol. It's much different than being in the backseat. No wonder he crashed into me. Being in a cop car is distracted driving itself. There's a laptop mounted to the dash. There's the radio going off. There's a shotgun right there between the seats. What cop actually has time to drive?

And here I am in a police car in the passenger seat, forming a budding friendship with the man who might not have caused all my problems but certainly amplified them. He's telling me about the Dad and Daughter boxing group down at Alexander's gym—the same place that I got a card from after I was cold-cocked on Jones Street! As we turn into the entrance of Percival Lake Park, he's telling me that he and his daughter have never gotten along better since they've started boxing. I only half hear him though because Jimmy Tripoli's closing the gate behind his idling SUV.

As Johansen flicks on his lights and grabs his radio, I try to explain that this is not the trespasser. One thing I do like about the cops— sometimes—is that they just don't mess around. He's already got his thumb pressed on the mic, asking about the Connecticut plate. Then he's out and he's asking for ID and registration. Tripoli has his arms in the air, not in surrender but in the "what the hell" way—palms at the sky. I should duck beneath the dash, but if Tripoli gets frisked, I have to see it up close. I get out as Johansen is coming back with the license and registration.

I have to hand it to Tripoli. Anyone else would have gone at least "huh?" seeing me come out of the cop car.

"Figures," he says. He's wearing a light overcoat and his hands are now in the pockets and he's so casual you might mistake his jacket for a robe.

I'm spun around again, trying to calculate a meeting between Tripoli and Mayor Dugus, and well I don't feel like beating around the bush anymore.

"How's the Mayor?" I ask.

"What?"

"I know the Mayor lives in there."

"Yes, of course, the king of the wood elves. We were all just dancing to pan pipes."

"Then what are you doing here?"

"You don't deserve an explanation but because I don't want to see it on the news tonight: Alogosh has never seen the park. He wanted to see what all the fuss is. It's not about much. That's for sure."

I try to see through the tinted glass on the passenger side. "If you guys had just done it right."

"Followed your vision better? I know you're the one that first pitched this park. And I just don't get it. You don't screw with what's already under cap. You leave it alone. It goes away. You wakened the sleeping fucking dragon."

"I thought this place was clean."

Tripoli snorts, "It is clean."

"It didn't freeze over."

"We did everything right here. You've seen the numbers."

"I keep hearing about something called PCX?" Look at me! I don't hold back. I wrap something up and then put it back out there. But why do I feel like I'm a little kid throwing pebbles?

Tripoli shakes his head. Alogosh must have heard those letters and the window comes down. He's got a phone pressed to his ear and in his other hand he's got one of the Mayor's golden Frisbees!

"Who's this?" he asks.

"Merit."

"Ah." The window goes back up.

"So what about it? What if Rachel brings it up tomorrow?"

He's shaking his head. He takes a deep breath, eyes the tinted glass and then continues in more of a whisper: "And you might as well tell her this whole place is going to be a solar field. We're done with Pontoosuc. We tried to do it right but everyone keeps fighting. Open up our pockets and keep pouring money in to mediate something that still isn't proven to be harmful. The new GE doesn't need this dinosaur footprint." He does a panorama motion with his arm to a bunch of trees. "No one has to worry about any of the shit because solar panels are going to cover the whole place. We are capping the riverbed for another mile. Then we're done. You might want to look at working for the sunglass hut at the mall. This place will glow."

"You're never going to get the city's approval."

"We've got it."

I look at Johansen coming out of the car with the papers. "And we're all gone? And Schaffeur's going to head up an office of one?"

"We're done."

Officer Johansen is looking at us.

"Sorry, sir. We just have to check things out since we got a report of trespassers."

"Go in if you want. But we just walked the entire grounds and there's no one."

The SUV's window rolls down again. Alogosh sticks out his head this time and smiles at Johansen, "Is there anything I can do?"

He doesn't seem cranky.

"No," says Tripoli, "Someone's just doing his job."

289

And that's when there's this vocalization, the kind of sound we used to make when we played cowboys and Indians: "Ah-oh-wah-ah-oh-wah-ah-oh-wah." I look for the mayor running down the greenest road in the world, with multiple Frisbees in hand. I'm ready for him to launch the first volley and I'm prepared to throw myself in front of Tripoli and Johansen and take two Frisbees in the chest for them. I'm that kind of guy.

But it's just a car that bucks its way by, the driver hoping to make it home.

After Tripoli leaves, Johansen and I search the grounds. He's unfazed that the guy in the SUV is the CEO of GE. Except for some Powerbar wrappers that I adamantly point to as well as one solar cell phone charger, there's no sign of anyone. Could the mayor have been in Tripoli's backseat? Johansen and I are no longer friends, but it is impossible to explain it all to him—none of it makes sense. I try to change the subject to the value of seesaws and he cuts me short. "I'm never going to step foot in the place again," he tells me as I close the gate. "It's everything that's wrong with this city." I don't quite get him, but apparently he's not going to be asked to step in here again. A solar field? All of GE? The lake? I know better to ask him for a ride home. I tell him maybe I'll see him at Alexander's Gym and I can tell by just the way he lingers in the fold of the car door, he wouldn't mind if Jess and I showed up. He just has to get back to work.

It's about a four-mile walk. It's turning out to be a beautiful spring day. People are out in their T-shirts. I soon have to remove my jacket. As I walk, my mind races past the sound of a man whose name starts with W, races past the idea of a conference call with Rachel and Nathan about solar fields, the image of Sam in his Camaro thinking deep thoughts about marriage, past the idea of asking Jason about PCX, past my future career options. Do you know where my mind lands? On the minivan. There's a car lot I'll pass on my way home. You never know what might be waiting for you. Imagine pulling into our driveway with a minivan!

With that addition to my plan, the open house extravaganza that I'll soon embark on with my wife will be a guaranteed grand slam. Plus, I should use my income before it goes away—there's bound to be a severance package. A minivan would certainly help get this day back to best day ever status. I pick up my pace. I'll browse. I'll chance serendipity. I'll buy.

36

That afternoon, I'm in the regular old Pontiac with my wife, idling in the driveway (I can't help but note that this is a long way from her slight push after my surprise kiss a couple days ago). We haven't been in the same car since therapy. And even more amazing, we're in the car alone—really alone—we've left our phones in the kitchen drawer—I'm not taking any chances. There was no minivan, but really that's for the best because we're off to a new start, and in this car we're a few inches closer together.

"I'm not sure I'm up for this," she says.

"Hey," I say, perhaps perkier than I scripted—it isn't easy playing this game, "I'm going to be a part of any house that you and the kids, all of the kids, move to. And we really need to iron things out. We have to figure out what we're doing. We have others to consider, just not us."

She scans me but doesn't seem to be able to get a reading. Here's the woman that I have loved for almost nineteen years and she doesn't know what to do with me. "Doug, you're looking a little bug-eyed."

"Really? It just must be my excitement for Rudd's date? And Jess, don't forget about Jess's prodigal return tonight. That would put bug eyes on anyone. Next stop, the Middle East for Nancy, negotiating that one—maybe GE could hire her for Monday. Plus Sarah will be here as part of the great compromise. When did they become friends again? And Tina, she gave me a great send-off hug." I take a deep breath and tell myself to tone it down. I put an upside down smile on my face.

"I don't see how you even have time for this with the town-hall meeting on Monday," my wife says again searching me one more time. We haven't talked at all about what's been happening at work or this morning—we haven't talked at all! She doesn't know that we have nothing to do with the planning. I don't even know if she thinks I'm guilty in this whole GE revelations mess. I take that thought back: there's no way she thinks I'm involved.

"I got a lot done this morning," I remind her.

She nods. That's what she does, nods. Great! She's mulling it all over and that's just what she should be doing.

"I'm just not ready for big steps right now," she says as she checks the mirror and shifts into reverse.

"These are just baby steps," I say and keep the frown for balance. I'm pretty impressed that she doesn't open up right here and ask me how I know. I'm already prepared: I've seen it three times before, I'll say. I'm an expert.

"OK," she says more to herself than me.

She's wrong of course: things are *better than OK*. In fact, they are about to be as good as they can get. She was stunned last night that I initiated this. And the thing is we do need to talk. Then we need to celebrate!

We are even dressed to celebrate. In lieu of the minivan, I dug out the blue blazer my wife bought me when I started at the tourist bureau years ago—I can't button it but that would be too formal anyway. I've got my softest Oxford on, my khakis and my black loafers. She was still in her pajamas twenty minutes ago. So when she finally got ready to go, I expected she'd come down in a T and jeans but instead she put on her long skirt that looks like suede but isn't (I love that skirt) and a light blouse with puffy sleeves (I love that blouse) and tempers these with her baseball cap and unfortunately those sneakers. But today I can handle those sneakers.

I was so stunned when she came downstairs, she even said, "What are you looking at?" In the car, right here, I begin to compose a note to Regina Samsonetti: "Dear, Ms. Samsonetti, I know you saw our family in its worst moment but if you saw my wife right now sitting next to me with that baseball cap and one hand on the wheel and the other holding my map over that belly of hers, that wondrous, glorious belly, you would know those predictions you made—don't deny it, I know you made them to yourself even if you won't admit it—were completely and utterly wrong."

"Just drive-bys," she says. "No going in."

I nod. The doors of the car will be sealed. Plus, we're getting off to a bit of a late start. Some houses just might not be that open by the time we get to them. But there will be the one at the end and there's no schedule for that one.

For the tenth time my wife's eyes catch on the brown paper bag at my feet.

"We do need snacks," I assure her. "We've been known to get hungry and thirsty. We can't hash things out dehydrated and on an empty stomach."

If she'll just back out of the driveway, that's all we need to jumpstart what I truly believe will be a jam-packed, uninterrupted afternoon. Just the two of us, the Pontiac, no phones, no minor crises to distract us from the two breathtaking revelations, one hers and one mine, both of which will put powerful positive stamps on our family's future. I have already practiced my look of utter surprise and utter glee when she reveals her secret.

Just as my wife lets off the brake, Rudd appears in front of us. He adjusts his glasses with both hands. I can tell he is here to cover his bases for the fiftieth time. You'd think he'd trust his parents—even if he protests the company his dad works for. "Six-fifteen," I call out the window, the time his mother is supposed to drive him on his date to the movies. Apparently protesting with someone all day long is not a date. He nods. "And don't forget to help Tina with Gazook. Make sure you shower afterward. You don't want to be all doggy on your date." The one thing that hasn't gone to plan today is my sit-down, face-to-face with son about how to make his first date momentous. I've mapped out the talk since my own first date with Jeannie Hebert twenty-five years ago. I need thirty minutes, but can do it in fifteen if we're running a little late. I still haven't been informed if I'm going to participate in the chauffeuring of my son's first date, but after all the revelations I can't see how I won't be in the car right here again next to my wife. We might end up celebrating this monumental day each year for the rest of our lives... maybe even down the line for centuries where the Merit family will gather from all over the country (hell, all over the world) and celebrate. I can picture green hair (I'm sure I'll have her name down by then) twenty years from now telling everyone about the look on my face each morning as she held up the sign and that time when Rudd got off the bus and how I even dared to be in the car on their first date.

By the third house—a nondescript rectangle of a house—my wife and I haven't spoken much. There's not much to talk about since the houses have been so-so (plus none of these houses matter to me, only the one that isn't on our map, the one that will be my surprise counts). But I feel her surprise must come first. Whenever she says something like *Right turn?* I can hear the strains of the revelations we are driving toward. A couple times I talk about what type of car seat Nick and Naomi will get for their baby. Baby seats are really impressive these days. But my wife doesn't take the bait. Hell, if she says, "I'm with child" again like she did when she finally told me about Tina, I wouldn't balk this time. With Tina, she absorbed the information first before landing it on me—we had agreed on the number two, replace ourselves. Should there be a number three? For a few weeks she didn't know what to do and then for a few more weeks we didn't know what to do—one of those things my wife has not forgiven herself for even considering. But it works out. *Things* work out. So today in this car I keep my palms up, I'm relaxed, I'm smiling (but not too big). My ears are open. My whole body says I'm ready to hear a particular piece of news.

When it still hasn't come as we pull away from our stakeout of the fourth house, I suggest that we take a break, eat our snacks, and chat. Distracted talking has been known to take lives, so we should do it in some safe place where steering and momentum are not involved. I wonder aloud if she knows a good place to relax and look at a view. You can't smash history from the fringes, you have to move right into the center of it.

"I'm not driving all the way up there," she says. "I'm never going there again."

I nod in agreement. I get it. I completely understand. Today is a day where people vow not to go to places ever again. I can do it too. She's right with me—we're smashing the past together!

When we pull up to 1224 Centennial Drive in front of a massive house in a budding development with a sprinkler system lawn that sprawls in that perfectly manicured way that aims to look exactly the same as every other yard in the development, one of those places with a committee and rules about grass height and garage doors, my wife stops behind a line of five or six cars and shuts off the engine and sticks her arm out the window. The afternoon has warmed considerably. Spring is here. Today is one of the warmest yet. Again, everything is going perfectly except that we haven't been able to start chatting. The engine ticks and pings, a bird here and there twitters, a jet crosses the sky with its hum chasing after it.

I pull out the Yoo-hoos I'd bought on my way home from work yesterday, and she takes a peek at all the bottles.

"You cornering the market?" she asks as she pops the lid and takes a few gulps. I feel as proud as a new father.

"It's incredible," I say. "These bottles are multiplying like rabbits."

She doesn't respond. We drink. People go into the house and come out of it. Cars leave and new cars come. Couples, all couples. The world makes sense in twos because twos can miraculously make threes.

"Should we at least take a look?" I ask.

The sunlight holds her arm still. The brim of the baseball cap directs her gaze as if it's the windshield in its entirety she's contemplating, just the windshield, nothing outside it. Her Yoo-hoo is wedged between the seat and the emergency brake. She adjusts the seat belt over her belly, which I think might be showing just a tiny bit; it will be either just three weeks or almost three months, but she is never one to balloon.

I, of course, have considered that this baby might not be mine and that is the reason for heightened tensions between us and her lack of willingness to relate her big news to me—maybe she doesn't even know for sure. But I've given this a lot of thought and it doesn't matter to me. Really. The kid can't help if he's got some fool for a father, a guy that would let this woman get away from him by essentially firing her. It's my kid. I don't care about genetics. It's my kid to bring all of us back together. I am human, though. That guy and Karen? My blood plunges. I think I'm going to drop with it. What I'm doing in this car with her is far from easy. But then, of course, there's a pretty good possibility that she lied about sleeping with him.

My wife fidgets in the seat and unsnaps the seatbelt and lets it recoil. I want to lay my ear down on her belly right then. Is she going to get out? Is this going to be our new house? No, she's just settled in.

The Yoo-hoos don't get her to start revealing her secret and that's fine. I've got phase two: I pull the scratch ticket I bought. I take a long, hard look at *Silver Spoons* before I hold it toward her and when she doesn't take it, I try to balance it on the stick shift, but finally have to place it on the dash between us. She's good; not even a restrained smile when she sees the name of the ticket.

I take a deep breath as the breeze swirls into the car. I struggle out of my blazer, roll up the sleeves of my Oxford, and stick my arm out the window and float it on the air too. Be patient. I can sense the big news is coming soon.

"I just have no idea what to do," she says after we float our arms for a few minutes. "I always know what to do."

This is great stuff. I'm not going to muck it up by saying a word. I'm nodding like crazy though.

"This is just so weird," she says after a few minutes.

It is certainly weird, but I'm ready for it.

"How did it happen?" she asks suddenly. "Were you drunk?"

Wait a second, I'm the one that's supposed to be smashing history! But at least I have an honest answer: "No, I was not drunk." I clear my throat. "I had some sips of wine. But I should have taken the breath—"

"I mean with Rachel." I could have nosedived right then and gave her the counterpunch asking after Wilt or Waldo or whatever his name is (I don't think I've ever liked anyone whose name started with *W* and I'm now sure I never will). I pull back on the controls and don't panic. Strip Scrabble, Aquaman blankets, news leaks, and the fact that we actually hadn't slept together make it too complicated to fully explain. But I do understand now where she's coming from. She wants to clear the air to open the way for our child. I drop my arm and cling to the warm metal of the door panel.

"No, not drunk," I say, directing my attention to the glove compartment. "It's like it really didn't happen. I don't know how to say it."

Her chin goes up and down in slow motion. We both stare forward.

"I wish I'd been drunk," she says and blasts a sigh. "Both times."

It's all fingernails on chalkboards and grinding gears. Talk about clearing the air! My lungs are so sucked dry they're like two vacuum-sucked Ziplocs, snack size.

298

"It was just twice. That's it. I think it is something you should know."

I'm having some trouble conjuring a *thank you*.

"It tells us something though," she concludes. "It tells us."

I'm shaking my head now. Shaking. Trying to locate at least a couple oxygen molecules. It doesn't tell us anything.

OK, it does tell me one thing: it might be tougher to raise some shit's kid than I thought. I really think I'm going to vomit. I hang toward the window. If I throw up though, that's it for my plan.

A young couple stands on either side of the car in front of us. They take one last long gander at the house, and then across the top of the car, the man says, "You think?" And the woman replies, "I think."

It's that easy.

The thing is that it is all out there in the world, like a puff of smoke. It lingers, it's right there, and then it dissipates. We've said it. It's over. We're ready for a fresh start. I start breathing again. I can't believe it. We made it through. We're still here.

The couple drives off, and my wife's fingers play with the side mirror. She leaves her fingerprints all over it. She clears her throat, and sliding her hand away from the mirror she stretches both arms so her wrists fold over the steering wheel. The sun's low in the sky and it fills up the car, but she isn't squinting under that cap. The realtor is in the doorway, gesticulating wildly at something in the foyer as the remaining couple nod and crane their necks.

I've known all along that there's another past, my wife's. A past, I have somehow not witnessed but one in which I've been a participant. But now, before anything else is said, I have no choice but try to snap these two pasts back together by throwing gas on the fire.

"Get out," I order.

"What?"

"Only I can drive us where we're going."

37

No police in hot pursuit in the rearview, the street narrows and I slow as soon as the house appears.

"Don't tell me," she says.

I jiggle the stick into neutral and we glide to a stop across the street from the house. The sun is sinking and its pale orange bathes the house, making its mustard color into something like gold. Birds are singing—a frantic hundred-pronged conversation before bed.

"What's this?" my wife asks, the same one who could have called a cab at the previous house, who could have refused to let me drive.

"I just wanted you to see it," I say. "See that it's not—"

"Is it for sale?" my wife asks, her hand falling on mine.

I stare at her hand there and I can hear Tina's voice: "Everything's possible."

The grass is greener, we used to joke all the time when we started going to open houses. But the thing is, here, it is. It's not summer lush but it's clearly grass that makes you want to rip your shoes and socks off and immerse your feet in it, so different from that perfect lawn at the house we just came from, that says, "feet off." A dogwood stands in the front yard. She's a big fan of dogwoods. The house has perfectly smooth clapboards as if each time it's been painted it's been sandblasted first. The porch swing is suspended on shiny chains. This is the house my wife has always dreamed of buying. And here it is. Here we are: my wife in the passenger seat with our fourth child growing at that very moment within her—the kid probably feeling pretty happy. A fetus can sense this sort of thing.

"You can't be serious," my wife says. "It can't be for sale."

I slide my hand out from under hers and step out of the car. Just twice? I slam the door and the sound passes the test 110%. I put my hands on my hips and face the house. My wife stays put. What am I doing? I can't smash this house. It *is* perfect. It *is* the house we would have been happy in. I wave to a neighbor carrying a garbage bag to the street and he waves back! We live here. Classical music filters from some nearby window, no kidding. The street is lined with oaks. Oak Street actually has oaks! The birds chatter a new bit of gossip and then quiet. I don't look back at the car. I don't look both ways before I cross the street. At the beginning of the walkway there is a sign, HARRISONS, a junior high woodshop creation, the name routered by an unsteady hand. I made one just like it for my own parents. I bend over and grasp the thin metal spirals that adorn the top of the sign. I feel bouncy.

The house isn't that much bigger than ours, but where ours has the long narrowness of a shotgun shack, this place is broad and thick—stout. The second floor doesn't look wobbly. The image of my wife and me and our new baby in the little windowed alcove drives me closer to the house. My plan is not working on me, the house is not revealing its flaws, it's not revealing our rose-colored glasses of youth, we aren't going to be walking away glad we never bought the house. I should jump back into the car at that moment and hightail it, but why would I? We aren't coming back from a sixteen-year journey. We already live here. We've lived here all along. I can enter it right here, go into the kitchen, and there we will already be, our family plus one.

Even the slight give and creak of the porch steps is damn welcoming.

There are gold numbers on the storm door. The main door has a half-circle window at the top. I grab hold of the doorknob. I hear the creak of the steps and my wife is at my side. She swallows hard.

"It's not for sale, is it?"

I turn the knob.

"What are you doing?"

"We forgot our keys."

"Doug."

On my tiptoes I look through the half-circle, and suddenly she is on tiptoes by my side, her shoulder presses into my arm as she balances herself, and together we look through the window.

The hallway has four rooms off it, its slatted varnished boards lining the walls to hip height until it opens into the kitchen, where there's a stainless steel dishwasher, coffee mugs and a stack of bowls. The back wall is lined with windows that look out over the backyard. Closer to us, shoes clutter the floor, coats hang from a rack nailed to the wall, photographs of the wrong lives line the hallway.

I push into the door with my shoulder.

"Doug!"

"It's a good door," I report. I turn around to find her headed down the steps. She keeps walking toward the car. She passes the Harrisons sign and crosses the sidewalk. Then something happens. She looks up the street and down the street and at the empty driveway and then straight up at the sky. She spins and comes back to the house, her sneakers in the grass, her long skirt shaping her thighs. She puts her hand around the trunk of the dogwood tree as she swings by it and disappears around the side of the house. I'm dumbfounded.

Out back the lilacs are still lining the riverbank. They are leafless, just a series of slender trunks and branches with weathered boards propping them. One branch has an actual crutch supporting it.

"Ice storm, April, what? five years ago?" my wife guesses as I catch up to her.

Her eyes meet mine for a moment, and there are tears. But beneath the tears I swear her eyes are weightless, flying with curiosity, the eyes of the girl who got into the car with me on that first date, the eyes that first became enchanted with this house.

She's on the move again. I follow her down the stone pathway around the bare tangle of a rose bush toward the riverbank.

"I don't remember the rose bush," I say.

"We'll dig it out, toss it into the river." She gives me a whimsical look I haven't seen in a long time. I dig into my pocket and hand her a tissue. She blows.

The river is about fifteen feet wide here. There's no fence. The water's moving, but you can't see it moving except for the swirling eddies near each bank. The way rivers should be. There's no way there are PCBs or anything else with daunting initials. It skipped this part of the river, it had to.

"Doug, I—"

"I understand completely." I reach for her hand and she doesn't pull it away. We are officially holding hands.

"Maybe it floods," she says, squeezing. "Maybe it fills the whole damn bottom floor."

I squeeze back.

I look over my shoulder toward the house because I think I hear a car. I will tolerate no interruption. If it's the Harrisons, there's a good chance they won't even notice us back here.

There's a plop.

"Did you see that?" my wife asks. "A fish jumped. We'd never get Tina to come inside."

Whatever has happened since we entered this yard, I have no choice but to like it. With her free hand she brushes her bangs aside. *Both times,* what? Harrisons, who? We were just doing something inside, like reading a magazine or watching TV and she said, *Let's go have a look at the river before it gets too dark out.* And here we are. We bought the house sixteen years ago and here we are nearing forty, as happy as can be. The sun setting.

My wife is on the move. She's right. It's time to go in. We look in another window. As we go around the other side of the house toward the front, there's a couple in the picture window next door. They are washing it together. Spring cleaning. We wave and they wave back. They are about our age. All four of our kids play with theirs. When we have them over for dinner we talk about growing old with them. One Christmas they will stop over, and we'll talk about our grandchildren and they will tell us how happy they are that we moved in, that they knew we were perfect neighbors. That is how it is.

I take the lead as we round the corner of the house. I sit on the porch steps. Standing in the grass just off the walkway, she looks at me and then up and down the street. Nobody's coming. The wood creaks under her feet as she sits next to me. The house is ours.

"I'm not sure about these steps," I say. "Get a couple kids on here with us and we're breaking right through."

"Tina won't want to sit with us much longer."

Emboldened by this (she did say "us," didn't she?) and not to mention the hand holding, I squeeze my wife's knee and she leans into me and lifts her face and I lean my lips toward her. But she snaps her head so that her hair is there. That's OK. Too soon. It's tempting to kiss even that hair of hers I'm so happy, but I back off.

"We'll get married," I say, "we'll have a baby, we'll own this house, we'll be happy."

"We're twenty-three," she chimes in.

We sit there and the world opens before us, all the potential, all the possibility, and then a set of headlights comes down the street, slows, my wife stands up, and when the car passes, she doesn't sit back down.

"We should go," she says.

I put my hand on her hip so she won't move any farther. "If they come home, we'll make them an offer they can't refuse," I say.

If I want to, I can grab onto the pause that follows and hang from it.

"I'll skip work," I try again, "and we'll drive right over here first thing."

"There's one thing I have to tell you," my wife says.

Great! It seems like the perfect time to tell her husband the good news.

"I've been happy most of the time," she says, watching her fingers. "I mean really happy. I'm lucky I had you."

She turns and puts her hand on my shoulder. Leans into it, but I don't look up at her because I already know what's next. I get ready to jump for joy.

"I think I'm going to stay with Nancy for a while." Her weight presses into my shoulder before she takes her hand away. "I'd like to make some arrangement. For the kids. We can share."

Lights shone from windows. It's dark. The air is cooling fast and my wife is hugging herself. I can hear the clank of dishes being washed. I bet this house has the best pantry. If we were just in that pantry in this house. If we were just. . .

"I just want to make things right between us," I say.

"I know." She swallows, shakes her head.

"We can make this ours."

She starts down the walk.

"I know you still love me."

She doesn't turn around, but walks faster.

"I know you could," I say.

I shoot up onto my feet and down the steps. I cut across the yard and grab hold of one of the dogwood branches, just hold it for a moment. Its bark is cool and smooth. She goes around the Pontiac to the passenger door. I cross the street after her and stand with my shins against the front bumper. The yellow streetlamp glows down on the car. The *Silver Spoons* lottery ticket is wedged between the dash and the windshield.

"We can do it," I say. "I know we can."

"Shit," she says, hitting the roof with her palm. She circles the back of the car and opens the driver's side. She flicks on the headlights before she starts the car. I'm still against the bumper, the beams of light on either side of me. I think of my shins against the bumper of the minivan when I packed it for our honeymoon. I'm not letting her go this time.

"Are you planning to get an abortion?" I yell.

Her mouth moves in the green glow. "What?"

I come around to her window.

"What? What are you talking about?" She has her hand on the emergency brake, and I can see her left knee move as she pushes in the clutch.

"I found the pregnancy test in the trash. The box wrapped in toilet paper. The strip." I pull it from my pocket and show her—she snaps on the interior light and looks at it. "I completely understand why you didn't say anything. I'm OK with it. You know with all that's happened I just thought you were— And coming here today. I thought— It would change. Changing around that everything was— I just think you should consider—"

"I didn't take any pregnancy test."

"I just think you should just—"

"I'm not pregnant. This isn't mine."

"But then. . ." The noise I let out was probably pretty close to the lamenting groan of a walrus.

"Jess."

38

Up ahead of us, just blocks from home, are the streetlight lit pipes where I used to think all my problems began, these pipes the city refuses to put in the ground probably because they are evidence against me that cannot be buried. My wife negotiates the corner, no problem, and the significance of this spot is lost on us both anyway when we see a police car parked on the curb in front of our house. We both pat our pockets to see if the phones we left at home have magically come back to us. Instead of going into the driveway she hops the curb with two wheels on the sidewalk and halts right behind the police car. Those sneakers carry my wife out of the car before I can even get my seatbelt unbuckled. And then as I shut the door, she's saying "Mom?" into the window of the cruiser. Spring is in the air for someone of course. There, in the cruiser, is Nancy fumbling with her blouse and Ray Roy smoothing his slacks with two strong hands. "Mom?" my wife says again so that her voice is that of a daughter, almost like Jess's. Nancy and Ray Roy start to talk, but there's no time for us to listen. My wife and I are up the driveway, my wife leading the way, the house key wielded in front of her. The driveway is brightly lit, not because of the spotlights I was supposed to install a couple years ago, but the light that is pouring out every window in the house. Shades are not pulled down, curtains are not drawn. At the very end of the driveway Nancy's Suburban is covered in smashed eggs. There are drips of yolk bleeding onto the pavement, but this does not give us pause. Nancy yells from behind us in fragments: where have you been, your phones, what are you two teenagers. "Wait," she yells. There's a strange sound coming from the house. We run faster.

My wife's unable to get the key in the lock because her hands are shaking so much. When I push open the door, the sound grows louder, like a waterfall. At the kitchen table, Jess is sitting behind a sewing machine and Sarah is at her side. The sewing machine's blasting, machine-gun-like. Both girls are intent on the corvette red fabric that Jess, with stretched fingers and thumbs, runs under the hammering needle.

Jess's hair is tied back in a ponytail that springs from the back of her head. She hasn't sported this uncool look for a couple years. She wears her sweatshirt and sweatpants and her mother's terry cloth robe. Seeing her like this—casually domestic? I don't know—knocks the wind out of me. Is she already taking on maternal instincts? Is she making baby clothes? Outside her phone and her reflection in the mirror, I have never seen her intent on anything.

Sarah's hair is pulled back too, but her ponytail droops. She also wears sweat clothes along with Jess's robe. She watches as if Jess is weaving straw into gold. Then I realize why I feel I have the wind knocked out of me: There on the table within easy reach of Jess is the bandage with its spindly, dirt-soaked strips of curled tape. Jess's nose is uncovered.

Jess and Sarah both turn their eyes up at the same time and at the same time back down to the bandage. In other circumstances their symmetry would have been comical. Jess takes her foot off the pedal and the sewing machine halts. Silence except for Nancy trying the back door. We must have locked her out and she doesn't have her keys with her.

There is coffee in the coffee maker and the orange light is on. The faucet's dripping. There are no dishes in the sink. The pathos plant hangs green. There is no bandage on Jess's nose. Her nose looks, well, just like her nose—paler, but every bit of it, the slightest ski jump, the bump, all the same. I expect her to reach for the bandage, but she just leaves it there, as if it's no big deal. The bandage isn't a big deal anymore.

"You ever heard of a phone?" Jess asks, looking past us at Nancy at the door's window. "We've been worried sick." She readjusts the wheel at the back of the sewing machine, renews her grip, and guns the power. "You were supposed to be home over two hours ago," she yells over the machine. "Rudd almost missed his date and then he and green hair got egged and Nancy called Ray and well, should we ground them?" she yells to Sarah, who takes one look at us and scoots her chair closer to Jess. "Clearly you just haven't been living up to your parental responsibility." Her eyes jump from my wife to me and stay there as if she's thrown one of my lectures back at me.

Egging and Rudd? It's too confusing for us to digest because there's only one thing on our minds. Is she actually happy to be pregnant? How could this daughter be pregnant? How could she have had sex? She's thirteen for Christ's sakes. As she continues to feed the red fabric under the pounding needle, the spool of purple thread dances in vibrating circles at the top of the machine. Sarah returns her eyes to us and keeps them there as if we are something that deserves more than her momentary curiosity, and then she refocuses on Jess's sewing. Nancy's no longer at the back door.

"We need to speak to you," my wife yells to Jess simultaneously as I ask, "When did you get home?" When you have one big question to be answered, it is my philosophy to start small. But my wife's philosophy is the opposite—she's on a spree tonight, cutting to the heart of the matter in every instance.

Jess stops: "Would you guys just get it together." Then she starts sewing again. Sarah, hunched over the table, shrinks in her chair. My wife and I take our daughter's advice and regroup at the outlet where the sewing machine is plugged in next to the where the TRUSTFUND jar had been (had my earlier donations financed the pregnancy test?). The cord stretches in the air from the counter to the table. I raise my eyebrows to my wife and she nods in assent. I pull the plug and let the cord drop to the floor.

"Cripes!"

Cripes? When did our daughter ever say that?

"The dance is in like three weeks and I still have to—" She must pick up on some strong parental vibes. The rough translation being: Jess, you won't be doing anything in three weeks, doing anything for the rest of your natural life—but you will be free in the spirit world to do as you please. "What? Am I in trouble or something?" Jess throws her hands into the air and the sleeves of her mother's robe fall down to her elbows. "It's good to see you too—so happy to be back. It wasn't supposed to be a big deal, remember?"

Are you pregnant? is all I have to ask, but I can't do it. Neither can my wife.

"Your mom," Jess addresses her mother, "said some pretty harsh things about you two. She's pretty angry. She gets about as red as Rudd. Together they were about as red as this fabric. That woman has a temper. Rudd was a wreck. I mean why was he nervous about a girl with green hair? He's already felt her up. Plus his fly was down."

Sarah covers her mouth.

I try not to think of my poor son on his first date with his fly down. I'm sure he noticed in time. I trained him early to always check and double-check. Life is tough, it's even tougher for a guy with his fly down. I reach over and turn off the coffee pot. My wife is leaning so hard into the counter I can see all the bones in her hands. Then I process the other thing Jess revealed: He felt her up? These words out of my daughter's mouth?

When did our children do all these things? When did they talk about them? I don't know my children anymore, just like I don't know my wife.

"Did you guys get a load of Nancy's car? Completely crazy. She says she's never seen anything like it and she was all like she's pressing charges on those juvies to the maximum extent, some kind of ambush because everyone thinks Rudd took money to throw the game. Nancy got Ray to come to guard our house and Rudd and green are in the cellar 'playing with trains'—yeah, right. . ." She nudges Sarah's arm, but Sarah just frowns.

I'm amazed with these events, amazed Jess is spouting off stories as if she's been zipped up for weeks. My wife, though, is able to stay on task.

"Jess," my wife says. "Your father and I would like to talk to you alone."

"Sarah's still sleeping over, right? You promised."

"No," we say together.

Jess seethes, but then controls herself. Something I've never witnessed: "She has to."

"Not tonight."

"Look," Jess says. "I freaked out. They were saying stupid stuff and it had to stop. No biggie. I'm like thirteen. Thirteen-year-olds freak out all the time. It's OK. It's normal. I got all Activated. I'm willing to pay the consequences. Sarah's up-to-date on it. She's helping me out. Nancy and I already had a talk. She told me you did whacked things when you were my age." Jess looks directly at her mother. "Skipping school, going out with bad boys, not coming home at night. You sounded pretty cool. But sewing, you never sewed. She said you wouldn't touch it. But sewing is pretty cool. Did I tell you we're making some kick'n dresses for the dance?"

"Sarah," my wife says turning to her. "Call your parents."

Sarah has the look of a trapeze artist who doesn't know whether to jump or keep hanging on.

311

"I'll call them for you," my wife offers.

The moment is cram-full of teenage girls' mental telepathy.

"Can't Sarah just hang out in my room or something? Does she actually have to leave the building?" Jess stops, smiles, thinks better of something and then thinks better of thinking better of it but before she can actually say anything my wife explodes:

"You had sex?"

Jess's eyes bulge.

"Are you pregnant? Oh my god, if you're pregnant," my wife continues. "How stupid can you be? Stupid, stupid. Wrecking your whole life. Wrecking everyone's life. You've always been so stupid. Idiotic. You don't even know how it will wreck your whole life."

Sarah screeches back her chair. She stares at my wife, with a horrible, twisted expression, and then sprints to the back door, fumbles with the locks and is gone. I too am staring at my wife. Cool air floats into the kitchen. I can't blame Sarah. If I wasn't the father around here I would've been two steps ahead of her.

Jess shoots to her feet and her chair falls. Her hands push against the table, her arms stiff.

"Don't you even think about it," my wife says.

Jess scrambles around the table, my wife, her arm reaching forward, comes after her. Jess slides out of the robe and is ready for action in her sweat clothes. I step between Jess and the door. She crushes her body against mine and tries to squirm and break from my grip, punching my sides and kicking at my feet, albeit not with much force, as her ponytail sways.

"You don't understand. You don't understand." Jess is crying. Her arms slowly stop fighting and she comes to rest so that I'm hugging her and she's more or less hugging me. "You guys don't understand," she's saying into my chest and I can feel the vibrations of her voice and her sobs run through me, a whole marching band. "Sarah. You can't let Sarah go. You can't."

My wife is facing me from behind Jess. She's rubbing Jess's back, trying to calm her. Here we all are, you can put a Hula Hoop around us.

"I'm sorry, Jess," she says. "This is just a big shock."

Jess pushes into me harder. She shakes her head until my wife stops touching her.

"It's OK, Jess," I say, patting her back. "We'll work this out. Everything will be fine."

She pulls back from me suddenly, bumping her mother and then squeezing out to the side. My wife and I each have one of her arms, and Jess hunches forward like she's harnessed, her arms bent back in each of our hands. She tries to pull us to the door as she repeats: "Let me go." Not making any progress, she pauses, tries harder, stops, and turns back to us, ripping one arm from her mother's grip, and half facing us.

"It's not fine. It's not OK. But it's not me. You're always fooling yourselves. Everything sucks. You guys suck. You always think the worst of me. I'm sick of you. You both are fucking cheaters and you tell me. . ." She can't finish whatever she's saying because she needs air. Then she finishes: "Why aren't you divorced?"

She turns her head so we can see her whole face. She isn't crying. I soften my grip and Jess pulls her arm away and looks at us both as if this is the last time she'll ever see us.

"Dad," she says, in the coldest voice, "your girlfriend called. Burty's missing." Then Jess is out the door.

I can feel my wife's eyes on me, a whole world of eyes at once. I turn and there is Rudd and the green-haired girl. His fly is up, thank god. She's wearing jeans and a shirt with two different color sleeves. I wait for her to look at me in disgust, like she's ready to spit on me or at least pull out the ASSASSINS sign because it applies to my home life as well. I can't even meet Rudd's eyes. His heart will be broken one day, probably sooner than later. She's holding his hand. She's got him for now. You can jump in front of a bus to save your kid but you can't jump in front of heartbreak.

But parents certainly can break your heart. I jog to the door. In the backyard partially lit by the glow of our house, Sarah is sitting on the ground, her back against the chain-link fence, her hands covering her eyes, her knees up, and her bare heels digging into the ground. Jess sits next to her and puts her arm around her and tugs her in close. As my wife comes through, I block the way.

"I think," I whisper, "we goofed."

I hold the screen door open with the back of my arm, and under Sarah's sobs, I hear the soft flow of Jess's words. They sound reassuring, whatever they are. The thing is she's not looking at Sarah, but back at us, challenging us; here are the two Jesses and I don't know what to make of either one of them. I do know I got both of them wrong. The light behind us from the kitchen makes our shadows large. Framed in the stretched doorway, my wife and I—the wife who possibly thinks kids ruined her life, who is about to leave me because there will be no reprieve now that my daughter is not pregnant—our shadows' heads bent against the rings of the fence, the crack of light dividing our bodies, and I'm glad our daughter and her friend are off to the side, in the dark. The spring whines as I let the screen door rest against my wife, who immediately leans into it.

If you believe you can get away from a true strikeout streak, like I did, by simply quitting Little League thirty-odd years ago after a second strike, you're sadly mistaken. My coach at every practice and every game told me to not swing with everything I had. Eventually he narrowed his criticism to "just for the love of god keep your eyes open!" My parents didn't care one way or the other if I hit the ball. "Being out there" was the important part. Dad loved being up on the ladder or up on our roof. Mom thought everything could be fixed with a glass of water. They planned for years to retire to Florida like everyone else but ended up near the Arctic circle with a Native American tribe (long story). They visit us each fall. They are happy up there. When I quit that day in the middle of a game, the umpire begged me to just at least stand there for one more pitch. Even as I was booed and parents said terrible things to little kid on a bad streak, my parents didn't say a word as they followed me out of the bleachers as the game went on without me. And I waited for it all the way to the car but it was halfway home before it finally came: "We'll get you a nice cold glass of water." At home, while I drank the glass with my mom's hand on my shoulder, I watched my dad out the back window getting the ladder out. And you know what? I didn't feel half bad after it. I just wish I had kept swinging because I know I would have hit that ball eventually and it would have sailed out of the field. I'd always have that but I quit. Two days later when the next game was scheduled my parents never even asked if I was going. "It's a good night for hamburgers out back." I nodded. I know there's no way to understand the small elements that we'll pass on to our kids. But at times like these you just have to go with what is at the bottom of your foundation. And that's why I'm counting heads to see how many glasses of water we're going to need and already looking forward to the next TPing of our house so I can get back up on the roof to erase those strands. Precedent is something that should not be ignored.

But before I can act, there's a strange sound. I know it well but my brain is racing for what it is. Gazook's nails on our driveway at full sprint. "Jess," I yell, but that's all the time I have. Nancy's at the corner of the house and Gazook cuts right behind her in a downhill skier stance tucking through the best line of a corner, paws forward, just right at Nancy's hamstrings so both her knees give out and she's toppling backwards over a dog that is already gone by. "Oh!" is all Nancy can manage as her arms shoot up. My wife jams open the screen door ripping the cylinder right out of the frame so the door smacks against the railing as she tries to stretch her arm for her mom who isn't even within reach. And now Gazook's mid-yard and Jess admits such a piercing cry that I'm absolutely sure that I can see the sound waves breeze against everyone and everything in the yard until it all halts at the percussion of Nancy's head on the pavement. Both sounds are pretty terrible, but they still rate just a percentage below your wife telling you she's slept with someone only twice.

Jess—someone who has thrown herself in front of a dog to save her sister—tries to scramble up the fence, pulling Sarah skyward with her. But Gazook pivots and hits the garbage can at full speed with his front paws near the top so it spills right under the one driveway spotlight that works. Tina needs a lesson on Pavlov. The lid goes flying off. In an instant he's in the can, his tail wagging. In the same instant, Ray Roy is down at Nancy's side. She's not saying a word. He automatically holds his hands on both sides of her head. He's saying, calmly, "Nance? Nance? Can you hear me?" My wife is at her side too. And green hair, now in the doorway behind me, is already on 911 passing her phone to Rudd as Jess and Sarah inch away from Gazook along the fence line. Karen kneels down and grabs Nancy by the shoulder and starts to shake her, "Mom!" Ray Roy commands her to stop. "Don't move her. She's going to be fine. Nance, you're going to be fine." "Head" I hear Rudd say into the phone. Then give our address.

I spot the broom we use to sweep the walkways and the cars after a light snow and I take it in my hands and I go right over to the garbage can and I bang and bang on it, but it is not a resounding drum of a sound, just a thud, and so I hit Gazook hard on his rump and there's a whimper and I hit him again but he's not budging from what he's found and I hit him again and I have it wound over my head like a lumberjack—my shadow spotlit across the can, his rump and the brown grass. When I go to swing I can't. I turn and it's Karen holding the other end of the broom and I let it go into her grasp. Gazook's tail is far between his legs but he's still busy in the trash. I haven't mortally wounded him. Then the bristles of the broom hit my arm. It's my wife. Again on the arm. Her side whacks start light and then pick up steam until they too are the overhead lumberjack fells and how, how can I explain to you as I cover my head from the blows, how can I explain these blows that hurt in so many different ways, but at the same time I feel like my wife will burst out laughing, laughing all of a sudden and I'll join her and we'll be laughing as we wrap ourselves around each other, laughing at the ridiculousness of all this, the mysteriousness and maze-y-ness of love. Hell, Gazook will probably come out and start licking us with his own kisses.

That doesn't seem to be happening though, and under the thwacks to my forearms as I try to get closer to her, the spotlight in my eyes, I can hear yelling which I can't discern if it's rooting for mom or a response to the terror that is happening. And I'm taking the blows in hopes of laughter. But it all comes to a stop when a truck races up the driveway, not an ambulance, its headlights illuminating the eggs on Nancy's car, illuminating my wife's face, as red as I've ever seen it. The KNNK van. Great, I'm glad they're here to cover this. My wife and I will experience prison together, for spousal abuse and dog abuse. Rachel spills out of the passenger door but she doesn't have a mic in her hand and Morgan, no high-five or half-smile in sight, comes around from the side. "Burty?" they both ask one after the other oblivious of the war zone they just entered as the ignition repeatedly pings its warning and my wife finally drops the broom.

I look toward Gazook again. Free range. Tina! I sprint past my wife whose eyes are on the ground, she doesn't understand anything. I pass Jess and Sarah—just kids, little girls still, why don't they just want to stay that way? Nancy's up on her elbows and Ray Roy is telling her to lie back down—he's already made his jacket into a pillow. I split Rudd and green hair as I shoot through the doorway. "She went to bed early," Jess's voice trails me. That has flags all over it. I hurdle the sewing machine cord in the kitchen, the knocked over chair, and accelerate toward the stairs.

317

39

Now after the snap of the light reveals Tina's empty bed, I wish I'd been the one knocked unconscious.

This is my third kid that has gone missing. This one I've got to get right. Her bed is covered with spilled dog biscuit boxes.

I'm down the stairs and by Rachel who's in the kitchen and understands. Then I'm out into the yard where everyone's close to Nancy, Morgan's looking at her as she protests. Karen looks like a woman who has just demolished her husband with a broom and is trying to figure out what that means. I zoom by them all. I've got a good head start and I'm hoping any followers will be discouraged because if I've got my wife, the woman she thinks I slept with, and her husband to boot, there's more room for error. Even still, I'm being pursued. Shoes clap the sidewalk behind me as I pass Nick and Naomi's. Gazook's gate is wide open. How Tina and Burty managed to get him tonight, and how Burty made it all the way across town, I can't quite imagine. I get one quick image of Nick and Naomi's look of disgust that they will forever regard me with. In the distance, the ambulance siren.

I cross the street with the same disregard for automobiles as any self-respecting dog. I'm sprayed by headlights and then my shadows run all around me. The seesaw park is dark except for two odd beams of light. The grass field is open and long and I wonder once again why Percival Lake Park has to be so complicated. Just needs grass and some playground equipment and let's be done with it.

I'm a man who can run really fast even in loafers, even after I've been beaten by a broom. As I draw close to the playground, there the figures are, the lights emanating from them. Two kids on either side of a seesaw holding Tina's two most powerful flashlights, and as I get closer I confirm that Tina and Burty are the two kids. I stop and catch my breath with my hands on my knees, and for a few beautiful seconds I'm clear of troubles.

Up Tina goes, up Burty goes. They are laughing. Their beams point to the sky, shorten and lengthen; then flash each other, and then glow right into the seesaw, muffled light. The sound of that laughter, real laughter, real fun. There's Gazook's leash right at my feet. Their plan has gone wrong. Their ambition of freeing Gazook has gone haywire. Clearly Gazook came to the park with them and then headed for home on his own and remembered our garbage. Their plans all failed, but they could just be here on the seesaw going up and down, trying to balance each other out. Laughing. Having a great time past their bedtimes in a park at this hour that probably isn't the safest place to be in the world. They don't care. I want to join those kids. I really, really do.

I stop Rachel and Karen and Morgan when they arrive, out of breath and full of questions. I put a finger to my lips. They flank me. The four of us—so entangled in each other's lives and not entangled at all—watch two kids with flashlights in the dark, seesaw.

It's not long before Tina catches us in her flashlight like escaped prisoners. She and Burty rush over—these runaways are even dressed properly, better than their parents as the night chills. "It worked, Dad, it worked. Gazook's free range now!" First Tina and then Burty give me their flashlights to hold as they rush to their mothers. The flashlights are heavy, something like ten D batteries in them. I switch them off.

Burty is in the air in a hug. His feet sailing out with centrifugal force as Rachel swings him side to side and Morgan claps his palm on Rachel's shoulder.

And I watch for Karen to throw at least one nasty look at Rachel, but she only seems to be aware of one thing. She's on her knees, hugging Tina in that way that says she's never letting her go.

I take a few steps back and drop onto the end of the slide, the flashlights weighing on my lap.

40

A few hours later, I'm up on the roof and I'm well armed. I have toilet paper—fight fire with fire, as they say. But I also have the hose, set on jet, the bane of TPers everywhere. I also have Tina's two super flashlights to both spotlight and blind the perpetrators. I've managed to balance most everything on top of the chimney. The chimney is close to the peak and on the street side of the house. Perfect cover as I wait for them.

The roof has a pretty good pitch but a manageable one. Night really is the time to be on the roof. Really, as I sit on the slant waiting, I can't help feel as if I'm on a high seesaw. I can't quite re-create the joy Tina and Burty were feeling in those moments I watched them, but at least there's a mountain top serenity. My neighbors' roofs, the open air of the cemetery, and the blinking far off light at the top of one of the real hills. Above me, clouds have a feel to them, a blanket, a protection from soaring too high. If you can't go on vacation I'd recommend the roof. Sure there's some danger up here but you don't have to worry about bears or ticks or poison ivy. With some rock climbing gear we'd probably get the blessing of Rick our insurance guy, statistically safer than in-home living, the most dangerous place, felled by some crazy dog, or more likely brought down by your own toe caught in your pajama pantleg. (Of course there are those other dangers that don't involve bodily injury that there should be insurance for: 100,000 property, 100,000 personal injury, 1,000,000 heartbreak.) So in a word, I'm feeling refreshed up here. Top of the world. Maybe I should have been a mountain ranger or airline pilot. I feel good.

Karen and the kids are sleeping at Nancy's tonight because they were all so concerned with her refusal to get into the ambulance or be driven to the ER. They plan to take turns watching her during the night. Tina was inconsolable when she found out Gazook had toppled her grandmother and she refused to let go of her hand even as they got into the Suburban. I hope Karen stopped at an all-night carwash on the way over there because if those eggs don't come off soon there's going to be a full paint job involved. I tried to go to bed and enjoy the emptiness of the house. I can't remember the last time I'd been alone at night in it. After five minutes, I was up and at 'em and after ten I was up the ladder.

When I hear the first car slow and then another and another, and then doors open almost in unison, I grab the hose and peer around the chimney. I'm expecting the toilet paper flaring in great arches but instead I hear the thwap of eggs on the house and windows. I should have guessed. Once you switch to eggs you can't go back to toilet paper. I pull on the hose to aim it but I haven't calculated the length quite correctly and can't spray these kids with their cartons of eggs balanced in one hand and their arms working with a quick precision of throws. I give the hose a good tug and along with more hose the ladder scrapes along the gutter on the Windchimers' side of the house and then hits the ground. It is an impressive crash and the kids are jarred and stop their throwing and that's just the moment of surprise I need as I aim the full jet power of the hose at them. A big football player type gets it right in the chest, the guy screams and his carton falls out of his hand. It's a great moment. I hit a girl in the baseball cap and the jet forces the brim over her face and she too drops her eggs. The element of surprise is

322

fading so I methodically spray across them all aiming for the cartons to unbalance them from their hands. I've got the kids in a panic, and one group piles back into the first car and takes off. The others take cover close to the house. I aim the hose into their open car doors and pile in the gallons. "Hey!" a voice calls up.

Then another voice reminds everyone that it is only water. Then there's the squeak of the faucet and my water runs dry. I'm impressed with their problem-solving skills.

"Go!" they yell. A volley of eggs, white ovals flying, it's like one of those movie scenes where bullets are fired in slow motion as doves flap. Though I'm quick to take cover next to the chimney I get hit right on the zipper of my jacket and both pants legs, one on the thigh and another on the calf. The roof is now a skating rink. I blast Tina's super flashlight toward the ground and there's a bunch of kids covering their eyes. "There!" one of them yells, another volley cracks to the right and left of me.

"It's his dad," someone yells.

Dripping with yolk, I'm only left the nuclear option: the parental lecture. I clear my throat. I plan to speak of love, respect, selfishness. "Listen up," I say, but before I even get started they're in their cars. It is, of course, a sign of victory that out of each car window there's at least one raised middle finger as they drive off. I don't think those kids will be back.

I step carefully to a clean part the roof and take a seat and savor my victory for a couple minutes, but I've got to get the hose on the house fast. Then I remember I'm stuck.

I note that on future roof campaigns to make sure I bring food, water (the hose drippings that remain at least keep my mouth from being parched), slightly warmer jacket, and perhaps a sleeping bag. I did pull my pants right over my pajamas so the eggs haven't soaked completely through. I do learn that lying on your belly with your armpits locked to the peak allows you to actually safely shut your eyes for a little while.

I do stare at my phone for a bit.

There's a lot to think about up here after this day, but I keep coming back to Rudd's spoiled first date. It is so important. It can set the tone for the rest of your life. And though Jess said he's already felt her up, I'm going to keep it simple—the way it all should be. Advice a dad needs to tell his son, advice I've been practicing all these years—with just a few new additions. As soon as I get a chance I'm going to write him this letter:

> Dear Rudd,
>
> Hold doors open. Pull chairs out. Since this is impossible, of course, at the movies, let her go into the row of seats first. Be precise where you would like to sit, but only after you ask her and she says it doesn't matter. Do not sit in the very back row or way off to one side. The center is always preferable. If someone tall sits in front of her, offer her your seat. But if she refuses, only ask twice more. It is better not to get any concessions if you can help it. Buttery fingers, crunching popcorn, slurping soda are never impressive. Of course ask her if she would like any of these, you don't want to seem cheap. Even if she wants to pay for the concessions or even the movie ticket insist on paying. You might hint that she could pay next time, a nice subtle option to pave the way to a second date. Bring some chocolates in your pocket. Highly illegal in movie theater terms, but romantic. And it never hurts to show that you are a rebel. If she happens to call you on it, just vaguely hint at the dangers of multinational corporations robbing the common man by jacking prices up when they

know they've got you. She'll eat that up. Do you know what kind of chocolates she likes? Always a good thing to figure out fast along with flowers. Chocolates and flowers still work and will probably always work— unless it is a royal screw-up. Hershey Kisses might be too forward. M&Ms might not be sanitary enough if she is concerned about that sort of thing. I'll think about this more. Your mother has always been a sucker for Milky Way bars. Remember don't put these in your pants' pocket because of awkward reaching, mistaken impression, and the possibility of melting. Wear a jacket if you can.

Rebels are good, but only to a point, so do not slouch in your seat or put your feet up on the seat in front of you. Do not talk loudly about other people in the theater. Do not try to hold her hand. Do not try to kiss her. (These are for later.) Do whisper funny remarks to her during the previews. Just make sure you are not too close to her ear and watch out that you don't spit. I'll show you how to check your breath before you go. Be careful to whisper during the movie only at very opportune moments, but this can still be risky. In lieu of whispering you could always look at her and nod to show she's more important than the movie.

What do you do if she drops her hand, palm up, on the armrest between you? First of all you should always keep your arm away from the armrest to provide such an opportunity, but you want to be careful it doesn't look like you're keeping away from her because you think she has germs. A good way to accomplish this is to put your elbow down on the armrest and hold your chin with your hand so you're leaning toward her. This leaves enough room for her open hand to be placed beside you. Once it is there, you don't want to hesitate too long, but you do also want to make sure she's putting it out there for you to hold and not just checking something on her wrist. Before you go for the hold, you might nudge her elbow gently. Now it is OK to slouch a little. Seem shy, even nervous because holding her hand is a momentous occasion. Girls like that. If she nudges you back, then go right for the hold, but first make sure your palm isn't sweaty. Of course you don't want to make a dramatic gesture of wiping your hand. Be subtle. You might want to just lay your hand on top of hers, very lightly and see if she closes her fingers around yours. Don't worry if you mess up getting each other's fingers in the right spots because it is something to laugh self-consciously about and she will find this endearing, that you laugh. A sense of humor is key in delicate moments. You might want to maneuver your knee closer to hers, in range for her knee to lean against yours. This you should do as you sit down. Of course you don't want to just make it obvious that's what you're doing. You might move and readjust occasionally but don't be annoying or loud about it—you don't want to seem like you're impatient. Gingerly move that knee into place. The knee tap will definitely be initiated by her, and most likely before the hand holding. So be ready. Keep that leg loose. You don't want to seem stiff and uptight.

Now I know this is uncomfortable hearing from your dad, but when you are close to a girl or even thinking of a girl sometimes natural things occur and your body reacts in certain ways even if you would rather it not. It is always a delicate matter and can be uncomfortable. Think about your trains if you get very desperate, for instance if you aren't quite ready to stand up. Keep your shirt untucked. The risk of seeming unkempt is worth it. This always has the rebel aspect, but make sure you are kempt otherwise because you don't want her parents to think you're a savage. A swift hand in the pocket can often save the day when you stand up, but try not to be obvious about it. Opening doors or climbing stairs are always the best place for adjustments. Leaks. Leaks are a difficult matter. Just be aware that it is natural, perfectly natural, and keep that shirt untucked. You might even consider an appropriately placed Kleenex as you get dressed, if you think this might be a problem.

Now as far as transportation. Obviously it is awkward with your mother driving, but you have to seem "cool" with it. You can be self-conscious but do not be hostile, because even if you are only fifteen your potential girlfriend could very well be seeing you as a possible mate for life. I know you are probably confused about your mom and your dad right now and you have a right to be, but don't let that put a damper on your date. How you treat your mother is telling her about you. Again, be funny, but don't be funny at the expense of the girl or your mother; you can be self-deprecating but don't be overly so. You don't want to seem down on yourself, though it is never terrible to seem a little dark and mysterious, but you don't want to go overboard. You also don't want to seem like a momma's boy. Rudd, it's a tightrope walk, this game of love. It's a tightrope and you're lucky that you're just getting in on the ground floor. You don't always have to have perfect balance, you can wobble a little, wobbling is fine, and eventually you'll acquire a pole and more skill and better balance, but I'll tell you right now, there are nets at first, plenty of nets, but these get taken away sooner than you'll expect, and you will be up there netless for the rest of your life. So take advantage of your nets, go out on one foot sometimes, try a handstand, use the net while it's still there. So being up on that tightrope can be exciting, great to watch, but when you start losing your balance and there are no more nets for you, it can be scary as hell, especially after all these years. And the thing is you're not even on that rope alone. That special person is up there with you. And one day you might discover that person is shaking the rope, maybe subtly, maybe in effort to keep her own balance and then you are stuck trying to keep your balance and sometimes you do anything you can do to find some kind of balance, but even that doesn't work and everything is still wobbling, making it as hard as hell for you both to stay up there. You have to keep the tightrope calm because it's already hard enough as it is. But if you keep it too calm that calmness even begins to vibrate.

But anyway when your mother drives you to the movies and picks you up, it would be awkward to sit both in the back when the passenger seat is empty. It is just as awkward for you to be sitting up front and her sitting in back. Being in the backseat together affords many opportunities for glances, touches, and maybe even your first sly kiss, but as I said if that passenger seat is empty then you really have no choice but to sit in it. One way to ensure those fine night-ending back seat moments of your young relationship, to keep the date going when inevitably it must end if you are in front and she is in back, to open all these opportunities, you might think of asking your mom if I could go and sit in that passenger seat so you can both slide right into the back. It's a great way to show that lady of yours how love can last for years. Even through the most difficult challenges. That balance is possible.

I know this may not seem possible with all that has happened and with some of the things you think you've seen and what you've heard but balance is always out there. Maybe we can earn back some of your admiration again. But as far as having both parents in the car, don't worry, we'll act as if you two are in another time zone. When you nudge your date, remember don't use any of your hockey skills. OK. Good luck. Be confident. Confidence is always good. And the great thing about it is you can always fake it. Ask your mom. Secure that back seat.

First thing in the morning, Nick and Naomi go by with Gazook, probably to go get the Sunday paper and some coffee. They do a quick survey of the mess and shake their heads, and then seeing me, give me a quick wave. I wave. Yep, I'm just up here working on the roof. Gazook sniffs at the egg cartons. He's not limping. I'm not a terrible person. He did nearly kill my mother-in-law. Maybe I'll catch them on the way home. I'm shivering pretty badly, but the sun is warming. Maybe I'm going for the unofficial world record for sitting on a roof.

It's Karen that comes next, in the egg-yoked Suburban. She pulls into the driveway extra slowly, surveying the mess. It's too slippery for me to go to the part of the roof where I can watch her get out of the car. I hear the back door open and close. She'll go through the house calling for me and she'll come back outside and look up based on a sneaking suspicion and I'll hear the ladder being set up. I'll see her face pop up over the gutter and it will be a wonderful moment, the expression she'll have.

It's a while before the back door opens again and I hear a rolling sound. It is rolling luggage. The hydraulics of the hatch hiss on the Suburban and then the bag slides in. But then the back door again. Another bag rolling. Then another. Finally one more.

She backs into the street and I can see her hands through the windshield unwind the steering wheel. Head injuries need watching so she's just gathering supplies for a couple extra days. I'm sure there's a message on my phone that explains.

Soon after there's another car in the driveway. Maybe my wife is back with the kids and the luggage! But there's a knock on the back door. A long pause and another knock. Maybe it's Rachel? I make my way across the peak as I yell out "hello!" and "up here" as I have to go down to my hands and knees and then lay down so I can look over the back door. The short gray hair, a woman, glasses, Mary Beth! I remember now that there was a brunch date calendared in with my wife. Today must be the day. "Hello," I call down. Mary Beth looks around, the broken door, the spilled garbage, eggshells and yolks, one pink shoe with splayed laces on the driveway. She fiddles with her glasses. I have to say, "Up here."

She cranes back. "Dave?"

41

So what if at the town-hall meeting Rachel waits thirty seconds after the introductions to utter initials a lot longer than PCB or PCX? What if Alogosh doesn't seem a bit surprised? What if Sam runs up the aisle and jumps onto the stage and takes the microphone from Alogosh? What if the school Activators! begin to chant *assassins* in foot-stomping unity that shakes a needle on a Richter scale? What if through the stomping and chanting, Sam tries to speak of the marriage of community and Rachel continues to grill Alogosh who stands firm as he tries to figure out what the pony-tailed man is saying—the microphone's power now cut. Sam's unheard question manages to lift one of Alogosh's eyebrows when Rachel's does not?

As I stand at the bottom of the stage stairs, demoted to one of the "ambassadors" that guard a microphone that even in the chaos audience members have begun to line up for, I scan the place for my children. I find Tina in the second tier of seats and she's yelling and stomping her feet with the best of them. I pray then for Frisbees to start flying, but none come—the mayor, smarter than the rest of us, doesn't make an appearance. And I have that same feeling as after the accident, rear-ended, knowing I need to act, that I need to be the one to jump on the stage and make things right. And it's just then that I meet eyes with Tripoli, who stands in the wings partially obscured by the curtain. He seems to be that general who does not flinch as bullets fly. He even seems to be relishing this moment that not even he will be able to dig GE out of. And what does he do? Gives me the thumbs up, two hands with thumbs up! He still thinks I'm the one. He thinks my plan has succeeded when all I want right now is for my children to find me, for my wife to appear, and for all of us to just hold on. I have the microphone in my hand and I yell their names into it. But there's just stomping. Rachel stops her questioning and turns in my direction. Alogosh puts his hands on his hips and shakes his head. I yell their names into the microphone again. Everything is stomping.

42

There we are with our orange vests, garbage bags, and litter sticks early Saturday mornings, in the median of the highway where the grass and weeds urge motorists to throw out whatever is within their reach immediately. There we are at the public parking garage where teens congregate the night before and work very hard to make sure the community service crew will never get bored because of the variety and scale of their refuse.

In the parking lot where we meet outside the courthouse, there are Audis and there are rusted Fords. We are the democracy of the back of the hand slaps. We were fortunate not to go to jail but unfortunate enough to end up here only to find out three things: 1) people litter an insane amount and will discard anything, anywhere, 2) poking out-of-place detritus on the ground with a sharp stick is immensely satisfying—I mean really really immensely satisfying, and 3) it's the best career move they've ever made. Whether it is side by side in the van or in our collecting teams on the roadside strip of grass, I've seen people with no jobs find jobs and people with good jobs find better jobs.

On my first day picking up garbage, I saw Rick my insurance

agent in the van, but I didn't say anything and acted like I didn't know him. But right when we stepped out, he recognized me and slapped my back and said how his father, the owner of the insurance agency, Hastern and Sons, loved me, absolutely loved me and he'd never believe we were "on duty" together. He might even want my autograph next week. After what happened at the town-hall-style meeting and after losing my job as GE pulled completely out of town, it was good to hear that I had one fan out there. And that next week came and there was Rick again, hardy handshaking Rick, and it turns out his dad didn't want my signature but wanted me to come in first thing Monday morning so we could have a chat.

In the fourth floor offices of Hastern and Sons, right downtown with a view of Park Square, Rick's dad, his bushy moustache rivaled only by the white moustaches over each eye, talked all of five minutes before he showed me my desk, plopped down some books in front of me, and said, "When Alice gets here she'll set you up on the computer." Four months later, here I still am. I do busywork at the office, shadow other agents, learn the ropes. At my apartment I read manuals and test-prep books and take insurance classes online to get all my certifications. I've already passed the Massachusetts Producer's Examination for Personal Lines Insurance with a score of 100! I'm waiting for my license to come, but I'm also studying for life and property. If I keep up at the rate I'm going, I'll be able to handle almost any line of insurance by New Year's. Last Saturday Rick said he was starting to get jealous of me. He said his father thinks I generally want people to be well insured and I don't really care about dollar signs. Then Rick stuck an empty bag of Doritos and his eyes urged me tell him that this could not possibly be true, that people can't possibly think that way. What was I going to say? He studied me a second before dropping Doritos into our garbage bag as I held it open for him. A little bit down the line, he said, "My father thinks I'm some kind of a saint too."

Insurance just makes sense. Everyone should have it, lots of it. It's the one thing in life you can't have too much of.

Right now it's two o'clock, and I leave my desk and head into the break room to collect my lunchbox. I check my phone again. I'm taking off early to get the kids. I'll get them one by one. Tina will say, "You learned to drive again!" I'm probably not going to hit the script—no "Where to, James?" or "bombardier"—I'm just going to take the kids' cue. It's the first day of having my license returned to me. And what makes it better is that it's my weekend to have the kids. I can't wait to pick them up from school for the first time in too long. I do know that we won't go right back to the apartment. It's Friday and we have a Camaro, Sam's Camaro, now mine. Whether we go out for ice cream or go to a park or go to the mall or make deliveries to the homeless, I'm up for it, though I have a feeling they'll want to just drive. We'll have all the windows down, Jess will pick out music, and I'm not going to go by the lookout or the roads we used to drive her on to get her to fall asleep. I think I'll head quickly across the New York state line and maybe take back roads to Vermont and then haul ourselves home—a great loop of open roads and mountain passes, all in a little over an hour. With the wind and the radio, we'll be quiet, just happy moving in this car together. Maybe we'll stop for ice cream every ten miles. No matter what happens after I pick them up, I know we'll have fun and we'll all be feeling good about the world (especially if we end up delivering supplies to the homeless).

The kids all love the car. It's the one thing they seem to agree on. It's been sitting in the parking lot of Lincoln Heights since Sam left on the first of June, headed west by bus for his job with a non-profit in a city where the car would just be a hassle. I took the car and his lease for his apartment. It's not quite the car or the apartment for me, but I wanted to help him out.

Over the summer on my days with the kids, I began to see how this car had the same force as the minivan. The kids loved it even though all we could do was sit in it. I could tell Rudd was becoming enamored with muscle cars so I presented him a new model kit each week he came and he loved building those plastic replicas so much I'd hardly see him. And when Karen left with the kids, there'd be this perfect model waiting for me on the kitchen counter, smelling of paint and glue. I bought a display case and I can tell he's proud. I never was invited on his first date or his second or third and it didn't matter because he decided to emulate his dad and fly solo. I don't know what happened but I do know working on the models does him some good even if I don't get to see much of him.

Jess doesn't want me to know how much she loves the car. But I know when she's standing out on the balcony with the car just below her, she's doing some calculations about driving it, cruising North Street in it, the windows down and the music blaring, eventually pulling into the parking garage with all the other teenagers and their cars and their littering. I know she's even thinking about pulling in way after curfew. And you know what, that will just be fine a few years down the line. I'll be sleeping like a baby. I completely trust here. The kid is a pillar and she can take care of herself. In our father-daughter boxing sessions, after a few good thunks on her poor dad, Mr. Alexander reminds her: "You don't box for the KO." She's her dad's daughter. I want to whisper to her to keep going for it, but I don't have to. She keeps punching. I really think Jess and I are just about due for a big breakthrough. Maybe even today!

It's Tina who sits in the driver's seat and she really drives that parked car, her throaty gear shifts as she winds out the engine, not to mention her tendency to catch air and drive on two wheels—but not for fun. She's driving pretend missions for the homeless. Breaking traffic laws to bring a guy a cardboard box, an umbrella, stuffed animals that smell good, and flashlights because it is her deep belief that the homeless should never be without one. It's been hard on Tina since she lost Burty this summer. His parents both got jobs in Philadelphia. Rachel will be hosting her own style of noon show starting in December, which her producer told her was just a test market before they ship her to New York. As for her other friend, Gazook, his name has been banished. She's unforgiving and I just hope to stay on her good side, always.

Karen and kids never returned to the house, continuing to stay at Nancy's, an arrangement that has been great for everyone. But the house was too much for me even if I could gloat every night that the TPing and egging never happened again. Nick and Naomi and Gazook live in the house now and I couldn't be happier for them. That baby is coming soon. They'll get it right.

I give myself another moment in the breakroom to really breathe in the magnitude of this day. I pour a cup of coffee out of the carafe. I even can project past our after-school driving adventure. Tonight we'll just all be a typical family again. We have wheels again, but they'll lead us home. Rudd will work on the new model I have ready for him, Jess will flip through channels, and Tina and I, we'll move the dining room table and set up the cardboard "tent" she's made for us. We'll plop down the newspapers and she'll fashion a nest. She'll open the windows wide for effect and I'll keep my fingers crossed that this doesn't carry into the winter months, but what if it does? She's always solemn as she pulls the newspaper up under her chin, but then we crack jokes and then silliness and newspaper crinkling will ensue. I still wait for her to pull out a flash-light before bed, but she doesn't use them anymore—most of them are in the trunk, ready to be dropped off to the homeless. Some people are concerned that she's pretty adamant about growing up to be homeless. Only I get it.

Tina will quickly fall into her even breathing and I'll pile a few more newspapers on her tonight and then I'll just lie there with my hands under my head. I'll remind myself to do the wash in the morning so

Karen won't ask about the newspaper smudges on Tina's pajamas. I'll hear the voices of Jess and Rudd talking as they watch some show in my bedroom. Maybe tonight I'll knock on the door and they'll let me in and we'll sprawl out in front of some bad movie like we used to when Karen was away.

But that's all later.

There's a window in the breakroom. We're up on the fourth floor in one of the oldest buildings downtown. If I press my temple against the window I can see one corner of Building 54 at GE. There's no solar field coming. Barbed wire has been added to the top of the fence around the land that used to be Percival Lake Park. Lawsuits and countersuits, new questions about new cleanups, arguments about who's responsible for what. The town-hall meeting didn't topple GE. It didn't topple Alogosh or Tripoli. It just toppled me and the rest of our office. GE was hit hard for a week or two internationally, but then the story just became a local one. The mayor is still the mayor and still is finalizing plans for some big announcement that will put Pontoosuc on its feet again— the consensus is that it will involve Frisbees, but maybe he'll surprise us. The only reason I look at the articles about GE at all is to see how Nathan Schaffeur is doing his job as a spokesperson and I have to say he's not half bad at it. He looks like he's handling it all just fine from Fairfield. We all are. The thing about *things* going wrong is that they can be cleaned up. True, they may never be quite the same, but they're almost the same.

I don't press my head against the window. I don't need to. Right out there is Park Square. Now that the leaves on the trees in the Square have changed color and started dropping, I can see Nancy's store pretty well. As Nancy predicted, it is only her store in name. Karen has taken it over and has big plans. Nancy makes a production about the coup d'état but you can see her enjoying her "executive" position as she rides her new bicycle alongside her newly retired officer Ray Roy as they leave the store to head to the bike path. While I'm eating a donut or drinking coffee, I don't stare out the window at Nancy's store. I just take a glimpse. It's a window with a good view. My fellow workers look out it too. I don't linger there. But I just take a quick snapshot. It's not like I'm stealing these glimpses of my wife. We see each other all the time when she's dropping off the kids or when there's some parents' activity at school. We make small talk. We avoid any mention of legal separation or divorce. We just keep each other up to date.

When I do catch her across the way, there's just something about seeing her there in the store. Last week she was in the display window tugging something heavy. Earlier this week she was out on the sidewalk with her back to me and her arms crossed as she stared into the store as if she were trying to transform it just by looking at it.

Today, in my quick glimpse as I pick up my lunchbox and have one sip of coffee before I drive the Camaro to get the kids at school and start our weekend adventure together—the game changer, mobile again—I don't see Karen at all, just the glass reflecting back a couple pedestrians and parked cars and the trees in the Square.

I've got this.

Acknowledgements

Thanks to everyone over the years that has devoted some time in helping making this book. . .but please don't tell me if you think the version you read was better than this one!

In particular to Meghan who is an amazing critic and far too patient with a slow writer and for whom I have to steady myself as I think of our first meeting at the MFA where I planned everything out and thankfully got everything wrong. Roan and Ada who I started to write about long before you entered this world and now you're writing yourselves in ways I couldn't imagine.

All the help and patience from Marc and Donna at Fomite. From all my readers who have played some part in making this what it is: Susan, Betsy, Jonas, Katherine, Warren, Adam, Roy, Judd, Matt, Camron, Corliss, Brian, Marymarc, Megan, Shonell, Billy, Nic, Mike, Darren, and Jeannie. And for those who have offered so much support in so many other ways: Eric, Shannon, Barbara, Keagan, Greg, and all the Woods, and all those at McNeese. And to Neil Connelly in particular who made this possible.

Fomite

About Fomite

A fomite is a medium capable of transmitting infectious organisms from one individual to another.

"The activity of art is based on the capacity of people to be infected by the feelings of others." Tolstoy, *What Is Art?*

Writing a review on Amazon, Good Reads, Shelfari, Library Thing or other social media sites for readers will help the progress of independent publishing. To submit a review, go to the book page on any of the sites and follow the links for reviews. Books from independent presses rely on reader to reader communications.

For more information or to order any of our books, visit http://www.fomitepress.com/FOMITE/Our_Books.html

More Titles from Fomite...

Novels
Joshua Amses — *During This, Our Nadir*
Joshua Amses — *Raven or Crow*
Joshua Amses — *The Moment Before an Injury*
Jaysinh Birjepatel — *The Good Muslim of Jackson Heights*
Jaysinh Birjepatel — *Nothing Beside Remains*
David Brizer — *Victor Rand*
Dan Chodorkoff — *Loisaida*
David Cleveland — *Time's Betrayal*
Paula Closson Buck — *Summer on the Cold War Planet*
David Adams Cleveland — *Time's Betrayal*
Jaimee Wriston Colbert — *Vanishing Acts*
Roger Coleman — *Skywreck Afternoons*
Marc Estrin — *Hyde*
Marc Estrin — *Kafka's Roach*
Marc Estrin — *Speckled Vanities*

Fomite

Fomite

Fomite

Stories

Fomite

Silas Dent Zobal — *The Inconvenience of the Wings*

Odd Birds

Micheal Breiner — *the way none of this happened*
J. C. Ellefson — *Under the Influence*
David Ross Gunn — *Cautionary Chronicles*
Andrei Guriuanu — *The Darkest City*
Gail Holst-Warhaft — *The Fall of Athens*
Roger Leboitz — *A Guide to the Western Slopes and the Outlying Area*
dug Nap— *Artsy Fartsy*
Delia Bell Robinson — *A Shirtwaist Story*
Peter Schumann — *Bread & Sentences*
Peter Schumann — *Charlotte Salomon*
Peter Schumann — *Faust 3*
Peter Schumann — *Planet Kasper, Volumes One and Two*
Peter Schumann — *We*

Plays

Stephen Goldberg — *Screwed and Other Plays*
Michele Markarian — *Unborn Children of America*